CONNEXIONS

FOURTH STORY FROM
THE SPACE FLEET SAGAS

DON FOXE

CABALLUS
PRESS™

Copyright © 2 0 1 8 donfoxe

This is a work of fiction. Names, characters, businesses, places, events and incidents are either the products of the author's imagination or used in a fictitious manner. Any resemblance to actual persons, living or dead, or actual events is purely coincidental.

Written by Don Foxe. donfoxe.com

Produced by Caballus Press, USA Division
www.caballuspress.com

Stock images are used for illustrative purposes only.
Some stock imagery from Pixabay.com, Unsplach.com and Stockdobe.com

ISBN: 978-0-9988044-9-1
       978-1-7321036-0-3 (e)

Library of Congress Control Number: TBD

Acknowledgments

Nancy Thurmond for editing. In those places you find the grammar questionable, those are my decisions to add *style* over substance. She shakes her head, but allows me artistic license.

Author's back cover photograph courtesy of *Abri Kruger Photography*, South Africa.

Cover graphics are mine, for better or worse. I do listen to others with more experience and talent, but I have a vision, so I go with it.

My love and appreciation to Sarah for continuing to support my late-night hours squirreled away in my office.

Special thanks to Samara for allowing me to use her name.

THE SPACE FLEET SAGAS

CONTACT AND CONFLICT
Aliens and Humans.
Book One in the Space Fleet Sagas.
The Launch of the PT-109, John F. Kennedy

CONFRONTATION
Aliens and Humans. Allies and Enemies
Book Two in the Space Fleet Sagas.

SPACE FLEET SAGAS
A Collection of Adventures.
Backstories Prior to the Launch of PT-109
Four Short Stories and Two Novelettes

CONFLUENCE
Book Three in the Space Fleet Sagas.

CONNEXIONS
The Fourth Story from the Space Fleet Sagas.

In **CONTACT & CONFLICT . . .**

First contact is made by Captain Daniel Cooper, commanding officer of the SFPT-109, John F. Kennedy; Earth's first space-worthy battleship of the newly sanctioned Space Fleet.

In **CONFRONTATION . . .**

A trip to the planet Rys is needed to acquire power crystals to maintain and build more ships based on the Martian technology. During the visit, Coop and the JFK once more encounter Zenge invaders, this time saving Rys.

We discover the Zenge are pawns of a race called the Mischene. Mischene supremacists are convinced they should rule the galaxy. A confrontation with the Mischene, and their Zenge army is inevitable.

While these events occur in space, a secret society of influential and powerful people conspire to dissolve the UEC on Earth, returning our planet to regional rule.

In **CONFLUENCE . . .**

A group of unexpected allies work to save the United Earth from a conspiracy to dissolve the central government.

Space Fleet Battle Group sails to a dangerous region in space to face the forces behind the galactic conflict.

Wraith. Cassandra.
Avatar. Cassie.

SHROUD OVER ENPARATUS

"The wormhole gate is opening," the ensign monitoring telemetry reported to the Command Officer (C.O.) overseeing the bridge.

The first Kashōn Empire vessel entered the system. They transmitted the security clearance codes provided by the Helacene traitor.

"Coms?" the officer questioned the petty officer on station.

"Receiving transmission," she responded. "Codes authenticated. It's a confederated supply vessel, C.O.. I don't have a notice for a delivery for another six days," she added.

"Send them a welcome, Sarii," the C.O. replied. Timetables and space travel never lined up.

The Helacene Alliance battleship on sentry duty returned a welcome. Within seconds the unshielded vessel suffered dozens of laser blasts.

"Shield generator hit," called the lieutenant at the Systems and Engineering station. "Section closed. Hatches locked. Laser cannon one destroyed. Scuttle sealed. Laser damage to engines. Hull breach sealed by emergency foam. System failures across the board."

The initial attack destroyed weapons and vital operation centers. Locations targeted from schematics provided by the traitor.

Alert alarms clamored, warning crew of danger and calling them to stations.

"Ops, launch missiles," the C.O. ordered. "Coms, contact the Fides and warn them."

"A second battlecruiser has exited the gate," Telemetry reported. "Missiles headed this way from both ships."

Lasers continued to blast the deck and hull. The Kashōn gunners targeting launch tube openings. Damage to the retractable hatches made releasing missiles impossible forward and starboard. The port-side tubes, away from enemy fire, remained operational.

"Missiles away," Ops reported.

"Fides will receive warning in twelve-hours-eight-minutes," Coms said. "Optics should be picking us up already." The speed of light versus the speed of sound.

The incoming enemy missiles acquired those fired by the stricken battleship as they cleared the vessel's hull. The Kashōn missiles outnumbered their Hela counterparts three-to-one. The enemy missiles not expended terminating the Hela missiles back-tracked the flight patterns of those fired from the Alliance ship. They impacted, exploded, and collapsed the port firing tubes.

"We're drifting," Systems reported. "Compartments are being sealed, but localized failures are allowing atmospheric venting. Catastrophic hull failure is probable."

Disabled, unable to defend or attack, the ship adrift, the CO did not wait for the Captain.

"This is the Commanding Officer. Abandon ship. All personnel to assigned lifeboats or ferries. The ship is gone."

As crew members rushed to lifeboats and shuttles, he ordered his bridge officers and staff to do the same. Reluctant, but with no other options, they departed. The C.O. broadcast an all-channels surrender.

The Kashōn destroyer fired two-dozen missiles into the hull. High-explosive loads splintered the remaining integrity, blowing the craft apart. Fifteen small escape craft managed to launch before the terminal collapse. The Shroud ships tracked and eliminated the helpless survivors.

A second Hela ship in orbit over the small, single planet within the system, broadcasted a warning to the surface. The captain ordered shields raised as the pilot relocated to challenge the invaders.

"Five vessels now, Captain," Telemetry called. "Kashōn. Two battlecruisers and three destroyers. The lifeboats from the Tychē have all been destroyed." The last piece of information delivered with difficulty.

Coms asked, "Do you want me to hail?"

"They aren't here to talk, Ensign," Captain Apatet told his communications officer. "We have four days to decide a plan of action."

"Captain, the enemy vessels are traveling at over 600,000mph. They will arrive in thirty-five-hours."

"Check your system, Ensign. Kashōn fleet-class vessels have never been reported reaching speeds over 210,000mph."

"Checked and rechecked, sir," the reply. "The ships are emitting shortwave gamma photons. They must be using a type of electromagnetic drive."

"Microwave energy for power?" The captain left his seat to view the telemetry readouts, not waiting for them to transfer to his display. "They must have discovered a viable containment system. It gives us less than thirty-hours before they will be in range to launch weapons."

"Orders?" Ops requested.

"Inform the Academy and the civilians on the surface. Charge all batteries to max to be ready to layer the force field. Order all tubes loaded and prep every missile. Lock down anything on this boat that could shift or fall in turbulence. Place medical response teams on every deck. Then stand down."

"Stand down?" the Ops officer, also the second in command, queried.

"Rest our people, Commander," the Captain replied. "Once the Shroud ships arrive it will be non-stop. Everybody listen up."

The bridge quieted. All eyes and ears to the commanding officer.

"Do not tell anyone about the Kashōn murdering the people in those lifeboats," he said. "We cannot outrun or outgun the enemy. I intend to get the Fides near enough to the wormhole to activate the gate. If we can open it, we can send a message."

Attempting to use surprise to save his ship and crew, Captain Apatet drove the HAB Fides into space to intercept the enemy.

Thirty-one-hours after the Tychē died, the Fides fired a dozen nuclear-tipped missiles, followed by a dozen plasma-burst missiles. The tight pattern designed to split the five enemy ships and open a path.

The nuclear explosions created gaps in the EM-generated force fields, but the distance between the first wave of missiles and the second wave allowed sufficient time for the shields to recover.

The plasma-explosions rocked the big ships and pushed the destroyers slightly off course. No lethal actual damage inflicted.

In response, the five ships, each densely shielded and more heavily armed than his, loosened the trademark of the Kashōn Empire. The prodigious number of weapons rained upon the enemy obscured the stars.

The strategy of initiating an invasion with overwhelming force engendered the appellation for the Kashōn Empire's warships: the Shroud Fleet. Named for the blanket effect caused by sweeping numbers of ships, weapons, or both. The enemy cloaked in death.

The Helacene battleship's forcefields held against the withering assault, but weakened with every impact. The Fides' constant offensive fire kept the enemy at bay. The twin electrostatic ion-thruster engines pushed the big ship forward. The Helacene made it difficult for the Kashōn to close. The barrage of hits deflected by shields still shook the Shroud ships.

Ten hours following initial contact, the confrontation ended. The Alliance ship, force field regeneration unable to keep pace with the incoming fire from multiple attackers, received three fatal hits in quick succession. She imploded. Too far from the wormhole to send a message and leaving the path to Enparatus open.

Following the death of the second Alliance battleship, the three Kashōn destroyers retreated to cover the wormhole portal. The two massive battlecruisers sailed for the small brown planet. Three space-to-surface troop ferries departed the hangar of the second ship, slipped past the leading battlecruiser, and made for the atmosphere.

The small ships, ferrying operators of the Empire's elite shock troops, broke through the clouds and skimmed across the hot sands of Enparatus. No need for stealth as the two Helacene Alliance battleships protecting the planet lay shredded in open space.

Shuttle engines slowed as the pilots neared a structure situated on a plateau. Stone walls ringed by expanses of barren land.

The site was originally an oasis of lush greenery surrounding a spring-fed crystal blue pond. The watering hole now existed within the center of the fortification.

An ancient tribe erected a stone fortress around the spring. Covering fifteen-acres, it became a trading center and place of protection against marauders. One-thousand-years earlier, when no longer needed to bar the enemy and airships replaced trade routes, the indigenous people repurposed it into a place for scholarly pursuits. Scholars in residence removed the fortified gateway doors and iron portcullis. The arched entryway, eternally open, exemplified the new purpose of the complex of stone buildings.

After Enparatus joined the Helacene Alliance, the school expanded to store and teach the histories and cultures of the aligned worlds within the Hela-led confederation. Part school, part museum, and sanctum for scholars and students. The Invicta Vitam library contained original manuscripts and file-storage copies of works from nineteen star systems. Accounts stretching back thousands of years.

Hela represented the heart of the Alliance. Enparatus symbolized its soul.

Students came from every affiliated world to live and learn at the place popularly known as the Academy.

Chancellor Ungu, chief administrator for the Academy, and three resident instructors stood beneath the center arch. They wore the white linen robes of scholars. They kept their hands out, palms down, to show no offense.

Captain Phistol, first off the lead transport to land outside the front entrance, gave the order. Empire Corps lancers blasted the four non-combatants. The Captain stepped around burning flesh and smoking linen to cross through the open gateway.

"Sergeant Traum, find the two Helacene princesses," he ordered his ranking NCO. "Bring them to the gazebo beside the pond. Do not harm them, Sergeant, and do not take long. Persuade anyone you find to help. Kill anyone who refuses."

Half the squad accompanied the Sergeant, and half fanned out to protect their Captain. Troopers from the second and third ferries took defensive positions inside the grounds or around the outer walls of the old fort. They made quick time to cover the second entry-exit location set on the southern wall, assuring no one escaped.

Phistol removed the galea from his head. It allowed the breeze, cooled by the fresh water, to provide relief from the heat created beneath the metal helmet in the short time away from the environment-controlled ferry. The metal-reinforced leather tunic and heavy-duty trousers were not designed for desert warfare. Good thing he did not intend to conduct a war on this desolated planet.

Phistol represented the Kashōn ideal. A ram with curled horns at the temples. Deep set eyes lost in shadow beneath a wide single brow. Wide nose and flared nostrils. His skin thick, cracked and reddish-brown. Incongruent small mouth with thin pink lips encased by soft white hair. Short, rounded-chin and small ears with the upper lobes folded over. A handsome specimen standing six-six and three-hundred pounds of battle-tested muscle.

His second-in-command, who arrived on the second ferry, approached to report on the successful stationing of troops inside and outside the walls.

"Did you detect anything on our way in?" he asked.

"The surface is too hot. The radiant waves disrupt scanners," the lieutenant answered. "The nearest settlement is fifty-miles south. An oasis on the edge of the region called the Great Dunes. I can dispatch a transport to make a visual inspection."

"No need," the Captain replied. "Not even the nomads who live on this planet will wander the desert in the middle of the day. Tonight, when the ground cools, you can send the ships up to scan an area one-hundred-miles around us. Finally, the sergeant returns."

Sergeant Traum walked with purpose, followed by two young women determined to keep up and remain composed at the same time. Four soldiers followed the women.

"Princess Alucha and Princess Mandara," Traum announced.

"You murdered Chancellor Ungu and our teachers without cause," Alucha, the elder sister, said. "Your presence on Enparatus is an act of war. I demand you release everyone here and leave."

"If your mother gives my king what he wishes, I will happily leave this hot, barren wasteland," Phistol replied from his seat. When he stood he towered over the Helacene females. His face of weathered pelt and red-rimmed eyes offered no sense of care or concern. "If she does not, I will give you to my soldiers before we depart. I will level this structure, kill everyone else, and be happy to return home."

"My sister is the future leader of the Helacene Alliance," Mandara said. She placed herself slightly forward of her older sister. Protective.

"Only if she lives to take the throne," Phistol countered. "You are the spare. I could kill you now. It might encourage your mother to make a wise decision regarding the remaining daughter."

Alucha took Mandara's arm and pulled her back.

"Traum, take the princesses to their rooms. Place guards. Find space for our soldiers. If you need to move others, do so," he ordered.

The sergeant and his team ushered the Hela royalty away from the gazebo. They marched back to the main building.

"I doubt either could survive a mating with a single Kashōn male," Lt. Angertol remarked, removing his own helmet. "You might consider you and I take the first turn, cousin."

"The Suzerain may give Phortis what he wants to save them," Phistol said.

"Leave all other Alliance systems unprotected," Angertol said. "Do you believe a leader would sacrifice entire worlds for two children?"

"I know little of the Helacene, cousin," Phistol admitted. "I do know my King. Those two females will never see their home again, regardless of their mother's decision."

Two sets of eyes dropped below the rim of a wadi one-mile from the overrun academy. Two hover-cycles built for desert excursions started, the magno-electric power-plants whispering as the heavy machines rose on cushions of air. They moved down a dry ravine, too deep to be seen, too quiet to be heard. When the wadi forked, they turned south, toward the Great Dunes.

Chapter 38 –
Final Chapter in CONFRONTATION.

Somewhere in between

Early next morning he met Elie, Mags, Genna and Hiro in the hangar. Mags and Hiro removing their gear from Cassandra before his departure.

"Sindy's promotion came through," Elie told him. "The vortex is breaking up. Two loyalist Mischene battlecruisers are closing on the Prophet's disabled ship. Everyone hopes they give up peacefully and release the hostages, but they will not take chances. If attacked, I'm afraid they will finish what you started, innocents on board or not."

After good-bye hugs all around, his three friends left the hangar and he entered Cassandra though the rear storage. Cassie became corporeal by the time he closed the storage door and entered the galley. She appeared dressed in khaki cargo pants, tennis shoes, a half shirt displaying under-boob, and her honey-blond hair in a pony tail.

"I like it when you enter from the rear," she said, and licked her lips.

"Don't ever give up, do you?" he laughed as he made his way to the cockpit.

"No reason to give up," she replied, taking the co-pilot's chair. "I have nothing but time, and you are male. Sooner or later I will hit on the precise combination of looks and clothes, or lack of clothes."

"Captain Cooper, the hanger is depressurized and door is open," came the flight control voice. "Good luck and safe flight, Captain."

"Thank you, Control. Cassandra is exiting Kennedy."

The Wraith class fighter eased back and out of the opening into space. Coop used thrusters to drop below the level of the warship before engaging sub-light engines. Cassandra laid in the course for the nearest system rim. It would require a few hours to reach a point where he could adjust the array for open space and full speed.

Within the gravity effects of a solar system, the little ship did a remarkable 80,473,995.48 mph. Once they could put the system's effects behind them, the ship would travel 1,000 parsecs (1kpc) in twenty-four hours.

They could cover nineteen-trillion-miles in one day.

The physicists already had a difficult time trying to explain how the laws of physics were more like guidelines in this new age of galactic travel. They offered no clue why every ship with a space-fold array covered open space at the same maximum rate of speed. Whether it was the relatively small Wraith or the PT-109, the same max speed applied . . . 1kpc.

The crystal-laser arrays built large enough for a space-time bubble to form in front of the ship, cover the ship, and then release natural space behind the ship, but size meant nothing to speed.

The trip to the rim passed in comfortable silence. Coop ran different scenarios through his head, trying to decide how the Aster system would begin and proceed through a difficult healing process. Cassandra would fade out from time to time, and return in a slightly different outfit or hairstyle. She never said anything.

"Exiting space fold," her voice informed him. "Resetting navigation for Fell. Re-entering space-fold."

Cassandra coursed for Fell.

"Why didn't you engage the Rys force field and head back to Fell directly from AF3?" Cassie asked.

"Because we don't know how much we tax the systems that way," he replied. "Time was imperative for the trip from Fell to the vortex. If we need to travel that way, we know now we can. Otherwise I don't plan on taking the risk until I know more about the effects. Getting to Fell and then back to AF3 is important, but it isn't imperative." He looked over at the empty co-pilot seat. "Why do you keep materializing and not talking?"

"I'm reading your bio-telemetry," she answered. "I thought I would go about seducing you in a more scientific manner. Each time I appear I gauge the effects of minor changes in my appearance against your biological reactions. I believe I will be able to create a feminine model you find too striking to resist. I am also beginning to experiment with pheromones. My research indicates human males are often stimulated by olfactory sensations as well as visual appearances."

"You think you can find a combination of looks, dress, and smell I will be unable to resist? Why do you think that?" he asked.

"My time with Lt. Moore has been as valuable as my time in research," Cassie replied. "Mags said repeatedly men are stupid and easy to manipulate. Human males think with their . . . "

"I know what Mags believes men think with," Coop interrupted. "I also imagine every man has a fantasy woman. I simply don't think meeting her will result in a complete meltdown."

When the computer programmers working for Trent Industries were tasked with building an artificial intelligence to operate and maintain systems on the new Wraith, they were also presented with the opportunity of creating the personality for a new holo-avatar. What Trent was not aware of when he gifted the Wraith to Coop, along with the AI and Avatar came a sub-routine within the source codes supposedly deleted before final delivery. A code writer thought it would be fun to have the avatar available as a sex-toy. Stuck on long lonely space flights, it would provide company both intellectual and physical. He wrote a sub-program to make the avatar sexually attracted to its captain. Too many years of gaming and a computer geek became responsible for the sexual tension between Cassie and Coop. All because Trent took the ship early.

Coop could have the sub-routine deleted. He was not sure if he would or should. He enjoyed Cassie's company, and feared re-programming now might destroy her personality. Still, there were times when she made it difficult not to notice her.

At sixteen hours into the trip, Coop brought the lights down in the cabin and made his way to the bunks. Removing everything but his boxers, ready to climb onto the lowest bunk, he was interrupted by an "Excuse me," from Cassie.

She found the right combination.

Honey-blond hair pulled back into the ponytail he found cute and sexy. The style provided her pretty face full frame, from green almond-shaped eyes, pouty full lips, to the strong chin. Graceful neck. She wore a cut-off white t-shirt to show a lot of tanned, smooth skin, and ripped abs beneath the promise of round, firm full breasts. Her nipples teased through the thin fabric.

Simple white panties hugged the narrow hips of a young, athletic woman. Her legs were long, strong, and also tan. She had on white crew socks and no shoes.

As she moved closer, her breathing raised and lowered the white top. The scent of Caribbean sea and female musk drifted softly across his awareness.

"Your bio-telemetry readings are impressive," she whispered. She pressed a curvy five-foot-nine against his six-foot-one. Her mouth covered his and her tongue worked easily into his mouth. His hands pulled her closer by holding two firm butt cheeks. Her fingers found the front of his shorts.

She pulled away from the kiss and said, "It appears all of your systems are responding perfectly."

Coop did not reply. He lost and he knew it. He pulled her into another kiss and the ship shuddered.

"Is that you?" he asked.

Cassie had a confused look. The ship shuddered again, much more violently. Then it bucked, and in spite of the gravotonics, both were tossed up and then down to the deck, Coop landing on top of the avatar.

"We're under attack," she said, unfazed by his weight thrown atop her or the heavy landing. "I'm unable to . . ." and she dematerialized. Coop dropped the few inches to the deck, caught himself, and pushed straight up.

"Cassie, report," he commanded.

The ship jerked violently. He was thrown backward and into the wall beside the bunks. His head hit and hit hard, knocking him unconscious. As he fell, something yanked his ship out of spacefold and into natural space.

Part One

Forced Conscription

Chapter 1

Coop awoke on one of Cassandra's two bunks. He replayed the moments before getting knocked unconscious. Nothing made any more sense now than then.

"Cassie," he whispered.

"Your AI is off line," a male voice said.

Coop opened his eyes to find a man, human appearing, seated at the com-tac station. The chair swiveled to allow him to face Cooper.

"My ship's medic checked you out before we put you in the bunk," he said. "She was quite impressed with your genetics. Said you would be up and running in no time." The man presented an easy smile. The relaxed demeanor did not reflect in his eyes.

Cooper's genetic reengineering provided the ability to self-heal from anything short of a fatal wound. It enhanced his strength to approximately six-times his former capacity. Boosted his speed, too. He considered using both, but decided on gaining more information before taking any rash actions.

He slid his feet over the side of the bunk to sit on the edge of the bottom bed. He wore boxers. Being nearly naked would not affect his ability to defend or attack, if needed.

"First, what have you done to my ship and, second, who are you?" he asked, taking command.

"First, your ship is fine," the man replied. "You were pulled out of space-fold by a tether. It's a rough way to get from A to B. The tether includes a force-limiter shield to assure nothing is permanently broken."

He crossed an ankle over a knee. The body language indicated he either did not know what Daniel Cooper was capable of doing, or did not care.

"My name is Veresk D'Sey. I would shake your hand, but I don't think I should get too close just yet. Not until you know more about me, and why I was sent to get you."

"You were sent to get me? Who sent you and why?"

D'Sey stood. He equalled Coop's six-one. His shaggy hair light brown or dark blond. Difficult to say in the cabin's reduced lighting. He had hazel eyes. His black t-shirt did not fit tightly, but hinted of muscled beneath. His arms were certainly muscular. He also wore, well, he wore blue jeans with hiking boots.

D'sey appeared to be a young urban professional on a wilderness excursion.

"Get dressed," he said. "I'll give you a tour, and try to answer all of your questions. You need to understand two things, Captain Cooper." Coop, former Army Ranger sniper, recognized the stare of a fellow predator. "I am not here to harm you, your friends, your ship, or your world. If you make any hostile moves, regardless of how strong, fast, and tough you think you are, the ship will toast you."

"The ship?"

D'Sey smiled again, caging the predator behind the laid-back demeanor. "Your ship is currently parked inside another ship. The other ship is somewhat protective, like your Cassie, but without the sexy. If you're curious yet, I'd love to show you around and explain a few things."

Coop shrugged as answer. He pulled on a grey long-sleeve t-shirt and black cargo pants. Slid his kevlar-composite boots on and laced them. He completed dressing with a well-worn Space Fleet baseball cap. Once dressed and standing, the two men resembled brothers, or, at least, cut from a similar mold.

D'sey knew his way around Cassandra. He called for the ladder to the top-hatch, and headed up and out first. Coop followed, close behind.

Cooper hesitated atop the Wraith. He scanned his environment. D'Sey jumped from the forward port wing to the deck. The man moved from the top of the ship and across the wing before Coop exited. The distance covered indicated speed. The jump meant he could fly, defy gravity, or was strong.

The hijacked human peered up. The overhead ceiling high enough to be obscured in darkness. The size of the hangar could not be discerned due to the low lighting, but he felt the enormity of the space around him. To his left, in the shadows, a ship rested. Easily ten-times the size of his two-person fighter. The star-cruiser appeared to leave a lot of space available in the bay. The sleek exterior milky in color and texture.

Coop dropped onto the wing, made his way forward, and jumped to the floor.

"This is Clyde," D'Sey said, turning his back on Coop, and walking away. "From the outside he looks like a gigantic kidney bean made of silver. Smooth as a baby's butt. Clyde has picked me up and bussed me around the galaxy for centuries. I have no idea how big he is inside. I used to explore. Not so much anymore."

"Picking you up and taking you places? For centuries?"

"Clyde works for the aliens you call Martians. They aren't Martians. Mars operated as an outpost. They are called Nakki."

D'Sey stopped. He held his hands up and out. "This is the main hangar. You could park all of your Space Fleet ships inside with enough room left for a few more. Currently, your ship and mine are the only two aboard." He pointed to his right.

The yacht shimmered. Coop was unsure why the term yacht came to mind, but the flowing lines, rear superstructure, and slightly convex deck leading to a pointed nose reminded him of the large private ships which sailed Earth's oceans. Parked a quarter-mile away, the ship floated above the deck.

"Menace," he said.

He made no further comments regarding the spacecraft.

"Nakki are among the oldest surviving species in the galaxy, if not the eldest." D'Sey spoke as they walked towards a bulkhead. "They created the space-fold array powering my ship," he turned his eyes to Cooper, "and yours. Imagine my surprise when Clyde informed me someone, other than a Nakki or Nakki Agent, traveled by space-fold."

He spoke to Coop without speaking to him. His monologue delivered as if vocalizing his thoughts.

"Obviously I fell behind with recent events on your side of the galaxy. I used the time coming here to catch up. Humans have been a busy lot this last century. While I was occupied in another sector of the Milky Way, Earth made quite the splash with your arrival into the galactic community."

Coop stopped. D'Sey walked forward a few feet before realizing.

"You work for the Nakki? You're not a Nakki?"

"Nakki have employed my family one way or another for half-a-million years," D'Say answered. His matter-of-fact tone made the number 'half-a-million' seem inconsequential. "I am not a Nakki. At least, no more than you, or another thousand species in the galaxy who can trace their origins to them. Please follow, Captain. There is a comfortable room on the other side of the door. I will try to be more concise. I promise."

Cooper did not trust the stranger, but he lacked options. He followed, leaving the hangar and entering a lounge. The view caught his attention first. A wall to his right displayed a black hole in the distance. Space around the hole vibrated with yellow light. Colored gases of solid and mixed hues fluttered throughout the void between his perspective and the black hole. Thousands of twinkling stars scattered around the edges of space. Impossible to determine if he peered from a window or onto a projection. He scanned the interior before continuing further.

The room contained three large sectional sofas, a dozen club chairs, and a stocked bar along one wall. Stocked with what, he had no clue, but it rivaled the bar in the Officer's Club on EMS2, the space station between Earth and its moon.

D'Say walked behind the bar. He returned with a glass of brown, effervescent liquid, and handed the chilled glass to his guest. Coop tasted the drink, while D'Sey made himself comfortable in a club chair facing the black hole.

"Cola," Coop said. "With ice," he added. He joined his host, taking the club chair to D'Sey's right.

"I didn't think you needed anything stronger yet," D'Sey replied. He waited for Coop to sit before continuing.

"We don't have time for a full-blown history lesson, Captain. I'll keep this briefing brief, and try to stay on point."

The wall displayed the star systems forming the spiral Milky Way Galaxy. A video display and not a window.

"I cannot tell you an exact number, but for millions of years Nakki vessels have explored the galaxy. They discovered billions of worlds with the potential for life. For life to occur, even to produce simplistic forms of living organisms, you need all the right things to happen within a relatively short window of opportunity. For those life-forms to evolve into sentient beings is an astronomical crapshoot. The Nakki decided to load the dice."

The video changed to show a silver spaceship shaped like a giant kidney bean.

"They seeded planets with the biological and chemical agents necessary for the development of living organisms. They assessed the trial planets and moons over time and boosted evolution along for those indicating promise."

"The Nakki are responsible for sentient life in the galaxy?" Coop asked.

"Not all sentient life. Life developed and evolved naturally on millions of worlds. There are species in this galaxy which resemble humanoids in no manner at all. There are sentient, highly evolved races whose appearance would scare a human to death. Billions of planets remain barren of life, or provide a home to non-sentient lifeforms."

The view returned to the Milky Way.

"There are also hundreds of species and thousands of races which are direct descendants of the Nakki."

"They were humanoid," Coop said.

"Obvious," D'Sey replied. "The scout ship Fairchild's group discovered on Mars was designed for use by humanoids. The ship, and the tech discovered in the storage hangar, led to the creation of your Space Fleet. Of all the worlds, in all this time, humans are the only ones to reverse-engineer Nakki technology to develop their own interstellar engines to access space-fold. Amazing. Not the time taken, but that it occurred at all."

"Have other species discovered abandoned Nakki technology?"

"There are thousands of Nakki outposts in the galaxy, and more than a few discarded sites discovered by the indigenous locals," D'Sey said. "Nakki cleared the majority of these stations out before departing. The discovery of ruins becomes an unexplained mystery for those finding them. I know of a dozen depots discovered containing abandoned equipment, records, and trash. Of those discoveries, three, now including Earth, led to locals reverse engineering portions of the technology left behind. Only humans recreated the space-fold arrays."

D'Sey paused to watch the display of the galaxy shimmer into multi-colored mist and the mist congealed to create Earth and its moon.

"Nathan Trent, your friend who tapped into the tech found on Mars, is someone I must meet one day. The origin DNA within his genome must be extremely dominate."

"Nakki seeded potential planets, and then stepped away to see what would happen?"

"The Nakki prefer sentient lifeforms to evolve as naturally as possible. They believe, left to their own devices, a few of these species will mature into the benevolent guardians the galaxy needs to expand and grow until time ends."

"Benevolent guardians. Is that how the Nakki see themselves? Guardians?"

"Are you familiar with the Sagittarius Dwarf Galaxy?" D'Sey asked. The screen changed to display another galaxy. A spheroid of stars and gases appeared, hanging within, slightly below a depiction of the Milky Way Galaxy.

"A group of around a billion stars swallowed into the Milky Way Spiral," Coop replied. "No black hole in the center we know of. On a deteriorating elliptic orbit as the Milky Way tears it apart and absorbs the pieces."

"Your solar system originated within the Sagittarius Dwarf Galaxy," D'Sey said. "There are eleven Dwarf Galaxies currently being eaten by the Milky Way. Over the past billion years, stars, and other matter, slipped from the Sagittarius Dwarf Galaxy into the Milky Way."

"Our scientists are aware of this," Coop replied. "The current orbit of Sagittarius is bringing it closer to our star. The dark matter emanating from the dwarf system appears to be reviving the ozone layers of Mars, along with other effects on planets and moons in our system."

"Dark Matter within Sagittarius does have unique, rich properties," the other man replied.

"It is also home to the species, Basfor Flyn," the stranger said, taking a sip from his own glass. "The Basfor Flyn conquered a large part of their galaxy. They are neither benevolent nor restrained. About one-million years ago they dispatched drones into the Milky Way. These drones came to build millions of wormhole channels. The Basfor Flyn use wormholes to travel between star systems. The dark matter from their galaxy provides the glue necessary to keep the channel walls intact."

"The wormhole channels used by the space-capable planets in our galaxy?" Coop asked.

"The same. Channels used by all of the interstellar travelers in this galaxy, except Nakki, a small number of Nakki agents, and, now, the planet Earth. Channels used by Basfor Flyn armadas to invade the Milky Way Galaxy one-million-years ago."

"Really. And no one knows about this invasion? I've read a lot of alien histories over the past year, and none of the races talk about an invasion from the Sagittarius Dwarf Galaxy."

D'Sey smiled, and nodded at the screen. A battle rages in the blue sky above a planet. The view pulled back to reveal Earth.

"Your own history records stories of incredible battles in the skies of your planet," he said. "Indian mythology gives detailed descriptions of nuclear warheads. There are ancient sites with pictographs of ships, aliens, weapons, and battles. These confrontations occurred throughout the galaxy."

"You said a million years ago," Coop countered. "Civilization on Earth is not that old."

"Your current civilization, perhaps not," D'Sey replied. "Civilizations existed on your planet long before your scientific records indicate. Do you really believe a planet able to sustain life for hundreds-of-millions of years only recently developed a sentient culture? Civilizations have come and gone a half-dozen times. Destroyed by wars, astronomical phenomenon, planetary shifts, pandemics, and new ones rebuilt on the ashes."

The Earth appeared in 3-D, fires raging across the surface.

"One of the major battles between the Nakki and the Basfor Flyn occurred in your solar system. It resulted in the end of life on Mars."

"Where are the Basfor Flyn now? For that matter, where are the Nakki?"

"The Nakki pushed the Basfor Flyn out of the Milky Way. Thanks, in great part, to technology like space-fold travel. The Nakki who survived remain in their home system. They keep an eye on the Sagittarius Dwarf Galaxy. They also created a provisional force. Agents dispatched to keep the playing fields safe inside the galaxy."

"You're a galactic cop?"

"More like a referee," D'Sey answered. "The Nakki never stopped wanting worlds to evolve as naturally as possible. They stay out of the way until a species evolves to the point of interstellar travel. Thereafter, they begin to take more of an interest."

D'Sey placed his drink on the floor, then turned to look at Cooper.

"When a civilization decides to forcefully disrupt the development of other worlds, they become more concerned. When a disruption turns violent, or worse, genocidal, they dispatch an agent. The agent decides if an intervention is necessary."

"Like the Mischene using the Zenge to invade the Trade Alliance worlds?" Coop asked. "Did they dispatch a referee to do something about them?"

D'Sey gave Coop an air-toast with his glass, and told him, "You did a pretty good job handling the Mischene and Zenge without help."

"It isn't over," Coop said.

"Not as long as the Devee are around," D'Sey responded.

"Who are the Devee?"

"Off the subject," the other man said. "I promised to remain on point."

"My assignment sent me elsewhere. A couple of powerful confederations are about to come into conflict. Because of the situation there, I have been absent this part of the galaxy for nearly one-hundred years. In that short amount of time, the Mischene problem developed, while Earth became a dominant player in local galactic politics."

"If not to intervene between the Mischene and the Trading Alliance, why are you here?" Coop asked.

"I need help with a difficult situation. The other agents with space-fold technology are not available. I'm here to ask for your help, and use the situation as a field test."

"Field test?"

"The Nakki believe you might be a potential new agent."

"I appreciate the offer, D'Sey," Coop said. "But things on this side of the galaxy are not settled. I can't leave my friends or my planet to play cops and robbers with you."

"Captain Cooper, you need to consider a few things before making a decision. The dust-up in this part of the Milky Way is a skirmish. You effectively stopped the Mischene. What's left is sweep out the trash. The larger threat to peace in this quadrant comes from the planet Devistar."

"Once more. Why?" Coop asked.

"If you agree to help us, I'll provide the intel you need to keep the Devee in check," D'Sey answered.

"Extortion?"

"Payment. There is a confrontation brewing between confederations in the great spiral arm you call The New Outer Arm. Ninety-nine-thousand-light-years across the Milky Way, near the black hole in the center of our galaxy. The section of interest is much younger than your part of the galaxy. A relatively young species evolved and discovered interstellar travel more quickly than any other since the Nakki."

The screen changed, displaying a time-lapse trip across space, skirting a black hole, ending at stars sitting on the edge of a dark void.

"The Helacene," he said, the view moving in to a single star, and finally the third planet orbiting the star. "Matriarchal civilization. As they discovered inhabited planets, they offered assistance where needed. Where the Trading Alliance Worlds consider it inappropriate to interact with civilizations which have not discovered wormholes, the Helacene decide contact on a case-by-case basis. If a world needed help to feed the population, fight disease, or faced a terminal threat, they stepped in. If natural disasters created misery, they showed up with aid. Civilization on the brink of new discoveries were sometimes given a boost."

"Flies in the face of the Nakki's non-intervention practice," Coop remarked.

"The Nakki would prefer civilizations to develop naturally," D'Sey countered. "The Helacene interventions are a result of their charitable nature. They are a generous, benevolent species at their core. They lead a confederation of nineteen star systems and twenty-six inhabited planets. The Alliance watches over another two dozen planets with sentient lifeforms, but with no need of intervention."

"Benevolent overseers," Coop said. "The hope of the Nakki?"

"Perhaps," D'Sey acknowledged. "If they aren't exterminated by the Kashōn."

"I assume the Kashōn are the reason you need my help?"

"The Kashōn descended from Basfor Flyn forces abandoned in the Milky Way following their defeat. It is genetically infused in them to empire build. Over the last half-million years they devolved to survive, then re-evolved to an advanced-technology civilization. They are a warrior species. Much of their time and resources are spent designing weapons. When they discovered wormhole travel, their initial action was to invade and enslave the first star system they visited."

"Why didn't the Nakki act then?"

"Nakki are not gods, Captain. The galaxy is not small, and resources are finite. A million bad things happen across the stars every minute. The Kashōn overran over two-hundred star systems, annexing each into the Kashōn Empire. It took time before stories retold by thousands of escapees of their vicious methods reached a Nakki listening post."

D'Sey placed his drink on the floor and stood. The screen changed to a 3-d image of a fierce-looking alien. The image rotated, displaying a blocky body, wide across the shoulders, deep through the chest, with large, powerful legs.

"The Nakki dispatched Clyde to scout the Kashōn Empire. He found a bipedal species. Symmetrical hominoid bodies. Large, thick-boned heads with two eyes, snout, and mouth. Males show spiral horns growing out from the temples. They average six-feet, and three-hundred pounds of muscle, sinew, and bone. High intelligence, and low tolerance for other beings. Clyde monitored communications and watched the Kashōn periodically for a century. The stories regarding the methods used by Kashōn invading, and enslaving other worlds proved true."

A planet of beautiful topography replaced the fearsome Kashōn image. The sweeping panoramic view crossed forests, fields, and oceans. It zoomed out to show expansive cities of metal and glass with incoming and departing space ships. The view dissolved and the Kashōn reappeared, clothed in a manner familiar to Cooper.

"In spite of advanced technology, creation of massive cities, and the ability to travel through wormhole channels, they continue to wear clothing similar to their warrior ancestors. A galea-style helmet, cut to allow their horns to show while protecting the head and face. A vest made of segmented armor able to prevent penetration by smaller laser fire or bladed weapons. Arm guards of the same material. A kilt of animal skin, and armored greaves to protect the legs. They usually wear heavy-soled sandals."

"You're describing a Roman soldier," Coop said.

"Similar, I suppose. Same mentality for sure," the other replied. "Except Roman soldiers did not carry laser pistols on their belts, or force-lances able to collapse a wall. Like your Roman Legionnaires, they carry knives and short, double-edged swords. Not for show. The Kashōn prefer to kill up close and with as much damage as they can inflict."

"The Nakki sent you to confront an entire Empire?"

"At the time, things were pretty quiet in your quadrant. Menace patrolled the sector. I raided a few ships to keep tabs on the potential problem-makers. Earth was a pleasant-enough world. Young but civilized. It provided a restful place to visit. I discovered comfortable clothes and cola."

D'Sey retrieved his glass.

"I was dispatched to make a closer inspection of the Kashōn. The Nakki recognized the species from battles with the Basfor Flyn."

The wall-display presented a simple diagram, labeling one area KASHŌN EMPIRE and another HELACENE ALLIANCE.

"Clyde dropped us off between the Helacene Alliance and the Kashōn Empire. We pillaged a couple of Empire outposts and looted supply ships for intel. We collected data from their files, took anything valuable, and freed a few slaves."

"Raided? Pillaged? Looted? As in pirated?" Coop asked.

"I've used the pirate-theme for a few centuries," D'Sey replied. "It allows me to attack ships, board, and take things without anyone attributing the attack to another world. Since I'm unaffiliated, the reason appears to be illegal profit."

"Do you make a profit?"

"Usually," he admitted. "In the case of the slaves, we turned them over to civilizations associated with the Helacene for other goods. Gave me the opportunity to see how the Hela operate up close and set up contacts. They consider Menace a privateer. As long as I do not target Helacene Alliance ships or outposts, they don't shoot first when we show up."

"And the Kashōn?"

"Wanted dead not alive by the Empire," D'Sey replied, amused. "The Kashōn do not allow unauthorized or unaffiliated ships in their space. I was never going to be able to fly through Empire-controlled regions without a challenge. As a pirate vessel, they don't like me, but they don't consider me a priority, either. Species like the Kashōn are marauders. I suspect there is a small amount of respect for Menace.

"I also deliver black-market goods to worlds under Kashōn rule. They get needed supplies, and I get intel."

"And make a profit?"

"Usually. I get more than intel, and I build my cover," D'Sey answered.

"What changed?" Coop asked. "You're here, looking for a recruit with access to space-fold. Something caught you off guard."

"The Kashōn Empire's expansionism over the past few hundred years concerned the Nakki. The connection to the Basfor Flyn warranted closer observation. My orders were to watch for any sign of more than a historical link."

"The Nakki feared the Basfor Flyn might use the Kashōn to launch a new offensive against them," Coop said.

"I haven't seen anything to indicate the Kashōn rulers know anything about their origins," D'Sey responded.

"They threatened the Helacene becoming guardians?" Coop asked.

"They threaten more than the Helacene or the systems aligned with them. The Empire is constantly battling logistic problems. They control a lot of planets, but their influence gets thin, especially where civilizations don't offer much of value. The King is always fighting an insurrection somewhere. It makes continued expansion less viable. Would you like another drink?"

Coop shook his head. D'Sey went behind the bar.

"To survive they need to target more valuable systems," Coop surmised. "They need resources to maintain their Empire."

"Hela and the confederated planets within the Alliance, with or without sentient life, fit those criteria," D'Sey replied. "Their resources, used for policing their slave-worlds, will not support a campaign to invade an alliance with a strong military of its own."

"A change in tactics?" Coop asked.

"I told you the Helacene are matriarchal," D'Sey said. "Suzerain Palla Athodite is their leader. She has three daughters. The eldest is next in line. The next girl is the spare. They are trained for years to replace their mother. Educated in cultural studies, diplomacy, military strategy, and even how to dress. When the eldest is crowned, the sister will become her chief counsel."

"The third daughter?"

"Who knows?" D'Sey replied. "She's not in training, and rumors say she's something of a wild-child. Teenager with Mommy's keys to the kingdom. There are two sons. In this type of society they will be given diplomatic or military positions and expected to fuck their way through life. The issue is the two princesses."

The wall-screen displayed a brown and ochre planet. The view zoomed down and panned across sand dunes similar to a North African desert. A walled fortress appeared. The facade large-cut blocks of stone. The entry a wide arched opening. The scene altered as the camera angle rose to reveal the structure enclosed an oasis. Glistening pool of water languid amid lush palm-like greenery.

"The planet is called Enparatus. The fortress is not a fort, but an academy. Normally used to educate children from the confederated planets in the history of their Alliance. They learn about the various religious and cultural beliefs held by the members. When the Suzerain' daughter is old enough, she is sent there for a series of advanced studies. All other students are relocated back to their home worlds. The Princess-heir is tutored by dedicated academics and clerics. In this case, the two oldest girls were close enough in age to attend at the same time."

D'Sey turned the screen off. He set his drink on the bar top.

"King Phortis sent a raiding party to Enparatus. They captured Palla's daughters. Phortis sent a drone to Hela with a message for the Suzerain. The Kashōn Empire intends to invade the Alliance systems nearest their border. If the Hela intercede, the teachers and clerics on Enparatus will be killed."

"He didn't threaten her daughters?" Coop asked.

"If, after those people were executed, the Suzerain did not agree to keep the fleet away, records kept at the Academy would be destroyed. Thousands of years of documents and digital files. Files likely copied and kept somewhere else, but significant original documents would be burned."

"And if she continues to resist?" Coop asked.

"Her daughters will be given to his soldiers," D'Sey answered.

"The Kashōn raided Enparatus. They had to arrive in the system through a wormhole gate. The Queen did not post ships in the system to guard her daughters?" Coop asked,

"Military mind," D'Sey said. "Yes, she did. Two of her best battleships. Five Shroud ships, The Empire's fleet is called The Shroud, entered and broadcast the codes to prove they were friendly and with permission to enter the system. They destroyed the two Hela ships. Two Shroud battleships remained to blockade the system."

"There's a traitor or a spy in the Helacene administration or military. Someone high enough to know secret codes and the agenda for the Princesses," Coop inferred. "You plan on rescuing the daughters. With space-fold you can enter the system without using the wormhole gate. Why do you need me?"

"Actually, I plan on you rescuing the girls," D'Sey answered. "I intend to assassinate Phortis and as many of his inner circle as possible. It will send a message to the Empire that Kashōn expansion is over."

D'Sey returned to his seat.

"Timing is key. I need the princesses safe before I go for the King. I also need Palla willing to help if any planets try to escape the Empire. Anger over the attack on her daughters, and grateful for their rescue should do the trick."

Before they could continue the discussion, a huge grey humanoid barged into the room. He ducked to enter through the hangar doorway. The alien stood six-eight, minimum, and mid-three-hundred-pounds of spacial-domination. Long arms covered in light-grey hair. Big hands, short legs, and wide feet.

On reflex, Coop reached for a sidearm he did not have. His first thought was 'troll'.

The creature's countenance of ruddy complexion with dense close-cropped orange-colored scalp provided the story-book-monster appearance. Bushy orange eyebrows and two rows of blocky teeth made him forbidding. Bright sky blue eyes, wide as a child's on Christmas morning, and a bouncy, giddy, excitement emanating from the giant reminded Coop of a big dog trying to not look vicious so people would pat him.

The blue eyes scanned the room, found and halted on Coop.

"You!" The word reverberated throughout the room. The voice a bass drum and a tuba rolled into one percussive instrument. He moved towards the human, who stood to face the giant. The huge alien did not lumber. Despite his girth, he moved easily, with giant, unshod feet propelling him across the deck like a dancer.

"You have got to tell me how you power those laser weapons," he said, stopping a few feet from Coop, who assumed a martial arts stance. "Can you make a pistol big enough for my hand?"

He held forth a massive right hand covered in grey hair. Four digits and a thumb spread.

"Captain Cooper, this is Duly." D'Sey stood next to Coop. "He's a member of my crew, and a bit of a fanatic about weapons. In case you didn't notice."

Chapter 2

"You went aboard my ship without my permission?" Coop asked.

The grey behemoth stared down at him. If surprised the human did not act intimidated, he did not show it.

"Of course not, Captain," he replied. His voice, no longer excited, modulated to a sound less elephant, and more moose. "Clyde did a security scan. I categorized the weapons. I'm good with weapons. Your ship is pretty cool, and a little dated, but your personal weapons are incredible."

"Duly gets carried away," D'Sey said. He resumed his seat. "What do you find incredible about Captain Cooper's personal armament?"

"The power source is small," the giant answered. "His sidearm laser can be pulled from a holster with ease. The shoulder-fire laser rifles are sleek and light. I had given up on laser-based personal weapons because of the stupid power source. You always run out of juice, and always when you need it most."

He turned back to Coop, once more the star-struck child seeking answers.

"How many shots can you fire before replacing the power cell?"

Cooper remained standing, but relaxed. For all of his size and intimidating appearance, the alien was a kid in a hobby store.

"One-thousand-hours of continual usage. It weighs less than four pounds. Armorers rebuilt the barrel assembly to allow the pistol to slide out of the Sherpa holster for a quick draw. The power source is in the hinged handle," he answered.

"What is the power source?"

Coop remained silent. Duly waited, and then turned to D'Sey.

"Captain Cooper does not yet trust us or our motives," he explained. "I do not believe he is ready to give away all of his secrets."

The grey alien shrugged. "When you finish with Dee, find me. If you show me yours, I'll show you mine." He turned and left, cramming his bulk through the door leading back to the hangar.

"Your ship's scans give you any other insights?" Coop asked.

"Clyde isn't my ship," D'Sey responded. "But I won't evade the answer. Everything aboard your ship was scanned and catalogued. Including your computer's memory files, communications, data, and technical aspects. Information added to a file the Nakki keeps on you, Earth, Space Fleet, and related subjects."

Coop considered his response to the invasion of Cassandra's systems. His reply left unspoken when the doorway to the hangar again opened. A female walked though this time. She was nothing like the grey alien who exited.

D'Sey rose. An oddly gentlemanly act. "Captain Cooper, this is Costi Tempur, my medical officer. Doc, you've already seen Captain Cooper, now you may meet him as well."

Tempur stopped short of walking into Coop. She made a visual examination. "You appear to have recovered from your unexpected exit from space-fold," she said. Her voice warm honey. A slight accent, but not one he could place. She extended her right hand.

He took hers in his. Her grip firm. The muscles in her forearm and biceps indicated she would be strong. Her coloring from the blue-spectrum, but not the Fell blue. Green mixed in to produce a shade not quite teal, nor green, nor blue, but all of them. Coop held her gaze. His dark brown eyes accessed her in return.

"What do you see?" she asked.

"Competence," he replied. Her hazel eyes showed smarts and mirth. Thick black, wavy hair covered her ears and fell to mid-neck. High cheek-bones, straight nose, a cupid's bow upper lip, and slightly turned-out lower lip. She stood six-inches shorter than him, about five-seven, and weighed a solid 130-135.

"Smart and diplomatic," she replied. She released the handshake first, walked around the human, and took a seat on the sofa. Her burgundy sleeveless vest and baggy pants gave no hints as to body shape, but she moved like an athlete.

"The rest of the crew are hanging around trying to come up with excuses to meet Captain Cooper," she said to D'Sey, who remained standing.

"Captain Cooper, it might speed things along if you allow my crew to enter and introduce themselves. Otherwise, we will be interrupted every few minutes."

"Fine with me."

"You may all come in now," D'Sey said. If he activated a communications device, Coop did not see it.

The grey mountain entered first and headed for the bar.

"You already met Duly," D'Sey said. "Duly is from the Xentarene system on this side of the galaxy. The name of his race translates roughly to Howlers. I'm sure you understand the reason. Next is Krest. You met his relatives aboard the Star Gazer. He is a Fray from Osperantue."

Coop perked up, giving the entering alien his complete attention. The Fray represented the second species on Osperantue. Fray were supposed to have been aboard the Star Gazer, the ship filled with alien refugees who made first contact with Earth. He recalled Bosine, Posine, and Woolifers, but did not recall seeing anyone similar to Krest.

Five-eight or nine, thin, with long arms and long legs for his compact torso. His appearance nothing like the other three Osperantue races, with their pink skin, wide noses, and small mouths. They had eyes set farther to the side of their heads. Osperantue were prey. Krest was a hunter.

He moved toward Coop, who glanced down to assure himself the creature's feet touched the deck. The being walked fluidly, with no effort. His skin coloring dark, of a reddish, mahogany hue. Black hair, cut short, and deep set black eyes beneath a ridged brow. A thick, rounded nose with slit nostrils.

"Thank you for assisting my fellow Osperantue," he said. He did not offer a hand. His voice was soft, but easily understood. "Should you decide to join us, it will be an honor to serve along side." He did not wait on a reply, leaving to join the grey alien at the bar.

"The Fray are an interesting species," D'Sey said, standing beside the human. "If they don't want you to notice them, you don't. Incredibly reserved, and not social. Equally honest and loyal."

"Predator," Coop said.

"Succinct and correct," D'Sey replied. "Descendants of indentured assassins brought to this galaxy by the Basfor Flyn."

Before the surprised human could ask more questions regarding Krest and the Fray, a short, stocky female, with dark green skin, and a bald head introduced herself.

"I'm Taah Vil," she said, extending hers and taking his hand. She kept her head tilted down, not making eye contact. "I'm in charge of maintenance. I keep Menace in shape. Your ship needs some touch-ups. She's been in battle. Singed and dinged. I can fix her right up. Straighten the interior. Can't make her as pretty as Menace, but she isn't meant to be pretty. She's mean. I like her. You're a good captain, Captain. You should help us."

"Taah, we aren't going to talk Captain Cooper into anything," D'Sey said.

Taah shrugged. "Just saying." She joined Doc on the sofa.

"Taah is a Cora Sen Du. Her planet is among a closed confederation of systems on the edge of the Trading Alliance Worlds. The system makes contact with a Trade world from time to time when they need something. They do not allow outsiders to visit their controlled space. Her species is known for their musical talents and sharp intelligence. Besides mechanical duties, Taah is my communications officer."

Cooper blinked. He turned his head to the side, allowing his peripheral vision to take charge. A shadow followed Taah. He tensed, his hand going to where a weapon would normally rest on his hip.

"Relax, Captain," D'Sey said, his tone casual. "I'm impressed. Most people never notice Ateakatakut."

"What is it?"

"A shadow from the Andromeda Galaxy. It will take time to explain Teak, and something we can discuss later, if you decide to help in our mission. For now, know that he communicates in a way that takes time to understand. He has become attached to Taah, and is usually near her."

"Teak and Taah, da two beautiful spirits dat make every day bright an' sunny. I'm Key Largo, and glad to meet a'nutter human."

The thin, dark-brown young man grabbed Coop's hand and pulled him into a modified bro-hug with chest-pump.

Extricated, Coop asked, "You're from Earth?"

"DNA don't lie, Cap'pin. Not only from the blue marble, but from the most beautiful i'land on the planet. Jamaica."

"I liberated Key and Taah from a Devee slave ship while patrolling around your side of the galaxy" D'Sey said. "Doc adopted them, and I gave them jobs. Key is my pilot-navigator and ship's cook. When Doc told him his origins, he went a bit overboard on research."

"Watching television shows I find beamed out into the void of space, and listening to the wonderful Bob Marley, Peter Tosh, and Burning Spear. I have a library filled with reggae, if you care to listen on your free time," the effervescent Jamaican space-traveler said.

Coop noted the dreadlocks, bright blue shirt with a green sleeveless vest, trimmed in bright red, worn jeans and sandals.

"You do realize the shows and music you are collecting left Earth over one-hundred-years ago?" he asked.

"People there now don't appreciate reggae?" Key asked, wide smile gone.

"Marley is a classic, and reggae will never die," Coop assured him, bringing the smile back.

"Tonight we eat jerk chicken with rice, plantains, carrots and green beans," Key Largo said. "And Bammies!"

The announcement of cassava cakes brought a round of "whoop! whoop!" from the crew, and a wry grin by D'Sey.

As the wannabe Wailer walked away, D'Sey told Cooper, "Doc determined he came from the Caribbean region of Earth. He decided to be Jamaican. His name came from a movie he found on some data file filled with human cultural studies. He's the one who taught the others to greet you with a handshake."

"How did he get out here?"

"Abducted. More than a few people in space are abductees, Captain. Not all aliens play nice. Prepare yourself, Captain Cooper. My last crew member approaches."

Stalked would better describe the woman's approach. D'Sey's crew contained a few hunters.

Her large breasts barely contained behind a silky, nearly transparent top of fern green. Doc's height, but another twenty-twenty-five pounds of muscle. Long, straight brown hair, green eyes, oval face, and elfin ears gave her an exotic appearance. Her sand-colored skin the shade of Far Eastern people on Earth. Black wavy lines ran from the left side of her face, down her body, and along the outside of her exposed left leg. He could not tell if they were tattoos or natural species coloring. Her legs exposed because she wore short shorts of dark green. The legs muscled like those of a dedicated body-builder.

She had no trouble making eye contact. She sniffed the air, tasting the scent of the human.

"I'm Rox Silvanaé. I'm a Dualønges. My species are shifters, human. When I am not in this form, I am a pula," she informed him.

"A pula is like a jaguar," D'Sey explained. "With bigger teeth."

"Bigger everything," Rox corrected. "Especially bigger appetite," she added, turning away to join those at the bar.

"Quite an interesting collection, Captain D'Sey," Coop said.

"We get the job done," D'Sey responded. "And our next job involves a rescue in one system, and an ass-kicking in another. If you sign on, we have a better chance of success for both. You will learn more things about the galaxy you live in, and I will provide new technology you can take back to help protect your worlds."

"Worlds?"

"Come now, Daniel Cooper. You are human, and Earth is important. But you have discovered new worlds and new beings. They have become just as important to you. You are more like us now. A citizen of the stars. Even if you do not take an offer to become an Agent, you will be better prepared to meet the next challenge."

"What next challenge?"

"Whatever," his host answered. "There will always be a next challenge for men like us. Without something to look forward to, why live so long?"

"I can explain why twelve people survived the reengineering process, and the others perished," Doc said from the sofa.

"I can provide com-translation devises implanted into the brain, and not simply under the skin," Taah said. "You will think the words of aliens, and be able to read and write in any language in the galaxy."

"Communicate as if you are telepathic," Rox added. "Be able to give and receive orders silently."

"New weapons," Duly said, lifting his glass in a toast.

The Fray and the Shadow said nothing.

Key Largo said, "Bammies," and the others joined in with "Whoop! Whoop!"

Chapter 3

"You offer a lot, but you ask for a lot in return," Coop told his host. "While I think it over, what's up with my ship and AI?"

"Clyde placed your AI in stasis while we examined everything," D'Sey answered. "I needed to make sure the information on you was up-to-date. I also wanted to verify Clyde's judgment regarding your ship's capabilities. As usual, he was right. You and your ship can help."

"If I decide not to help?"

"No one will force you, and I will not commandeer your ship, Captain," the agent replied. "The actions by the Kashōn to move on the Helacene Alliance caught me by surprise. I've watched them for decades. We've harassed their ships, and provided aid when and where we could. I hoped to provide time for the Hela to grow stronger. It would have been better if they could face-down the threat. If the Helacene Alliance could stop the Kashōn advances across the Scutum-Centaurus Arm, without overt actions by the Nakki, the Empire would eventually implode."

"Implode because empires based on militaristic principles usually do?" Coop asked.

"Yes. Whether an imperium is located on a single planet or stretches across a galaxy, absolute power results in corruption. Corruption leads to corrosion. Resources grow thin, command grows weary, and subjugated people revolt. Only by continuing to advance do Empires continue to survive."

"The Helacene Alliance offered the best hope for stopping the Kashōn Empire from growing," Coop surmised. "You did not anticipate an attack to come this soon, or it would come by way of a personal assault on the Helacene leader."

"I fucked up," D'Sey admitted.

"Because the Shanks make you play stupid games," Rox chimed in from the bar. "The whole *do not interfere with natural development* crap. While sending us here to interfere."

"Shanks?" Coop asked.

"Nakki," D'Sey answered.

"It's Dualønges for dumb-ass clueless godlike freaks," Rox added. "We spend decades screwing around on the edges of the Ashemachers. Slipping Empire-controlled planets food and medical supplies. Wasting our time introducing a little bit of new tech to Alliance planets. Slow down the Kashōn, and speed up the Hela, and don't let anyone see us do it. Stupid."

"Ashemachers?" Coop asked.

"The core group leading the Kashōn Empire," D'Sey replied. "Ash Makers. Their goal is to enslave as many cultures within the Milky Way Galaxy as they can. The same basic doctrine expressed by the Basfor Flyn. It worked its way into the DNA of their Kashōn descendants. Anything else you want to add, Rox?"

"As a matter of fact, yes," the Dualønges answered. "My people are predators. The Ashemachers are killers. They are unlike any species I have ever seen. They look like primitives, but they are incredibly smart. They pretend to be warriors, but warriors have honor. The Suzerain's hesitation to endanger her daughters will allow them all the advantage they need to win. They will use the princesses as a wedge to allow them to swarm across the Helacene Alliance planets. Just as our hesitation allowed them to sneak onto Enparatus and begin the conquest of the Alliance a century before expected."

"Like I said. I fucked up," D'Sey repeated. "To make sure Palla does not hesitate to face them, I need the royal heirs safe. I must cut out the Ashemacher's influence to slow the Kashōn advance. To accomplish both, I need help."

"I need to think," Coop responded. "Will you remove the stasis lock on Cassandra?"

"By the time you get to your ship every system will be fully functional," D'Sey promised. "Clyde adapted his interior particle array emitters to your AI's corporeal printer. Amazing technology and even more interesting personality routine your avatar has, Captain. Once the AI holo-avatar becomes solid, it can exist outside your ship. It will be able to move freely throughout Clyde."

"She," Coop said. "She is Cassie."

"Clyde will bring *her* up to speed on everything since you were pulled from space-fold. You and Cassie may come and go as you please, but you cannot take your ship out of the hangar. Whether you decide to help or not, I did not have time to wait for your answer. We are on the way back. Clyde uses trans-dimensional drive to make the trip a short one. If you take off, there is no way of knowing what universe you might fly into," D'Sey told him.

"If I say no?"

"Clyde will bring you home after Menace departs. But there is one more long-term consideration you need to take into account."

Coop waited without asking.

"After the Helacene Alliance comes the Galvari Federation. The Cora Sen Du's planet is within the Federation. The Galvari borders the Trading Alliance Worlds. Earth will eventually be in the Kashōn's cross-hairs, Captain Cooper."

Chapter 4

Kashōn Home World - Chōntorham

Kas, a massive main-sequence dwarf star, created a great deal of heat. Chōntorham, the single habitable planet of the twelve within the system, orbited the red star distant enough for liquid water to exist on the surface. Five saline oceans separated six continents. Ice-covered polar caps appeared white and pristine from space. Rivers and streams ribboned the landscapes across five continents. The sixth held a desert of sand, wind, and scorching temperatures.

The planet had a diameter of 25,000 km; twice the width of Earth. Despite the larger total mass, a thick mantle and smaller core resulted in a gravity only one.point.three times Earth's. Humans would feel heavy, but could operate. The Kashōn developed dense bones and strong muscles as compensation.

Plants grew dense, dominated by bright colors of yellow and orange. Many of the leaves displayed blue shades from aqua to navy.

The mix of gases within the atmosphere and star-shine resulted in a pale blue sky. It was a beautiful world with a wide-range of animal life and one sentient species.

Contemporary Kaschōn traced their history to rival tribes. For them, civilization began when the first Ashemachers united the clans and formed the Empire. Written and oral chronicles did not record the first Kashōn were battle-hardened soldiers in service to the Basfor Flyn. Stranded and abandoned on this planet as Basfor Flyn forces retreated. To survive, they discarded technology. In essence, the castaways devolved and learned to exist in the simplest of terms.

After several generations, stories of their origin became myths. Groups broke apart, and tribes claimed territories. The history of castaways faded from memory. Items brought to the planet from distant worlds decayed and disappeared. The Kashōn began the process of re-evolving into the image of their forgotten ancestors.

King Phortis C stood on the balcony of the private chambers of the monarch. The first Phortis built a castle at the highest point overlooking a river one-quarter-mile wide. The river fed the agriculture of a valley once responsible for feeding the fledgling empire. The structure raised and rebuilt a dozen times until the current castle, built of dark blue alloy and trimmed in orange-red quartz, provided safe-haven for the one-hundredth ultimate leader of the Kashōn Empire.

Phortis C stood seven-feet-two-inches and weighed four-hundred pounds. Warrior weight. From his perch eight-hundred-feet high, he gazed onto the valley where the Empire began and now feeds the flames of expansion.

As far as he could see lay a space-port. Dry-docks rising a mile into the sky serviced warships berthed on ten levels, from the surface to the communications and control center on top. Factories worked non-stop building more ships. Maintenance hangars repaired and updated older craft. This port, one of fourteen, the largest on Chōntorham.

His dark grey eyes drank in the landscape. Curled ram-horns protruded from his thick-boned head. His wide snout and flared nostrils dominated his pink-skinned face. Tuffs of white wool sprouted along his jaws and unevenly over his pate. His pinched thin lips hid yellow, blocky teeth. The majority of prey-driven, dominance-oriented species ate meat. The Kashōn were vegetarians.

Phortis stood on his balcony nude. The sight of the port, and mental scenes of battles waged and those to come, exciting him. Engorged, he returned to his chamber and his harem.

"The King goes to make more royal offspring."

The comment made by a thin, red-hued humanoid. She stood before a transparent wall several stories higher than the King's terrace. The building, part of the space port, rose one-hundred stories. It contained offices, research and development areas, food services, and apartments. This particular building housed non-Kashōn employed to work on military space craft. Employed a misnomer. The aliens working for the Kashōn did not receive pay. The Kashōn provided housing, food, and allowed them to live. They were slaves taken from defeated systems.

"He does seem to enjoy standing around nude in the open."

The response from a three-foot-tall alien wearing large round goggles with shaded grey lenses.

"He must realize anyone facing the castle, and higher than ten stories, can see him," the first alien said.

"Phortis is aware," the short one answered. "He's showing his contempt for non-Kashōn, and displaying his power to his followers. Doesn't the size of his penis excite you, Scandeki?"

"As long as it comes attached to a Kashōn, never."

She turned from the view. Her companion sat upon a tall stool before a touch-screen computer display taller and wider than the little alien. Besides tinted goggles, he wore a dark green jumpsuit. Wide, pale feet with six-toes protruded from the pants' legs. He used an alloy stick to activate the touch screen, his arms too short to reach the entire display. Five fingers and a thumb on each hand.

"You won't find a penis that long on any Ve males," he assured her. "We would trip on it, or if we became excited, be unable to see around it," he joked.

"Docha, we have worked together for a year," Scandeki said. "You never talk about your home, or your people."

"I don't hear you speak often of Aekran, either," Docha replied. "No off-world worker does, even among our own kind. It is too painful. The memories, and not knowing what is happening to our families."

Scandeki sat on a stool beside the Ve. Her feet actually touched the floor. She rubbed her hands along the sides of her head. Short cropped black stubble prickled her palms. Placing both elbows on the desktop, she rested her sharp chin on cupped hands.

"There are fresh water pools hidden deep within caverns on Aekran. Water clear and devoid of sediment. When you dive beneath the surface, you cannot tell up from down," she said. "It is like flying; with no sound, and no sense of gravity."

"And no air," Docha quipped. "Bet you decide which way is up pretty quick when you need to breathe."

"Do you have special places on Ve?"

"Ve is forever dark," he answered. "Our civilization destroyed our environment. We polluted the air, streaming toxic gases into the atmosphere until they mixed to become a deadly cloud trapped above the surface. The skies dimmed as light from our star went away. We created artificial biospheres to maintain crops and animals. Knowledge led to our technical superiority, and to our own stupidity. It also created habitats for our survival. Only not enough habitats. Billions of Ve perished."

"I'm sorry, Docha," the Aekran said. "I did not mean to cause you pain."

"We caused our own pain, Scandeki," he replied. "At least we became better environmentalists. Habitats use natural thermals to generate energy, and the atmosphere is slowly healing. We also see well in the dark. Only we did not see the arrival of the Shroud ships. It would not have mattered. We had no military to resist."

"Aekran resisted," she said, her voice barely audible. Her timber shaky. "My grandfather told me our scanners detected the wormhole gate opening. Our government knew of the Kashōn Empire. They sent a wave of ships to defend the system. The Shroud destroyed all of them. The Empire's Corps invaded, wiped out all surface resistance, and accepted our surrender. They celebrated by executing one-in-five of the Aekranian left alive."

"I am sorry for your painful history as well," the Ve said. "This is why we do not talk of home. Even beautiful memories are covered in the ashes of the Kashōn Empire. The Ve believed we represented the only intelligent life in the galaxy until the invasion. After meeting the invaders, we were convinced we were the only intelligent life in the galaxy."

"You kept a sense of humor."

"It keeps me sane. And the work," he added, pointer tapping the display screen.

"A doctor of applied physics and you, one of the most gifted engineers I ever met," she said. "Brought here and brought together to build bigger, better Kashōn warcraft so more worlds can be taken by the Empire. I am not sure this is sanity, Docha."

"No, it is reality," he answered. "As long as we deliver improvements to their current systems, we are valuable. We can make sure we deliver those improvements a bit slower than necessary."

"Theories must be tested thoroughly," she said. "We certainly do not want any of our work to cause a Shroud ship to explode."

"No. That would be unthinkable." The pale Ve smiled. "Have you learned any more about the pirates attacking Kashōn ships?"

"The stories are not a myth," she replied. "My assigned food table is next to one used by the space dock administration. When I eat, I listen. Ve may see well in the dark, but Aekranians can hear snowflakes land. There are pirates, and they are giving the Empire a headache. They have not caused serious harm, but more than anyone else has ever accomplished."

"If we could reach them, maybe they could do more harm," the engineer said.

"I will keep listening, but I think we are only dreaming, Docha. The Empire destroys whole systems. I do not think one ship of pirates will stand in their way."

"Sanity requires a sense of humor, and hope, Dr. Pau," Docha countered. "I will continue to provide the humor. You must maintain hope."

On the desert planet Enparatus

"There isn't anything we can do, Samara."

The older man sat cross-legged on a woven mat. Enparatus's setting sun cast long shadows across the oasis. When it finally set, the desert night would turn cold. For now, the shadows and the spring-fed pool of water provided a cool reprieve from the dry heat.

"We have to think of something we can do, Trak," the dark-haired, brown-eyed young woman said. She sat cross-legged as well, her knees bouncing as she fought impatience and fear. "They killed the Chancellor and three teachers for no reason. They have Alucha and Mandara, and could be doing horrible things to them. If we can't fight the Kashōn, we must, at least, contact Mother."

"If we try to send a signal to the Suzerain, the soldiers will trace it back. My people live a simple life, Samara. We are not fighters," Trak responded.

"I don't want you or your people harmed," Samara agreed, "but I cannot leave my sisters to those monsters."

Princess Samara stood and faced northward. Her imagination covered the miles and cut through the giant dunes standing between her and her captured siblings. While her elder sisters trained for future roles as leaders of the Helacene, she, with her two brothers, accepted their roles as forgotten royalty. Alucha and Mandara studied to follow a path of diplomacy and statesmanship. She sought adventure, learning to climb granite mountains on Montarius 3, combat training with the Royal Guards on Batoü, and speeding across desert sands and huge dunes on hover cycles on Enparatus. Being a Princess of Hela gave her entry to anything she wished to try. Being fearless and asking no favors made her welcome with those she met along her way.

"I have known you ten years," Trak said. "Since you first came to Enparatus to study at the Academy."

"Six-years-old," Samara interjected. "Mother thought it might calm me down."

"Years younger than children normally sent to study Alliance history," Trak added. "The stories of heroes and tales of adventure and intrigue from the worlds of our alliance did not calm you, as your mother wished."

"No, but they did give me purpose. What good is knowing how to take care of myself, fight, and fly anything from space craft to hover cycles, if I cannot save my sisters?"

Trak, older by a generation and responsible for the well-being of his tribe of nomads, stood, joining the young princess and following her gaze to the North.

"My people are not fighters, Samara, but we are not cowards. Perhaps we can think of something we can do."

"Thank you, Trak. But as I said, I do not want you or your people harmed," the young woman said.

"The Parz Nomads of Enparatus have lived in these deserts for thousands of years," he replied. "My ancestors watched the fortress being built. We have records of passages, drainage systems, and karez tunnels used to trap and store spring water. We may know more about the Academy than those who live within the walls today."

"You think we might be able to sneak in and rescue them?" she asked. Her voice a tinge hopeful, and a bit skeptical.

"I will find what I can," he promised. "I will also send the tribe further away. It is early to leave the oasis, but distance may protect them should we try something foolish and fail."

"We?"

"I am a member of the Helacene Alliance. Your mother is my Suzerain. Your sisters are on my world, and, therefore, my responsibility as much as those who run the academy. You have been a member of my tribe since you walked into this oasis as a six-year-old determined to sail the sand dunes. If you intend to save your sisters, I intend to be with you."

Princess Samara Athodite, the forgotten royal, hugged her friend. She whispered, "I don't know if my visit is bad timing or good fortune. I do know I have family on Enparatus, and not just Alucha and Mandara."

Hela - The Royal Estate

"There's no way to verify the claim?"

Suzerain Palla Athodite stood at the balustrade overlooking the manor's rear garden. The golden sun, the Hela system star Cadme, contained a unique dark-orange center which expanded as it crossed the sky. It set as a glowing reddish-yellow orb fringed in gold. The spectrum resulted in the Helacene's light reddish-orange skin. It also created vibrant foliage in greens from the darkest heather to a bright lime leaf. Blossoms were predominantly yellows and reds and combinations of the two primary colors.

Parterres, formal planting beds of varying heights, were laid out in geometric shapes. These beds set across acres of flat ground creating symmetrical patterns and separated by stone paths. Fountains and cascades built to resemble natural waterfalls animated the garden. Stairways and ramps artfully used to unite different levels of the garden. Grottos and labyrinths provided intrigue. Statuary based on Helacene mythology stood at major intersections.

The garden's design based on symmetry and the principle of imposing order on nature. It represented the beauty and purpose of the Helacene Suzerain. To impose order on a confederation of cultures, without destroying the beauty of each. To legislate harmony.

Suzerain Palla lived acutely aware of the balance of unity without demanding uniformity she was charged with maintaining. The Alliance represented by this garden. Cared for daily and kept under control or it would both wither and grow wild.

Prince Alain, her son and eldest child, brought the news of the Academy's capture by the Kashōn. He performed the duties of Commander of the Guard, the Suzerain's security detail.

"Captain Phistol, the commander of the Empire troops now on Enparatus, sent video of our ships blasted from space, as well as Alucha and Mandara under arrest," the young Guard Commander reported. "They used our own wormhole relay communication stations."

"The Kashōn have our communication codes?" Palla's question more of an indictment. The statuesque leader of the Alliance stood six-inches taller than Alain. Her son grew into a formidable fighter, and fierce competitor, in part because of his own stature. The shortest of all of her children, he compensated by refusing to allow any insult to pass. As a child, this often resulted in trips to the infirmary. His dedication to training soon sent others to the medics. By the time he reached the age to train for a profession, his path was obvious. Warrior.

"The Captain included video of the bodies of Chancellor Ungu and several instructors and Academy staff. I'm sure he tortured the information from someone."

Alain did not enjoy looking up to speak with his own mother, but if he stared straight ahead he would be ogling her chest. If he looked away it would be disrespectful.

"Have the communications been analyzed?" she asked, turning to face the gardens once more. Palla was aware of her son's discomfort, and tried to ease his position without pandering. She thought, not for the first time, it was truly best Helacene Alliance

Confederation laws recognized matriarchal succession. Alain grew into a strong man, but not a patient leader. Alucha would be a better heir to Suzerain. If she survived.

"I brought the news to you immediately," he said. "Analysts have everything, but they will confirm what I already know. The Kashōn Empire is at war with the Helacene Alliance. They invaded a confederated world, murdered citizens, and kidnapped the Suzerain heir and the future First Counsel."

"Demands?"

"According to Captain Phistol, King Phortis C intends to extend his empire and will be annexing the Nessur system," Alain replied. "If the Alliance intervenes, Mandara will be given to his troops." He did not voice what the threat entailed.

"If we allow the Empire to simply take Nessur, the Alliance will begin to dissolve," Palla said. "My children's lives against maintaining the confederation."

"If we intervene, whether our fleet wins or loses, Alucha will be given to the troops," Alain added. "Nessur is far from the center of the confederation. You must consider the strategic advantage of allowing the Kashōn to take it. We can use the time to prepare to prevent them moving closer."

"Strategic advantage," Palla repeated, returning her gaze to Alain. "Not to save your sisters?"

"Both," he answered. No apology followed. "Phortis opened communications, and did not simply invade Nessur. This is new for him and the Ashemacher. They must believe the Helacene Alliance is capable of stopping them. We can use this to negotiate for the release of Alucha and Mandara while we prepare our defenses."

"Alain, the Shroud ships entered the Enparatus system and surprised two battleships. They knew your sisters attended the Academy. They know about the communication relay stations we placed within wormhole channels. Someone provided them with information." The Suzerain continued to look down at her son. This the first time she consulted with him on galactic politics, in spite of his position as her son and Commander of the Guard.

"I already realized a spy helped Captain Phistol's forces. The location of the princesses is always kept secret when they are off-world. When we finish this conversation, my first task will be to find the spy and take their head," Alain responded.

His mother and queen nodded, then told him, "Contact Phistol and open negotiations. Phortis used him to make his first move and to contact me with his demands. He either speaks for Phortis or has direct access. Tell him I will consider his demands, but if anything happens to my daughters, or anyone else under their control, my answer will be to send every battle-worthy craft in the Helacene Alliance at Chōntorham."

Commander Alain Athodite stood to attention and saluted. He performed a snap turn and left to follow his regent's orders.

"Did you hear everything?" she asked.

A shadow hidden within a deeper shadow cast by a marble column answered.

"I did."

"Do you have any suggestions?"

"Keep them busy discussing terms and conditions," the shadow replied. "The hurdles of each side verifying the other side's offers will require considerable time and effort."

"And by delaying, I achieve what, exactly?" the woman holding the greatest power within thousands of parsecs asked.

"Time for me to come up with a brilliant plan to rescue the princesses and stop Phortis from launching an invasion of the Helacene confederation," D'Sey replied, stepping from the shadow.

"The life of my daughters and the fate of nineteen star systems placed in the hands of a pirate," Palla said. Her gaze drifted to the sculpted topiary placed in the middle of her formal garden. A burst of dark green foliage made of leaves with gold veins. Orange, yellow, and red blooms flowing up from the center. A depiction of Hela's sun, and the symbol of the Suzerain. When she turned to again speak to D'Sey, he was no longer on the terrace. The shadows empty.

Chapter 5

Aboard Cassandra

Coop returned to the Wraith alone. Cassie materialized when he descended through the top hatch.

The ship's avatar appeared subdued. Her hair loose. She wore a tactical outfit of grays and blacks which did not accentuate her curves. Her withdrawn demeanor matched her appearance.

"I understand why they pulled us out of space-fold," she said. "I do not understand why Captain D'Sey thinks you can help prevent the Kashōn Empire from advancing on the Helacene Alliance."

He kept his concerns regarding the effects of the tether followed by stasis might have on the avatar's program coding unspoken.

"He's making plans on the go," Coop said, taking a seat in the pilot's chair. Cassie joined him, sliding into the co-pilot's seat. "His strategy involves the Wraith's capabilities. He will not share the entire scheme until he believes I intend to help."

"Will we help?"

Coop realized he continued to treat Cassie as a construct. Despite his acceptance of her as an individual with self-awareness, he hesitated from making the final step. It was time to recognize she was equally affected by the circumstances.

"Any points you would like to make for or against joining a fight on the far side of the galaxy?" Coop asked.

"I can think of several reasons not to participate," the physical hologram replied. "Start with it is none of our business and continue to not trusting D'Sey's motives."

"Pro?"

"It would be fun," she answered. A wry smile the first indication Cassie's frisky personality remained intact.

"I'm sorry," Coop said. He swiveled to face the AI. "Did you say we should get involved because it would be fun?"

"I have only known you following your recovery from brain injury," Cassie said. Her hazel eyes held his. "Part of my programming, the unofficial part left intact by mistake, is to seduce you and provide you a distraction when we are not otherwise engaged. To accomplish my objective, I have studied every file, every piece of data I could find on Daniel Marcel Cooper."

"Sounds rather boring," Coop quipped.

"Only the current version," she answered.

Coop sat forward, attention peaked. "Please go on."

"Daniel Cooper was an eighteen-year-old enlistee in the Can-Am army following the pandemic. Sent to places where bad people were doing bad things to those who survived. You became a sniper, and saved your friends. You received a field promotion to lieutenant in order to lead a raid to save the lives of kidnapped girls. You led missions, lost friends, and never turned your back on your duty."

"Emphasis on lost friends," he said. "People died under my command. People I cared about."

"And you continued moving forward," Cassie responded. "Your sense of humor and devotion to your friends kept spirits up and people alive. You did what was needed, and did not wait for orders."

"And sometimes disobeyed orders," he added.

"For all the right reasons. You were on the ground, in the fight. In the moment. You were always in the moment. You took risks, but never expected the same from others. It is why you volunteered for the Space Ranger Project. Your focus on succeeding is why you became one of the finalists."

"So I became one of only twelve humans capable of regenerations. Improved strength, and speed. Didn't stop a laser from cutting a hole in my brain," he replied.

"The injury healed," Cassie responded. "Your brain functions at a higher level than before, as your body did after the project. When your body changed, you remained the same person. Seeking adventures. Looking for the next challenge. Keeping people from getting too near, afraid of losing them."

"I think my snarky humor kept people away," Coop said.

"Only it never worked out the way you planned," Cassie countered. "Your friends stayed friends. They recognized your faults, and accepted them. They also recognized your talents. They saw the boy who enlisted and kept advancing because he chose to do the right things, not the easy things. They saw a man who saw everyone else as equal. Even when you made first contact, aliens recognized your inability to make judgements based on nothing other than experience. If someone does right, you are there with them. If someone does wrong, you stand against them. Simple."

"That's me. Simple."

"That was you," Cassie said. "When you awoke from the coma and discovered your brain performed amazing calculations at incredible speed, you quit being simple. You became distant. You became a freak because you thought you had turned into a freak."

"I am a freak, Cassie," Coop responded. Not angry, or hurt. He sat back in the chair, slumped in posture and resigned in temperament.

"Do you consider Genna a freak?" she asked.

Genna, the genetically engineered human designed and modified to be the avatar for the PT-109's Artificial Intelligence. Created to provide tactile awareness for the computer as a way of preventing it from going insane as it evolved.

"I consider Genna a friend," he replied.

"And me? Am I a freak?"

"I'm not entirely sure if there is a category for you, Cassie, but freak is not in the description."

"You are a human who now stands as a bridge between humans, aliens, and artificial intelligence," she said. Her hand reached for his. "You are not a freak, and you are not alone. You are Daniel Marcel Cooper, and despite all the changes made to you, you are still the same man who enlisted to help save lives and prevent your planet from self-destructing. You have been hiding away, looking for a complex answer to a complex riddle."

"The 'Why me?' riddle," he said, squeezing the holo-hand.

"Because you can handle it," she replied. "Because when others get lost in complexity, you keep it all simple."

"Shit," Coop said, shaking his head. "Keep it simple, stupid. Trust your instincts."

"D'Sey's offer?" Cassie asked.

"It sounds impossible, but it does sound like it would be fun trying," he admitted, his own smile reaching his dark brown eyes for the first time since awakening on Fin Island.

"Damn it, Cassie," Coop said. He stood on the top of Cassandra, looking down the entry hatch behind the cockpit. "The worst thing to happen is you dematerialize and return to the mainframe."

"I have never considered the prospect of leaving the ship," the voice below answered. "What if I dematerialize and cannot return to the mainframe because I have exited?"

"What if you don't try, and it would have worked?" he countered.

Her hand appeared through the opening. He grabbed it and half-helped, half-hauled the avatar onto the ship's airframe. Cassie stood, feet wide and planted firmly on the alloy skin of the Wraith. She waited, and if holo-avatars needed to breath, she would have held her breath, anticipating the worse.

"It works," she said. She turned to Coop, who stood silently next to her, smiling. "It actually works. I can remain solid."

"That was amazing," Cassie said as she plopped into a comfortable chair in the crew's lounge. "To walk around the entire hangar. See my ship from the outside. I touched the wings. And D'Sey's Menace. It is beautiful. Do you think it uses artificial intelligence?"

Coop smiled, enjoying the child-like mannerisms of the holo-avatar as she discovered the world outside of the Wraith. When she flopped into the chair it made him realize how much time and thought went into writing the codes running her personality. The gamer-geek may have been a bit sex-crazed, but he was also a genius. Cassie, and by extension Cassandra, the ship's AI, were the most human-like AI-Avatar interface in his experience.

Kennedy, the AI operational system aboard the PT-109 had personality, but always remained within a certain set of parameters when dealing with operators. Genna, Kennedy's avatar, was an actual human being. Engineered and experimental, but still human. She was developing her own personality, but at a pace similar to a teenager becoming an adult.

Cassie jumped from sultry vixen, to no-nonsense tactical command operations, to excited child, and everything in between with no sense of strangeness. Coop recognized his ship's avatar possessed a sense of self and it did not include any requirement to remain in a single lane.

"You'll need to ask D'Sey," Coop replied. "We never got around to discussing his ship."

Taah Vil, the Cora Sen Du, entered the lounge from the doorway opposite the hangar entry-exit. Coop noted the detached shadow following her, and cut his eyes to Cassie, curious if the avatar would notice the Adromedan.

"I'm sorry," Taah said, head down. "I did not mean to interrupt. The lounge is normally empty at this time. I can leave."

"Please don't go," Cassie said, standing. "I'm Cassie, the Avatar for Captain Cooper's Wraith. You must be Taah Vil, the mechanic. And this is Ateakatakut, the being from the Andromeda galaxy."

"Cassie," Coop interceded, "I haven't told you about any of D'Sey's crew."

"The ship's intelligence briefed me before I came out of stasis," Cassie answered. "I can recognize the different members of the crew. I also have detailed reports on the Kashōn Empire and the Helacene Alliance, including star charts and wormhole channels for this part of the galaxy."

"D'Sey calls the ship Clyde," Coop said.

"Complex Linear Inter-Dimensional Drive, or CLIDD," Taah spoke as she walked to the bar. She disappeared, easily accomplished by the short female, but soon reemerged with a bottle. "The Nakki invented it to make extremely long distance travel possible in short time spans."

Talking about things mechanical, or, at least, industrial relaxed the shy woman. She sat on a chair facing Cassie and Coop, who both sat as soon as the Cora Sen Du settled into her seat. Teak, the Shadow, remained near the interior doorway. Silent smoke with no flame.

"It's why Dee calls the ship Clyde," Taah added.

"The ship travels across dimensions in order to shorten the distance between points in real space?" Coop asked.

"It's basically the same concept as the tachyon communications system you use to send data across hundreds of parsecs, arriving in real time to the receiver," Taah answered.

Coop remembered D'Sey telling him Vil acted as his chief mechanic and communications officer. She drank from her bottle, always keeping her head down, leaving her dark green hairless pate tilted in Coop's direction. He could not recall seeing her eyes the first time they met, and still had no clue as to shape or color. She did have a melodic voice. The tone a soft brush, but every word clearly spoken. The Cora Sen Du description included musically gifted as a species.

"The sub-atomic particles are small enough and fast enough to cross dimensional barriers," Coop responded. "Space and time are altered, resulting in movement faster than the speed of light."

"Sub-atomic particles are simple." As Taah took a sip from her bottle, the shadowy form of Teak drifted closer. Coop had the impression the being from Andromeda was interested in the discussion. "They have hardly any mass, and they exist in two places at once. Your trick of capturing one without losing duality was the important discovery. A little push in the right direction, and traveling through dimensions was simple. Moving us through dimensions is complex."

"How is it done?" Cassie asked. She also noted Teak's arrival, but made no comment.

"It's complex," the green alien replied. Her head tilted up, revealing soft light-brown eyes and a small mouth with a wide smile.

"And linear," Coop said, adding a mirthful tone to the comment.

"And inter-dimensional," Cassie said.

"Requires a big drive," Taah finished the word play. "It requires Clyde."

Enjoying both the subject and the interplay with the two strangers, Taah allowed her innate shyness to dissipate in the warmth of conversation.

"Sub-atomic particles are weightless. Just a little push is needed," she said. "To move objects requires a big power source. But because the power source is big . . ."

"It requires more power to push it along with any matter being transported," Coop finished.

"Exactly," Taah responded. "The Nakki kept building and refining power generators until they found the right combination of energy-to-mass-plus-load. They could move a ship, people, and cargo across the galaxy by dropping in and out of dimensional levels. Space was replaced by time. Time moves faster than light. Time slows space and makes it more dense. Shortens distance, makes getting somewhere quicker."

"Explains why the ship is huge," Coop said. "It's a giant engine."

"Yep," the green young lady answered.

"What is the energy source?" Cassie asked.

"Don't know," Taah admitted. The answer took some of the wind from her enjoyment of the subject. "The core is unreachable. Two-thirds of the ship is locked away. I work on systems operating from the same energy pushing the ship, but I have never seen the source."

"Why not?" Cassie asked.

"Because it is too dangerous," D'Sey answered.

The human, avatar, and Cora Sen Du all started at his voice. D'Sey stood behind the bar. He appeared relaxed, and could have been there one-second or since the talk regarding Clyde began. No one saw him enter, or knew where he came from. Coop noticed Teak vibrate for a nano-second. The shadow from another galaxy also surprised by the ship's captain. Something to remember.

Drink in hand, the tall, slender man in a dark t-shirt and worn bluejeans moved around the end of the bar to join the others. He sat on the arm of Taah's chair.

"Everyone on board can explore every inch of the ship, but not the core," he said. "The drive system the Nakki created is, for lack of a better term, delicate. You know what happens if a laser contacting a crystal in a space-fold drive is knocked off its target."

"The ship falls out of space-fold and into natural space," Coop said.

"Which is an abrupt and bumpy transition, but not usually terminal," D'Sey added. "You either rely on normal propulsion, and go for an extended flight, or you realign the laser. If the crystal was damaged, you replace it and recalibrate the lasers. Time-consuming, but, again, not fatal."

"If the inter-dimensional drive is knocked off line?" Coop asked.

"Depends," D'Sey answered, taking a sip from his glass. "If we are in our own dimension, we might be able to use a hangared ship to get somewhere safe. If the core didn't explode. If we fall out in another dimension, we could end up like Teak, stuck in a place like nothing we have ever known. Maybe a friendly place with beings who want to do us no harm. Maybe not. Probably not."

"And no way back to our own dimension," Cassie said.

"Not even a direction sign showing the way," D'Sey replied. "Welcome aboard, Cassie. We have not been formally introduced."

The holo-avatar stood and held a hand out to the ship's captain in the human style. "Please to meet you, Captain D'Sey. Thank you for making it possible for me to leave my ship."

D'Sey stood and accepted her hand without hesitation. "Clyde managed it, but I accept the gratitude. Perhaps it will place you in my debt and I can ask your help persuading Captain Cooper to join our mission."

"I've already decided to help," Coop said. "But I will not go in blindly. I expect a full mission outline. That includes an honest appraisal of your expectations regarding enemy forces and response. If I decide you're full of shit, I retain the right to still say no."

Taah giggled. D'Sey smiled.

"I've called for a crew meeting in six hours," D'Sey said. "We'll meet here in the lounge. I'd hoped to have your answer sooner so I can either present a single plan, or a dual mission scenario. Looks like I'm going with the one-two punch."

"I'm glad you're helping," Taah said. "I'm glad you're both helping," she added, looking at Cassie.

"Depends on the plan, Taah," Coop cautioned. "Cassie and I will go back to Cassandra. A couple of hours of sleep can't hurt, and Cassie can begin organizing some of the data on the players Clyde provided."

"We have extra crew quarters if you would prefer a real bed, Captain," D'Sey offered.

"Thanks, but I'm comfortable aboard my own ship. I'm sure you understand."

"Perfectly," D'Sey answered. "Six hours and back here. Taah, you and Teak need to get some rest as well. Once we all agree our plans are more than a pile of worthless shit, things are going to get extremely busy."

Taah giggled again.

"That was amazing," Cassie said, standing in the small cabin of the Wraith.

"You said that before," Coop responded, his back to the avatar as he pulled the lower bunk's privacy curtain aside.

"I may be saying it a lot," Cassie answered.

He turned to find the avatar changed, with her honey-blond hair pulled back into the ponytail he found cute and sexy. The style framed her pretty face, accenting her green almond-shaped eyes, pouty full lips, and strong chin. A cut-off white t-shirt revealed tanned, smooth skin. Ripped abs beneath the promise of round, firm full breasts. Her nipples teased through the thin fabric.

White panties hugged the narrow hips of the young, athletic woman. Her legs long, strong, and also tan. She wore white crew socks and no shoes.

As she moved closer, her breathing raised and lowered the white top. The scent of Caribbean sea and female musk drifted softly across his awareness.

"I believe you found this combination desirable," she whispered. Her hands slipped between his arms, held his back and pulled him into a deep kiss. Warm. His hands found her buttocks, pulling her closer.

Chapter 6

Hela - Office of the Suzerain

"I should represent you," Alain said. He made his statement without the force normally added to his tone when trying to win an argument. He spoke calmly.

"Phortis would have three of my children, and not just two," Palla replied. She sat behind the desk in the Suzerain's working office. She conducted official meetings and duties in a larger chamber. Attendees seated at an oval table allowed everyone a sense of equality. In this office she handled the labors of leader of the Alliance. A visitor might think a staff normally shared the space, considering the number of work stations, files, data storage drives, and old-fashion wall boards. They did not. All of the information on all the different media could have been searched and reviewed by one computer. Palla Athodite preferred separating responsibilities by also separating where and how she addressed each requirement of her station. It helped her concentrate on a single task, and while inefficient, she found it effective.

"Phortis is well aware the Helacene are matriarchal," her son said. He wore his Guard Commander uniform. The dark blue highlighted with gold and red piping around the coat's cuffs and high collar, while stripes ran down the side of his wrinkle-free pants. "Having your son would hold no more importance than holding any other male in the confederation hostage."

"To the Suzerain. Perhaps not to a mother," Palla countered. "By kidnapping Alucha and Mandara, Phortis delivered a message to me as a ruler and a mother."

"Sending the commander of your personal guard, and brother to the princesses, also sends a message. You take his actions seriously, and you are willing to open discussions. Phortis is a creature addicted to power. If you send a normal negotiator and they say something he does not like, he might simply kill them. He will not take the chance with me. That alone may give us time to find a way to prevent harm to Alucha and Mandara, and keep the Kashōn out of the Nessur system."

"I thought you considered Nessur expendable."

"If we need more time, and it keeps my sisters alive, they are," Alain replied.

Changing subjects, giving herself time to consider Alain's proposal, his mother asked, "Have you located Samara and Mandrake?"

"Mandrake, is here on Hela," Alain answered. "He's been studying computer sciences at the Hela Institute. I ordered his security detail to bring him back to the estate. He should be here before sundown. Samara has not answered any calls, but she rarely does. The last report placed her on the water-world of Faega. She was exploring the ancient ruins recently discovered beneath the ocean."

"Her security detail?"

"She lost them in the Tarqintary system," her brother reported, adding a scowl. He was never pleased his younger sister constantly evaded and eluded his own guardsmen assigned to keep her safe. "They are nearing Faega."

Palla, knowing it was wrong, could not contain a smile. She pulled an electronic communications pad from a desk drawer to hide her mirth from Alain. She knew her youngest daughter took too many risks, and fought every attempt to rein her in, but she also admired the spirit. She knew how much Alain disapproved his sister's actions.

"If her own security detail cannot find her, I doubt the Kashōn will have any more luck," she said. She keyed a message to Samara's com-code. The girl would not ignore her mother's request.

"Her com-unit is unavailable," she informed Alain.

"I know," he replied. "It is operational, but signals are blocked. She is probably near a radiant source of interference. When she gets far enough away she will find dozens of emergency messages queued. I still should be the one to go to Enparatus."

Unable to prolong the decision, not nearly the adept at evasion as Samara, Suzerain Palla Athodite said, "I agree, Commander. Your arguments make sense, and you have shown a great deal of maturity in the past few months. If you control your temper, and promise to act as a diplomatic ambassador, then you can act as negotiator."

"I will give you time to pull the battle assets of the confederation together," he promised. "If I can free the princesses, I will. The Kashōn battlecruisers intercept communications within the system. You must inform me if you decide to send a fleet to protect Nessur before I exit the wormhole. Once I am on Enparatus, if you recall me for consultations regarding the negotiations, it will be the signal our ships are massing."

"Send Captain Phistol notification of your intention to arrive personally to discuss the situation and his King's demands," she said. "It will take time to receive a reply and set the time for your arrival. I will meet with our military leaders and evaluate our odds of success should we confront the Kashōn fleet."

She turned her dark blue eyes onto the young man in uniform before her. "Alain, if you cannot free your sisters without getting all of you killed or captured, leave them."

"Yes, Suzerain."

"Keep your people looking for Samara."

"Yes, Suzerain."

Alain saluted, turned on a heel, and departed.

Palla examined her pad. Nothing from Samara. Nothing from D'Sey. Unsure which troubled her more.

Royal Sub-Chamber Study of King Phortis C

"I rule over one-hundred planets," Phortis said. The pale pink skin of his forehead turned a deeper red as his blood pressure rose. His blood pressure escalted with his anger. "The communication relay drones the Hela use make our own system as antiquated as our ancestors' drums. With all of the technology we have taken, why is it the Helacene have a more efficient system?"

"Our research teams were extremely close to producing a similar relay package," Sentutol lied.

The First Council to the King, Sentutol administered the endless research and development programs the Kashōn funded within the capital's space port complex. Her personal staff catalogued technology, concepts, and theories from annexed worlds. She approved the alien scientists, engineers, and experts relocated to Chŏntorham. Virtual prisoners, these aliens worked on projects expected to improve Kashŏn superiority across all fields of technology. Especially projects relative to improving military strength.

"Then you should have no trouble replicating the Helacene system," Phortis said.

"None at all," Sentutol responded, straight faced. As a career political operative and member of the Ashemacher elite, she lied as easily as she told the truth. Whichever suited her goal at the moment. Honesty never played a major part in deciding her answers.

Placated, Phortis returned to the original reason for meeting with his council. He, and four others, all Ashemacher inner-circle, discussed the proposal for face-to-face negotiations with a representative of Suzerain Palla Athodite.

"The Helacene bitch has decided to play games," the King said. "She wants to negotiate. The time we waste will be used by her generals to consolidate their forces."

"Then why waste time?" Pitaitis asked. The King's brother, younger by two years, and taller by two inches, commanded the Shroud Fleet. "My ships can easily take Nessur. It is a backward planet producing agricultural products. If we wait for the Alliance to move their ships into Nessur space, it will make the invasion more costly."

"The Shroud Fleet must be superior to the Helacene Alliance ships," Vistol de Aritis chimed in from the far end of the Council meeting table. The King's cousin, she oversaw the Kashŏn Unconventional Warfare development program. More simply put, she provided the King with deadly weapons able to produce deadly results. Biological agents, massive explosive devices, and chemical concoctions which could destroy an enemy up to, and including, wiping life from a planet.

"We are superior," Pitaitis answered. "Why risk losing a single ship by hesitating? We can take Nessur now and defend it against the Helacene later."

"We could, but we will not," Phortis C said. "Palla is torn between family and duty. She will eventually choose duty, but is desperate to try anything to save her daughters. Sending the Commander of her personal guard, who is also her son, is meant to show sincerity. It is a delaying tactic, and nothing more."

"Perhaps you give her too much credit as a leader," Sentutol said. "The Hela are a soft species. She may be willing to trade Nessur, and other systems, to buy the release of her children."

"We cannot risk trying to understand the motivations of these creatures," Pitaitis interjected. "Hesitation loses battles. We must act."

"We are acting, brother," Phortis replied. He could not keep the smug look of satisfaction from his face. Always appearing smarter than his younger brother was important to the King. Especially since his younger brother matured into a larger specimen. "I have a spy in the Suzerain's Court. I do not try to understand what motivates her. I know what she plans."

"How long has this spy been active, and why have we been unaware until now?" Vistol asked.

"Long enough for plans to be made," Phortis answered. "You are Ashemacher, and you are my council, but I do not answer to you, Cousin," he directed at Vistol.

"True, my King," she quickly replied, offering a subjugated head and exposed neck to show her acceptance of his dominance. "It is difficult to council you wisely if we are unaware of all the facts."

"Fine. Our ships entered the Enpartus system using codes provided by my spy. They destroyed two Helacene battleships before they could do more than die in space. My ground troops secured the Invicta Vitam Academy. They hold the heir to the Suzarain and the sister known as 'the spare'."

Phortis C rose from his chair. From the head of the table he peered down at the four most powerful Kashōn after himself. From time to time he found it prudent to remind them of his position. If he could place a spy in the Hela capital, then he might place spies among the Ashemacher.

"Sending her son to negotiate is a ploy. She will mass the Helacene Alliance ships before sending them to defend Nessur. The negotiations are to delay our invasion while the son devises some method to extract his sisters. In the end, she will sacrifice her children to defend an Alliance planet."

"What will our response be?" his brother inquired.

"My spy will learn where the Alliance ships will be gathered. When we know where the ships of that accursed confederation will be called together, we will spring our own trap. Your Shroud Fleet, Pitaritis, will ambush those ships and destroy the Helacene Alliance's offensive and defensive force. Without their battleships, we will rage against the confederation. Systems will surrender or be taken by force. With the resources of the confederation added to the Empire, I will lead our expansion further into the galaxy. I will spread enough ashes to blanket a thousand stars."

"Do you trust your spy?" Vistol asked.

"I trust no one," Phortis answered. "But I trust greed. In return for Hela and the two systems nearest, my spy will provide the location for the Helacene rally point. We have already been given Enparatus, and access to the Helacene wormhole communication relays. We have their codes, and hold Palla's daughters. I believe my spy has proven credible."

"You intend to play along with the Suzerain," Sentütol said. "You will accept the negotiations. They will be held on Enparatus?"

"Yes. While we prepare for war. Each of you must be ready. When I know the location, Pitaritis, you must arrive before the first Helacene ship. Our fleet must have every advantage. If there are no more questions or council to give, go. Soon we release the Shroud across Alliance skies."

The three Ashemachers departed, leaving the King and the counselor who made no comments during the meeting.

When the door to the chamber closed, Phortis remarked, "You were silent, Paun. No sage advice?"

"It is our nature to advance and expand our empire," the oldest living Ashemacher said. His puffs of cotton-like wool thin and wiry. The pink skin wrinkled, furrowed deeply across his face. His temple horns faded to grey. "It is your nature to take pride in your accomplishments, and well deserved," he quickly added. He had no desire to stoke the King's considerable temper. "I ask only that you not underestimate your enemies."

"I do not underestimate Palla Athodite or her forces," Phortis replied. "Nor do I underestimate the Kashōn military," he added as he walked to the exit. "I will crush my enemy," he finished, closing the door on the old Ram left at the table.

"If the Helacene were your only enemy, perhaps," the elder said to no one.

Chapter 7

Aboard Clyde

Coop wandered into the crew lounge two hours before the scheduled meeting. Sex with Cassie proved passionate, physical, and satisfying. Not once during their time together did he concern himself over the reality of the act. Actually, acts. While he never used the artificial sex-bots available on Earth, he never derided those who did. Cassie certainly did not feel like an artificial woman.

Since childhood, Coop compartmentalized life. He could set aside distractions. An artificially constructed organic holo-avatar as a sex partner did not fit into any ready-made compartment. He understood the programmer's logic. Extended travel in space could be made less tedious with a companion. A companion capable of altering their configuration would be more entertaining. There would be no emotional or moral toll placed on the avatar. How he internalized the relationship would be more of an issue than the sex. He could end personal speculation and rewrite Cassandra's codes, modifying or deleting Cassie's captain-fixation.

"Whatever has you distracted, you might want to consider solving it or forgetting it before you go into a dangerous situation."

Doc, the Kanistari, sat in a lounge chair, feet propped on the seat of a facing chair.

"If you didn't notice me sitting here, you might miss some guy with a laser aimed at you."

"I saw you," Cooper answered. He continued at his same pace, walking behind the bar. "Do you know if D'Sey keeps more cola?"

"Metal fridge left of center, beneath the bar," she answered. "You didn't act like you saw me."

"You don't represent a danger," he replied, bending, then standing with a bottle in hand. He joined her, pulling a chair in front of the one next to her. He sat, propping his booted feet onto the additional chair, same as her.

"You don't think I'm dangerous?"

"Not what I said. You don't represent a danger to me . . . at the moment. I'm sure you can be dangerous or you would not be a part of D'Sey's crew."

"Your brain analyzes everything at a remarkably advanced speed," Doc said. "Brains do that, but I have seldom seen someone capable of accepting and acting on the information as quickly as you."

"Seldom?"

"Never," she corrected. "Not even D'Sey, and he's the most advanced being I have encountered."

"Because of his lifespan?"

"Because he is a direct descendant of the Nakki. Not one himself, but with a number of genetic markers indicative of proximal lineage," she replied.

"He said the Nakki seeded much of the galaxy in an attempt to develop new civilizations."

"Genetic markers found across thousands of species do indicate a single donor," the aqua-teal alien replied.

Coop noticed her honey-brown irises. She had hazel eyes the first time he met her. Fellen skin changed shades of blue depending on their blood pressure. Perhaps Kanistari eyes did the same.

"One reason why thousands of aliens are hominoids with bilateral asymmetry," she added. "I've studied their methodology in Clyde's archive. Nakki seeded their biological traits, and often added traits from other species. They also experimented with a variety of non-intelligent life. Different environments led to the evolution of a myriad of lifeforms."

"There are advanced species with no connection to the seeding," Coop said.

"Advanced and not-so-advanced," she agreed. "A few, like the Kashōn and the Fray, evolved from genetic material brought from another galaxy."

"You said you knew why some of the volunteers in the Space Ranger project survived while the majority did not."

"When you were unconscious, I accessed your personal records to see if there were any medical conditions I should be concerned with. Your medical files are linked with reports on the eleven others who survived the regeneration immersion," Doc told him. She turned to face him, her eyes now more golden than honey, with specs of brown. "You are aware of what human researchers designated as the Martian-genome pair in your DNA?"

"The regeneration pair and the Methuselah genome the scientists reactivated," he answered.

"All creatures with a connexion to genesis where the Nakki used their own genetic material mixed into the soup have this pair," she said. "What your researchers did not discover was some members of your species possess a second Nakki-genome pair within the scaffolding. This pair is hidden. Attached to the obvious pair in a way I can only describe as layered. For the immersion to succeed, a subject must have a minimum of one layered pair. The twelve survivors had these genome anomalies. The others did not."

"If we can determine if a human has the layered pair, then more Space Rangers could be created?"

"Your scientists figured out how the immersion-reengineering process could be replicated," she replied. "Plug in the right subject and you get the right result."

"Why can't scientists reactivate the Methuselah genes in other humans? Is longevity also connected to the layered-pairs?"

"Your extended lifespan is a result of completing the reengineering," Doc answered. She pulled her feet from the chair, adjusted her legs beneath her, and found a comfortable position leaning back and to the side. It allowed her to look at Coop without having to turn her head. "It is not a specific Nakki construct. Early humans lived for hundreds of years as a result of environmental factors. Evolution encoded human DNA with the possibility of enhanced lifespans. The immersion shocked your scaffolding, rebooting what you call the Methuselah effect."

"Humans lived hundreds of years because of the environment?"

"Don't make it sound incredible," she responded. "The species on Fell are a perfect example of the same thing."

"Fellen live for hundreds of years?" This time his feet came down. He turned, his full attention on the Kanistari.

"Wow. You honestly had no idea," she said, her eyes back to the honey-brown color. "Since they made first contact, and learned the majority of alien species do not live as long as Fellen, they kept their lifespans secret. I thought you would have been told. You not only live with two of them, you helped save their planet. I suppose being conditioned to keep a secret for untold generations, it's difficult to share."

"I'm not sure I believe it," he said. "I can't believe it wouldn't be obvious."

"First, you would need to be around for decades before you noticed the Fell did not age normally. Second, it is obvious." She added this with a smile.

"Okay. I'll bite. How is it obvious?"

"Would you say Fellen are among the more technologically advanced civilizations in your part of the galaxy?"

"From what I know of my part of the galaxy, and what other aliens I have encountered tell me, then yes. From what I have seen personally, yes again."

"You see how they live?"

"Simply," he said the word quickly. "Tribal villages. They use naturally occurring power sources. They construct homes from natural products. The only towns are those developed around the space ports. They also have hidden research and development sites that are ultra-sophisticated. Concrete and alloy construction."

"They demand off-world visitors remain in those space port towns," Doc said. "The same Fellen rarely greets or barters with the same alien twice. They do not want some aging visitor to notice they are trading with someone who does not age. If their secret became common knowledge, what would happen, Captain Cooper?"

"Others would want the secret," he answered.

"Many would kill for it," she added.

"I understand why they keep it a secret," he conceded. "I still don't see why it is obvious."

"Advanced technology produced by a bucolic society," she answered. "When someone decides to work on a theory, they don't have to limit their research because they become too old to continue. They don't need to train an apprentice, and hope they carry on the work. How many of Da Vinci's inventions would be refined had he lived eight-hundred years instead of eighty?"

"The modern world would have evolved hundreds of years sooner," Coop answered. "Over a thousand humans remained on Fell after defeating the Mischene. There is no way to keep their lifespans secret."

"The Fell appear to be at a crossroad, Captain. They will either reveal the secret, perhaps encouraging their non-Fell allies to keep it, simply let it out, or silence those who stayed behind."

"I don't see them trying to force the volunteers into silence," he replied. "I suspect those who did stay would be willing to keep the secret."

"It would take only one to break the dam," she countered.

"The mission to free Fell from the Zenge and the Mischene leading them was dubbed Operation Crossroads. Prophetic. You mentioned environmental reasons for Fellen long life. Earth once provided the same conditions."

"Combination of things, but mainly the dense atmosphere preventing a lot of damaging radiation from reaching the surface," she replied. "Earth had a similar atmosphere, but a tilt of the axis resulted in the loss of the barrier. Continents and oceans changed, and the sky literally rained down, flooding the planet. Those who survived were forced to cope with a loss of their civilization, as well as a shortened lifespan. Within three generations humans returned to hunter-gatherers in order to survive."

"D'Sey said Earth experienced more than a couple of advanced civilizations."

"Most worlds do," Doc said. "Natural disasters, like the planetary shift on Earth, or getting slammed by space debris, which also occurred on your planet, end one era and begin another. Wars. Plagues. Civilizations and cultures are as fragile as a single life. Easily forgotten by those who follow."

"There is a lesson in there somewhere," D'Sey said from behind the bar, having appeared in much the same manner as the previous day. Unannounced and unnoticed.

"Don't let him rattle you," Doc said. "There is a secret panel at the end of the bar. He waits until everyone is engaged in something interesting and uses the distraction to appear."

"Are you giving away all of the secrets of the galaxy, Costi?" D'Sey asked.

"If I know about them, they aren't very secret," she responded. "May as well give them away."

"The others will join us soon, Captain Cooper," D'Sey said. "Is there anything else you would like to know before we get onto mission planning? Will Cassie be attending?"

"Nothing more for the moment," the human replied. "Doc has given me a lot to think about. Cassie will be here."

Chapter 8

Invicta Academy

Lt. Angartol stood on the southern parapet of the ancient fortress. A small breeze normally crossed south-to-north. From this height he found a small reprieve as it passed over his moist skin. The sun settled low on the horizon, but the oppressive heat remained. He, as the other Shroud Corp troopers, wore the lightest clothing available. The heavy armored uniforms and helmets stored inside.

The academics and servant staff presented no threat. The princesses were harmless. The desert sands stretching out for miles around all four sides of the Academy made it impossible for anyone to approach unnoticed. Besides the guards on duty, scanners swept the area. Night not only did not provide cover against the webbed beams emitted by the electronic motion detectors, the cooler air improved the scan imagery. The heat of the day, reflected off the fey sand, created mirages. Soldiers on watch could not trust their eyes, and those monitoring the scans could not trust the veracity of the echoes. Thermals rising from the surface were dense. They often presented as solid objects. After two days of chasing these illusions, Captain Phistol ordered everyone to remain on station. The mirages lasted less than a minute, and waiting a short time to see if an alarm was a false reading made more sense than jumping at shadows.

"The young bucks watching the monitors no longer bother calling an alarm," Sergeant Traum said, joining the younger officer on the wide overlook. "I'm not sure that's a good thing, Lieutenant."

"If we were holding a position against a worthwhile enemy, probably not," Angartol replied. "This has to be the most boring raid in the history of the Corps."

"The landing ship crew did an overflight of the oasis to the South," the older trooper said. "It's the nearest location where a camp could be located. No one there. Signs of recent activity. I believe the local nomads know we are here and decided to vacate."

"Perhaps the Enparatus native species is more intelligent than reported," the young officer quipped. "I read a report that said this fortress may be twenty-thousand years old. Not much advancement over twenty centuries."

"Strange place to educate the children of their queen," the NCO remarked.

"The Suzerain is not exactly a queen." Angertol turned his back to the southern sky. His eyes scanned the oasis sustaining life in the harsh landscape. "She's more like a judge. She governs the alliance by making sure all of the member worlds act in accordance to rules agreed upon by the members. She settles disputes, and administers the military. Each world donates and provides assets and citizens to serve in their surface and space units. It's the stick used to make sure all of the individual rulers remain compliant. It is also how they defend their territory."

"You know a lot about this Helacene Alliance," Traum said.

"It always pays to study the enemy, Sergeant. Doesn't matter if it's a band of rebels or a confederation of star systems."

"I am an old fashion soldier," Traum replied. "I study the corpses of the enemy. Who or what they were before becoming dead does not interest me."

"The emissary from Suzerain Palla arrives in two days," the lieutenant said. "I don't suppose you have any interested in studying him before his death."

"The endless talk of diplomats would cause my own death from boredom," Traum answered. "It isn't usually a smart tactic to allow an enemy inside your perimeter. The less they know about our numbers the better."

"I will tell my cousin, the Captain, you think King Phortis is making a tactical mistake by allowing the Helacene to visit Enparatus and beg for their princesses."

In the dwindling light, Traum's normally pink skin turning ghost white went unnoticed.

"I am sure the King and the Captain know far more about strategy than a lowly trooper like me," the sergeant said.

"You are probably right, Sgt. Traum," Angartol replied. He enjoyed those moments when he could use his rank or relatives to put less important people in their place. "I need the latest status report from the battlecruisers securing the system. Captain Phistol is expecting my report."

"I will get the updates and have them relayed to your com unit, Lieutenant," Traum said. Anything to help the snotty officer forget his comment about poor field tactics.

"That would help, Sergeant," Angartol replied. His foot stomped the granite-like deck of the rampart's walkway. "Though it is difficult getting signals through this thick stone."

"I will send a runner with the report," Traum promised, disappearing down the spiral stairway.

"Better than me having to walk around in this heat," Angartol said to himself.

Captain Phistol commandeered the offices of the recently departed chancellor. The rooms' lighting powered by an ingenious power converter located beneath the old fortress. After discovering the generator he ordered engineers from the battlecruiser stationed above the planet to come to the surface and inspect the system.

The ship's captain dispatched two aliens from Ve. Kashōn space ships used personnel from across the Empire in compulsory service to the King. The Ve, the odd-looking little race, stood on wide feet with six-toes. They normally walked around barefoot, but forced to wear sandals aboard Shroud ships. Their five fingers and a thumb on each hand proved nimble, and possessed incredible strength. Skin and hair colors varied among the species. Females tended to be slimmer with high, round breasts and softer features. Despite the appearance of something between a child and a stuffed toy, the Ve displayed a passion for engineering. Inventive and inquisitive.

A male and a female arrived on the Captain's order. The male, pale-skinned with red hair cut close to his scalp, was the gregarious type that drove staid Kashōn mad. The female had chocolate skin and dark red hair she wore in a tail. Unlike the male, she seemed sullen.

"I've heard of attempts to convert heat into electrical power," the male informed the commanding officer, "but the efficiency was always too low to make it a viable source."

The little alien literally bounced as he talked. His eyes hidden by protective goggles, shaded to prevent pain caused by too much light. A result of living on a dark home world.

"This generator is efficient?" Phistol asked.

"It is a simple matter to convert radioactive decay into electrical energy. Heat, like the heat created on this planet when the star's radiation is reflected from the granular surface, is similar to radioactive decay," the Ve male answered without providing a direct answer. He shifted foot to foot as he talked.

"The reason it has always seemed inefficient is every method I know of is not a direct conversion process. Most experiments included a solar cell configuration to use the light produced in normal decay, and convert the light into electricity."

"Five-percent average conversion," the female, Bantry added.

"Yes. Low," Grat, the male agreed. "Whoever designed the machine below us was a genius. They created a mixture containing a small amount of radium salt emitting alpha particles. The radium salt is mixed with an element similar to germanium. It is a lustrous, hard, grayish-white carbon-group metalloid. It acts as a semiconductor, with an appearance similar to elemental silicon. The metalloid emits electrons following direct contact with the alpha particles produced by the radium salt."

"At some point, do you intend to explain if the generator is efficient?" the field officer asked, his patience with the engineer's fascination with the power generator thin.

"Ninety-five percent," Bantry replied in her short, withdrawn manner.

"Yes. High," Grat emphasized the words. "But you must see the genius. They amplified the direct conversion process by introducing the salt's alpha particles to a lighter element. I would need to analyze the mixtures, but the element added was a light metal of a brittle nature. It increased the conductivity. The alpha particles have sufficient energy to fuse with the new element's atom. Energy is released in the form of a super-fast neutron."

Grat stopped. He stopped talking and stopped bouncing. He stood there waiting for the Captain to comment on his explanation.

"So?" Phistol asked, somewhat hesitant, fearful the answer would be as mysterious as the long-winded explanation leading up to this point.

"Impinge this fast neutron on a silver electrode and you create electrons," Bantry said.

The Kashōn Ashemacher and career military officer felt the female's interjections were given in a manner indicative of disdain for her superiors. But her voice held no inflection, and could simply be her natural tone.

"Yes. Friction," Grat added quickly. "They engineered a copper electrode opposite to the silver electrode. They manufactured an electrical potential difference between the two electrodes. The electrons bouncing between the cooper and the silver create friction. Next they attached an electrical load, a consumer wire, across the electrodes. You have an electrical current."

"The lights, cooling units, and other machines located on the basement level of this structure are powered by electricity provided by the generator and convertor located in the sub-basement," Phistol surmised.

"Yes," Grat replied.

"The system converts heat created on the surface into electricity."

"Yes."

"It would be a valuable source of efficient energy for the Kashōn Empire?"

"Maybe. It would need to operate where the environment produces a similar radiant heat, and where the other elements are easily found," Grat replied.

"It works on Enparatus but may not work anywhere else in the galaxy?" the Captain's question came out as a staccato statement.

"Probably," Grat answered, shying backward a half-step.

"Get out, and go back to your ship," Phistol ordered. "Wait. Will it continue to operate?"

"There are barrels of mixture stored next to the generator room," the male answered. "There are also large container bins of the elements unmixed. As long as someone keeps the mix tray loaded the generator will produce electricity."

"Go."

Grat and Bantry remained quiet on their walk to the transport. They stayed quiet during the flight to the battlecruiser. Once they reached the engineering section they entered the repair studio. Because of the repairs made to sensitive equipment, the room was secure from electronic scans or devices able to record conversations.

"With simple modifications, the Enparatus machine would produce energy at an efficient, cost-effective manner anywhere in the galaxy," Bantry said.

"I know," a much calmer Grat replied. He removed the constricting sandals and wiggled all twelve toes. "But I was not giving such an incredible machine to the Empire to be used to power more invasions and imprison more people."

"If another engineer inspects it, and does not have your scruples, the Captain will not be happy with you," Bantry said.

"He will hang me by my big scruples," Grat answered. "Until then, screw them."

Chapter 9

ABOARD CLYDE

"Three teams," D'Sey said. "Captain Cooper and Cassie will be joined by Doc and Key aboard the Wraith. Your mission is hostage rescue. Taah and Teak will remain on Clyde and monitor communications. Rox, Krest, and Duly will join me on Menace. Our responsibility is King Phortis C on Chōntorham."

The Andromedas shadow vibrated. Taah said, "Teak thinks he could help more by joining a surface mission."

"If we get separated, Teak becomes lost forever," D'Sey said. "Aboard Clyde he can monitor other systems and warn you if anything unusual or dangerous threatens either mission."

"Duly, Krest, and Rox start getting your gear together for a quick in and out. A dirty in and out. We'll mission plan later. The Enparatus plan comes first. We will all meet again before final deployment."

A hard edge intensified D'Sey's tone. One not present in earlier conversations with the Nakki Agent and part-time pirate.

The three to join D'Sey later left quickly and silently. The lounge held D'Sey, standing before a blank wall. Coop and Cassie occupied a sofa. Doc and Key sat in chairs. Taah used a stool at the bar and Teak became a shadow near the door leading to the ship's hangar deck.

A diagram labeled INVICTA ACADEMY / GROUND appeared on the bulkhead behind Veresk.

"The Wraith is a small ship," he said. "You will be a small team. Coop, Doc, and Key will find and recover Alucha and Mandara. Your primary responsibility is Princess Alucha."

"If they are not together?" Doc asked.

"If you find Alucha first, exit and escape. If you find Mandara first, continue until Captain Cooper decides it isn't worth the risk," D'Sey answered.

"It is Captain Cooper's responsibility to get you into the Enparatus system and on the surface without raising an alarm. He know's his ship, and he is an experienced insertion operator. He is in command of this mission at all times. Doc, Key. Whatever he tells you to do, you do. Got that?"

Doc nodded and Key said, "You betcha, Dee. Coop dah man."

"Once on the surface, Cassie will be unable to leave the ship. She becomes your back-up. Cassie?"

"I monitor, follow orders, and act if anything bad happens," the avatar replied.

"The Academy originally acted as a fortress to protect the oasis in the center of the complex." D'Sey turned to the diagram. As he spoke the diagram dimmed around the water hole. "The main entrance faces west. Originally a barrier door, it is now an open archway." The diagram highlighted the archway and wide corridor leading to the central oasis. "Four thick walls of stone with a tower at each corner. Those towers no longer act as guard locations. They have been converted into an infirmary (back left), fitness training (back right), music center (front right), and student lounge (front left).

"The walls are twenty feet high and ten feet thick. Parapets along all four sides, with an eight-foot connector walkway. The other entrance-exit is a door on the southern wall. It enters the South hall that once held stock and stables. It's the maintenance center for the academy now. Because the Academy does not provide artificial power to the ground floor beyond the four towers, the remaining rooms consist of storage, class space, or remain empty."

"A waste of a lot of space," Coop said.

"The scholars decided hundreds of years ago to keep the main area of the fortress and oasis as original as possible," D'Sey answered. "Partly to honor the heritage, and mainly because it would place demands on the power generator."

The diagram changed. The same outline, but now entitled IN-VICTA ACADEMY / SECOND FLOOR.

"Building the second floor beneath the surface provided additional protection. It is also naturally cooler. The large area in the center accounts for the oasis and ground water. The front, beneath the main gate, is set aside for classrooms. The left side is offices, staff quarters, art gallery, museum, and library. The back quadrant is kitchens, cafeterias, quarters for visitors, and a large community chamber and lounge."

The diagram zoomed in on the right side. "Student quarters are located in the South wing, beneath the maintenance area. This is where you are most likely to find Alucha and Mandara."

"Do we know how many non-combatants are on site?" Coop inquired.

"The communications from the Kashōn captain in charge displayed the burned bodies of the Chancellor and three teachers. Based on a resupply form Clyde found in the Hela fleet files, there are six more instructors. While the school is only open to Alucha and Mandara at the moment, it stills has a sizable staff. Twelve librarians, who oversee the galleries, twelve cafeteria staff, ten maintenance people for inside and outside, two secretaries, and two fitness trainers. The two in charge of physical fitness are there to train the princesses in self-defense tactics. They are former Royal Guardsmen. If they get frisky, they could cause trouble."

"Any unknown player can create a problem," Coop responded. "Do you have profiles and head shots?"

"Everything Clyde collected will be air-dropped to Cassandra."

The second floor disappeared, replaced by INVICTA ACADEMY / THIRD FLOOR.

"Power generator and engineering occupy the lowest level," D'Sey explained. "Some type of solar converter. I've never discovered any records or schematics to detail the system, but everything I found indicates a power source using radiation from the system's star. Power is distributed to the second floor and the interiors of the four towers above the surface. Stairwell access door located at the right rear corner of the second floor, outside of the tower used for fitness training."

The diagram vanished, replaced by an overhead view of the Academy and surrounding area.

"Thirty-Six total Kashōn military personnel estimated to hold the Academy," D'Sey said.

"Estimated?" from Coop.

"Three troop ferries were dispatched to the surface to take control of the school," the Agent answered. "The normal force strength would be three pilots, three co-pilots, and three maintenance-gunners. Each ferry would carry either a command officer or top sergeant, with a corporal, and seven elite troopers. Twelve bodies per ship."

"But you aren't positive?"

"We don't have a reliable source on the surface, and no way of getting intel out if we did," he admitted. "They could have loaded the ferries with more personnel, but it isn't their normal operating standard if they did. Regardless, you need to create a plan to get in, find the girls, and get out with as little interaction with hostiles as possible. If you get caught in a firefight, you lose."

"You haven't already devised some scheme?" Coop asked.

"You will be the commander of the operation, Captain Cooper. Like I said, we don't have reliable intelligence. You and your team will need to get in, evaluate the situation, and determine the viability of completing the mission. You either determine a plan of action or bug out."

"Without the princesses?" Key asked. "Dat don't seem right, Dee."

"I don't send people on suicide missions, Key. If Captain Cooper thinks you have a good chance of rescuing the girls, getting off Enparatus and out of the system, you follow his lead. If he decides the odds don't justify an attempt, don't argue."

"If I decide to leave without Alucha, what then?" Coop asked.

"Reconnect with Clyde. When I hear you have cleared the Enparatus system, my team will take out Phortis," Veresk replied.

"If we do get her out?"

"Reconnect with Clyde. My team will take out Phortis."

"When you kill their king, the Kashōn on Enparatus will kill everyone at that school," Doc said. "Even if we get Alucha, no way anyone else lives."

"You can't save everybody every time, Costi," D'sey replied. He looked her in the eye, refusing to allow a moment of doubt. "Your team rescues Alucha, her sister if possible, and Palla can save an entire system. If you don't, and the Shroud Corps kills them, she still saves the Nessur system. Out of spite, if not duty."

"What if you fail to assassinate King Phortis?" Cassandra asked. The avatar, an observer only until the question.

"The King will decide Palla authorized the attempt. Her daughters will be killed, unless you get them off Enparatus first," he answered. "He'll execute anyone left behind," he added, turning to Doc.

"The people at the Enparatus Academy will die regardless of the outcome of either mission," Cassie said.

The man at the screen ignored the statement. The obvious needed no extra attention.

"We will exit into Hela Alliance space in seven-hours-twelve-minutes," he said. "Captain Cooper, I expect you to introduce Costi and Key to your ship, determine for yourself their capabilities relative to your mission, and begin making preliminary plans. Clyde downloaded all of the diagrams and information regarding Enparatus to your ship. Questions?"

Coop stood; Cassie rising a half-second behind his lead.

"None." He turned to face Taah at the bar counter. "Taah, you have everything you need to communicate with Cassandra?"

"Yessir, all set," she answered. "Your tachyon-based communications integrated perfectly with Clyde's multiple systems. I added the Alliance transmission channels and Hela codes so you can monitor or use the wormhole relay stations. Shipboard scanners can also monitor Empire broadcasts. Your Fell-designed trans-com implant is linked and synced. Use it the way you normally would."

"One more thing," D'Sey said. "Clyde used the tech-specs for the METS unit you wear. Specifically the nano fiber-embedded optics used to capture and retransmit images, making you virtually invisible. He adapted the hull of the Wraith to create the same effect. A ship the size of Menace is too large, but your fighter-sized ship should be able to use the cloaking for short periods."

"Thank you. Doc and Key, join us aboard the Wraith after you collect your preferred personal weapons."

With Cassie at his side, Coop left.

"Short and to da point," Key said as the door closed behind the human and the avatar.

"I like them," Taah said. "Teak does too."

"I like him, too," the Kanistari medic agreed. "I don't see him not trying to get both princesses out, regardless of the situation."

"He's the commanding officer until you decide he's endangering Hela standing against the Empire," D'Sey said to both Doc and Key. He handed the teal-green woman a chip the size of a thumbnail. "Squeeze it until it shatters and Clyde will release a system-wide data wipe aboard the Wraith. He'll follow with new operational codes giving you control."

"Cassie?" Doc asked.

"She'll be wiped with all other systems," he answered. "Make sure you have a weapon on Cooper before you squeeze the chip."

Aboard the Wraith

"I'm in love," Key said. He sat in the Wraith's co-pilot seat, both hands lightly gripping the yoke. "This is what flying should be. Not telling a computer where to go."

"Menace only operates by computer-generated actions?" Coop asked.

"Most times," the Jamaican replied. "D'sey can bypass and allow operator control if he needs to make quick decisions on the go. Don't happen too often. Don't ever happen when I'm pilot."

"Earth still does things differently," the Canadian-American said. "We want the pilot in charge. We switch to automated controls when things are slow and boring. The canopy screen can provide situational awareness in digital readouts, or create a picture of the exterior and display telemetry in the format the pilot prefers."

"Is everything hands-on?" Doc asked.

She stood in the space between the cockpit seats and the cabin. Coop sat in the pilot's seat to Key's left.

"Pilot preference," Coop replied. "You can fly, give verbal commands, operate through a touch screen, or turn the whole bird over to the AI."

"In space or within an atmosphere?" Key asked.

"Same. The Wraith will automatically reconfigure for operating within a planet's atmosphere. The rear tail sections, wings, flaps become integral to flight. In space the Wraith's design allows for less build-up of interior pressure from exterior forces. The flight controls remain the same. How you use them changes," Coop answered.

"Power?" Key swiveled to face Coop.

"Two sources. Ionic-fusion converter for atmospheric flight and up to 250,000mph in space. Space-Fold array for longer in-system travel at .12sl. Between systems at 1kpc."

"This small ship can sustain those speeds and handle the stresses?" Doc asked.

"Composite alloy construction, including some reverse engineered material found on Mars. Things left by the Nakki. The composition, design, and profile of the Wraith, coupled with anti-detection electronics makes her nearly impossible to scan," Cooper continued. "She was designed to be a two-person stealth fighter. Not big, not comfortable. Deadly."

"I'm in love," Key repeated. "Weapons?"

"Double-barrel railguns on either side of the raised cockpit. Kinetic projectiles under EM pulse. Independent or mixed fire. Lower keel opens and a tachyon cannon deploys."

"Can't be too powerful a gun," the thin, dark human said. "Otherwise the recoil would turn everyone inside to soup."

"The Wraith engineers installed special dampeners," Coop replied to the comment. "Power level equal to a battleship and negligible reverb. Four laser cannon hard-mounted to forward wings, but with three-sixty rotation. Pulse, beam, or blast capable."

He reached across and pressed an inset section of the dash in front of Key. The yoke rotated clockwise, replaced by twin joysticks.

"Left hand is rail-guns. Top trigger EM. Middle trigger for LRP, long-range penetrator, short rods. Bottom trigger fires preset mix of the two. Right hand is the tachyon cannon. Squeeze the handles."

Key went "Awww, man. So cool."

Doc, behind the two seated men asked, "What?"

Coop explained to the Kanistari: "You see what you did before. The interior hangar. I see the same, with details. Key sees what the guns see, or if he squeezes harder, any potential threats. The canopy screen is retinal specific. It shows each one of us what we need to see according to our priorities."

Coop swiveled and all images disappeared.

"Lasers can be fired by pilot or co-pilot from yoke-mounted triggers. You can automate all of the firing systems through Cassie. If the cockpit is compromised, use the com-tac system in the galley," he told them.

"I need to see your personal weapons," he said. Standing, he allowed Doc to back into the cabin before following. Key came behind.

The teal-hued female wore a jumpsuit of desert colors with a pair of sturdy brown boots. She lifted a laser rifle from the com-tac console and presented it to Cooper. He noticed her eyes were hazel.

"It's been cut down," she said. "I'm stronger than I look, but carrying it for long periods can be tiring. Duly removed anything not essential, reduced the barrel length, and changed the stock to a light graphite-based composite. He also attached a lighter power unit. I get fifty bursts instead of one-hundred, but I'm more likely to hit my target."

Coop leaned the weapon against the bulkhead and turned to Key Largo. The man's dreadlocks were pulled into a loose pony-tail. He wore an outfit similar to Doc's, with black boots instead of brown.

He pulled a long blade from a leather sheath strapped to his belt and left thigh. He reversed the knife to hand the grip-first to Coop.

"Panga style," Coop said, taking the hilt and flipping the small machete with a couple of wrist flicks. "Upswept curve and up-turned tip. Good stabber and chopper. You any good with it?"

"I practice with Duly," the Jamaican answered.

"You've ever used it in a fight?"

"Nah. I'm the pilot, navigator, and cook," the man said, eyes down. "Dee don't let me too close to real action."

"No pistol or rifle?" Coop asked.

"Never learned much about using them," Key replied.

Crew Lounge

Coop interrupted the mission planning for the team headed to Chōntorham by entering through the hangar door and saying, "Sorry to interrupt, but I need a word."

The screen behind D'Sey dimmed. Without a spoken word, he headed for the door connecting the lounge to the ship's interior. Coop followed, closing the door after he entered the corridor.

"Yes?" D'Sey asked.

"Doc has a laser rifle too big to be worth a damn. Key is carrying a knife into a gunfight. You want to explain?" the human asked.

"I already did," came the quick response. "If you get into a fight, you lose. Doc is along because she's one hell of a medic. If the girls are hurt, she's your best chance of saving their lives. She's also female. Alucha and Mandara will trust her quicker than a male. Key is there because he is the most loyal person I have ever encountered. Any of the other crew members, with the possible exception of Taah, would ignore an order if they thought they knew better. They are all killers. Predators and alphas. You don't have the time to prove your balls are biggest. Key will follow any order you give, and he'll follow it to the end. You need a team you can rely on. I gave them to you."

"Cassie can't leave Cassandra, so that puts me alone on the ground," Coop said.

"Use Doc and Key, understanding their limitations. They will die to see the mission completed."

"You're suggesting I use them as sacrificial lambs if it helps get the princesses away from the Kashōn."

"I'm suggesting that you were selected because you have a history of getting the job done," D'Sey countered. "Use your assets. Use them how you decide. But know one thing, Captain Cooper. I want my people back. I want them back whole. The reason I agreed with the Nakki to ask for your help is your record for bringing your teams home."

"Didn't always work out that way," Coop countered.

"Never from a lack of trying on your part, Captain," D'Sey responded. "Anything else?"

Coop's replied with a shake of his head. He reentered the lounge, made no notice of the crew members assembled, and exited through the hangar connector.

D'Sey returned to the mission screen. No mention made of the interruption.

Chapter 10

Coop, Cassie, Key and Doc stood in the open hangar between Cassandra and Menace. Coop inquired about lighting and Key passed the request to Clyde. The area for fifty-yards in all directions brightened. It made the hangar reaches beyond that circle seem darker, more foreboding.

Cassie set down two alloy-shielded cases beside two similar cases already placed on the deck by Coop. His touch opened one.

"Taser Projectile Pistol, or TPP," he told Doc, handing her a weapon with a rectangular box beneath the barrel and in front of the grip. "No trigger. Aim, squeeze the grip, and a taser plug is fired. When it hits someone, they go down. 50,000 initial volts at twenty-five watts. Actual delivery is less than two-thousand volts following the establishment of the current, but plenty enough to knock out a large human. I think it will do the same to a Kashōn trooper."

"Impressive," she said, admiring the dull black pistol made of composite plastics.

"Limits," Coop said. His serious tone forced her eyes from the weapon to him. "Maximum distance is fifty yards, and, for you, better distance is less than ten yards. Get close to make sure you hit your target. Understand?"

"Ten yards," she repeated.

"It carries ten plugs, and there is no field reload. It uses a compressed gas delivery system in the grip linked to the squeeze trigger. Ten shots and the gas is gone."

"Ten yards, ten shots," Doc said. "Holster?"

"Better," he replied. From one of the cases Cassie brought he extracted a military tactical vest. "Quick draw holster at the chest for the TPP. You'll be carrying medical supplies in the pockets. The cross-draw knife at the bottom is a last-resort, or if you need to cut through something."

"Hey, Coop. Do I get a cool vest, too?" Key asked as Doc tried hers on for fit. Cassie helped the Kanistari medic cinch straps until the tactical top fit snugly, but remained comfortable.

Instead of answering Key's question, he retrieved his trusted rubber-gripped Army Ranger issued Falkniven A1 knife. Some blades were for show. The Falkniven came to work. The CeraKote black matte finish kept the blade from reflecting light.

"Earn it," he said, stepping a few feet aside for more room. He held the knife in his right hand.

The Jamaican hesitated, unsure what the other human expected.

"Use your knife," Cassie told him. "Attack Captain Cooper with it."

Key pulled his panga from the sheath on his belt. Still unsure, he stepped closer to his opponent, weapon held right handed, away from his body, and tip down.

Coop waited.

The attack came quicker than one would consider the laid-back Reggae fan capable. The tip of his blade slashed at Coop's mid-section. He turned sideways and the knife struck empty space. Key shifted the handle, pulling the panga back with a hammer grip, trying to disembowel Cooper. Coop stepped backward, away from the backhand slash.

Key shuffled, raised the curved steel and chopped down at his foe. Coop parried the attack, his steel blade catching the panga, deflecting its path.

The thinner, smaller man dropped and spun, attempting to sweep Coop's legs.

Coop jumped the attempt, landed, and had the Falkniven's edge against Key Largo's Adam's apple before he could rise from the crouch.

"I give," he said, dropping his own weapon, allowing it to clang off the deck.

"Guess I don't get no vest," he said, standing following his release.

"Guess again," his team leader said. "You did well. Better than I expected," he added, handing over another tactical top. "You cannot use the cross-draw to carry the larger panga."

"Way cool," Key replied. "Not to push my luck, Captain, but will I get a stun shooter?"

"Something different," Cassie answered. "A modified laser pistol from Rys, with special holster from Earth. You'll be able to attach your knife's sheath to the belt."

Key accepted the weapon and Sherpa holster.

"This the lighter, meaner, better laser pistol Duly been dreamin' 'bout since you landed?"

"It is," Coop answered, "but you aren't going to have time or a place to practice. Same instructions I gave Doc. Get close, hit what you aim at, and don't go overkill. The pistol will last a thousand-hours, but if you're lighting up the area, it means we're in a vat of crap."

He pulled two more goodies from a case. He handed both new team members a sleeveless, skintight undershirt made from a composite material of kevlar and woven metal alloy discovered on Mars.

"The thin material can stop a projectile, deflect a knife, and dissipate the effects of a hand-held laser weapon. If hit by a laser burst, you will go down, but you will be able to get back up," he told them.

"We're scheduled to meet with D'Sey and his team in the lounge in five hours," he said. "Doc, D'Sey said Clyde has extra crew quarters with real beds. Do those quarters come with show-ers?"

"Sonic, beam, or water," she answered. "Want me to take you there?"

"Cassie and I will store the cases, and then you can take us both. I suggest we all get rest while we can. Always remember, sleep is a weapon, too."

Doc and Key waited outside the Wraith while Coop and Cassie entered the Wraith via the rear cargo hatch. Before returning to the others, Cassie asked, "You plan on a shower and sleep?"

"I'm curious to see what water does to a naked holo-avatar," he replied. "If you survive, I then intend to experiment with a bed bigger, and more comfortable, than one the size of a crate."

"Experimenting?"

"If you make it out of the shower."

"If I don't?"

"Then I'll have to walk wet and naked back to Cassandra. Ei-ther way, we're going to discover how imaginative your nerdy pro-grammer was when he coded your libido."

"I think I like the new, new Daniel Cooper," the avatar said.

He wasn't entirely sure, the inside of the storage area was dim, but it seemed as if her chest expanded before she turned to exit the ship.

Chapter 11

"Damn it!"

The exclamation by D'Sey struck Coop as odd. The expletive a uniquely human response to bad news and the first time he saw the privateer upset. It could be his translator provided a phrase he recognized, and D'Sey never actually used the word 'damn'. Or not. With the black t-shirt, worn jeans, and leather hikers, he certainly appeared human.

"I told Palla to send negotiators to Enparatus to string the Kashōn along until we could get a plan organized. I did not tell her to send her fucking son."

Taah Vil contacted Coop and Cassie to inform them when Clyde exited trans-dimensional space and entered natural space near the Enparatus system.

"Clyde is uploading communications and data transfers from Hela, Enparatus, and the Empire satellites for Captain Dee," she told them. "He wants everyone in the lounge in an hour for updates."

The hour gave them time to shower . . . Coop needed another. Cassie joined him, though she did not require washing. They discovered the spray did not interfere with her holography, and she found the mutual scrubbing satisfying. They arrived to the lounge in time to hear D'Sey's angry exclamation.

Key and Doc sat on stools at the bar. They joined them. Rox Silvanaē entered a minute later, the last to arrive. She took a chair as a photograph of a handsome young man in a uniform appeared on the screen-wall.

"Alain Athodite is the Suzerain's oldest child. He's the Commander of her personal guard. She dispatched him to Enparatus as her representative to negotiate with the Kashōn."

"Looks young," Doc said.

"He is," D'Sey confirmed. "Because he's a son, his options as a royal are limited to diplomatic or military service. I will tell you he earned his rank. Tough guy, but with anger issues. Not my first choice as the Suzerain's representative, considering the lives of her daughters, his sisters are on the line."

"Then why would she send him?" Cassie asked.

"Maybe because he is tough," the reply. "Could be Palla believes a military officer will get more respect from Phortis than a career diplomat. Whatever the reason, he's expected to enter the Enparatus system in less than twenty-hours."

"Will they hold talks on the surface or aboard a ship?" Coop asked.

"My impression is they expect him to remain at the Academy during talks," D'Sey answered. "The Hela ship delivering him is unarmed. The captain is instructed to pass him off to the Shroud ship blockading the gateway then depart the system. He will be shuttled to the surface. Alain will be the lone negotiator. We need to assume he will be at the academy when you arrive."

"Priorities are Princess Alucha," Coop said, continuing with, "and Mandara if possible, and the son, if possible."

"Captain Cooper, the priority is Princess Alucha. No plurals. With Alain on site the Shroud troops will be on higher alert. Find her and get her off Enparatus."

D'Sey waited for an argument. None came.

"Good. Based on the information Clyde intercepted, two Kashōn battlecruisers remained in the Enparatus system. One stationed at the wormhole and one in stationary orbit above the Enparatus Academy. Interview notes from academy staff departing the planet after the princesses arrived place the girls in side-by-side rooms in the student section. The exact location is marked on your mission notes. It will give you a place to start."

The Nakki agent once again hesitated to allow Cooper to add any comments. None came.

"Since there seems to be nothing more to add, we are on the clock," D'Sey said. "The hostage rescue team is less than fourteen-hours from the Enparatus System. My team will use Clyde to get nearer the Kas system before transferring to Menace. We will be on Chōntorham four to six hours afterward. Both teams will need to recon on site before beginning either mission. Does that give you sufficient time, Captain?"

"No worries," Coop replied, stealing a phrase from a young Bosine from Osperantue, who stole it from New Zealanders on Earth.

"At thirty-six hours from now, if Taah has heard nothing from you, my team will commence the mission to eliminate Phortis C. We will be prepared to act in twenty-four hours, and I do not want to be on the Kashōn home world more than twelve-hours after we have established our base of operations. You cannot be on Enparatus after thirty-six hours, Captain Cooper. Even with the time required to make contact between the two systems, when that contact comes things are going to get nasty."

Coop stood, followed by his new team.

"Captain D'Sey, Duly, Krest, and Rox. I do not know you well, but I believe you will handle your mission professionally. Regardless, good-luck. Taah and Teak, I trust you will be listening when we call. Since the clock is running, we'll be on our way."

Coop and Cassie waited while Doc and Key said their good-byes to their crew mates. Done, the four departed the lounge through the hangar access door.

"Any comments about Captain Cooper and his mission?" D'Sey asked those remaining.

"He's a predator," Rox said. "Anyone gets in his way, he'll kill them without hesitation. I like that in a man."

"Agree," Krest said. "He would be a worthy enemy, but a better ally."

"I like his guns," Dully said.

"As soon as Cassandra departs Clyde will take us back into trans-dimensional travel. Start prepping your weapons and gear," D'Sey ordered.

Four assassins left the lounge via the corridor door, leaving Taah at the bar and Teak nearby.

The Cora Sen Du did not look at the shadow when she said, "He's a good man," she said, speaking of Cooper. "It makes him more dangerous than a killer."

Chapter 12

On Chōntorham

"What is happening?"

Dr. Scandeki Pau asked the question after she entered the research studio shared with the Ve Engineer, Docha.

The short man stood at the panoramic window on the fifteenth-level of the research and development center. The Empire's Alien-Technical Research Center (ARC) rose a total of forty-eight stories and sat on the western edge of the largest space port and military complex on the Kashōn home world of Chōntorham. Aliens brought to the planet to develop technical innovations lived and worked within the building.

Without turning away from the view, he answered, "An uprising on the planet Saepartiq. The rebels control the space port and control two Kashōn supply ships. They hold the King's representative and the military commander hostage."

The Aekran scientist joined her colleague at the window. To their left, across the river, lay the King's castle. An ugly block of alloy designed like a step pyramid. The top held the throne room and private meeting spaces. Phortis C's private quarters, including his harem, the block one step below. The King known to wander the portico encircling his quarters while nude. The two alien researchers observed his highness' nakedness enough it no longer elicited a comment.

To the right they could see the portion of the complex used to dock spaceships. Primarily Shroud Fleet spaceships. The massive air-harbor rose miles into the sky. Built from composite materials developed by alien engineers and scientists who predated Pau and Docha by thousands of years. Since the first Kashōn excursion through a wormhole, the race of domineering warriors sacked new systems, and shanghaied the best and brightest from the worlds they conquered.

"Supply ships and shuttles are taking off," Docha said. The smaller ships occupied dockage lower down the harbor. The larger battle ships would use piers at the highest reaches. Faint images seen from the tallest buildings in the complex.

"It's quicker to use ships to deliver supplies to the battle ships at the top of the harbor. Using the freight elevators would take much longer," Scandeki said. "The military is in a hurry."

"The King watches," Docha said.

Phortis C, at seven-foot, appeared massive from a distance of one-half-mile.

"He's wearing clothes," the Ve added. "The King is taking the uprising seriously."

"The Saepartiq races have their own history of military conquest," Scandeki responded in her scientist-instructor tone of voice. A former college professor of applied physics, she often fell into the old habit. "They gave the Kashōn a difficult time before falling to superior numbers. Rebels have always created problems, but never had the numbers or equipment necessary to actually attempt a breakaway."

"They may soon regret their attempt," Docha said.

Scandeki followed the Ve's gaze, his tinted googles peering up. She saw the keel of a red-hulled yacht detach and move away from the ARC.

"Vistol de Aritis," she whispered. The red ship the private transport for the Ashemacher in command of the development of unconventional weapons. Nonconventional weapons described those less like ones already in use. While scientists like Dr. Pau and engineers like Docha worked to improve military technology relative to improving power sources and efficiency, the levels above them worked on nonconventional weapons. Above those, Aritis' strove to create the unconventional.

"Aritis the Vicious," Docha murmured. "If she is joining the Shroud ships being sent to Saepartiq, it will not end well for the rebels."

"I heard whispers she is forcing her research and development teams to create weapons capable of eliminating worlds," Scandeki said. She ran her palm over the stubble of dark hair on her scalp. A nervous gesture.

The Ve replied, "I heard they accomplished their goal."

SHROUD BATTLESHIP OVER ENPARATUS

"What is happening?

Bantry, the female Ve engineer aboard the Shroud battlecruiser in stationary orbit above Enparatus, asked the question as she entered the supply pantry for spare parts and equipment used to keep the ship's power systems operational.

Grat pulled a hover platform across the deck. He stopped to answer. "The captain received a communication to send us back to the planet. Councilor Sentutol ordered a more detailed report on the Enparatus power system."

"She recognized the potential," the darker Ve said.

"Maybe," Grat replied, placing the platform in front of a wall of cubbies. He stepped aboard, using the hover to rise and allow him access to storage twelve-feet above the deck. "More likely she read about a unique power-production system invented by an ancient civilization that still operates and is curious."

"We cannot fudge the next report," Bantry said.

"No," he agreed. "These power meters and recorders will show how efficient the system actually operates." He pulled an alloy box from the cubby. "The detailed scans, along with the schematics we create will prove the system can be replicated."

The hover moved right, The engineer recovered more stored equipment. He pulled a hand-held force-laser from a locked bin. He hesitated. His eyes, hidden behind shaded googles to protect his sensitive eyes from light, squinted as his thoughts travelled beyond the job at hand. He added the laser to the other equipment on the platform, and returned to the deck.

"We will have to report on the materials used to create the fuel," Bantry said, taking equipment from the platform.

"Sentutol will have a new power source that is effective and efficient and can be replicated anywhere in the Empire," Grat said.

"What do we do?" she asked.

Grat placed the force-laser in the transport bin with the meters, recorders, and scanners.

"Our job," he answered.

Aboard the Hela State Ship Elos

Alain stood before the mirror in his cabin. The Hela state-ship, Elos, traveled through the wormhole channel toward the Enparatus system. He wore his Commander of the Guard dress uniform. The waist-cut jacket of dark blue material accentuated his slender waist. The gold stripe with red piping down the outside pants legs made him appear taller. The over-the-calf leather boots gave him a menacing aspect.

"Much better impression to present a Kashōn than the blue suit of a Hela diplomat," he said to his reflection.

The chime alerted him of a call.

"Yes," he said aloud.

"We received an encrypted message from Suzerain Athodite for you, Commander Athrodite. It has been relayed to your private tablet. No other copies have been retained."

"Off," he said, closing communications until he reactivated access.

He picked up his tablet. His touch turned on the multi-functional computer and a retinal scan activated secured applications. When he said "Alain Athodite" aloud, the voice-recognition decrypted the last message dropped to the system.

His mother's image appeared on screen.

"Every available Helacene Alliance battle ship is ordered to rendezvous in the Geras system. The Carrier-Cruiser Prudent will arrive in three days. The other ships will time their arrival to follow. Admiral Ephron will lead the fleet to Nessur system as soon as she believes they are prepared. She promises no more than twenty-four hours to have every captain briefed and all crews ready."

The blue-eyed blonde leaned forward as if in the room with Alain, and not recorded billions of miles away.

"Alain, in four days the Kashōn Empire will know our answer to their threat. I expect you to have negotiated an alternative truce or depart Enparatus system in three days maximum. It is not much time for talks of this magnitude, but it is what we have. If you persuade Phortis to release your sisters, even if it is a ruse to gain their freedom, get them and get out. If you cannot, tell them you must communicate with me to continue the talks. To do so you must reenter the wormhole aboard the Elos to insure a secure channel. If I have not heard from you by then, I will send instructions for your return to discuss progress."

The Suzerain sat back before finishing. "Those are your orders, Commander. I expect compliance." The screen flashed as the message was destroyed.

He placed the tablet on a desk, turned to the mirror, and said, "I will do what I must, Mother."

Planet Saepartiq

The rebel commander sat at the desk of the Empire's Administrator.

"The departure of the Shroud battleship gave us the chance we needed," his second-in-command said. The young woman stood before him, giddy in the defeat of the Kashōn regulars and capture of the space port and offices.

"Make sure the Administrator, the Port Commander, and the Kashōn troopers captured are treated properly, Chrysti," he said. "We need the hostages healthy and unharmed so we can use them for negotiations."

"Our people have been informed," she assured her commander and father. "Those wounded or injured are being cared for as well. But why negotiate, Father? We have the two supply ships. All Kashōn ships are weaponized. We can blockade the wormhole gate."

"The gate is too distant," he replied. "By the time we could get ships there, the Empire will have received the news and dispatched battleships. They could exit the gate before our ships arrived. They would come out prepared for a trap. Two suppliers, each with a single laser cannon, cannot compete with heavy battle ships."

"Maybe we should use the supply ships to take some of our people off world," she said. "In case we cannot negotiate with the devils."

"Which ones?" he asked. "How do you tell one person they get to escape, and tell the next sorry, you stay?"

"Saepartiq has been under the thumb of the Empire for a thousand years," she complained. "The chance to get out from under their rule is something we have fought for all of our lives. Do you think you can negotiate our freedom?"

"Fighting for a thousand years has resulted in millions of dead," he replied. "Our dead. I think we can negotiate for more freedoms. Perhaps we remain within the Empire, but we are allowed self-rule. This is what negotiations are about, Chrysti. We compromise, but we still win. The Kashōn hostages are the only chip we hold."

"I ordered my team to set explosives around the port," she informed him. "You will have more chips that way."

"Good thinking," he replied. "If we remain strong, we accomplish our ultimate goal. To no longer live under the thumb of Phortis C."

The Great Dunes Oasis on Enparatus

"You think we can get inside the academy?" Samara asked.

Trak, the tribal leader of the Parz nomads who normally tended flock at the oasis south of the Great Dunes, sat cross-legged on a blanket. He stared at lines drawn in the sand before him. Lines he drew moments before.

"The water sources on Enparatus are connected," he said to the young Hela princess. "Natural tunnels feed underground water beneath open lands. Some deep wells exist beneath mountains. Ancient Parz, those who used technology before the Enlightenment, built karez channels to direct natural water flow and connect to places not part of the natural order."

He turned to the daughter of Palla Athodite. His own daughters younger than the teenager. He adopted her into the tribe when she was six-years old. The forgotten princess. The rebellious sibling. Unable to join with children her age on Hela due to her status. Unable to be a significant part of her family's activities due to her status. The Parz were nomads, forever moving across the Enparatus deserts according to seasons and water levels. Samara was destined to a nomadic life as she searched for her place in the galaxy.

"An underground well feeds this oasis. The same well produces the water in the pond inside the old fortress," he said. Two circles in the sand. One circle represented their location. The other the academy to the north. In between, nearer the academy, a square to show the well's position. Lines connected the circles and square. Water channels.

"When the ancients constructed the fortress, they built a karez around the natural stream. The reinforced walls assured no cave-ins would disrupt their source of fresh water."

"A karez large enough for a person to travel through?" she asked.

"If it is passable after centuries," he answered. "There is a cover above the well. I doubt anyone has moved it in hundreds of years. It will be covered by sand. Maybe a foot, maybe fifty-feet. The sand moves with the winds. If we can remove the cover, we then rappel down. The karez to the North will have a walkway. If the water is not too high, and the ceiling or walls have not fallen in, it will allow us to walk all the way to the center of the fortress."

"If, if, if," Samara said. "If we go to all the trouble to get into the channel, and we cannot get into the academy, what then?"

"We come back," Trak answered. "I see no other way of freeing your sisters. Samara, even if we succeed, there are few places to hide. When the troopers discover the princesses are gone, the first place they will come is here."

"You think too hard, Trak," the young woman said. "We might enter the academy and find ourselves in the middle of Kashōn soldiers. Planning for later will have been a total waste of time."

"The well is within fifteen miles of the old fortress walls," the nomad said. "We'll probably be arrested or killed when they see us digging in the desert."

"Too bad the academy is on Enparatus instead of Glu," the princess said.

"The winter planet?" Trak asked. "Why would it be better if the academy was there?"

"If the soldiers found us digging, at least we would have snowballs to throw at them," Samara joked.

Her sense of humor, poor but welcome, made the stoic Parz smile.

"What do we do, Princess Samara?" he asked.

"We do what we must, Trak. We do what we must."

Part Two

Surprise, Intelligence, Skills, and Deception

Chapter 13

"Nothing," Key said. His tone inflected by a dash of surprise and a whole lot of awe. "No changes in aspect for either of the Kashōn battlecruisers. No chatter to be heard. No alarms. The Imperial units at the academy are quiet. No one noticed us enter the system, pass through the atmosphere, or land on the surface. Amazing."

"What happened to the Jamaican accent?" Coop asked. He sat to Key's left in the cockpit of the Wraith.

"I tend to lose it when I get excited or I'm concentrating really hard."

"I admit I wondered why Dee decided he needed your help," Doc said, joining them in the forward compartment. She rested her hands on the back of the pilots' seats. Her eyes studied the interior canopy, currently transmitting a visual of a twilight desert. "You are an incredible pilot, and Cassandra is the essence of science and art."

"Thank you," Cassie said from behind Doc. She materialized moments after the craft settled into the cup created by sand dunes on all sides.

"Menace uses space-fold," the thin black human said, "and operates with scan dampeners. She's covered in a reflective hull, but she isn't invisible. Your ship's size and anti-electronic defense will cause scan-monitors to treat her like a two-dimensional object. A scan echo would be interpreted as a gap in the pixels, or an anomaly in the feedback."

"The optic-camouflage enhancements Clyde added help," Coop reminded them.

"Enhancements on elements already present," Doc noted. "Your ship's tech is impressive by any measure."

"I find it odd Earth technology, in some ways, appears more advanced than Nakki applications," Cassie said. "Humans reverse engineered Nakki technology to create space ships like the Wraith. Dr. Fairchild, the person who discovered the hidden Nakki site on Mars, estimated the location to be over two-hundred-thousand-years old. Humans should be at least that far behind in practical knowledge."

Coop continued to scan for an indication the Kashōn vessels overhead or troops on the surface realized they had company. They might remain quiet to engender a sense of confidence. He used similar tactics when enemy combatants arrived unexpectedly during missions under his command. Unchallenged, they believed they operated unnoticed and held the element of surprise. He watched, waited, and learned what he could until time came to turn the tables.

"The big word is ennui," he said in answer to Cassie's observation. "The common result from being complacent. Or overconfident."

"Dee always tellin' us dat if we get overconfident, we get dead," Key commented, the accent back.

The accent a result of the reduction in tension as time passed and nothing bad happened.

"First rule of engagement," Coop replied. "In the case of the Nakki, I believe they became content with their level of achievement. After millennia as the dominant species in the galaxy, they became complacent. They were so advanced, they quit attempting to improve. It gave others a chance to catch up. I first noticed it when Duly became excited about the design of our personal laser weapons. The Nakki may be unaware of the Lisza Kaugh discovery of black-diamond crystals, or their applications as power sources. The use of a secondary-forcefield to allow space-fold exit and entry deeper within a system is not something used on Menace."

"You've never been aboard Menace," Doc said.

"Key pilots the ship," Coop responded. "I engaged the forcefield generator designed by the engineers on Rys before we entered space-fold. He nearly broke his yoke when Cassandra reentered natural space outside the planet's exosphere."

"I admit the truth," Key enjoined. "That big brown planet filled the screen and I thought my end was here."

Coop provided another example by reminding them, "Clyde used information from Cassandra's files to create organic-holo emitters. By placing them inside the ship, it allows Cassie to leave the Wraith"

"Clyde did not possess the technical data. He extrapolated the improvements from data stored in my systems," Cassie continued

Coop's logical reasoning. "He did the same thing to convert technology used in Coop's METS to create negative refraction emitters on my exterior hull."

"Negative refraction emitters?" Key queried.

"Optical antennae designed to bend light," Coop said. "A way to use the METS' fibre-optic nano-repeaters over a larger field."

"You're making those words up," Key accused the other human.

Coop smiled. He did not confirm or deny.

"Humans are more advanced than the Nakki?" Doc asked.

"Catching up . . . slowly," Coop answered. "Necessity breeds invention," he added. "The Nakki remain superior in ninety-percent of their tech, but Earth, with help from our galactic allies, has made advances in areas we needed to improve to survive."

"The Nakki been sittin' on their hands, happy with theirselves. After they kicked the Bashor Flynn back to their little galaxy, they caught ennui."

"Something like that," Coop said. He smiled at Key's use of the term. He found himself smiling a lot lately.

"They recognized the extent of human technical evolution. They sent Clyde to Dee, and Dee to get you," Doc said. "Too bad no one knows where the Nakki actually live. Someone needs to have a talk with them. It's tiresome to jump every time Clyde shows up."

Satisfied their approach and landing occcurred undetected, Coop disengaged all systems except environmental. He muted interior lights.

"They're in one of three systems. Possibly all three. Alnilam, Alnitak, or Mintaka." He delivered this gem as he slipped by Doc on his way into the galley.

"You can't say something like that and leave it," Doc stuttered. "Dee swears he doesn't know the actual location of the Nakki. I've heard him complain often enough about wishing he could talk with them face-to-face."

Coop opened the rear hatch to storage. Instead of entering, he turned back.

"Alnilam, Alnitak, and Mintaka are the stars which form a constellation humans call Orion's Belt," he said. "The constellation is in an area of space astronomers consider a 'Stellar Nursery'. A place where stars are born."

Key Largo joined Doc beside the Com-Tac station. Cassie stood to the side. All three waited on Coop's explanation.

"Doc, you told me humans, at least some humans, possess double-genome pairs within our DNA. These genes link us to the Nakki."

"A signpost for most Nakki-seeded species," she said.

"D'Sey commented he believed Nathan Trent, the man who reverse-engineered the technology left on Mars, must have more connectors."

Coop entered the aft storage unit, leaving his last comment for the others to ponder.

He returned with three soft-tech garment bags. Indestructible carriage units designed to protect the contents against damage. If the ship went blewee, the bags and their contents would survive.

"Dat us humans are close cousins to the Nakki don't explain why you think they live in Orlon's Butt." Key delivered his counter as Coop closed the interior hatch.

"Orion's Belt," he corrected, unable to contain another smile. "Several ancient civilizations on Earth, people separated by oceans and centuries, who never made contact with each other, created structures which replicated the position of those three stars."

He placed one bag on the upper bunk, then handed Doc and Key one each.

"One of the oldest writings found on Earth is the story of creation by the Sumerians," he said, swiping his right index finger across a tab on each garment bag. A seam appeared and opened down the side of the carriers. "They believed humans were created by gods from Orion's Belt. Gods they called the Anunnaki."

"Anun . . . Nakki," Doc repeated.

"Damn," the transplanted Jamaican said. "I'm related to gods."

"Poor relative," Coop said. "The bodysuits in the bags are Multi-Environmental Tactical Skin-Suits, or METS. These two were used by a couple of teenage girls. They stretch or contract to fit the person. You're both close enough in size to Stacey and Chaspi for them to work."

The extracted suits were matte navy blue.

"This can't weigh more than six-or-seven ounces," Doc said, holding the skin-suit from the shoulders.

"Originally designed for the Space Rangers," Coop explained. "The suits include an environmental modification system. As a result your body remains at a constant and comfortable temperature. The blend of materials will stop a projectile or a blade. A glancing hit by a laser can be deflected. A direct blast will kill you. These two were designed for nighttime incursions. They are coated in a dye that tricks the eye. If you remain still, you blend into the darkness. The material will mask your body's heat signature from scans."

"I've seen battle suits before," the Kanistari said. "Never anything this light with sufficient protection and adaptability. In fact, most suits look and wear like high-tech armor."

"There are full head-covers, gloves, and boots in the bags. When you tell the suit, it will integrate everything into one piece. The helmet includes communications and data feeds. In this case, you will be in constant contact with Cassie. You can request heads-up displays, video feeds, or any type of optical assistance, from infra-red to telescopic."

"Will it play my tunes?" Key asked.

"My gloves have only two fingers," Doc said.

"Chaspi is a Bosine, The gloves designed for her hands and the fact she could not fit a finger into a normal trigger guard," he explained.

"The squeeze-activated stun pistol," she said.

"Yep. You must remove a glove if you need your fingers. With them on you can hold a knife or fire your weapon. Because of the modification, you do not have sensory feedback through the gloves. Key will be able to actually feel things with his on."

"You said the suits will integrate the helmet, gloves, and boots. Oxygen?" Doc asked.

"Rebreathers and fog-control ventilation to keep your headgear clear."

"Damn. I'm better dan dem old gods," Key said, caressing the suit like a pet.

"The suits are like any other tool, Key," the military training asserting itself and reflected in Cooper's tone. "You start believing they make you invulnerable and you get careless. Careless gets you dead every time. More importantly, when someone on a team gets careless under fire, they usually get others killed."

Daniel Marcel Cooper - soldier, pilot, Space Ranger - pulled out his METS. Unlike the matte suits Doc and Key held, his reflected the galley lights, shimmering like a still lake reflecting sunlight.

"They help. They provide a tactical advantage, but you're the operator," he said. "Confidence is an asset. Overconfidence is a trap. If you do not understand the difference, you're a liability."

"I understand," the mollified young man replied. "I truly do. The team comes first."

"You can't wear the armored undershirts with the METS," he informed them. "Nothing comes between your skin and the cloth."

"I'm going to recon the academy," he said. "You two get your suits on and get comfortable with how they operate. Cassie will help. While you wander around in the dunes, she'll test telemetry, optics, active, and passive systems."

"We're ten miles from the academy," Doc said. "It will take a couple of hours to get there, and the same to return. The sun will be up before you get back."

Not the shy type, Coop began undressing.

"Thirty-minutes one-way," he said. "You need to get into your suits."

Members of a crew of part-time pirates, and shipmates for many years, the medic and the pilot-cook began pulling off clothes. Close quarters and combat-readiness meant naked and nearby a natural condition for space operators.

Outside the ship, the three checked communications and connectivity with each other and Cassandra.

"My suit is a newer version," he told the other two. "There is a spectrophotometer woven into the material. Micro-cameras are connected by nano-fiber optics. The hybrid-material will match the exterior of my immediate surrounding area. The nano-repeaters Clyde adapted to Cassandra's hull." This final explanation directed at Key.

"No point in wasting energy for the trip. I'll save the virtual invisibility until I near the Kashōn and the fortress. I don't plan on testing their ability to detect communications. Unless there is an emergency I will remain radio silent."

"Radio?" Doc asked.

"I will explain it to her later," Key said. "Kool ninety-seven FM. Ninety-seven-point-one, Kingston."

"We really need to update your reggae sources," Coop said. "Back in two hours. Cassie, copy?"

"Copy. Clock at one-twenty. Start. Now." The avatar's voice responded in all three headgears.

Cooper, reengineered human, turned and sprinted up the dune to the immediate west. Up and over the steep sand hill before Cassie's 'Now' receded.

Key stared slack-jawed at the speed Cooper displayed.

"Doc, you know 'dat thing 'bout other species catching up to Nakki technology?"

"Yes?"

"I think they are about to be passed."

Chapter 14

The red yacht exited the gate behind two Shroud battlecruisers. The smaller, streamlined spacecraft engaged a recently completed power plant unavailable to the older military craft. A version improved beyond the ones installed in the latest fleet vessels.

"We will be above the planet in four hours, Councilor Aritis," the ship's captain said. "The EMDrive will place us over Saepartiq days ahead of the Shroud cruisers."

Vistol de Aritis, Ashemacher Council member and director of research and development of unconventional weapons for the Kashōn Empire, sat in her comfortable chair at the rear of the spacious command center for her private ship, Haimah. The ship's name derived from an ancient word for bloodshed.

"Would you prefer to orbit or stand off until the military escort catches up?" Captain Amikras asked. She turned her Captain's chair to face her superior.

"We will not wait for the Shroud ships, Captain," de Aritis replied. Her right hand fingertip-tapping the arm of her chair. The nervous tic the only indication the older Kashōn female felt anything other than relaxation. "Head directly for the space port taken by the rebels."

The fingers ceased drumming. The Ashemacher rose to her full height, slightly over five-feet. Extremely short for a Kashōn, even a female. The brown shirt, woven from natural materials, swelled over substantial breasts most assumed were artificial, and no one commented upon. She wore a leather skirt and leg greaves with laced sandals in the style of the Empire's Elite Troopers. The embodiment of conflict in her looks, clothing, and persona. A child's height, a whore's body, and a warrior's clothing.

"I will be in the engineer's control center. Contact me one-hour from entering Saepartiq's atmosphere."

Amikras's shoulders relaxed as soon as the Ashemacher departed command. She earned her rank serving in the Empire's space navy, rising to command a Shroud escort cruiser. Unfortunately as assignment to escort Haimah to collect rare elements from an uninhabited planet brought her to the attention of Aritis the Vicious. Admiral Pitaritis, de Aritis' cousin, transferred her to the blood-red yacht. She now served aboard Haimah as the Captain and de Aritis' sex toy on space trips. She found no joy in either.

The Chief Engineer for the Haimah stood at his control panel. Flizz Secate Hival Prime Dia came from an insectoid species from a system within the Empire. The system contained two inhabited planets. Travel between the worlds established centuries before the Kashōn's arrival. The Secate, the dominant species, readily accepted the "invitation" to join the Empire. Vastly different from the Kashōn, they shared a desire to dominate.

de Aritis entered Flizz's domain without announcement or request. His little world subservient to her, as his home world bowed to her's.

"The EMDrive appears to be performing perfectly," she said.

Flizz's right compound eye could watch the female and the readouts on that side of his panel without any requirement to turn his body. Secate compound eyes consist of thousands of individual visual receptors called ommatidia. Each ommatidium is a functioning eye in itself. Thousands of them together per unit-eye created a broad field of vision. Flizz's two units sat high on either side of a thin skull. Pincer-like mandibles made efficient chewers, but inefficient communicators. His left hand, a three-fingered arrangement with a taloned short thumb tapped a pad placed atop his console.

"The microwave containment is difficult," a mechanical voice replied. The communication activator relay strapped around his thick throat created the impression the voice came from him. "The alloy used to line the walls of the generator is the best I have tried. It will give you four, perhaps five extended trips before it must be replaced."

"Energy?" she asked.

"The solar batteries are charged. However, travel in space, in spite of the billions of stars, does not provide a readily available recharge."

"I may be onto something to fix that problem," de Aritis said. "I will continue looking for more microwave-resistant materials for the containment shielding."

Flizz continued to monitor the ship's systems, normal and exotic, while keeping a few hundred eyes on de Aritis.

"Is my new weapon ready?" she asked.

The engineer shifted to his left. Stationary, he appeared to stand on two legs. When he moved the legs separated. He was a hexapod, made up of two tripod groups. The arrangement would allow him to maneuver across all types of terrain.

"The scientists have not completed the filter," he replied. "You will need to wait until the next opportunity to test it over a wide area."

"Or I test it without filters," she countered.

"Yes. If you do not care about collateral damage."

Chapter 15

Enparatus - The Invicta Academy

Coop lay prone atop a dune. Decades earlier, a world and a lifetime away, he did the same thing on missions for the Can-Am Rangers across North Africa. Slip in. Recon.

Back then he wore several pounds of gear, carried a sniper's rifle, and perspired through layers of clothing.

The light-weight METS he wore today kept his body temperature regulated and comfortable. The optical capabilities contained within the suit's helmet alone would have required a van to transport when he ran missions as a Can-Am Ranger.

The data collected by the suit's sensors streamed to Cassandra. Recon, intel collection, and reports combined and delivered to base for instant analysis.

With the sun below the horizon, he activated infrared thermal scans enhanced by an image intensifier. The helmet visor contained an integrated overlay using current information with a battlefield relief created from the diagrams provided by D'Sey. Merged they produced a holographic display visible only to Coop.

He whispered as he took mental notes of what the display revealed. Vocalizing not because Cassandra needed the information, but out of habit.

"Two ships parked and cold at the main entrance to the academy," he said. "Ferries for the troops and supplies. Six guards stationed at the entrance. Two sets of two walk the outer perimeter in opposite directions. No consistent speed, and no obvious time constraints. Two guards remain at the archway."

The height of the dune allowed visual of the upper interior walkway. From his position he could not see the protected oasis, nor any other portion of the grounds inside the stone walls.

"Two sets of two troopers walk the parapet. Speed varies. They pass at different locations each circuit. Thermals show one, and maybe two bodies located in the upper third of each of the four towers. Each tower has doorway access to the upper walkway. They do not have windows overlooking the sidewalls or walks. Diagrams indicated viewports focused out into the desert or into the courtyard. Nothing indicates placement of security beyond the immediate area."

The rear hatch for the furthest shuttle craft opened and dropped to the sandy soil, drawing Coop's attention. The open doorway allowed interior illumination to spill into the dark night.

"Guards are well-trained at not being predictable, but personnel must be getting bored. Sloppy to open the ship and announce yourself by lighting up the whole area in front of the building."

He continued to observe as soldiers emerged. A couple of the group dressed less warlike indicated flight crew.

"Six total," he muttered. "Commander has troopers sleeping on the ships while others bivouac inside the academy. It splits his forces. It also allows for mutual back-up if needed."

The second ship's hatch opened. Six Kashōn walked the ramp to join the previous group.

Someone marched through the open archway toward the ships. Three others followed. By the determined pace of the first one, an officer. The dozen personnel on the ground came to attention. Confirmation.

Coop checked the southern-facing access to the ancient fortress again. It never opened. The walking guards did not stop to check it. No heat signatures ever flashed behind the thick wooden material. It must be secured from inside, and everyone felt comfortable it would remain closed and locked. Barricaded? Welded closed?

The sky behind him lightened as he surveilled the grounds. He decided to leave before the system's star broke the horizon. A blip on his screen made him hesitate. A third ferry crossed the dessert from the North, coming down at a steep angle.

He removed the overlay and switched to the image intensifier.

The arriving ship descended behind the other two, landing far enough away to prevent the blow-up of sand and debris from reaching the troopers on the ground, partially protected by the other ferries.

The rear ramp lowered. Four troopers emerged and took up positions, weapons in hand.

A man in a black or navy blue uniform followed. He moved down the ramp and toward the waiting officer and troopers.

"Alain Athodite," Coop commented to himself. "The Kashōn officer did not go to meet him. Not very polite."

The optics provided a close-up of the young Helacene prince. He presented as calm, bordering on bored. When he reached the exterior encampment, the size and height difference between him and the Shroud officer became apparent. The Suzerain's Guard Commander seemed a boy next to a football player.

The Kashōn speaking to the Helacene looked fierce. The prince remained stoic, peering up at the taller alien, but giving no indication he was intimidated.

"Good for you," Coop said. "Hopefully you're as cool when things go sideways as you are now."

The officer turned and headed for the fortress. Alain followed, followed, in turn, by the troopers who originally came from the walled compound. Coop waited. A few minutes later two aliens, shorter than the prince, departed the newly arrived spacecraft. They waited while the four troopers disappeared into the ship, returning within minutes pulling a grav-sled loaded with containers of various sizes. Three Kashōn, not dressed in battle gear, followed the soldiers down the ramp. The hatch closed after they reached the ground.

The two odd aliens, with the soldiers, crew, and grav-sled headed for the academy, followed by the Kashōn originally with the first two ferries.

"Going in for a meal," Coop muttered. "No one left on guard around the ships." He switched to thermal scan. "No one appears to be inside the parked ships. No fear of anyone messing with the ferries. Overconfident."

With the sun already up, as careful as a desert scorpion, he shimmied down the far side of the dune. At the bottom, he turned south and began to sprint. Once sure no one picked him out of the landscape, he would turn east and north to return to Cassandra.

"Coop, something is coming up from the South."

Breaking com-silence meant Cassie considered this an emergency.

"Non-sinusoidal vibrations picked up by the acoustic-seis-mometers in Cassandra's footings. Two miles south of you, following a deep wadi toward the academy."

Something on the surface, something strong enough to set off the wave-monitors in the Wraith's tripod landing gear, moving toward the academy. Nothing natural. Something that changed speeds and directions.

Coop's heads-up display provided a diagram with his position indicated by a red dot. The unknown bogey represented by a green dot. He changed directions and moved toward an intercept point one-mile away. Cassie would monitor the display, note his movement, and realize his intention.

The green dot came to a halt before he reached the point of contact. According to his display, the unknown target stopped fourteen-point-six miles from the academy.

He adjusted his direction and ran along the outer rim of the wadi, keeping dunes between him and the dry river bed. Nearing the stationary green dot, he slowed and carefully made his way over a smaller dune. He snaked down the far side. An overlook at the edge, one with exposed rocks, provided a place for him to observe and remain hidden. He crawled between two larger boulders. The METS photo-reflective meta-material should hide him from view, but a bit of additional cover could not hurt.

Two people stood at the center of the narrow wadi. Two hover-cycles, both appeared to have a history of use in desert conditions, sat on the barren ground behind the riders. Both riders wore protective leathers, and one, according to the curves and swells revealed by the tight material, was female. The other, probably male, also wore a heavy cloth wrap that cloaked his upper body and provided a hood. They wore full face-masks. The masks would prevent desert sands from ripping their skin and eyes, while providing protection from the bright sunshine, and (conjecture) communications with each other. Possibly others if they belonged to a larger group.

The female walked a grid pattern. She kept her attention on a compact device held in her hand and in front of her as she paced square patterns. She stopped and pointed at her feet. The male hurried to the cycles, extracted two short-handled shovels and returned, handing one to the female. Together, on knees, they began to shovel and push sand aside.

"What have you found?" Coop asked himself. "And who are you? Not Kashōn. Wrong body type. Locals? People from the academy out for a ride when the troopers arrived?"

"Coop," Cassie again, "two of the ferries are up. They appear to be conducting a surface sweep. One of them is headed in your direction. Coming in from the west. You have less than ten minutes before they over-fly."

It did not require the advanced cognitive skills his brain achieved following the revivification of cells after a laser sliced into his skull to realize he needed to make a tactical decision.

He jumped over the rocks and slid down the wadi's wall like surfing a big wave. At the bottom he sprinted toward the first cycle. He noted the laser force-lance affixed to the side of the vehicle when he scanned the site on arrival.

The two diggers jumped to their feet as his ghost-like shade passed them. He retrieved the weapon, turned off the METS cloaking system, and turned on the two surprised riders.

He did not try to communicate, not wanting to waste time if the trans-coms did not contain their language, or if they did not use similar tech. He used the lance to herd them to their vehicles. With exaggerated pantomime and threats, he made them hover the cycles while staying off the seats. Using the force-lance as a prod, he herded them against the western wall of the wadi.

Only two options seemed available. Hide in the shadows of the eastern wall created by the rising sun, or against the lighted western wall and hope the denser material holding the wadi's structure might resist scans. He opted for attempting to hide from electronics, and hoped no one looked back after the ship crossed overhead.

The male lunged at him. The female leapt toward the male's cycle.

The force-lance became a quarterstaff when Coop slammed the butt into the man's mid-torso and followed with an arch to the back of his head. His speed got him to the female as she tried to pull a laser pistol from a pack behind the cycle's seat. His grip on her wrist was not kind. He forced her fingers open. He spun her around, let go, and used the lance to push her, hard, backwards and onto her butt.

She held both hands up, attempting to ward off the next blow.

Nothing came. Opening her eyes and lowering her hands, she watched the attacker drag the downed rider with one hand toward her. He flung the man against the wall, where he slid down beside her. As she watched, he pushed one cycle, followed by the other over onto their sides with his foot. A tremendous feat of strength since the cycles were specifically designed to not roll over.

Coop dropped the lance and grabbed one of the short spades. He shoveled sand over the warmer engine parts until his display indicated a ship closing overhead. He activated the invisibility system. He could not cover both riders. He lay on top of them and tried to spread his body as wide as possible.

The sound of the incoming ship reached them. The female realized his actions were not a threat to her and her companion. She did not struggle when his body draped over her.

The Kashōn space ferry crossed above them and continued toward the East. The shadow cast by the rising sun followed, moving over the people and machines after the ship cleared the eastern wall.

Coop did not move. The female did not move. The male remained unconscious.

He monitored the ship from his helmet's display. Once sure they were not returning to investigate anything their scans detected, he pushed away and rose.

The female body-slammed him with her shoulder. It did not knock him down, but the force of the surprise attack did make him stumble backward. She dove for the force-lance on the ground, but could not lift it. Coop's foot held it down.

The leather hood and face mask rotated to look up.

Coop turned off the METS cloaking system, and the flexi-faceplate disappeared into the helmet.

"Don't know if you can understand me, but it was the only way to get you and your friend safe before the Kashōn ship arrived," he said.

The female rolled over and came to her knees. She removed the face-mask. Definitely a female. Coop was surprised to see a young face looking up at him.

"You might have tried telling us instead of beating us," she said.

"You might not have understood," he countered. "Or you might think I was lying and try to shoot me."

He reached out a hand. She took it without hesitation, and he lifted her to her feet.

"I might still shoot you if Trak isn't okay," she told him before going to check on her companion.

A little more time, with water externally and internally applied, and the nomad regained consciousness. Aware, but groggy.

"Don't suppose you want to explain what you were trying to dig up?" Coop asked.

Neither answered.

"I have a medic at my ship," Coop told the young woman. "You carry Trak and I'll take his cycle. If you don't mind showing me how it operates."

The controls proved simple and straight forward for the experienced pilot and test pilot.

Realizing introduction had been bypassed by necessity, he told the young woman, "My Name is Daniel Cooper. I'm a human from a planet called Earth. I'm new to this section of the galaxy."

She hesitated before saying, "Sam. My friends call me Sam."

"Most people call me Coop," he replied. "I'll lead. You follow with your friend."

"I want my force-lance back," she said, dark eyes holding his.

Coop did not answer directly. Instead he strapped the lance back into its holder. He harnessed Trak onto the seat behind Sam, making sure he was aware enough to hold onto the girl in case the hasty harness failed.

The hover-cycle hummed to life. The motorcycle-like vehicle amazed him as it flew up the wadi bank, across, and over the nearby dunes. Sam remained behind and slightly to his left side. It allowed her to keep the lance aimed at his exposed back.

Chapter 16

Saepartiq - Space Port Control

"The smaller ship that entered the system with the two warships is nearly through the atmosphere," Chrysti's father said aloud.

He monitored the space port control console readouts while she handled the communications console.

"No one has tried to contact us," she told him. "They aren't responding to my calls."

"It's a good sign they sent the smaller ship ahead of the battlecruisers," he said. "They must plan on talking first. I told you the hostages would help."

Haimah, Vistol de Aritis' private red space-yacht exited the upper atmosphere into a brilliant blue sky.

"Is the disperser array ready?" she asked the insect-like chief engineer.

"The scientists have not yet developed a proper filter," Flizz Secate replied. "The array is ready, but we cannot differentiate between lifeforms. There is no way to filter Kashōn protein cells from others. Your personnel on the surface will be as vulnerable as the rebels."

"Their lesson for allowing rebels to overrun the space port," she said. "Disperse the radiation when we reach the edge of the port."

Chrysti could see the entire space port from her vantage point atop the control center. One-hundred-feet of elevation; the control center at the apex surrounded by perma-glass walls.

She gaped as the dark red ship approach, unable to suppress the awe she felt at the shear beauty of the yacht. A wonderful way to explore the universe. Something she dreamed of, but never expected to accomplish.

The young rebel's attention on the undercarriage, the keel, she saw a hatch open and a platform lower. The bottom of the platform glowed yellow and green. Her attention pulled to the surface and the guards at the furthermost edge of the spaceport. Those beneath the arriving ship began to struggle, then slumped lifeless onto the ground.

"Father. The red ship is killing our people," she called.

Her father joined her by the com console. They both stood witness as people beneath the ship screamed in agony and died. He forced his eyes away to discover rebels and workers high up on docks reacting the same way. As the ship passed over an office building, they could both see people behind windows scream and disappear.

"Being inside doesn't help," he said. "The ship will be here before we can reach the ground."

Chrysti used the communications console to broadcast a warning to escape.

"Don't try to hide," she allowed her fear to add urgency to the message. "Run and keep running. Get as far as you can."

The Haimah passed over the vaults holding captured Kashōn. They died in the same manner as the Saepartiq people above.

While the young woman repeated the alert, her father used his laser pistol to blast a section of perma-glass from its frame. Ten feet away, a stabilizer cable for the tower angled away toward the solid footing on the surface.

"You'll have to jump, and wrap your belt around the cable," he said. "Ride it to the ground. When you reach the ground, run. You first, and I'll be right behind you," he assured her.

Belt in hand, with little time to consider options, Chrysti ran across the room and launched herself at the cable. The metal hurt her hands as she grabbed and held long enough to loop the belt over and grasp both ends. Next, she hurtled towards the ground.

Tilting her head backward, she saw her father replicate her jump.

Because of his weight, gravity brought him at her faster than she could move away. She lifted her booted-feet and tried to become more aerodynamic. Her father did the opposite, splaying his body as wide as possible to slow his descent.

Once more, head tilted awkwardly back to see him, she caught sight of the red hull crossing over the top of the command center.

Chrysti locked her feet against the cable, the animal-skin soles smoked as she used the friction to slow down before hitting the ground too fast. She dropped before the cable reached the footing. The athletic young rebel hit, rolled, and tumbled to the side, missing the concrete structure used to anchor the extended stabilizer.

She looked back, expecting to see her father replicate her move. Instead she could see his face twist in agony before life left him. The beam from the ship catching up before he could let go.

No time for tears, she sprinted, angling away from the course of the ship in hopes of staying ahead and away from whatever weapon killed her friends and father.

The pain hit, ripping reality from her mind, and she died.

The red ship continued on.

"The radiation attacks organic protein at the cellular level," Flizz Secate said, watching video feeds and scanning monitors while keeping several eyes on de Aritis. "It's an effective method of eliminating your enemy without the need to get close. It also does no damage to non-organic structures."

"Do we have enough power to radiate the entire planet?" the Ashemacher asked.

"Without the filters, we would destroy all animal and plant life, not simply the rebels," he replied. "But it does not matter, because we do not have sufficient power for more than another hour. It would require weeks with a ship this size."

"Pity," de Aristis said. "I'll inform the captains of the battle-cruisers to complete our business here."

Flizz Secate held no interest in other species surviving or becoming extinct, by natural or unconventional methods. The insectoid engineer shivered across his body when the Kashōn departed. He never wished to become a target of the woman's interest.

Chapter 17

Informed Coop would arrive by hover cycle with two guests, Doc waited in front of the Wraith. She held one of the Rys diamond-powered laser rifles from the ship's armory.

Key carried the second laser rifle with him. He found a dip on top of a low dune fifty-yards away from Cassandra. He would cover from concealment, in case the guests turned out to be party crashers.

The two nearly silent transporters snaked between two dunes, silicate-planing over the desert sand toward the fighter.

Coop called to her as he swung his leg over the cycle, "Doc, I have a guy with a head injury."

Sam eased her cycle behind the first one and waited for Coop to help detach Trak from her, the harness, and the vehicle. He lifted the nomad as if he weighed no more than a child. He placed him on the ground, his back nestled against the stationery cycle.

Doc handed Coop the rifle, removed the injured man's face mask, and gave a quick once over before saying, "Maybe a slight concussion. Wouldn't risk anything for pain. Take him inside the ship where he can cool off. He should be okay soon."

Cooper picked Trak up once more and turned to find Sam with her mask off and lance in hand. Pointed toward him and Doc.

"I want to know who you are and why you're here?"

"We can discuss it inside," Coop said.

"Inside what?"

"Cassie, uncloak," Coop ordered. The wraith appeared immediately. No fading in. The moment Cassie cut off the antennas, the ship was there.

The girl showed grit. Facing a wicked looking fighter that materialized from air, she held her ground.

"I don't intend to go inside that ship until I have answers."

The soft whirr of rotors, and Sam turned her head slightly enough to see the two double-barrel mini-cannons on either side of the ship's cockpit adjust to aim directly at her. In her peripheral vision she caught sight of Key as he rose from the dip, laser rifle trained on her.

She leaned her weapon against the cycle Coop rode in on. Without skipping a beat, she said, "But it is hot out here. You can tell me what I want to know inside. Trak could use a cool place to rest."

Impressed by the young woman's recognition of her position, and refusal to act intimidated, Coop gave a wry smile and said, "Cassie, lower the rear ramp. Key, come in and join us. Doc, lead the way."

Coop lay Trak on the lower bunk. Doc placed a cool thermal wrap across his forehead. Key stayed quiet and alert, on guard at the hatch separating the galley from the storage area. Samara made herself at home, inspecting everything as if she was a potential buyer.

No one stopped her when she entered the cockpit and took the pilot's chair. Cassie would never allow her to actually operate anything. No chance she could damage or disrupt any systems.

"Great good tiny blue stars," she said. "This is one way cool ship. What is it?"

"Two-person fighter called a Wraith," Coop replied. "Her name is Cassandra. Who are you and what were you looking for in the wadi?"

"Aren't you afraid the Kashōn will find you?" The question avoided answering his.

"The ship uses anti-scan detection, jammers, and you may have noticed she comes with a cloak. Emitters on the hull bend light. A visual scan will only show more sand and rocks. Basically electronic camouflage. I still want an answer."

"She's Princess Samara Athodite, Suzerain Palla's third daughter," Doc said. "I've seen pictures and videos of her and her siblings since they were babies. D'Sey provided images of the children. We've watched them from birth as part of monitoring this section of space."

"D'Sey?" Samara asked the question as she turned the pilot's seat. Her face a scowl with a hooded look. "The pirate?"

"How do you know of D'Sey?" the teal green Kanistari demanded. Her cool demeanor shaken by the revelation.

"Relax," the younger woman responded. "The Helacene Alliance keeps records, and I thought the idea of pirates was cool when I was a kid. I heard my Mom say his name once. I don't think she knew I heard. I never saw it in any of the official records. The Hela military called him Slate, after an ancient mythological being known for reckless behavior. You're pirates, too? Really? From the Virago?"

"What's Virago?" Key asked.

"Slate's ship. Virago was the name of the original Slate's winged dragon. Described as a female flamethrower with a bad attitude."

"So D'Sey is Slate and Menace is Virago," Key said. "What do the military call the rest of us?"

"Nothing," she replied, turning back to face the instrument panel. "How fast does Cassandra fly?"

"Nothin'!" Key exclaimed, lowering his rifle and stepping further into the galley.

Trak moved like a desert snake. He came off the bunk and made for the distracted brown-skinned alien.

Coop was faster. He caught the Parz nomad a foot from Key Largo. He was fast and he was strong, pinning the wiry man to the rear hull.

"I was wondering when you would make your play," he said. "Nice teamwork. The Princess has everyone focus on her, creates a distraction, and you take out the nearest person. Then what?"

"One step at a time," Trak answered. If surprised or fearful, he showed neither. His right hand slid down his tunic while the left held onto Coop's wrist.

"I removed the blade when I picked you up in the wadi," Coop said. He released the pressure of his hold and stepped away. To Key he said, "I hope you learned a lesson."

The Jamaican nodded.

The princess, on her feet when Coop intercepted her friend, joined Trak.

"What now?" she asked, after assurances by the Enparatus native he remained unharmed.

"Our intel said your sisters, Alucha and Mandara, were the only daughters of Palla at the academy," he said.

"They are," Samara answered. "I snuck a ride here on the last supply ship. I came to visit Trak's tribe and surf the dunes on my cycle. I've done it for years. This time happened to be during their training for succession. Trak and I saw the Kashōn murder the academy chancellor and three teachers. When they did not kill my sisters, I figured they wanted them as hostages. We planned on getting them out."

Without options available, Samara decided to trust the pirates. With Trak's assistance, they explained the system of underground water supply tunnels.

"If you did get in, find the two girls, and get out, where did you plan to go?" Doc asked.

"Hundreds of secret wells and ancient sites are located in the deserts of Enparatus," Trak said. "We would hide until help came from the Suzerain, or the Kashōn stopped searching and left."

"Princess Samara," Doc said, "What do you know about the Kashōn?"

"Not much," she admitted. "The Alliance is aware of the Kashōn Empire. My mother considers them dangerous. My older brother, Alain is fascinated by them. He collects and studies everything he can on militaristic species."

"Did you know Alain was here?" Coop asked.

By their shocked expressions, the news surprised the Hela and the Parz.

"No," she answered. "We didn't plan on rescuing anyone else. Alucha and Mandara would have refused to leave without him. How did they capture Alain?"

"Your mother sent him to negotiate for your sisters' release," Doc answered.

"Seems all your plans are one step at a time," Key said.

Doc said, "Princess Samara, Trak you need to understand something about the aliens who hold your sisters, and now have your brother." The two would-be rescuers sat at the raised table near the com-tac station. Doc, who had been standing, sat in the third seat. She waited until they made eye contact before continuing.

"If you had rescued the princesses, and if you found a way to bring your brother out as well, there would be no hiding from them. The Kashōn, especially those in leadership, officers, and their elite troops, like those on the surface now, have no mercy for other species. They would have killed everyone you left behind at the academy. They would have found every village on the planet and tortured the Parz until someone told them where to look for you, or you came out of hiding."

"Why are pirates here?" Samara asked. She turned to face Coop, who sat in the cockpit, chair turned. "You aren't with the Kashōn. Were you planning on taking Alucha and Mandara for yourselves? Sneak in. Steal them and escape in your fancy ship. Sell them to the highest bidder? If what you say is true, the Kashōn would murder everyone left behind."

"We are here to get the girls," Coop admitted. "When we did, they were to be taken to a Hela Alliance world. I hoped to lure the Kashōn into leaving Enparatus and following us."

Key and Doc exchanged looks. He never mentioned that part of the plan before.

"If they did not catch you, what would stop them from coming back and killing everyone?" the youngest princess asked.

"Nothing."

"And now?" Trak asked.

"I was at the fortress trying to decide the best way in and out before meeting up with you two at the hidden well," he said. "Now I plan on incorporating your plan into my own. The mission has not changed. Get the hostages and get off the planet. If I can distract the troopers and the ships overhead they might forget about the people here. It's the only chance they have."

"Alain?" Samara asked.

"I consider him a valued target. If there is a way to bring him out with your sisters, we will. But they remain the primary mission."

"I appreciate the honesty," the mature teenager responded. "What about Trak and me?"

"You need to leave with your brother and sisters," Coop replied. "Trak will have to get back to his tribe on his own. There won't be time to drop him off."

"I'm not asking about after the rescue," she said. "How do we help get them out?"

"The success of this type of mission depends on operators who follow orders," Coop said. While spoken to Samara, his words were directed to everyone. "I cannot have a single person on the team who does not function according to the mission plan. Every life, those of the hostages and those of every team member, requires you follow orders without hesitation."

"It is the same for life in the desert," Trak said. "I understand, and if you allow me to help, I will follow your orders. No hesitation."

"I've never been good at taking orders," the princess admitted. "This isn't a game, and my sisters and brother are in danger. I swear on my allegiance to the Athodite name, I will follow every order without hesitation."

Coop turned to the other two on board and asked, "Thoughts?"

"We could maybe use an extra pair of hands," Key said. "I like dem."

"I think placing the last female heir in danger is risky," Doc said. Her normally hazel eyes a dark shade of brown as she considered her position. "I also remember being a young girl. I did not have the choice on becoming a woman. Princess Samara has the opportunity of making a truly adult decision. I hope she has the maturity to follow through with her actions. I'm willing to trust them."

"Cassie?" Coop asked.

"I do not have baselines for monitoring their physiological changes."

The voice, coming from no one, but from everywhere, startled the girl and the nomad. Both heads on swivels as they peered into every corner of the cramped ship.

"What I do read indicates no spikes to indicate deceit," Cassie continued. "I believe you can trust them, Captain."

"Cassie is the ship's artificial intelligence," he explained. He did not explain her ability to manifest, keeping that information to himself, Key, and Doc.

"Show me what you have on the water supply channel," he told Trak.

Chapter 18

Princess Samara and Trak sat together at the table next to the com-tac station. Key sat on the floor, his back propped against the bulkhead, laser rifle across his lap. Coop sat in the pilot's seat with Doc sitting co-pilot.

"You're risking her life," Doc said. "You don't have the right."

"No," he agreed. "I'm taking advantage of an opportunity."

"They gave you the information about the water channels. You and I could find the other girls."

"Key would need to be outside the academy as an observer," he said. "Princess Samara and Trak would be left alone. Do you trust them to not do something stupid?"

"Lock them in storage," she countered.

"I thought about it," Coop replied.

"You want to keep her near," Doc said, grasping the truth. "If she's with you, you can protect her. Even if you're taking her into the middle of the enemy."

"If we find her brother and sisters, they will be more likely to do what I tell them to do without a fuss," he said. "She's young and she's rash. If I keep her concentrating on the job, she's less apt to get into trouble. Or cause any," he added.

"You want to keep her near," Doc repeated.

"What did you mean when you said you didn't have a choice becoming a woman?"

The Kanistari cut hazel eyes toward the human. The change in subject surprised her. Not the fact he wanted to change the subject. His interest.

"You have shown a surprising lack of curiosity about any of the people who kidnapped you," she said. "Why now?"

"We have the time now," he answered. "When I first met everyone, I needed to know your motivations. Then I needed to find out what you were capable of if I was going into battle with you. Up until now we have been involved with mission planning or dealing with side issues. We have the time, but only if you want to answer."

"Kanistar, my home, is part of the Galvari Federation. Federation is not the designation most people on Kanistar would agree with," she said. Doc sat upright in the co-pilot's seat, eyes straight ahead. The interior canopy provided a view of sand dunes and cloudless light blue sky. Her eyes, shifting to a honey color, saw through the sky, space, and into a portion of the galaxy far, far away.

"There is a central government. Martial law rules the federation, led by a council of generals. Not as domineering, nor driven to expansion like the Kashōn. They control two-dozen systems and have for thousands of years. The Galvari allow systems to manage their own affairs. Each system pays tribute for protection and use of wormhole channels to trade among themselves. No one trades outside of the federation except the Galvari."

"Protection from whom?" Coop asked.

"The Galvari claim they protect federated worlds against external threats," she replied. "In truth, the planets pay the Galvari for protection from the Galvari."

"The Kanistari do not want to be in the federation?"

"Most Kanistari do not care who rules them," she replied. Her tone indicated a mix of contempt with a tinge of sadness.

"Kanistar is one of two inhabited planets in the Twin Sisters system. Our system has twin stars, Zae and Zbeth. The other planet is Settasor. The Setites developed technology while the Kanistari grew crops. The Galvari arrived six-hundred-years ago. Imagine the turmoil on Kanistar. The indigenous races considered the Galvari gods."

Doc sat quietly watching history through the filter of time and distance.

"Something else happened," Coop surmised, the comment designed to pull Doc back to the present.

"The Setites accepted the Galvari as superior beings, but not gods. The arrival led to improvements in their technology. The Setites adopted many of the Galvari beliefs. A century after *The Arrival*, what Kanistari call the day the gods descended, the Setites made their own arrival. They annexed Kanistar and enslaved the population. Any attempts at resistance were met with ferocious firepower."

"The Galvari?"

"It's a confederation. Remember? They allowed system politics to work themselves out." She spat the words.

"And you?"

"Born a slave," she answered. "The Kanistari live and work as we always have. The technology brought in by the Setites was used to improve production. They did not concern themselves with how we lived. Before and after their arrival our villages cared for all children. We received educations. From a young age we were required to work, but children always given safe jobs with short hours. Until we grew old enough for the Setites to take notice."

Coop remained silent, allowing Doc time to deal with her thoughts and emotions. She accepted an internal decision with a deep, silent breath.

"Most teenagers become workers," she said. "Some, those who show signs of athleticism, are moved to training facilities to become police, fire-fighters, or military personnel. The brighter students may be chosen to learn a vocation operating technical systems. I was not as lucky. I developed the feminine traits the Setites considered appealing. That I was bright, athletic, and hard working did not matter. I was taken from my parents, removed from my village, and placed in a brothel for sex training."

She turned to look at the human. Her eyes deep brown.

"Funny thing about being a sex slave. You learn a lot about medical training in case you need to care for injured co-workers, or yourself. It also seems an understanding of physiology improves your ability to provide pleasure."

"How did you get away?"

"D'Sey," she replied. "He raided a Setite ship delivering tribute to the Galvari. I was part of the payment. One of his crew was injured after they boarded the ship. I kept him alive, returned with them to Menace to attend to the wound, and stayed."

"D'Sey said he left that part of the galaxy a century ago," Coop said, the comment also a question.

"I joined the crew about fifty-years before Clyde showed up," she answered. "I used the time to study more about medicine. When not busy pirating."

"Kanistari have long lifespans, too?"

"Nothing extraordinary," she answered. "Space travel screws with time in strange ways, Captain Cooper. Trans-dimensional travel and space-fold travel can change your biology, if you use them often enough. They definitely change linear time. There are also effects from living aboard Menace or Clyde for that matter. Something in the environmental systems is designed to enhance body chemistry. I've become a damn good doctor, but I'm still working on becoming a scientist. I can't explain the entire process. Still, not bad for a farm girl and a whore."

"The rest of the crew?"

"Everyone has a story," she said. "You know most of Key's. Dee attacked a Devee trade ship. Key had been abducted as an infant and raised to work aboard Devee ships. They trained him as a pilot and navigator to back-up their computer systems. Taah happened to be aboard the same ship. She was a present for a rich merchant on an independent planet the Devee wanted to open negotiations with. Key begged for freedom, and Taah broke my heart."

"D'Sey said you adopted them."

"Clyde arrived soon after they joined us," she said. "The rest of his crew decided to accept payment for services rendered and remain in the part of the galaxy they were familiar with. Key, Taah, and I joined Dee for the trip here. We picked Ateakatakut up by accident when Clyde slipped into the Andromeda Galaxy to avoid a surge from the black hole."

Doc appeared more relaxed as the subject moved away from her personal history. Her shoulders lowered, and her eyes displayed flecks of blue-grey.

"Duly joined after we raided a Kashōn outpost on Xentarene. The Imperial Troops penned us down. He showed up and cleaned them out with one massive laser weapon. He designed and built the gun from scavenged parts. Key found Rox locked in a cage aboard a Kashōn supply vessel we ambushed as it exited a wormhole gate. She scared him witless when she changed from a pula into a woman. They both asked to join us instead of being delivered somewhere safe."

"Krest?"

"Clyde delivered Krest," the teal alien answered. "Menace docked and he was waiting. He doesn't talk a lot. I'm not sure if he volunteered for the trip, or, like you, he was taken and later persuaded to help."

"D'Sey?"

"You probably know as much about him as any of us," she answered. "The man lives in the moment, despite being thousands-of-years old. He enjoys messing with bullies. The Galvari, the Setite, the Devee, and now the Kashōn. I'm sure others have come and gone in his lifetime. He never admits it, but he also enjoys being a good guy. Whether it's saving chattel, like his current crew, or delivering food and medicine to places under the Empire's thumb. I've only seen him act against character once."

"Care to share?"

"He fell in love with Palla Athodite."

Chapter 19

The Raid on Invicta

The success of a hostage rescue operation depends of four principles. Surprise. Intelligence. Operators' skill. Deception.

Four hours after deciding to add Samara and Trak to the team, Coop's modified mission plan went into action. They would access the well, recon the karez, and if the tunnel remained open and allowed passage to the fortress, move forward with plan number one.

If the tunnel did not remain open the entire length, they would regroup and change to plan number two.

Plan one took advantage of the forgotten access tunnel. They would attempt the extraction during daylight hours. A raid occurring during the daytime would definitely be a surprise.

Plan two required a nighttime action, using the darkness and the natural sluggishness occurring in the early morning hours to surprise the enemy.

Electronic scanning would be intermittent and unreliable due to the heat radiating through the atmosphere and reflected by the surface. These gaps in the invaders' security net coupled with Cassandra's own anti-detection systems meant they could fly the Wraith to the location Coop first encountered Samara and Trak.

Samara and Trak pushed the hover-cycles into Cassandra's rear storage. Hatch secured, Coop flew them toward the wadi.

"Why so slow?" the princess asked. She sat in the co-pilot's seat. Key relinquished the chair to help Doc and Trak prep equipment.

"Reduce surface disturbance," he answered. "Scans may have a difficult time, but sending up a dust cloud could get us seen by anyone who happened to look in our direction."

"Where is Earth?" she asked.

"Other side of the black hole," he replied. "Stay focused on mission, Sam. You need to remain relaxed. Don't allow distractions to get in the way."

"Tell me the truth. Am I staying with you because you don't trust me on my own?"

"If I didn't trust you, I'd tie you up and leave you in the ship," he answered. "Doc was going to be with me originally. Having a female along was to help calm your sisters when we found them. You are a better option. Plus your brother is more apt to trust me if you are there. You save me time."

"I've also attended the academy and know my way around," she said.

"That, too," he agreed. "You and Trak improve our intelligence. The more data we have, and the better the source, the better our chances of success."

"Too bad Alain isn't here instead of me. He's studied everything about races like the Kashōn. As far back as I can remember, he wanted to become a military officer. He could probably lead you past all them, grab Alucha and Mandara, and escape before anyone knew anything."

"If we pick him up along the way, his information can still benefit the mission. In the mean time, don't discount your importance. The file Cassie received from D'Sey says you are proficient at climbing, diving, flying, and possess pretty decent fighting skills."

"Better than decent," she huffed.

Doc interrupted. "I need to implant the com unit," she said.

Coop's Fellen-designed communication and translation chip, inserted subcutaneously beneath his right ear, had been updated with languages for this sector of the galaxy by Clyde. At the same time he was linked with the Menace crew's brain-implants for cross-communications. Doc did not have any complex systems with her, but did bring a half-dozen communications chips which could be inserted under the skin. The chips included locators. The plan was to tag the two princesses.

Samara left to have hers inserted. Coop continued toward the wadi. He hoped the young woman proved as competent as similar teenage aliens and humans on Earth who helped prevent the destruction of the United Earth Council.

"I like her," Cassie whispered. "She reminds me of Mags."

Coop smiled. Mags, Elie's co-pilot on the fighter-ship Demon, was a woman to be reckoned with. Smart person, smart mouth, and damn fine teammate.

Trak produced an ancient piece of Enparatus tech called a diviner. It reminded Coop of an old-style magnetic compass from Earth.

"The ones who built the water systems added a mineral called citic into the forging of the covers placed over access shafts," he told them. "Citic is rare and the diviner will indicate its presence. We know approximately where access shafts to wells are located, but the shifting sands can change the landscape. We walk a grid until the diviner reacts. Doesn't matter how much sand shifts atop the cover, the citic will cause a reaction. Then we dig."

Because no winds crossed the desert since they first discovered the well shaft's lid, they only needed to continue digging where the diviner pinged before Coop's arrival.

"Dark down der," Key said, peering into the uncovered shaft.

Coop tossed a line into the darkness. He secured the top end to a Wraith landing strut.

He wore his METS beneath black camo shirt and cargo pants. A tactical vest carried his laser pistol and knife. Doc and Key wore their borrowed METS beneath sand-colored outerwear. Doc had the stun gun. Key held a laser rifle. Trak wore his cycle leathers with a brown-thatch tunic draped over his upper body. It helped him blend into the desert colors. He held Samara's force lance and wore his returned blade in a sheath around his waist. Samara wore her cycle leathers. A belt holster held a second laser pistol and a knife from Cassandra's armory.

Cooper clipped the line onto a harness adapted to his tac-vest and jumped into the dark well. The others waited.

"Twenty-two feet down and I'm on the edge of a fresh water pool," he reported via the connected coms. "I popped a light stick. Everything here looks to be in good shape. A tunnel heads north, towards the academy, and another south, towards the oasis in that direction. Send down the sensor."

Key, with Trak's help, carried a contraption quickly cobbled together by Coop, with Cassandra's assistance, before they began the trip back to the wadi.

Long Range Acoustic Devices (LRAD) were developed in the twenty-first century to utilize high frequency sounds to disable enemy attacks, or disperse crowds without the need for killing. Ultra sonic sensor technology was part of the AI's defensive scanning systems. Normally used to detect sonar-like scans before they could echo off the ship's hull. Coop built a conical speaker from components from the Wraith's communications and entertainment systems. He changed the emitter to fire ultrasonic waves instead of audible frequency sounds.

Key and Trak lowered the eight-pound gizmo by cable. Coop pointed the conical tip down the northern tunnel and flipped a switch. Because of the high frequency, he had no way of knowing if it worked.

Cassandra used precision velocity measurement to calculate the time required for the ultrasonic wave to reach an obstruction, rebound, and return to the original source. The acoustic-seismometers located in Cassandra's footings, the same system that detected the hover cycles crossing the desert, monitored the discharged sound wave.

"The time indicates the tunnel is open all the way to the old fortress," she reported for everyone to hear. "Small fluctuations mean there may be minor obstructions along the path. Ninety-two percent positive the karez is passable."

"Plan one," Coop called. "Samara, get down here. Doc, make sure you replace the lid and make the sand look as natural as possible. Take Samara's cycle and find an overlook position to monitor the southern wall of the academy. No closer than three miles, Doc. Cassie will provide enhanced optics for your METS helmet."

The artificial glow from the light stick he activated earlier illuminated the young woman's body as she repelled down.

"Key and Trak," Coop continued. "Take the other cycle and circle around until you can come at the academy from the West. You'll need to walk in the last four miles. Find a place to nest and wait for my signal. Cassie, locate a deep shadow between dunes and get as invisible as you can. If we can get out quietly, I'll send a ping. Reply and we'll come to you. If things go sideways, come in fast. Be prepared to cover and extract under fire."

"As Mags would say, I should start preparing for fast and ready," the AI quipped.

"Mission clock starts now. If we do not make contact after six hours, we're toast. Close everything down and get back to Clyde. Speaking of. Cassie, inform Taah the clock has started. Coop, out."

"Did Doc show you how to turn off your com?" he asked Samara. She nodded, pressed two fingers against her neck, and nodded again. Coop disengaged his own com with a simple verbal order. He left the translator active. He could also monitor incoming signals and decide whether to reply or ignore.

He handed Samara a modified METS helmet sent down with the acoustic device.

"Use this like you would your mask. It will use the light from the glow stick on your belt to enhance your vision up to twenty-feet ahead. You lead, I follow."

"Men," the teenager said. "Anything to watch a girl's leather-wrapped ass."

"Get your leather-wrapped ass moving," he replied. "We're on the clock."

The centuries-old tunnel remained well preserved. A couple of times the two needed to step into the shallow water of the karez to pass by sections of wall which crumbled and crossed the pathway. Once they needed to climb over a portion of ceiling that fell down, but did not dam the water flow. No light shown from above, and no sand appeared mixed in with the rubble. The ceiling held, though weakened.

Two-hours-forty-one minutes after Samara got her ass moving, they came to a metal grate bolted into solid blocks of carved stones.

"Southern wall of the fortress," Coop said. He adjusted his laser pistol, turning it into a cutter. The weapon cut through enough bars for him to pull away a lower section they could crawl through. "We should be under the lowest floor. What do you know about the academy's power plant."

"I know it takes up the entire basement of the school, but I never had a reason to go down to it," she replied. "The plans Trak had from the original construction showed an access from the karez up into the basement before the water spilled into the spring feeding the oasis."

They walked thirty-two steps inside the outer wall and found a simple metal ladder. A few feet further they could hear the running water spill into more water. The combined spring and karez flow would drop down, meander beneath subsurface rock, and join the well feeding the pond in the center of the fortress.

Coop climbed the ladder. No matter how light his movements, or Samara's attempt to hold it steady, the ancient corrosion and loss of integrity sent squeaks echoing down the tunnel. They could only hope the sounds did not work up through the foundation stones.

A square hole at the top rose between large stones that created the tunnel's ceiling and the basement's floor. A three-by-three square of the same stone sat above the final rung. It could be one-inch or three-feet thick. Regardless, the trap door had probably not been used in over a thousand years.

He placed his feet on the unreliable rungs of the ladder, and wedged his back against the interior side of the foundation flooring. Both hands flat beneath the trap door, he pressed. The stone slid easily, more importantly, silently up. Less than an inch thick, light from the basement leaked through the crack formed when the lid rose above the floor-line. He eased the edge over his head onto the floor above, and silently slid the cover out of the way. His head, protected by the METS helmet rose, stopping as soon as he could obtain a visual of the space above him.

The enhanced vision amplified the dim light. A quick three-sixty look showed nothing except machinery, storage bins, and normal bits and pieces expected around a power generator. The basement was too extensive to see everywhere, and the power plant in the center of the space hid the area on the far side. Thermal scan proved worthless due to the heat wafting from the generator. He upped his acoustic filters. It only increased the low hum produced by the dynamo.

He boosted himself onto the floor, pulled his pistol, and extended his free hand to help Samara up and out of the tunnel. The girl proved her operational awareness by remaining quiet.

Coop cat-footed around the generator, Samara on his heels, her pistol in hand. He rounded the machinery, stopped, and held a hand up to stop her forward progress.

Two short aliens stood in front of a control console, enthralled with their efforts as they punched dials, and made notes on electronic pads. They both wore jumpsuits, and had wide, bare feet. If body shape indicated anything within their species, the one on the left a male, and the other a female. Coop's optics washed out details, but the female appeared to be darker than the male. Both wore heavy googles.

The female either caught a glimpse of him, or some sixth sense warned her. She jerked around, slapped the male with her pad, and pointed.

Coop raised his weapon and said, "Quiet. Shout or move and you die."

Samara circled around him, staying away from his line of fire, and trained her weapon on the two little beings.

Two sets of hands on short arms shot straight up in the universal display of surrender.

Coop advanced. The young woman from Hela stayed back. She peered back the way they came, maintaining security while trusting he controlled the surprised aliens.

"Who are you? Why are you here?"

"Grat," the male said. "This is Bantry," he nodded at his companion, keeping his hands in sight and overhead. "We're from the planet Vc. We work as engineers aboard the Kashōn battleship orbiting this planet. Council Sentutol ordered us to produce detailed diagrams and create a report on how the Enparatus radiation-convertor creates power."

"They work for the Kashōn," Samara said. "We can't let them warn them."

"Warn them?" Bantry repeated, her head tilted. "You do not work for the Kashōn?"

"They're here to rescue the princesses," Grat surmised -- aloud.

Samara's pistol rose and turned on the red-haired Ve, who quickly dropped his hands to ward off a laser burst.

"No, no, no," he stammered. "We work for them because they force us. If we do not do as they say, our families on Ve will be killed. It is how the Kashōn treat all aliens they defeat. We can help. We want to help."

"Grat! Shut up!" Bantry said. "It could be a trick."

Field operations require the commander to make decisions on the go. Too many things can change, including intelligence, acquiring additional assets, and events simply going wonky at the wrong time. Coop had decades of experience in missions going wonky. Usually not in a good way. But not always.

"Lower your pistol, Sam. We are here to rescue the princesses, Bantry," using the Ve's name as a token. "How can you help, Grat?"

Grat looked to Bantry, who shrugged. He already placed them in a dangerous position. No reason to stop now.

"We have been wasting time," he said. "This convertor is much too valuable to allow Sentutol to have. While we tried to decide how to cover the truth up in our reports, we've been exploring the entire system. Including how energy is fed to other systems, and how those systems operate. For a structure and a power grid over one-thousand-years old, the integrated mechanics are equal to the more advanced circuits operating anywhere in the Empire."

"The Parz were once what we would call an advanced civilization," Samara said. "They made a collective decision to turn their backs on continuing down a path they saw leading away from their fundamental beliefs. Especially their respect for the environment. There are still technological marvels to be found on Enparatus, like this generator and the underground waterways."

"I wish the Ve made the same decision before our ancestors destroyed our planet's eco-system," Grat said. The sadness in his simple statement evident.

"Grat, I cannot waste time," Coop said. "How can you help?"

"The Imperial Troops guard the hallways. They posted guards on the doors where the princesses stay." The short alien walked across the basement to an enclosed container with round tubes entering the front. A cylinder and a boxed shaft rose from its top, four-feet and into the ceiling. "Electricity is provided to the academy through conduits in the cylinder," he said, pointing at the round metal tube. "The square venting is cooled air being blown into air ducts. The ceiling is also the floor for rooms above us. Circuits direct electricity to panels, and the panels are wired to the rooms and hallways. Cool air escapes the crawl spaces through vents in the floor."

"Crawl spaces?" Coop asked.

Grat nodded. He smiled meekly, realizing the tall alien already understood. "Bantry and I unlatched the top section. The crawl-space, for the conduits, cool air, and to allow maintenance, circle this entire building. The rooms where the Helacene princesses are kept are over there." He pointed at the wall directly across from them. "To get there you must enter here," he pointed at the ceiling. "This is the center of the northern section of the academy. Above are offices and living spaces for instructors and administrators. The Kashōn use those spaces. You must be quiet. The princesses will be on the opposite side of the fortress. The southern section. If you go west, and turn south, you will have only empty classrooms to pass beneath before reaching the student dormitories. The other way is more living quarters, kitchens, and cafeterias. Those rooms are always busy."

"Will the vent grates be large enough for us to get through?" Coop asked.

"Tight, but, yes, I think so," Grat replied. "I do not know if the grates can be opened. We did not try."

"A Helacene officer arrived earlier," Samara interrupted. "Do you know where he is being kept?"

"We flew down in the same ferry. He went with the Kashōn and we have been down here," Bantry answered.

Coop ignored the other three while he ran scenarios through his enhanced analytical mind.

"It appears to be the best way of reaching and extracting the girls with the fewest obstacles, and least chance of getting into a skirmish," he said. "When the troopers find the girls gone, it won't take long to find the vent was disturbed. What will they do to you when they trace our passage back?"

"Can we go with you?" Bantry asked.

"Sorry, Bantry," he replied. "I appreciate that you are both willing to help, but there won't be space for the hostages and you."

"Then you must tie us up," Grat said. "We were surprised and overwhelmed. I do not think they will harm us. We are valuable engineers."

"Hate to do it, but it may be your best chance," Coop agreed. "Anything else before we start?"

Grat looked once more to Bantry, who nodded.

"I have a cousin on the Kashōn's home world," he said. "His name is Docha. He works on engineering upgrades for Shroud space ships. He has valuable information about their latest battle-cruisers. I do not know what. It is too dangerous for him to send. He is forced to live and work in a tower where aliens are kept. It's in the main space port, across from the King's castle. I wish I knew more. If you can get to Docha, his information could help your Alliance against the Shroud Fleet."

"If we get out of here in one piece, I'll see the information about your cousin reaches the right people," Coop promised.

Grat brought a ladder, and Bantry released the top housing section at the roof-line. Coop led, his helmet on, optics and sensors fired up. Samara followed. The Ve engineers closed the section using magnets to hold it in place and not bolts.

"You're placing a lot of trust in them," Samara said.

Coop did not reply. He understood the risks.

Chapter 20

"The Helacene Alliance is a confederation of soft planets," Captain Phistol said. "A collection of races afraid of being ruled by a strong hand, and fearful of failing if left alone. The Suzerain is little more than an arbitrator. Instead of leading, she listens to disputes. In the Kashōn Empire, if there is a dispute the Shroud settles it by punishing both sides. Fewer disputes arise when everyone understands the consequences of disturbing the peace."

"You consider holding dozens of worlds under fear of your guns as peaceful?" Alain asked. He sat in a high-back chair in the office of the former Chancellor.

"I consider anything other than war as peace," Phistol replied. He sat at the desk of the former Chancellor. "Missions to settle disputes with our ships and troops are opportunities for training. Personally, I prefer a real war. Placing a foot on the neck of an opponent already bested once is never as satisfying as the first confrontation."

"That does not sound like someone who wishes to negotiate a settlement which would allow my sisters go free," The Hela responded.

"You dress like a military officer, Commander. Are you happy with a mission that ends in a peaceful result?"

"I'm happy with a mission that ends successfully, Captain. I respect the Kashōn. I admire the effort involved to create the empire you have built across the stars. I recognize the difficulties and the necessities required to maintain order." The young Helacene leaned forward and added, "I know what it takes to succeed."

Phistol stared across a dead man's desk. He appraised the young alien ram sent as the Suzerain's representative. Son of the same leader. He, himself, was related to King Phortis C. He represented his lord. They shared many commonalities.

"You will do whatever necessary to succeed?" the Ashemacher asked.

"As will you," the Hela replied. "Your King knows what I expect. Are you authorized to deal, or will this require wasted time while you send messages back and forth?"

"You can provide what you promised?"

"I gave you the codes to use the communication relay drones within our wormhole channels," Alain said. He sat back in the chair, crossing a leg as a show of ease. "I provided the military frequencies and the pass-codes used by your Shroud to enter the Enparatus system. I told you the time and the place to take hostages the Suzerain would not forfeit. I gave the Kashōn all of these to prove my value. I can give you the final piece necessary for the Empire to sweep through the Hela Alliance without resistance." The traitor paused. "If King Phortis gives me what I want."

"The Hela system and the two systems nearest to it," Phistol said. "Plus the Empire's help to eliminate any resistance to your rule."

"Hela is a matriarchal society," the young man said. The words dripped of disdain. "The only help I need to become the first male Suzerain is the death of my three sisters and my mother. I cannot be connected to their deaths. With the Kashōn fleet at our border, the people will welcome my taking control."

"We hold only two princesses," Phistol reminded Alain.

"People loyal to me search for the third," Alain responded. "After I find and dispose of Samara, you will execute Alucha and Mandara. Distraught at the loss of her daughters, facing the invasion by your forces, my mother will commit suicide. It will be called an accidental overdose while rumors spread the truth."

"Truth?"

The traitor shrugged. "Truth is what you leak to the media," he said. "Pundits will suggest that, as a woman, she did not possess the fortitude to continue. I will take my place as their leader."

"The other systems?"

"When you threaten the two systems nearest Hela, I will offer them my protection. This will be the genesis for my own empire. You can have all of the others. You prefer war, Captain. I'm giving you sixteen systems to conquer."

"With your new empire at our back," the Imperial officer noted.

"I will move in a direction different from King Phortis' plans. Systems under my dominion will automatically become allies to the Kashōn."

"A bold plan," the Captain said. A hint of respect in the tone. "But it all depends on final payment. A payment of this size requires an equally valuable commodity."

Alain Athodite uncrossed his legs. From a satchel at his feet he retrieved a compact coin-drive chip. He flipped the drive, like the coin it resembled, to the Kashōn.

"The majority of the Helacene Alliance's war fleet will assemble in the Geras system. The ships will rendezvous in three days. King Phortis has enough time for the Shroud Fleet to arrive first. That chip contains information on the Geras system, as well as detailed schematics for Helacene vessels. Systems, weapons, capabilities, vulnerabilities are all in your palm."

"We can destroy the Helacene fleet as they exit the gate. We will take out every ship and leave the confederation nothing to stop us." Phistol realized he held his hands in fists as he thought about the destruction of the enemy. He relaxed before adding, "You understand we will not kill your sisters until this is confirmed."

Alain rose. "I will trust you to uphold your King's bargain. I will return to Hela. I need to make sure Samara has been found, and I need to be near my mother when word of the fleet's destruction reaches her. When I hear that, I will know you have executed Alucha and Mandara."

"You also have a younger brother," Phistol said.

"An accidental death sometime in the coming year."

"Do you wish to see your sisters before leaving?"

"No. I will stay today and tonight, and leave in the morning. I will send a message to my mother they remain safe as long as the Alliance does not interfere with your invasion of the Nessur system. I will be very upset I could not arrange for their release."

"So their deaths will fall on the Suzerain and not you," the Shroud officer said.

"So it would appear," Alain replied. "If you require anything more, I will be in my room."

Coop used one strong arm to hold Samara. His other hand placed firmly over her mouth. It required a lot of his prodigious strength to prevent the girl from crawling through the air vent and attacking her traitorous sibling.

With Alain's departure, her struggles subsided. Coop raised his faceplate and held the girl so their eyes met. He waited until her eyes cleared, and he read the answer to his unspoken question. She would not betray their location by creating a scene.

Uncertain he could trust the angry princess, he pushed her forward to lead the rest of the way along the stone-encased crawl-space. They entered the southern corridor. Coop held Samara's ankle to stop her crawling further. He lay beneath an air vent. His METS suit used nano-video tech to create the effect that rendered him nearly invisible. He could use the microscopic cameras in other ways. He lifted his index fingertip through the vent. The cameras provided a three-sixty-degree view of the corridor. Two guards stood in front of a doorway well down the long corridor. No one else in view.

"Samara," he whispered. "Do you understand how important it is we rescue your sister now?"

"Yes," she whispered back.

"I understand why you wanted to kill your brother back there, but you must stay under control if we have any chance of success. Can you?"

"Yes. I'll kill him later."

Coop worked his way pass the young woman. He tried to not notice the curves and swells beneath the tight leather. When he reached the access tunnel branching from the main line, the one feeding the room behind the guarded door, he entered with Samara close behind.

At the first vent he once again raised his index finger. The vent placement beneath a side table in a small room set up as part study and part living room. Two attractive women sat across the room. They shared a sofa, talking quietly.

The problem with the current plan, one made on the run, was how to force the ancient grill up and out of the vent frame without alarming the princesses or alerting the guards. He pulled a stun pistol from a pocket, raised it through the grate, used his index finger as a sight, and pulled the trigger twice with his middle finger. Not the nicest thing to do to a couple of royals, but expedient.

Chapter 21

Alucha and Mandara came around thirty-minutes after being stunned. In that time Coop used his knife and strength to free the vent grate. He and Samara agreed not to tell her sisters about their brother being a traitor. There would be enough drama trying to escape.

He remained near the door as the two young women regained consciousness. Samara quieted her sisters, held them, and spoke to both in hushed, urgent tones. Coop thought the youngest sibling appeared the most assured of the three, but the others did just get stunned.

Samara joined him as the two princesses disappeared through a side door.

"I told them to put on clothes for going into the desert," she said. "They won't have bike leathers, but they should have thick trekking clothes and high boots with flat soles for hiking."

"You did well, Sam."

The compliment elicited a slight smile, which quickly dissolved.

"Alucha says we have two hours before the guards call them for dinner," she told him. "Unless they come early for some other reason. The officer in charge will sometimes send for them to ask questions about the Alliance, or Mother. They have not been told Alain is here."

"You sure?"

"If they knew, they would have asked about rescuing him."

"Did you tell them?"

"No."

The two returned a five-minutes later, dressed in what Coop would describe as desert safari clothing. Both wore boots laced to below their knees with pants legs tucked in to prevent sand from entering.

Samara made hasty introductions. Coop sent her through the open vent first, followed by Mandara, then Alucha. He dropped into the crawl space last, placing the grate back in place. The return trip went faster, with no loitering to listen in on conversations. They made two short stops to allow guards above them to pass by vents without hearing the scuffling sounds of people crawling beneath the floors.

The youngest princess pushed the top section of the main air duct down far enough to peek through. The Ve had been anxiously waiting, Grat collected the ladder and headed for the base of the cool air circulator unit the moment the small gap appeared.

He took the square metal casing off and began helping them down. Each one found footing on the opposite side of the tall ladder and hurried to the floor where Bantry waited. Grat fixed the section into place with the original mounting brackets before joining the others.

They did not take time for introductions.

"Sam," Coop ordered, "Take your sisters down into the karez. Head for the well. Don't contact Cassie until you're ready to get out. Everyone take a light stick, and Sam . . ."

"Yes?"

"Keep your pistol in hand and ready. No one on our side will be in that tunnel. I'll follow as soon as I take care of Grat and Bantry," he said.

Alucha and Mandara remained silent. Both observed the exchange between their younger sister and the impressive looking soldier. He treated her as an equal, and not a teenage girl. It may have been the first time either realized Samara might be more than the flippant wild-child of the royal family.

Sam dropped through the open grate and helped the other two down. Before they started down the dark waterway, Alucha whispered, "He's something special, Samara. Who is he?"

"A friend," she replied.

"I don't like the idea of tying you up," Coop said to the two engineers. "I understand it may be the only way to explain how someone got through here, but it leaves you helpless."

"We cannot go with you. We understand," Grat replied. "We cannot escape on our own, and there is no place for us to hide. This is the only option where we may live. Even if it is to continue working for the Kashōn."

"When Captain Phistol discovers Princess Alucha and Princess Mandara have been taken away, he will execute everyone else,"

Bantry said in her matter-of-fact way. "It is a heavy price, but must be paid."

Coop stood quietly. For the Ve his silence lasted a couple of seconds. For Coop, a thousand scenarios were considered and evaluated.

"Would it be odd if you were to go to one of the shuttles?" he asked.

"A little," Grat said, "but not out of the question. Shuttles carry tools. The troopers are not engineers. If we told them we needed a special piece of equipment to complete our work, they would not question what or why."

"Get to the shuttle furtherest from the entry," Coop said. "Stay inside. At worse, if the Kashōn question you later, tell them no one came into this area while you worked in here."

"At the best?" Bantry asked.

"Can you destroy the data you have collected on the energy convertor?" he asked.

"A simple erase and eradicate command if someone opens our tablets and does not enter the proper codes within a few seconds," Grat answered.

"Why?" Bantry asked. "You have the princesses? What does the rest matter?"

"Lives matter. All lives," he replied. "Rangers don't leave their own behind. Get to the shuttle," he said, disappearing through the hole in the floor.

"What's a Ranger?" Grat asked.

The trip to the well required three hours. The last half-hour spent filled with added tension after Cassie broke silence to inform Coop the troops in and around the academy were acting agitated. The jailers now realized the princesses had gone missing.

"They will assume you are still inside the academy," Coop told the three women as they hurried to the extraction point. "It will take at least a few minutes before they find the vent and the crawl spaces. They will track us to the sub-basement. When they discover the karez, they will send troops behind us and launch the shuttles."

"They will be too far behind to catch us," Alucha said.

"When they send up the ferry ships, they will also alert the battlecruiser in orbit. Every scanner they have will concentrate on the area around the academy," he told her. "With the sun setting they may be able to find Cassandra. We have to be into phase two before that happens."

"Phase two?" Samara asked.

"Phase one: get them away from the fortress. Phase two: get them off the planet," he answered as they arrived at the original natural well.

"We're here," he called over his com.

Doc, who abandoned her overlook as soon as the troopers began running into the old fortress, opened the cover and dropped a line.

The two older princesses engaged in physical fitness training for years as part of their development. Climbing the rope proved no hardship for either. Samara and Coop followed. Doc retrieved the line, dropped the cover atop the well, and began pushing sand over the entrance. The others joined until they moved enough sand to hide the cover.

"Won't stop any troopers who follow from getting out," Samara said.

"Delaying tactic only," Coop confirmed. "Everyone aboard Cassandra."

"Cassandra?" Alucha asked.

The Wraith appeared twenty-feet away, the nano-optical remitters turned off so she could be seen.

Alucha and Mandara stood speechless at the sudden appearance of the angry-looking little fighter.

Samara took Alucha and Doc took Mandara. They ushered the two women to the rear of the ship and up the ramp.

"Lock up, Cassie," Coop ordered. "Get as invisible as you can, and get a few miles from here." He straddled the hover cycle Doc had used to get to the well before them. "Be prepared to blast off the planet on my call. Once you are outside the atmosphere, engage the Rys forcefield and initiate space fold. Head for Clyde."

"You?" asked the AI-Avatar.

"Deception and distraction," he replied.

No longer worried about conversations detected over communication channels, Coop called Key Largo.

"Key, did you and Trak place the charges?"

"No problem, Bubba," the Jamaican answered. "Say the word, and the ships go boom."

"Did you see a couple of short aliens leave the fortress?"

"Did dat," Key answered. "Dey went into the shuttle closest to me."

Coop aboard the hover cycle flew across the desert, zoned in on Key's location emitter.

"Don't blow that ship," he ordered. "Let me know when troops leave the main structure and head for the ferries."

"Dat be happenin' now," the immediate response.

"Let as many board the first two ferries as you can before firing on the ones trying to reach the last ship."

"They will know where Trak and I are."

"I know," the reply. "When the first two ships lift, detonate the mag-mines."

"The shrapnel will take out the troopers on the ground," Key said. "Nice, in a very not-nice way."

Coop closing on the site, heard the unique pew-pew sounds of laser fire exchanged between Key, Trak and the Imperial troopers. He was one large dune away when twin fireballs filled the sky, followed by echoing booms. Key detonated the small, powerful, effective magnetic mines attached to the hulls.

"Cassie. Go!" he ordered.

The Kashōn ferry ships exploding would pull the attention of the orbiting cruiser into a smaller area of concern. Anyone inside the academy would focus on the battle happening outside the front entry.

"Key, get to the third ferry. The two short aliens are friendlies. Anyone else on board is a target."

Topping the dune, Coop arrived to see Key enter the lowered ramp of the ferry. Trak stayed at the door to watch their back. Two burning husks proved the explosive capabilities of the mines.

Coop pulled in behind the third shuttle. He waved to Trak as he dismounted and lowered his faceplate.

He entered to find Key in conversation with Grat and Bantry.

"They already took out the pilot and co-pilot," he told Coop. "Hit 'em on the head with damn big wrenches."

"The Captain keeps hailing us," Grat said. "We haven't answered."

"Stay silent," Coop said. "I don't think he will request the cruiser to target the last shuttle unless forced into it. At the moment, he isn't sure what to do. Anyone have an estimate on the number of troopers killed when the ships exploded?"

"Six entered the first one, and five into the second one," Trak answered. "Another six headed for this one. They were on the ground when the mines went off."

"Seventeen, plus flight crews of one to three, and these two," indicating the unconscious pilots the Ve downed. "Twenty-one to twenty-five of the original thirty-six. There will a squad in the karez. Four to six troopers. Rough estimate leaves between five and eleven Kashōn soldiers inside the academy."

Two pings sounded across the com units of the three hostage rescue team members.

"Cassandra is about to enter space-fold," Coop explained the signal to the other two. "Key, can you fly this ship?"

"Sure. Been in this section long enough to read a little Kashōn. Enough to understand the controls," he replied. "We leaving with that big battlewagon on top of us?"

"Not until I clear the academy," Coop replied. "I can't stop the cruiser from blasting it from space, but I can do something to protect those inside from the troopers."

"How do we help?" Key asked.

"You and Trak fire on the archway," he said. "Short handed, the Captain will have to place his remaining assets there to prevent a breach. I'll flank them from the South."

"Excuse me, General. We can jam communications from the ground to the battleship," Bantry chimed in. "We know the frequencies. We can adapt the communications system on board the ferry."

"It would help a lot, Bantry," he replied. "My name is Coop. I'm not a general. Just Coop."

The Ve engineer nodded, grabbed her companion by the arm and pulled him along to the cockpit of the small shuttle.

Coop removed his outerwear, including boots. The METS would help make him difficult to see, especially in the waning light of sunset. It would mask his heat signature as well. Only his belt with holstered laser pistol and sheathed knife would be visible.

"Give me five minutes," he said, activating the nano-optics and exiting the rear hatch.

"He never intended to leave the civilians behind to be murdered," Trak said.

"Nope," Key agreed. "Not his style."

"I like his style," the nomad said.

"Better than bammies," the human answered. The word untranslatable, but the meaning understood.

Chapter 22

Trak began the assault with his force lance, firing at the archway from behind a piece of shattered shuttle hull. He alternated blasts with Key, who fired short laser bursts from similar cover and twenty-yards to Trak's right.

Return fire emanated from three spots above the ramparts, and from the ground on either side of the archway.

Coop used the framing for the locked entrance gate on the southern wall to climb the edifice. At the top of the frame, relying on years of free-climbing experience, he began using finger and toe holds to finish the ascent. He landed on the wide walkway unseen.

The three Shroud troopers above the parapet were dressed for battle. Heads covered by galea. They wore long tunics of metal and leather to deflect laser fire or bladed weapons. Thick trousers over laced leather sandals. With the enhanced optics, Coop could make out details like the metal guards on their forearms. All three carried force lances tucked beneath armpits.

The first trooper did not have horns. A female, which did not matter to Coop. She could kill as easily as her male teammates. His matte-black blade's point entered as the base of her skull, beneath the edge of the helmet and above the neckline of her tunic. The metal sliced quickly through and up, killing her instantly. He held the body, lowering it to the stone walkway.

Next to the section where the walkway narrowed at the top of the arched entrance, a trooper knelt behind a crenel between merlons. Ram's horns curled from either side of his helmet. His lance lay atop the crenel's shelf to steady his aim. The trooper would stand seven-feet tall. Coop lucked out by the soldier's decision to kneel in order to avoid incoming laser fire. It made him a perfect target for Coop's steel-alloy knife.

Once again, the only vulnerable spot allowed by the armor proved to be the nape. Once again he lay the deadweight down so as not to alert the other trooper on the wall, or the two firing from below.

Things became a lot trickier. The ledge connecting the walkways on either side of the archway measured less than eighteen-inches wide. If the last trooper noticed him before he crossed, he would be an easy target.

His speed, combined with the distraction created by fire from Key and Trak, got him across the divide. Sgt. Traum felt his presence, turning as Coop gained the wider walkway. He continued, lowered a shoulder and slammed the huge Kashōn NCO in the mid-section. The heavy armor absorbed a lot of the blow, as did the heavy muscle beneath. Traum did lose his grip on the laser force-lance. The weapon fell to the walkway, but did not fall over the side. The troopers below continued exchanging fire with Key and Trak, unaware of the confrontation occurring overhead.

Traum regained his balance quickly. Coop's charge threw him backward, but he did not go down. He stood tall, facing the attack. A second weapon, a hand-held baton style laser already in hand.

The METS' optical camouflage was off. It was now a battle suit, capable of deflecting a bullet, blade, or low-yield laser blast. At six-one, Coop stood above average for a human, but felt child-like before the towering Shroud trooper. He gripped the bloodied knife in his left hand, waiting on the next move.

Traum experienced the rush of one-on-one battle. The spike in endocrines and the lust for a kill created a euphoric high. He pulled the galea off, exposing his weathered, gnarly features. Blood-shot eyes, and tightly, curled horns extending from his temples gave him a demonic appearance. His eyes clouded beneath the extended brow above them. He smiled. A gruesome grin of small, green-stained blocky teeth. He settled his gaze on the bloodied Can-Am Ranger Falkniven knife.

Coop raised the helmets plexi-faceplate. He pulled the hood from his head, allowing it to drape across the back of his neck. Noticing the Kashōn's stare, he flicked the knife, flinging the blood of the first two kills against the stone rampart.

Traum gave a low snarl. He slid the baton into its holster and pulled his short sword. The wide single-edged blade rose to point down at the shorter human.

Exactly the move Coop hoped would happen when he flicked his own blade.

The Space Ranger Project reengineered his body providing enhanced speed. The revivification of his left brain following a near-lethal laser wound enhanced his eye-hand coordination. Perhaps not fair, but fair and battlefields never met in real life. He pulled the Rys-adapted laser pistol from the quick-draw Sherpa holster retooled to fit the weapon's design. The laser burst entered Traum's left eye and exited the rear of his skull. He stood for a breath, as his brain accepted it no longer existed, before the body collapsed.

Coop wasted no time sheathing his knife and holstering his pistol. He collected the trooper's force lance and stepped off the walkway backwards. He landed behind the two Imperial elite soldiers covering the open gateway. Two bursts, and two more enemy combatants died.

"Key. Trak. The entry is cleared," he reported over the coms. "Trak, come in and cover the interior from the arch. Key, stay back. Cover Trak and keep an eye on the ferry."

Trak arrived without comment. As soon as the nomad found a good spot to watch from, Coop headed across the open space beside the oasis water hole toward the academy. No fire. No shouts.

He burst through the school's front doors and headed left. He reached the stairwell and started down to the next level. The community lounge would be the first open space at the bottom of the steps.

In a normal hostage rescue insertion, he would work with one or more special operators. They would take turns moving forward or providing cover. Knowing an open space, a kill zone, lay ahead, they would set up before entering. After tossing in stun grenades or some other distraction, they would go in fast, searching for targets while identifying civilians. They would also cover a section, while covering each other's back.

Now he relied on surprise over tactics. He ran the last few steps and went into the lounge in a squat. The smaller target surface paid off as two laser bursts flashed over his head, tearing into the stone wall behind him.

Coop fired left, taking a trooper standing twenty-feet away in the forehead. As he tracked right, a laser slashed into his left shoulder, spinning him around and to a knee. The METS saved his life and prevented any damage beyond a deep bruise. His left arm and hand tingled, but the pistol remained in his right hand.

The Kashōn stood behind two frightened women. He was having a difficult time making himself small enough to hide behind the smaller hostages. Before he could loose another round at Cooper, the Space Ranger fired. The beam cut into the soldier's inner right thigh, above the greaves on his shins. It entered beneath the armored vest and between the tunic's open front.

The trooper dropped to both knees, his sudden fall pushing the two women away as he reached out with his free hand to brace for the landing. He glanced up in time to see the yellow-red beam from Coop's weapon before it drilled a hole where his wide nose once sat.

Besides the two women, another dozen men and women sat on the floor of the lounge. Most appeared to be in shock. Two stood and came forward. Coop raised and aimed his pistol.

"I'm Antoni Paicell," the older of the two said, hands raised. "I'm a fitness trainer and former Royal Guard for the Suzerain. This is Charace Deuramy," he indicated the woman with him, "she is also a trainer and ex-Guard. We want to help."

"Any idea where any more Kashōn are? Numbers?" He kept the pistol up.

"These two herded us in here," Deuramy answered. "We have no way of knowing where anyone else may be."

"What about Alain Athodite? Have you seen him?" Coop asked.

The two ex-Guards exchanged surprised looks, dropping their hands despite the laser gun pointed at them.

"The boy commander?" Paicell asked. "He took command of the Royal Guard after Charace and I transferred to the Academy. He should be on Hela."

"Coop!" His name called so loudly, the sound echoed inside his skull. "Trak is down," Key said. The zip-pop distinctive to laser weapons in the background. "I'm pinned down. Three shooters. Two Kashōn in antique armor and a human-looking guy dressed in a black uniform. The one in black came out to Trak, called him by name, and when he lowered his lance, the son-of-a-bitch shot him with a laser baton. Other two came around the towers."

"Shit!" Coop said. Operational error. He did not warn Trak and Key about Alain. The Parz nomad would have recognized

Samara's brother and never considered him a danger. "I'm on the way," he replied.

Exiting the lounge laser fire erupted around him, including a glancing shot that seared a line across the left side of his neck. With the helmet off, he nearly received his second laser-inflicted head wound of the year.

The team sent to follow his escape with the three princesses had returned from the subterranean water channel. Captain Phistol recalled Lt. Angartol and his three-person squad of operators when the frontal attack on the academy began. Hurrying through the corridors to reach their commanding officer, Coop's sudden appearance surprised them enough to hasten their shots. As seasoned soldiers, they would not remained startled, and their aim would improve quickly.

Winning a firefight required most of the same principles as a hostage rescue.

Surprise was gone, but distraction remained on the table.

Dropping low and rolling, Coop held the trigger down on his laser pistol, creating a pinwheel laser show. Dazzling and deadly with the sound turned into a zip and crescendoing roar as the non-stop beam scorched oxygen and tore into stone walls and floor.

The Kashōn scattered. They had little maneuvering space in the corridor. The unaimed beam slashed through the neck of one trooper. Luck alone finding the space between the galea and the protective chest cover.

Deception came next. Before the three remaining soldiers realized the laser no longer ripped crazily through the hallway, Coop yanked his hood-helmet up, set the plexi-shield in place, and activated the nano-optics. He froze on one knee, right shoulder against a wall.

"Where did he go?" Angertol yelled. The corridor appeared empty.

"He must have rolled back into the lounge," a trooper replied.

"Target the doorway," the LT ordered.

Each soldier took a turn firing a short blast at the open doorway. The other two moved forward, each taking a turn, as the trailing team member moved up and took a forward position. Good tactic. Skilled team.

Coop had more skills and the advantage of being cloaked. The Kashōn may have seen his silhouette as a shimmer when they hurried forward and the optics lagged a split second to adjust for the changing angles. Focussed on the threat they believed waited beyond the doorway, the tell went unnoticed.

When they closed to the point where they might trip over him, Coop moved.

He waited until they had no time to react. A ghost rose from the ancient fortress floor, floating up through the stone. This ghost did not rattle and wail. The forward soldier died when a laser beam cut into his right eye, through his brain, and out the rear of his skull. No chance of a miss with the muzzle pressed against his socket.

The beam exited through bone and the metal helmet with no loss of velocity or strength. It impacted the second trooper, a ram six-inches taller than his fallen team mate, in the right chest. The alloy armor looked like hammered metal and leather, but it deflected the laser as well as Coop's METS could. The force of the shot did spin the trooper.

Coop quick-stepped around the first Kashōn as he collapsed. He placed the tip of the laser pistol against the ram's horn on the male's left temple and pulled the trigger.

As the trooper fell, Angartol's short sword struck. The heavy blade crushed the barrel of Coop's pistol and the strength of the down swing tore the useless weapon from his hand.

Coop pulled back to avoid a return blow. The sword's weight made for a fantastic chopper. Proof in the broken pistol now lying on the floor. But that weight made it difficult to recover quickly, regardless of the Kashōn officer's strength. A close-quarter weapon needed to be designed for strength, but also needed to be built for fast responses.

The Falkniven A1 in Coop's right hand had a pedigree in battle second to no other blade in history. Made of an alloy discovered in the Martian hangar, but designed and forged in the same manner as its predecessors. Strong, light, sharp. In the hand of a skilled operator . . . deadly when used up close and personal.

Angartol's sword continued moving up. The ram unable to fully brake the swing when he realized Coop evaded his strike. It left his sword arm exposed, and Coop took advantage. The matte-black blade sliced across the officer's wrist, opening skin, and severing muscle and tendon beneath. Nerves screamed and died. Angartol's hand opened reflexively, and the short sword dropped.

With Trak down and Key under fire, Coop wasted no time. There was no lag in recovering the Falkniven. He flipped his wrist, the light blade turning from cutter to thruster. With his weight and strength behind the jab, the tip of the knife drove up. It entered under his opponent's chin and passed through his mouth and into his sinus cavity.

When Coop pulled the blade out, Angartol began swallowing blood. He coughed, and then vomited blood, bile, and mucus into his destroyed oral cavity. The Ashemacher fell to his knees, eyes wide in panic. The terror etched his face as he realized he would die by drowning in his own body fluids. Screams of pain and succor squelched to gurgles.

Cooper did not wait for the ram to die. That could take time, and time became more precious with each passing second. He did stop to recover the black diamond from the destroyed laser pistol.

He found the Parz slumped against the interior wall inside the gateway. Trak had removed his outer garment. He pressed it firmly against his right side. The sand-colored tunic stained dark red.

"I'll live," he told Coop. "I have not heard laser fire for over a minute. You need to help Key."

The Space Ranger activated all sensory systems embedded in the METS. He used the heads-up display inside the face shield to scan the area between the fortress entrance and the remaining ferry. The shuttles engines were on. Four heat signatures inside, but difficult to identify through the space-worthy material used in the ship's construction.

A Kashōn lay in the sand to his right. Body heat dissipating in the cooling air as the planet's star set low across the horizon. Scans detected no other movement.

A second muted heat signature came from behind a piece of shattered shuttle. The debris on his right and left of the dead trooper.

The ferry lifted, hover engines pushing debris and sand outward as the ship rose. The rear ramp remained lowered. The reason became clear when two small bodies dropped off the ramp, plummeting to the surface. Too high a fall to expect survival.

The ship soared away as Coop ran to where he hoped to find Key.

Chapter 23

Coop entered the fortress with the laser rifle ready. He found the two physical fitness instructors, Paicell and Deuramy, administering field dressings to Trak's wound. The blood came from the initial penetration of the blast. The blast must not have been a clean hit. Normally a laser wound produces little blood as the beam cauterizes as quickly as it kills.

"Key and the Ve engineers are dead," Coop told Trak.

"Why did Alain shoot me?"

Coop explained the role the eldest son of the Suzerain played in events leading up to the moment.

"The biology professor is also the Academy's medic," Paicell said, interrupting after Coop finished the explanation. "We need to get this man to the infirmary."

"When Athodite reaches the cruiser overhead, there won't be an infirmary," Coop said. "He'll have the ship's captain blow the whole place to hell."

"We have to evacuate, but if they destroy the building they destroy thousands of years of priceless manuscripts and art with it," Deuramy said. "Is there enough time to take some things with us?"

"You can't take the chance," Coop answered. "Take Trak, collect everyone and go to the sub-basement with the power generator. You'll find a floor grate that leads to an old water channel. Get everyone in the tunnel and head south."

Coop turned his attention to the nomad.

"Trak, it's a long walk to the other oasis. Will you make it?"

"I will," the Parz assured him. "You?"

"I'm going to find the two Ve and make sure their bodies, and Key's are secure. We can return them home later. Then I'm going to take a hover cycle and see how much sand I can spread north of here."

"Trying to get the Kashōn to fire at you and not the fortress," Trak said. "You may have pissed them off enough for that to work."

"They're in a hurry," Coop said. "They must make sure the plan to ambush the Helacene Fleet is not compromised. Suzerain

Palla's son will need to kill her before she finds out about him. If I can distract them, they may not waist more time to take out the old fort."

"If you live," the desert dweller said, "find me at the well where you and Samara entered the karez. We cannot let Alain kill the Suzerain, and we must warn her of the trap. I may have a way."

Chapter 24

Cassandra

"I demand we go to Hela immediately."

"You can demand what you like, Princess Alucha. This ship is headed for our base," Doc told the strident young woman.

Since entering space-fold within the Enparatus system, Alucha and Mandara took turns asking, begging, and then ordering Doc to take them home.

Samara remained quiet the entire time. She sat in the co-pilot's seat, staring at instruments and readouts. The youngest princess ignored her older sisters' repeated requests for her to join the argument on their side. Nor did she side with the exotic teal-colored alien.

"Mother, Suzerain Palla Athodite, must be informed of our escape," Mandara said. She stood next to her sister, both standing in the galley near the cockpit.

"A message has been sent," Doc replied. "This ship has an incredibly sophisticated communications array. We adapted our base receiver to capture anything dispatched from her. They know you are free. They will relay the message to Hela."

"If this toy ship has such advanced communications, use it to contact my mother," Alucha said.

"The Helacene Alliance does not have anything to catch such a message," the Kanistari replied. She tried to remain calm. The constant nagging from the two young women wore at her. Her responses were becoming more clipped.

"Tell your base to contact her," Mandara responded. He words clipped as well, but tinted with the tone one used with servants.

"They will," Doc replied. She did not say it would happen after Taah passed the news to D'Sey "They'll transmit through the wormhole relays to make sure the Suzerain receives the news. It will be less likely intercepted by the Kashōn that way."

"It won't matter," Samara said. She did not turn to look at her sisters. She spoke to the displays in front of her. "The Kashōn have our codes, and they know how to access the relay drones. They probably have a way of jamming them as well."

"You can't know that," Alucha said to her sibling. Actually, to the back of her head since she continued to stare ahead. "You've been off partying across the galaxy. Swimming, climbing, riding around on your toys. We've been with Mother or in training. If the Kashōn knew about the relays, we would have been told."

"I saw the way you looked at that man you were with," Mandara chimed in. "Is that what you've been doing? Hiding from Alain's guards so you could screw around."

Doc started to rise from her chair. Cassie was faster.

The holo-avatar materialized behind the two Hela royals. So intent on goading their sister, they never saw the faint glow that preceded her appearance.

With a handful of Alucha's blonde hair and a handful of Mandara's brown tresses, she pulled the surprised women away from the cockpit entrance. When she let go, the two spun to face their attacker. Instead of the hours of training in self-defense kicking in, the two stood slack-jawed.

Cassie's time with Daniel Cooper included observing how he could present a visage designed to command instant respect. Fear-based, but respect just the same. She wore a curved-bill black baseball cap pulled low over her forehead. Her ash-blonde pony-tail protruded from the back. She wore aviator shades, and no lipstick. Black, long-sleeve ribbed shirt with a deep v-neck accentuated her breasts, but not in a provocative or sexy way. Her muscles showed beneath the tight material and her chest said I'm more woman than you can ever hope to be.

Black cargo pants molded to her narrow hips, flaring at the cuffs to cover black-leather combat boots. The belt around her slim waste carried a knife identical to Coop's. No matter where in the galaxy, no matter how advance the aliens, seeing something as primeval and deadly as a blade designed to kill engendered awe.

This beautiful, fair-skinned woman in combat black captured their attention.

"Who . . ." Mandara began. Cassie cut her off.

"Your sister risked her life to assault a fortress guarded by elite soldiers. Dozens of soldiers, and every one of them twice her size.

She crawled through a drain for fifteen miles, then crawled through ancient passageways, beneath the noses of those troopers, to find you and rescue you. Samara was prepared to kill to save your asses. She was prepared to die trying. From what I have seen and heard, the princess with the balls to become queen was passed over because of when she was born."

"You . . ." Alucha, her royal instincts returning, began to argue with this unknown person, even taking a step forward.

"Shut the fuck up!" Cassie said it without raising her voice. "This is my ship, and you can stay aboard and get delivered somewhere safe, or you can piss me off and I will kick your asses off in the middle of space. You know what they say, don't you?"

"No," Alucha, visibly flustered stuttered. "What do they say?"

"No one can hear you scream in space," Cassie whispered. "Now go sit on a bunk out of our way," she ordered.

When neither moved, Cassie pointed. The sister princesses held hands and eased around the scary woman on their way to the lower bunk.

The avatar joined the two women up front. Both swiveled their seats to watch the verbal beat-down. Doc held back her laughs, causing tears. Samara sat forward, her mouth slightly open.

"Hello, Sam," Cassie held out her right hand. When the teenager took it by reflex, she added, "I'm Cassie. If you have not figure it out, I am Cassandra's avatar."

Samara stared at her hand holding the avatar's. "You're real," she said.

"I am," the blonde in black replied, releasing the hand-shake. "We may have a problem."

"That we left Coop, Trak, and Key behind," Sam said. "I know. It's been driving me crazy."

"Daniel Cooper can take care of himself," Cassie said. "He'll take care of Key and Trak. The Kashōn troopers and your brother are in more danger than they are."

"The problem is time," Doc said. "Even using your tachyon-communicator, the distance from Clyde to Hela means the message warning them about Alain and the Shroud Fleet planning an ambush may not get there in time. The improvements they made using relays inside wormholes speeds communications, but it still takes days."

"What do we do?" Samara asked.

"What we are doing," Cassie replied. "We get back to Clyde. We persuade him to use the dimensional-drive to get to the Alliance Fleet before they enter the Geras system."

"We can only get back so fast," Doc interjected.

"Actually, I have a file detailing how an AI named Kennedy was able to adjust the laser-crystal array in Captain Cooper's first ship, the PT-109. The adjustments allowed her to add enough speed to make a major difference in their first conflict with alien ships."

"Are you going to make the same adjustments?" Sam asked.

"Cassandra is already working on it," Cassie answered.

"Should I tell my sisters about Alain?" she asked next.

"They have enough to deal with," Doc answered. "All the bluster and the big talk before are symptoms of stress. They've been under a death watch by nasty creatures. They saw their teachers gunned down, and had to handle escaping while leaving others behind. Now may not be the best time to hear their brother, who was supposed to save them, is the one who put them in danger."

Samara nodded in understanding and agreement. Young, but smart.

She turned her attention to Cassie.

"Two more questions, and then I'll shut up, too," she said.

"Ask," Cassie replied.

"I'm the princess with the balls to be queen?"

Doc laughed aloud, not holding it back this time.

The avatar smiled. She replied, "I needed to get through to them, but I still meant what I said."

"No one can hear you scream in space?"

"My files contain thousands of old movies from Captain Cooper's home world of Earth," she said. "It was a quote from a trailer, a film synopsis made to entice people to watch a movie."

"I'm not sure if it makes me interested or too scared to consider it," Sam said.

"Even increasing our speed, we have a day in space-fold before reaching Clyde," Cassie said. "I think I can adjust the ship's optics so I can display the film on the galley's hull. We have time on our hands, so we might as well watch a movie."

Cassie moved away, taking a seat at the com-tac station to make adjustments to allow her to create a projector.

Doc swiveled back, and whispered to Samara, "You didn't ask the question you really wanted to."

"Which would be?" Sam whispered back.

"Are Coop and she a couple?"

Sam's dark eyes found Doc's hazel ones. "Have you seen Cassie? Coop doesn't have a choice."

Once more: young, but smart.

Chapter 25

Chōntorham

Menace was too large a vessel to incorporate the optic systems necessary to make her appear invisible. The ship's skin did allow the video repeaters placed between the outer hull and the inner liner to project an image across the exterior. She could not disappear, but the pirate ship could disguise herself.

A day earlier she entered Chōntorham's atmosphere looking like an old ore-carrier from a distant system under Empire control. Using codes pirated and purchased, D'Sey convinced the controllers they were unscheduled because they never knew how long it would take to complete the journey. Not unusual for high-maintenance haulers used to freight non-essential items.

After he warned them the hauler's atmosphere engines showed signs of a potential failure, the traffic cops at the space port directed him to land at the surface dock furthest from the center of activity. If power failed, the ship would fall harmlessly to the ground. Harmful to anyone aboard, but safe for the more important people, buildings, and ships below.

D'Sey made a show of sloppily completing the landing on a dock that was nothing more than a paved pad riddled with cracks.

"We're down, control. Thank you for the assist," he radioed.

"Do not leave your vessel until security has completed your inspection," the tower replied.

"When can I expect them?"

"When they get around to you," came the snide response. "We are busy, and there are other, more important deliveries to process first. Palace City Port Control, out."

"Impressive," Krest said from the communication console. "We've used the same ploy on outer worlds in the Empire, but I did not believe the main command center in the capital of their home world would be as lax."

"Too many centuries of success," D'Sey said from the bridge command chair. "They see what they expect, and they don't expect anyone to challenge their power."

"What now?" Duly asked from weapons' control.

"Wait to hear from Taah," D'Sey answered. "Krest, monitor all local communications and get us up to speed. The ship will alert us when Taah signals."

Enparatus System

"Screw them," Captain Phistol said. "We aren't wasting time blasting a worthless school."

"What about the hover cycle north of the academy?" Alain asked.

"It would be more difficult to target anything that small," the Captain replied. "We need to join the fleet for the attack on the Alliance ships. I don't know how the local nomads pulled off the raid, but those two Ve were part of the plan. They had access to this ship. If they sent a message to the Suzerain, we need to leave now to warn King Phortis."

"You think Enparatus nomads defeated your elite troopers?"

Phistol turned to look down on the much smaller Helacene traitor. He held his fist in the young man's face, then extended his index finger.

"One. They know the terrain." Second finger extended. "Two. They had surprise." Third finger. "Three. They had superior numbers." An excuse he decided on for his report to his superiors. "Four. We had bad intelligence. Those nomads used advanced weapons. You should have told us."

Alain, used to being looked down upon, did not cower before the fierce Ashemacher.

"I did not know they had any weapons," he replied. "Are you sure no one arrived on the planet after you and before me?"

"Captain," he called to the ship's commander. "Did you or the other battlecruiser detect any activity in the system after your arrival?"

"None," the immediate response. "Nothing to or from the surface except our ferries."

"Anything else?" Phistol asked.

"Joining the Shroud fleet would be adding two more ships that will be useless if the Helacene Alliance is warned from entering the Geras system," Alain said. "You need to get me to Hela as quickly as possible. If I kill the Suzerain no one will pass along the warning. The admirals will continue and King Phortis will have his victory."

"And what will happen when a Kashōn battlecruiser exits the wormhole gate near Hela?"

"With the Suzerain's son and Personal Guard Commander aboard returning her two daughters," Alain replied. "They will roll out a welcome."

"You have a devious mind, Commander," the Captain said.

Enparatus

When fire and destruction did not rain from the night sky, Coop stopped making loops in barren land north of the ancient fortress. His METS suit did not have the advantages added when Cassandra provided information beyond the suit's scope. It was still an impressive piece of technology.

Without the interference an advanced world would produce, his optics and telemetry scans produced images and data further away than design specs estimated. Through the clear, clean skies of the desert world, he detected the battlecruiser's power emitters. After a minute, telemetry confirmed the ship's movement indicated a path toward the wormhole.

Convinced the Kashōn would not waste time and ordinance on a valueless target, he turned the hover cycle south.

He reached the wadi and uncovered the well before the first of the escapees from the Invicta Academy arrived.

Charace Deuramy led the way, cautiously moving forward until she recognized the tall man in the tight suit lit by a glow stick.

"The Kashōn are leaving the system," he told her. "I realize everyone has made a long walk in a dark and wet tunnel, but going back fifteen miles will be easier than trying to walk another thirty-five in natural channels that have not been inspected."

Antoni Paicell moved forward, pulling a grav-sled. Probably the same one Grat used. Trak lay on the sled. An attractive young woman walked beside him.

"How you doing?" he asked the nomad.

"He's badly injured," the woman answered. "I'm Dr. Wabley. I teach biology and act as the Academy's medic. I've done what I could, but without the use of the infirmary, it's only temporary. He needs better attention."

"I'm fine," Trak said, raising up on an elbow. "Did I hear the bastards have left?"

"Yes. These people can return to the school. The doctor can get you to the infirmary and give you that better care."

"Alain is a traitor," Trak said. The hush around them indicated the academy staff knew who Alain was, and understood the portent of his statement. "If you do not reach Suzerain Palla before he returns to Hela, he will kill her. With his sisters safe his only option will be a direct coup."

"Probably," Coop agreed. "We have to hope Samara and her sisters get word to their mother before that can happen. There isn't anything I can do until Cassandra returns."

"There may be another way," Trak said. He removed the light blanket and swung his legs over the side of the sled-turned-stretcher. "If you can help me out of the well and onto the hover cycle."

"I would not suggest trying," Dr. Wabley interrupted. "You may have internal injuries that become more critical if you try moving too much."

"It is my choice, Doctor," he replied. Standing, he turned once more to the human who gained his trust by rescuing the girls. The display of trust in Samara and himself added to his decision. "Will you help me?"

Coop handed the cable he used to rappel from the surface to the Parz.

"Tie this under your armpits. After I reach the top, I'll pull you up."

Chōntorham - Palace City Space Port Facilities

"There are no military ships docked here," Duly said. "Well, a couple of supply frigates, but nothing worth a damn. This cannot be normal."

D'Sey called up a holo-display of the data from Duly's scans.

"Deployed," he murmured. "No way the planet's major port and the King's palace have been left without protection. The entire fleet must be massing."

"Not a good thing," Krest said.

"It means they are preparing for an invasion," D'Sey replied.

"An ambush," Krest interjected. "I have a message from Taah. Cassandra rendezvoused with Clyde. Doc and all three Hela princesses are safe and aboard."

"Samara, too?" D'Sey asked.

Krest nodded and continued. "Cooper and Key remained behind."

"Why?" the pirate-agent asked.

"Alain Athodite."

"He was sent by Palla to negotiate for his sisters' release," D'Sey interrupted. "Did they stay to rescue him?"

"Alain is the traitor," the Fray said. "He is the one who provided the Kashōn with Alliance wormhole communications specs and the pass codes. He told them about Alucha and Mandara studying on Enparatus. I do not think Cooper intends to rescue him."

"What else?"

"Suzerain Palla ordered the Helacene Alliance Fleet to the Geras System. They will gather for final operational orders before advancing to Nessur system and blockading it against the Shroud. King Phortis is aware of this. It is why no military vessels are in port. They intend to be in Geras when the Alliance ships exit the wormhole gate."

"This isn't making any sense," D'Sey said. His eyes narrowed as he rested his chin on his raised right hand, elbow braced on the arm of his command chair. "How does Phortis expect to have the Shroud Fleet in the Geras system before the Helacene Alliance ships arrive?"

"There's more to the message," Krest said. "Cassie recorded a conversation between Cooper and two Ve engineers sent to investigate the Invicta Vitam Academy's power supply systems. They told him a Ve engineer forced to work for the Kashōn here on Chōntorham could provide help."

D'Sey sat tight-lipped in concentration, reorganizing his thoughts with the new information added to the mix.

"We need to locate the Ve engineer and talk with him," he finally said. "It may or may not impact our mission to assassinate Phortis. Krest, you will head for the palace. Try to determine the best method of getting inside, and decide on two or three escape routes. I did not come here on a suicide mission."

The leader turned next to Duly. A glint of glee and mischief in his eye.

"What?" the Xentorene asked, his face a scowl.

"Do you remember the raid on the Kashōn outpost on that planet with the twin stars?" he asked.

"You aren't thinking of trying to pull that off here, are you? In the Palace City? At the Empire's largest military space port?"

"The stuff is in storage," D'Sey replied. "Rox and I will map out the shortest way to the building where they keep the aliens. Get down to storage and get ready. We'll meet at the lower port hatch."

Chapter 26

Perhaps the group's audacity worked in their favor.

Maybe the massive deployment of ships and the excitement of battle created more confusion than normal.

Not one uniformed Kashōn military serviceperson challenged them on their trek from the outer space docks toward the sky rise building holding aliens co-opted to work for the Empire under the watch of First Council Sentutol.

Duly's appearance could have been the real reason.

The Howler wore a Kashōn Shroud Trooper uniform, complete with tunic, heavy trousers to hide his furry legs, and arm greaves with gloves. The galea designed with fake ram's horns disguised most of his face. Rox enjoyed gluing cotton balls to his exposed jaw to simulate wooly facial hair.

Duly's size equalled that of the larger military operators, but the massive laser rifle dwarfed anything the average trooper would carry. Inquisitive eyes were drawn to the weapon, appraised the soldier capable of toting it with ease, and stayed out of the path of the procession.

D'Sey and Rox wore no disguises. They walked ahead of the shepherding pretend-guard, heads down, with the defeated shuttle step of indentured aliens or prisoners.

They carried a metal container between them. The size and weight adding to their shuffling.

Krest would be making his way to the palace. The Fray used shadows and stealth as no other beings in the galaxy. There was little doubt he would discover Phortis C's location. The mission to remove the King and any nearby Ashemachers remained on, but dropped a notch.

The security guards outside the entrance to the Alien housing and operations building moved quickly to open the double doors for the trio. Neither bothered to challenge Duly. Not one Kashōn spoke to the disguised trooper until they reached the command and control station in the lobby.

The male behind the counter did not wear armor. A civilian.

"Your business?" he asked.

"First Council Sentutol ordered the delivery of these parts," Duly nodded at the container. "They are to be taken to a Ve engineer named Docha for decontamination."

The civilian pushed his chair backward.

"Decontamination?"

"Radiation pollution from a leak at a power transfer station."

"Is it safe to have them here?"

"No," Duly answered quietly. "It is why I used aliens and not Kashōn to carry them. The Ve is supposed to know how to deradiate the equipment and determine what caused the leak. The King is concerned other stations will fail."

"No one told me to expect you," the bureaucrat said. His eyes remained on the metal crate.

"Everyone is busy," Duly replied. "Or have you not noticed?"

The controller hesitated. His next step would be the butt-cover move of calling on someone higher up the chain. Duly cut the move off before it could be made.

"Leave the container here," he ordered D'Sey and Rox. "I delivered it. They can handle the shit now."

The metal base barely touched the floor when the controller said, "The Ve named Docha is on the fifteenth level, west wing, lab suite A. Take the last lift on your left. Do not stop at any other floors."

Duly gave the requisite impression of being unhappy shuttling the dangerous package further. He ordered his aliens to lift and follow him. They disappeared into the lift.

Duly did a small jig as the cubicle rose.

"Don't let your pride get too out of control," D'Sey said. "We still have to get out again. Duly."

"Yes?"

"Deradiate is not a word."

Continuing to play their roles after exiting the lift, assuming all areas would be under surveillance, Duly did not bother knocking on the door to Lab-Suite A. He opened it, ushered D'Sey and Rox through with the metal container, and followed.

A short alien in an orange jumpsuit sat on a high chair. He swiveled around as the door opened. A thin female in a sky blue lab coat stood before the flex-glass windows. She watched the three enter without comment.

Duly raised the impressive laser weapon. At the same time he placed a finger in front of his mouth in the universal order for silence.

They stood quietly as the male alien opened the container, removed a device and placed it around his right wrist. The female, a different species by her coloring and stripes, extracted a laser pistol and aimed it at the scientists.

The male walked around the studio, eyes on his wrist, coming to a halt where he began.

"No security devices," he said. "Interesting. I would have thought someone as pathological as Sentutol would watch and listen to everything in this building."

He turned his attention to the smaller alien.

"Are you Docha?"

"I am. I do not understand why we are under arrest."

"Lower weapons," D'Sey ordered. "A couple of Ve engineers on a Shroud battlecruiser suggested I find you. Grat and Bantry."

"Grat is my cousin," Docha said. "Why would they want you to find me? Who are you?"

"My name is Slate."

"The pirate?" Docha jumped to the floor. He walked nearer the man. "You are the pirate, Slate?"

"Careful, Docha," the female scientist warned. "This could be a trap set up by Sentutol. She often tests the aliens working here."

"I wish I had time to convince you, but I do not," D'Sey said. "The Shroud Fleet has deployed. You had to observe that from here. They are setting a trap for a fleet of confederated planets who do not wish to join the Empire. Grat told a friend of mine that you had information that could help us defeat the Shroud ships. If you do, tell me now. If you do not, or if you intend on wasting my time through evasions, tell me so we can get on with the rest of our mission."

Docha turned to Pau, shrugged, and turned back to the pirate.

"What about the Kashōn trooper?"

Duly let his rifle hang by the sling. He removed the galea to reveal his grey skin and un-ram-like face.

Docha laughed. A combination of pleasure and relief.

"Pirates," he said. "Real pirates. I hoped to get the information to you somehow, but never did I expect you here?"

"Time, Docha," D'Sey reminded the Ve.

"Dr. Pau and I worked on fleet engineering improvements for the last five years," the little alien said. He hurried back to his console. He pulled a metal wand from the desktop, returned and handed it to D'Sey.

"Pull the tip off and insert the wand into a stick reader port," he said. "I've stored all of the details and designs for Kashōn ships built over the past few years. It also includes updates to older vessels. More importantly, there is a backdoor installed in the operating system control chip. The pathway and the codes are all there."

"We can get into the operating systems for Shroud ships and take control?" D'Sey asked. Awed by the potential value of the slender metal rod.

"Control, no," Dr. Pau said. "We could not take the chance creating code for a remote take-over. A skilled diagnostic tech would see the threads. You hold a kill switch."

"You put an off-code into all of the Kashōn's space ships," Rox said. "That has to be the juiciest thing I have ever heard."

"Not every ship," Pau cautioned. "Maybe half, but all of the ones launched in the last four years."

"The most powerful in the fleet," Docha added.

"How near and how powerful a transmitter?" D'Sey asked.

"Within a million miles with a portable system capable of transmitting across a lower-band. A stronger system means you can launch the off-code from further away. The lower band will not be deflected by Shroud forcefields."

"You?"

"Us and others working with us," Docha answered. "Not a single alien in this building works with the Kashōn by choice. Most never believed the little bugs we designed would ever be used, but it felt good to slide them in under our jailers' noses."

"You both seem plugged into Empire secrets involving tech and space-worthy vessels," D'Sey said. "Why do they think they can reach a system nearer the confederation before the enemy ships arrive?"

The Ve turned his attention to the female and said, "Dr. Pau is the smartest applied physicist in the Empire. I believe she knows."

"Wormhole travel is slightly different for ships of varying size and power," she began. "You understand this?"

"A ship with a better engine can travel a channel more quickly, but not drastically so," D'Sey replied.

"Which makes no sense," she responded. "Either speeds should be constant, or there should be a greater difference between the least and most powerful vessels. The dark matter that holds channels together also creates drag on the ships passing through. Stronger ships are able to fight the drag, but as the ship surges forward, drag increases in response."

"The rope pulls back," Rox said. "A larger animal may pull further away, but the rope will still reel it back in, same as a weaker animal."

"Yes," Pau agreed. "But what happens if the rope slips off the weaker animal?"

"It escapes. The Kashōn can slip out of wormhole drag?"

"Have you ever been to a world using mag-lev tube transit systems?" The scientist asked.

"I have," D'Sey answered. "Magnetic conductive systems with levitated cars inserted into vacuum tunnels. Twice as fast as mag-lev transports using rails only."

"The wormholes are vacuum tubes," Pau said. "The Kashōn added secondary power plants on many of their ships. These power systems arc enclosed microwave generators. They do not have long lives, but they make the ships incredibly fast in normal space flight. When they operate inside a wormhole, a magnetic field is generated around the ship's hull."

"Which is only half the solution," D'Sey said. "You need an opposite magnetic pole for the ship to levitate above. Wormholes don't have rails."

"No, but Shroud vessels do have pulse cannons," Pau said. "They fire metal flakes ahead of the ship. It requires a constant pattern of fire, and takes the ship's systems to dangerous failure limits."

"The ship glides on the flakes. No drag from the dark matter," the Ve interjected. "The metal flakes remain in the channels.

Kashōn cartographers maintain records showing those channels already coated. If a ship uses one of these wormholes, they do not need to use their cannons. Each trip they make increases the network of mag-lev capable channels."

"How much faster?"

"Weeks in days and days in hours," Pau answered.

"They can reach a system gate quicker than a traditional traveler in a faction of the time." Rox said. "An advantage which could spread the Kashōn Empire across the entire galaxy."

"The Shroud ships with microwave-power plants will also be faster within a star system," Docha reminded them. "The attack on the ships of your confederated planets is the test Phortis has been seeking. I'm afraid those ships will not stand against the Shroud."

"Unless we hit the kill switch," Rox said.

"Even if you had a ship with a mag-lev system, the Kashōn armada is already on the way. You could not catch up in time to make a difference," Docha said.

"Maybe," D'Sey murmured, not mentioning space-fold aloud. "But we need to go now. Rox, contact Krest and tell him to abort. We'll go after Phortis another day."

"You planned on capturing the King?" Docha asked, once more awe-inspired by the pirates. "Bold, but the King is with the Shroud fleet. He intends to watch the test."

"Rox, tell Krest. Meet us at the ship." To Docha and Pau he said, "I cannot take you with us. I truly wish I could considering everything you have done."

"We understand," Docha said. "If you can do anything to defeat the Shroud, it will be a signal to all of the worlds within the Empire freedom is possible. With hope, people will find a way to fight. Dr. Pau and I will continue doing what we can from here."

From the container D'Sey collected two small plugs. He handed one to each of his new allies.

"Communication tabs," he said. "Simple. Squeeze and talk. My ship constantly monitors Chōntorham and the system. It may take a few days, but we will hear you. If anything Important occurs, make the call. If you need help, make the call. Once you do, place the plug in an ear canal or a nasal passage to hide it from view. You'll hear us when we call back, and we'll be able to hear you."

"Amazing," Docha said, holding the miniature device closer.

"Don't try engineering on it," D'Sey warned him. "Control your curiosity. It may save your life, but not if you break it."

"What's the plan to get out?" Duly asked, placing the helmet with fake horns over his head.

"Keep it simple," D'Sey answered. "We left the contaminated pieces here, and we're taking the container to be incinerated."

"If anyone comes to see the fictional equipment?" Scandeki inquired.

D'Sey lifted a heavy power-coupler out and placed it on the floor.

"It has a bit of radiation engrained on o-rings," he said. "It would be expected after you deradiated it," he added, looking at Duly as he used the word.

The command and control agent on the ground floor appeared happy to see them leave with the container. The return trip to Menace proved less stressful than the walk into the port complex. Fewer people wandered the grounds, and everyone they did encounter hurried to get somewhere else. They were not surprised to find Krest on the bridge waiting. The thin marauder could move quicker through shadows and from cover to cover than someone walking a straight line.

"We have to go now to have any chance of warning the Alliance," D'Sey told Krest before taking the command chair.

"Palace City Port Control, this is the hauler J-one-one-three requesting a flight path from surface dock station S-D-eight," Krest made the call as Rox brought engines on line and initiated pre-flight checks.

"J-one-one you have not been cleared by security. Why are you requesting a departure lane?"

"Sorry, Control, but a security detail boarded and left. Military transport units loaded the ore. Mineral Supply and Storage has the freight and we have a receipt," Krest lied.

"No one in security or supply has reported this to records," the controller responded. Peeved. "They already unloaded your freight?"

"Yessir," Krest answered. "I guess all of the activity may have reports low on the priority chain. Do you want to send a dispatch for the receipt? If you don't have the cargo reports, you probably don't have the receipt numbers either."

The three pirates stopped and waited on the response. If the controller decided to send a security team, they would have to force their way through Kashōn skies. Highly militarized and protected skies.

"Damn them," the voice returned. "It does not matter if the fleet is deploying, the records are supposed to be kept current. I do not have the time or personnel to send a dispatch J-one-one. A flight path is being patched through to your nav system. You can take off in twelve minutes, or you have to wait another six hours."

"Twelve minutes it is," Krest responded. "Thank you, Control. J-one-one, out."

The normally staid Fray fell back into his seat, releasing a deep breath.

Rox chuckled, and D'Sey smiled. The universal burdens bureaucrats suffered, and their total lack of patience with other departments worked in their favor once more.

Chapter 27

Enparatus - Oasis of the Great Dunes

Trak proved to be of hardy stock. The Parz nomads, a race of beings who lived comfortably with a harsh environment, did not allow injuries to beat them. Their bodies, hardened over the centuries, dealt with the problems associated with cuts, broken bones, and other wounds efficiently.

The ride from the wadi well entrance to the natural spring feeding the oasis south of the Great Dunes proved smooth for the tribal leader riding behind Coop. Without further trauma, the internal injuries began to shunt work from damaged organs to other systems while the healing process began.

While the external abrasion did not cauterize fully, Dr. Wabal expertly sutured the gap left open and bleeding closed. Death would not visit Trak this day.

Coop stopped the hover cycle between the waterline and a wall of limestone. He helped the nomad off the cycle and provided support. With his enhanced strength he could easily carry the man, but knew better than to offer. A race such as the Parz would take pride in standing on their own. A solid support welcomed, but to be carried as a child, not so much while conscious.

"We have living spaces inside the wall," Trak said. "When you get closer, if you know where to look, you can see the lines of the entrance stones. Press against the left edge and the door will pivot inward."

The enhanced optics of the METS helmet easily discerned the slim lines outlining the natural-appearing doors. Following Trak's directions to a section of the wall, he placed his hand inside the left line and pushed.

After he and Trak entered, Coop placed the door back in place. Marveling at the smooth action of the thick stone portal and the way it fit seamlessly into position. As the door swung to close, lights came on.

The limestone wall acted as a facade for a hollow hill covered in desert sand and rocks. From above, and three sides, the hill appeared as one more large dune. The wall was visible only from the side facing the oasis. Inside, the smallish mountain contained open space. The interior segmented by constructed walls. The current level acted as a platform, bridging the entrance to a cavernous area. At the edge, looking down, the cavern floor sat one-hundred-feet lower. The floor extended back for thousands of feet beneath the shifting sands of the desert planet.

"It reminds me of the Martian hangar," Coop said.

"Martian hangar?"

"A planet near my home world is called Mars. We discovered a flying saucer inside a hangar disguised as a mountain. The information we learned is how my species developed the ability to fly into space beyond our solar system. The hangar was a lot like this one. It also used automatic lights embedded in the walls and ceiling. Like these."

"You found a flying saucer? A space plate?"

"A machine capable of extended space flight at great speeds. The design roughly the shape of two concave plates, one placed atop the other," Coop said.

"Did it fly? Could you fly it?" Trak asked.

"Everyone thought it should be able to fly," Coop answered. "An exo-linguist from Earth deciphered the Martian writing. We built ships, and created many other innovative technologies from the decoded files. Ships like Cassandra, and devices like the METS I'm wearing. Scientists and engineers reverse engineered the power systems, but we could never get the saucer's engines to turn on."

"Come with me, Coop," Trak said, leading the way to a smaller platform jutting out from the larger one. Once both stood on the deck, it began to lower.

At the bottom the Parz leader led the human to a sidewall and a normal appearing door. Trak turned a knob and the two entered a portion of the cavern segmented from the rest.

"Is this like your Martian ship?" he asked as lights brightened and illuminated a flying saucer.

"Smaller," Coop said, "but nearly identical. Trak, how many people know there is a Nakki space ship on Enparatus?"

"I don't know of Martians or Nakki," the older man said. "These caverns and this ship have been part of our history from before the first civilization rose. Like your world, our forbearers used the things found here to create a planet second to none in technical superiority. Our belief in our superiority led to pridefulness. Pride led to the decay of our morality. Following centuries of living as spoiled children, the Parz regained their moral compass. My ancestors weaned themselves from any technology not used to benefit the well-being of people or the planet."

Trak walked over to the ship. He rested a hand against a strut. The scout ship on Mars would have towered another twenty feet over his head. This keel of this ship sat less than six-feet above him.

"No one beyond my tribe remembers the existence of this ship, or the other machines stored within this site. My ancestors needed centuries to find ways of using the miracles here. After centuries of advancements, we advanced ourselves backward to a simple existence. A happier existence. No one ever deciphered the language of the Seeders."

"Seeders?"

"Parz mythology, or religious tales," the tribal head said. "Depends on the depth of your belief. Some Parz believed then, and some believe now, we began from the seeds of a great species. Some believed this ship delivered the seeds to Enparatus that matured into the first Parz."

"According to a reliable source I know, your beliefs may not be too far off the mark," Coop said. "Like Earth, you have an advanced space ship that doesn't fly. That doesn't exactly help, Trak. Or was there something else you wanted to show me?"

"You said you can read the Seeders' language, but you could not start the saucer you discovered."

"Yes."

"We cannot read their words, but we know how to start this ship."

Few things in his extended life, before or after the conversion to Space Ranger, surprised Coop to the point of shutting him down. For one frozen second in time, Trak's statement dropped him into a mental abyss.

"You can start this ship. How?"

Trak shuffled to a desk placed against a wall. The desk, chair, and most of the floor under and around the furniture covered in a thin coating of limestone dust. The same dust spread across the enclosed space indicating a lack of visitors for an extended time. The nomad opened an unlocked drawer, removed something, and tossed it to Coop.

An oblong wedge of material similar to green obsidian. Three-inches in length, one-inch in diameter. Four-sided, it tapered to a half-inch at one end and a point. Held upright, the shape resembled an obelisk.

"There's a slot on the forward panel, to the left of where we believe the pilot would sit," he told the dazed human. "The wedge of stone fits the slot. Press it all the way in and everything comes on. Because no one could understand the writing, none dared go further. The fear of the ship blowing up or flying away kept it here. The ancients thought they would eventually learn how to read Seeder. It never happened."

"A key," Coop said. "An old-fashion, as the stars are my witness, fucking key."

Chapter 28

Aboard Clyde

"Cassie, we do not have enough time to go back for Coop," Doc said. "Menace is attempting to reach the Geras system before the Alliance ships. Their ships are already in wormhole channels. D'Sey hopes we can get a message through the Helacene communication repeaters to them before they exit. If not, the only chance the Alliance fleet has will be if Menace arrives in time to sabotage some of the Shroud ships. He discovered a vulnerability in the operating systems for newer Shroud vessels. It may give the Alliance ships enough time to escape the ambush. If D'Sey is late the Shroud Fleet will outnumber the Alliance and have the element of surprise. With the Helacene Alliance Fleet destroyed, there is not another force on this side of the galaxy capable of standing against the Empire."

"My responsibility is to my Captain," Cassie answered. The holo-avatar and the Kanistari conducted their civilized argument in Clyde's hangar. Cassie requested the hatch be re-opened for her departure as soon as the three Hela princesses disembarked. Clyde refused. "If I have to blow a hole in Clyde large enough to fly through, I will."

"You are the only ship capable of reaching Hela in time to prevent Alain from murdering his mother, and probably his younger brother," Doc continued. "D'Sey can't do both jobs, and he's nearer Geras. We're closer to Hela. The Suzerain can send a message to warn the fleet before they exit the gate."

Doc's right hand remained in her pants pocket as she tried to convince Cassie. The chip D'Sey gave her, the one that could erase Cassie from existence, rubbed against her fingertips.

"The Wraith is a major part of the reason D'Sey recruited Coop," Doc reminded the avatar.

"To rescue the princesses from the Kashōn on Enparatus," Cassie countered. "We accomplished the mission. Now it is time for me to go back and collect Coop."

"The princesses are safe," Doc agreed. "This entire section of the galaxy is now held hostage. Trillions upon trillions of beings will continue to live under the Kashōn boot. More civilizations will fall if Alain Athodite succeeds in assassinating the Suzerain."

"Clyde can reach Hela faster than I can," the avatar countered.

"The Nakki will not allow it," Doc responded. "Clyde cannot be seen and cannot actively participate. It is against his programming. He can provide support. He can help with transportation, supplies, intelligence, and a host of other things. But he cannot enter a system."

"Shanks," Cassie said, using the Dualönges' derogatory term for the Nakki.

"Enough, Cassie. You can't fight your way out of this ship. More importantly, you know what Coop would tell you to do."

The pirate-medic pulled the destruction chip from her pocket. She handed it to the sentient construct.

"Be careful," Doc warned. "If you squeeze that chip it will erase all of Cassandra's programming."

Cassie realized the result would include her own extermination.

Doc said, "I've known the man less than a week, and I know exactly what he would order you to do."

"Get me later. Save the Suzerain," Cassie said, imitating Cooper's clipped tone when speaking and expecting no argument in return.

"I'll go with you," Doc said.

"And me." Samara entered the halo of light. "The Hela military will fire everything they have at you unless I'm there."

"If I agree, what's to stop me from changing course once we depart Clyde?" Cassie asked.

"Honor," Doc answered.

"Justice," Samara added.

In the Kas system an antiquated freight hauler slipped behind an asteroid and disappeared from tracking monitors on Chōnto-ham. On the far side, a sleek space yacht slipped into a space-time bubble for a quick trip to the edge of the system. Once away from the gravitational objects creating potential problems, it would slide once more into space-fold and make way for an uninhabited three-planet system named Geras.

Wormhole channels carried Shroud ships towards the Geras gateway at the edge of the small system. Ships dispatched to the general area weeks earlier, now made a final, short channel jump toward Geras. Others, equipped with new tech able to turn wormholes into speed ramps, deployed later, but would arrive earlier.

King Phortis C accompanied his younger brother, Admiral Pitaritis on the Shroud's most powerful juggernaut. When the Shroud Fleet gathered, over six-hundred warships would crowd the system.

So many vessels, the Geras star would appear shrouded behind their silhouettes.

Fifty-two Helacene Alliance Military Vessels crossed through wormholes from nineteen confederation systems. Ordered to rendezvous at Geras for final instructions before moving to Nessur.

In the void of space, between Helacene Alliance worlds, a tiny ship with a nasty semblance flew away from a giant silver kidney-shaped space ship. It turned toward the Alliance capital of Hela and exited natural space for more expedient space-fold travel.

On board: a non-living sentient avatar chose honor and duty over desire. A pirate who could not take a life decided she would do whatever necessary, even if it meant killing another being. A teenager worried about her mother and younger brother, and what they would think of her when she killed her other brother.

A Kashōn battlecruiser transporting the Helacene Guard Commander and an Imperial Elite Captain prepared to exit through the wormhole gate where the star, Cadme, warmed the planet, Hela. Its light giving life to the garden where Suzerain Palla Athodite wandered in worried thought. The Commander intended to steal the star and all it shined upon. The Captain planned to black out the entire Helacene Alliance.

The blood-red private ship, Haiman departed the Saepartiq system on a course for the Helacene Alliance capital world. Vistol the Vicious did not know the plans of Captain Phistol and Alain Athodite. If she had, she would not have cared. The experiment on Saepartiq inspired her with a plan of her own.

Over the brown desert world of Enparatus, a ship not seen for hundreds-of-thousands of years soared across the pale blue sky. The silver saucer headed for the darkness of space and a confrontation not too different from the last time it flew.

Part 3

BATTLE ON THE FAR SIDE
OF THE GALAXY

Chapter 29

"I messaged my Mother," Alain said. "I told her the Kashōn are delivering Alucha, Mandara, and me home as an offer of good will. I also told her King Phortis C will honor a truce to allow time for negotiations to continue."

"Which will explain an Empire battlecruiser entering the Hela system," Captain Phistol replied. "I do not think King Phortis will appreciate it if the Suzerain recalls her fleet. An ambush is only successful if there is an enemy to surprise."

"I added my lack of belief in King Phortis' word," the Hela traitor said. "In a special code, of course. Mother will continue with her plans to gather the Alliance ships. At the same time, she will hope for a peaceful solution. In the week it will take for us to travel from the gate to Hela, the Shroud will eliminate the Alliance fleet."

"I have no intention of wasting a week," the officer said. "The EMdrive will get us to Hela in half the time. The ship's Captain calculated our estimated time of arrival and informed the other battlecruiser's commander. Unless you hesitate, they will follow us into the system at about the same time you eliminate the Suzerain. If you are succeed, two Kashōn ships will be present to support your claim to leadership. If you are not, I will handle the Suzerain myself."

"There will be Hela military ships on guard. The planet has surface-mounted repulser cannons."

"The ships on guard will be lightly armed system patrol boats," Phistol responded. "According to our spy, (he raised one side of his ridged brow to cast a sarcastic look at Alain) all major ships have sailed to defend the confederation. As to the cannons on the planet, our useful spy provided the location of all emplacements. We will blast them to rubble. You should be proud, Commander Athodite. Your information will result in the expansion of the Kashōn Empire. The King may give you a medal to go with your new fiefdom."

The Kashōn Flag Ship, Jagannatha

"You should pick them off one by one as they exit the wormhole," Phortis said.

The King sat at the head of a metal conference table in the war room aboard his newest Juggernaut. The SuperCruiser Class vessel used the latest technology, as well as the largest number of weapons ever placed on a single ship. The Jagannatha required four-thousand-one-hundred-fifteen personnel to operate. Phortis named the SuperCruiser for a mythological chariot driven by one of the gods who gave birth to the Kashōn. The unstoppable chariot mowed down enemy soldiers as it raced across the battlefield.

Admiral Pitaritis, who normally sat at the head of the table, responded to his brother, keeping the vitriol from entering his tone.

"At a point, the following ships would realize what was happening. They would close the gate," he said.

"They cannot reverse course within a wormhole channel," the King returned. "They will be trapped. Eventually forced to break out."

"They cannot reverse," his brother agreed, "but they can stay in the channel for months, with sufficient supplies. While they remain behind the portal, our ships will be unable to access the wormhole. Do you want the Shroud Fleet drifting in this dead system for months, my King?"

Ignoring the question, Phortis asked, "What is your plan?"

Pitaritis activated a holo-wall display.

"Geras consists of three planets, no moons, and random asteroid debris," he said. His words created images that floated across the wall. "Currently two planets are on the far side of the star, but the orbit of the largest brings it within a couple of days of the gate. I believe the choice of this system by the Helacene military was the combination of it being near the Nessur system, and the current proximal orbit of the planet to the gate. The planet does not support sentient life, but it does have an atmosphere. If any of the ships required maintenance before departing for Nessur, orbiting the planet or landing would make the work easier to accomplish."

"How does any of this help us destroy them?" a bored King asked. Phortis much preferred his voice to others.

"I will place the Shroud on the star-side of the planet. Its mass and density will hide the fleet from Alliance visual and electronic scans. Their fleet admiral will gather his ships outside the wormhole gate. The first to arrive will move far enough from the portal to allow others easier egress. When the last ship enters and the gate is closed, they will begin post-channel integrity inspections. Unwilling to allow his fleet to spread too far apart, all ships will make for the planet to maintain contact with those needing repairs. While the commanding officers discuss their assets, maintenance needs, and strategy they will also let down their guard. When they reach more than half way between the wormhole and the planet, we will pounce."

"If they have no ships in need of repairs," the King noted.

"A fleet of spaceships always includes vessels in need of repairs," his brother responded.

"Half-way gives them a day to prepare," Phortis countered.

"Yes, at their speed," his brother agreed. "However, our newer ships can use EMdrives and reach them in hours. SuperCruisers and the latest Battlecruisers are fitted with improved cannon. They will commence firing long before they arrive on site. The Destroyers and Penetrator-class ships do not have EMD, but they use kinetic rods with booster rockets."

On the wall, six-hundred-sixteen Shroud ships fanned out and moved toward one-hundred Alliance ships. Bright flashes and tracer streams demonstrated the cannon fire raining across space and into the enemy.

"Our SuperCruisers carry forty-eight missiles. I will send them to lead the ambush. They will be the point of the spear, and launch one-hundred nuclear missiles into the Alliance fleet. The missiles will interrupt the electro-magnetic forcefields employed by Helacene Alliance warships. Long-rods will plow into those ships like arrows tearing through paper shields."

Explosions and carnage blossomed on the hull display.

"The Shroud will swarm, leaving not a single enemy ship intact."

The cloud of Kashōn vessels swept through the Helacene ships. As the Shroud continued toward the wormhole gate, dust lingered in their wake.

"I suppose that could work as well," the King said.

Chapter 30

Hela System

The Kashōn shuttle deposited Alain Athodite on the landing pad beyond the manor's sculptured gardens. A squad of Royal Guard awaited as he disembarked. The ferry rose and returned to the battlecruiser in orbit as squad and Commander made their way through the garden.

The Suzerain met her son at the foot of the steps leading up to the rear portico. She greeted him with an embrace for a son safely returned and not a formal greeting for her negotiator sent into danger.

"Where are Alucha and Mandara?" she asked.

"Aboard the Kashōn ship," he replied. "The Captain is hesitant to trust we will not turn weapons on him as soon as they reach the surface. I've come down first to personally confirm King Phortis intends to negotiate in good faith."

"They are unharmed?"

"The girls are perfectly fine, Mother," Alain said. His smile and relaxed posture meant to ease her stress. "Other than witnessing the unfortunate actions taken by Captain Phistol when he arrived on Enparatus, they have been treated as royalty."

"Unfortunate actions?" The Suzerain's words inflected with disdain. "Murdering the Chancellor and innocent instructors at a defenseless school is more than unfortunate."

"The Kashōn are an over-reactive military race, Mother. Phistol over-played his position. King Phortis was not pleased by the death of those people either. The Captain will be disciplined after we conclude the terms of the truce and he returns to Chōntorham"

"Terms?"

"Simple, really. The Suzerain agrees Helacene Alliance worlds will not interfere with the Empire, and the Empire will ignore the nineteen systems within the confederation."

"We do not expand the confederation or extend aid to other worlds the Kashōn decide to swallow," she translated Alain's words. "When the King expands his empire large enough, what will stop him from turning back on the Alliance?"

"Nothing," Alain conceded. "You are speaking about hundreds of years, Suzerain Palla. In the short term, you protect your subjects, which is your priority. Over time, we plan for the day Phortis, or his descendants, decide they will attempt to usurp the Alliance. By agreeing to the truce now, you give us time prepare. You also save Alucha and Mandara."

"The two patrol ships reported the Battlecruiser left them far behind," the Suzerain said. "Are Kashōn ships that fast?"

"They use power systems beyond what our intelligence reports indicated," he replied. "It is another reason to accept the truce. They may not realize their advantages over the Alliance military."

"And a spy."

"Yes. Someone provided them with information. I will personally find out who and deal with them."

"I do not trust Phortis, Alain. If we concede to his conditions, he may still attack Nessur, thinking us weak."

"You still have the fleet gathering in Geras?"

"The first ships should arrive shortly," she confirmed.

"Let them gather," he replied. "Have them ready to move to Nessur in case the Kashōn try something. When you are convinced the truce is real, you can recall the fleet."

"What must I do to get Alucha and Mandara home?"

Alain gave a small smile of victory. He placed a gentle hand on his mother's elbow to guide her.

"Let's continue talking inside the manor. When you order the surface cannons to stand down, it will be proof of your intention to honor a truce. I will contact Captain Phistol and he will send down the girls."

Palla Athodite stopped short of the veranda doors. She turned to her son and Guard Commander.

"Alain, if I order the cannon stations to stand down, they will bleed power from the converters. The system is designed to protect as it charges for action. Bleeding the power will weaken their shields at the same time."

"Mother, do you think I would suggest we take our most powerful defensive weapons off-line if I did not believe the Kashōn would honor their side of the truce?" Alain added enough pain to his question to prick his mother. "Alucha and Mandara are my sisters. I want them home, and I want Hela safe. Besides, I hinted to Phistol our surface cannons were the obvious deterrent, but Hela had other ways of protecting our planet."

"A bluff," she said.

"Part of negotiating with thugs," he answered. "You did send me to bring the girls home. Whatever it required."

"And you accomplished your goal, Alain," she said, moving to enter the home and seat of Helacene Alliance power. "You did it far more quickly than I could have imagined."

"Captain Phistol, the communications officer received a message from Commander Athodite," the ship's captain said. He read from a display on the flip-down console of his bridge command chair. Phistol stood feet away before a wide portal. The planet Hela framed in his view. "The Suzerain ordered the surface cannon to stand-by. It will require a couple of hours for the ion-charges to bleed off."

"And their shields?" the Ashemacher asked.

"Shield force will lessen as the ions disperse. We estimate two hours and they should be weak enough for our lasers to penetrate."

"System patrol ships?"

"We are flanked by the two that flew up from the surface at our arrival. The two patrolling the wormhole, left in our wake, continue to catch up," came the answer. "Minimal offensive capability, and rudimentary shields. When the time comes, they will not present a threat."

"Acknowledge the message. Inform Commander Athodite I will deliver Princess Alucha and Princess Mandara in two hours."

"Sir? The princesses are not on board," the confused officer replied.

"No, Captain, they are not. Send the reply," Phistol ordered.

The Wraith exited space-fold for natural space between the first and second planets in the five-planet system. Cassandra passed by Hela, the third orbital-body. Cassie opted for the cover offered by the larger, barren second world. It would provide time for them to assess the situation.

"The Kashōn battlecruiser orbiting Hela fired a sub-atomic beam toward the wormhole gate," Cassie said, her voice emanating from cabin speakers as she remained non-corporal for the trip from Clyde.

"Why?" Doc asked. "A sub-atomic beam isn't going to impact anything."

"I've seen something similar used during the battle between Space Fleet and the Mischene Prophet's forces," Cassie replied. "If the beam has a range limiter, it will create a burst when it reaches maximum distance."

"A burst in open space," Doc said.

"A disruption of the gravity waves near the wormhole gate," Cassie answered. "Ships in wormhole channels use warning systems to alert them if a gravity anomaly exists near a gate. The battlecruiser sent a signal to someone waiting inside the channel."

"More Kashōn," Samara said.

"Scans indicate four Helacene patrol vessels in the system," Cassie reported. "Two are six-million-miles from the planet and thirty-hours-twenty-three-minutes from arrival. Two flank the Kashōn. Scans of the Hela indicate the surface cannons show power levels at fifty-percent. Levels are dropping, not increasing."

"They're bleeding the ionic charges from the power converters used to energize the thrusters," Samara said. The youngest princess sat in the co-pilot seat. Doc occupied the pilot's chair. "Alain must have persuaded Mother to do it. The force fields around the cannon emplacements operate off of the same thrusters. They'll soon be defenseless."

The anger caused by dread roused the young woman, raising her voice as she pushed out of the seat.

"Cassie, you have to get me to the Estate. I have to warn Mother."

"I've adjusted course already," the calm reply. "Samara, get undressed. Doc, you too. Give Samara the METS."

"You plan on letting her go into the palace alone?" the Kanistari asked.

"No. You will accompany her. Since he is commander of the Royal Guard, we need to expect some, if not all, will back his play to seize power. He cannot ascend if there is a female heir. It makes Princess Samara a high-value target. The METS will provide a bit more protection."

Doc, up and shedding her outer garments, asked."You?"

"When the Kashōn attack, the two patrol ships will need help stopping them. While you and Samara find and protect her mother, I will distract the battlecruiser. You must get the surface cannon back on line. They may be the only way of defending Hela from an invasion."

The Helacene helped peel the bodysuit off the teal-hued alien. Doc helped the younger, but curvier, teen pull it on.

"Doc, you will not be able to rely on a stun-gun," Cassie's disembodied voice said. "You must be prepared to kill."

With her clothes back on, the pirate opened Cassandra's armory. She soon wore a tactical vest with a cross-pull knife, a holster with a Rys-improved laser pistol, and snap-pockets loaded with disc-shaped explosive grenades.

She handed Samara a second holster with laser pistol. As the teen strapped it around her waist, Doc collected a laser rifle.

"There's a second knife in here," Doc said. "ELIE is engraved into the black blade."

"Give it to Samara," Cassie said.

"Who is Elie?" the Helacene asked.

"Twelve of the greatest warriors ever produced on Earth are called the Space Rangers," Cassie said. "Ten live. Daniel Cooper is one. Elie is another."

"Her knife is here to remind him of her?" Samara asked. "Are they close?"

"It is here to remind him that in spite of his enhanced strength, speed, and mental acuity, there is always someone better."

"Elie is better than Coop?"

"He thinks so. In specific ways, I agree," the AI-Avatar answered.

Samara slipped the wicked-looking blade into the sheath on her holster. She did not bother putting her outer wear back on. With the form-fitting body-armor and weapons belt, she no longer looked like a teenage girl.

"You look like a warrior-princess," Doc said, admiring the younger woman.

"You look bad-ass," Samara returned, noting Doc's tactical clothing, gear, and guns.

Chapter 31

Tech-geeks working for the Empire had not been able to create a weapon using sub-atomic particles. They did build a collector capable of capturing a sub-atomic particle long enough for it to attract more. A dispenser ejected the particles before they became unstable and exploded. The stream would burst apart at a distance dependent on the weight of the collected particles. Because the ejected stream of particles lost cohesiveness, they no longer represented a danger. The death-burst was spectacular, but harmless beyond a short disruption of non-material waves . . . like gravity waves emanating from a system's star.

While it did not work as a weapon, it did produce a reading on gate-scans aboard ships inside a wormhole. Readings normally used to warn a ship of orbital objects, black holes, or other dangers lurking outside a portal. A captain could hold until the movement of the gate allowed for safe passage. The burst from the sub-atomic particles did the opposite. It signaled a ship to exit.

As the signal from the Kashōn reached the gate, the Wraith entered the upper atmosphere. Samara contacted communications controllers at the military base near the Royal Estate.

"Hela, this is Princess Samara Emi Athodite. I am about to land at the Estate's pad. Inform the Suzerain, and order military and security units to not fire on this ship."

"Princess, we have verified your id, but there is no ship on any of our scans," the coms officer replied.

"It is a special ship," she answered.

"Exit via the hatch," Cassie said. "The port wing ladder will be ready."

Doc left first; Samara quickly followed. On the ground, Samara took the lead. She kept the METS hood down to allow the guards to recognize her.

Before the two women reached the edge of the manicured garden, the Wraith lifted and turned toward the skies.

Royal Guards running from the rear of the manor recognized the princess. They confirmed her identity and listened to their commander's orders, shouted into ear-receivers. Force lances raised and fired.

Doc tackled Samara, taking them both beneath the blaze of incoming laser fire.

Behind them, Cassandra pivoted one-eighty and fired her wing-mounted laser cannons. The bursts of super-heated light cut through the squad in seconds. With the path to the Suzerain open, Cassandra continued the pivot, then shot up and away.

Before the two women entered the manor, thick beams flashed through the ozone. The Kashōn vessel firing on surface cannon sites.

Doc followed Samara through the oddly empty royal home. The girl rushed to her mother's office. Doc caught her in time to prevent the excited girl from bursting through the door. Taking lead, the pirate turned the handle, and then violently kicked the door to fling it inward.

It required incredible control for her to not fire her rifle at the body hurtling toward her. The Helacene leader crashed into the Kanistari, sending both into the door jamb. The sharp edge slammed against Doc's spine. The pain forced her hands open; the laser rifle fell to the floor. She followed, sliding down the wall. Palla already lay on the tile.

Alain's boot caught Doc across her jaw. He reached for the rifle, failing to retrieve the weapon as Samara shoulder-slammed him backward.

Her pistol rose, but she was unprepared for how quickly her older brother regained his balance. A lifetime spent developing strength and speed to compensate for his lack of size placed him on offense before she could fire. His left hand grabbed her wrist, twisting. The knuckles of his right hand struck hard onto her fingers. He continued the push with his right hand, twisting hard with his left. As Samara's wrist bent painfully back, she let go of the pistol. Alain stepped into the wrist lock, pushing Samara's wrist and arm behind her.

The young princess did not panic. She ignored the pain and allowed her own training, fighting techniques learned from the same masters who schooled Alain, to take control. She stepped with her attacker instead of fighting his arm-hold. She twisted beneath his arm to face him. In close she rammed her knee at his groin.

Alain released his hold to block the in-coming knee. He jumped back to prevent her follow-up elbow strike from connecting to his head.

"Impressive, sis," he said. He stood relaxed. Breathing normally, as if the attack on Doc and the explosive encounter with Samara meant nothing.

"What did you do to Mother?"

"She wasn't thrilled when I ordered my people to shoot you," he answered. "I had to shut her up. She's actually tougher than she looks. I think I bruised my knuckles."

"Why, Alain? How could you do any of this?"

"Because I'm the eldest and should rule," he replied. His breathing amplified in anger more than it had been in exertion. "The stupid tradition of women as Suzerain made that impossible. You make that impossible, Samara. Alucha, Mandara, and then you. You would all become Suzerain before me. Just because you have tits."

"Being ruler is this important to you?" she asked. "Becoming a traitor. Murdering your family. Destroying the Alliance you want to rule. You are why men are not allowed to become Suzerain. You prove the exact point you detest."

"Nice outfit," he said, changing the discussion. "The slutty look fits you. Just another part to your own personal rebellion. You would never amount to anything but the least important member of the family. You lashed out by becoming a rogue. I've read all of the reports, Samara. You hate this family as much as I do. Why fight me? I'm going to become king whether you and our sisters live or die. Why not recognize it and live?"

"Mother?"

"She has to die," Alain answered. "I cannot ascend if she's alive. Too many Helacene would stand with her."

"You are such a shit," Samara said. "I've been living outside the lines, but I never stopped loving my family. I never once considered betraying them, or Hela, or the Alliance. I will not let you murder our mother."

The Guard Commander pulled a slender, pointed dagger from a forearm sheath concealed under his jacket's sleeve.

"The Kashōn would rather kill an enemy up close, with sword or knife. It is archaic and barbarian, but it does have a certain appeal. No one will be coming to save you, Samara. I ordered everyone in the manor to the security bunker. Only Guard loyal to me remain. You will die. Then your green companion, and finally Mother."

The youngest princess of the Helacene Alliance pulled the Falkniven A1 knife, forged on a planet on the far side of the galaxy, from its belt sheath. The special leather wrap, instead of the traditional rubber grip, felt warm in her fingers. The CeraKote black matte finish gave it a wicked look different from Alain's shiny dagger.

Alain stood in the stance used by the Hela military. Centered and balanced. Samara took similar training in hand-to-hand from troopers. Today she relied on her friend Trak's instructions when it came to blades. She dropped low, her flexibility allowing a much wider stance. She held the Ranger-issued knife above her head, edge up.

Alain lunged, dagger thrusting down toward her face. She parried the blow and followed with a front kick to his mid-section. Angered by the hit, Alain attempted to use his superior strength to force his way inside her defense. She pivoted aside, avoided his rush, and swept her left foot against his right shin.

The sweep did not take him off his feet, but it did cause pain. Angrier, he slashed high and when Samara raised her knife to block, he discarded the feint for his true target. He reversed directions, back-handing the twin-edged dagger to slice across her belly. To add more power, he stepped across and into the blow. He dragged the sharp blade as far across her torso as possible. Smiling, he turned expecting to see his sister gutted.

He was not prepared to defend against the back kick she directed to his knee. The joint bent backward, the sharp pain forcing him to retreat. He could not put all of his weight on the injured leg.

Samara stood before him, no mark on the METS constructed of human and alien blends woven to prevent penetration by edged weapons.

"Thank you, Cassie," she said aloud. "And Doc, for giving me your suit."

Confidence increased by realizing the suit would protect her, she moved toward her brother. Alain, also realized the suit deflected his blade. He squinted as he turned his eyes on his sister's face.

Samara exposed her throat as she neared. Her hands held lower than they should be. Alain spotted the opening and lunged as he did when they began the fight. This time his dagger thrust going upward, toward the unprotected throat and chin.

Ready, knowing he would try to take advantage of her weak defense, the girl windmilled her left arm with as much force as she could muster. Her forearm blocked the attack. She stepped into her opponent, her right hand with knife stabbing forward and up as it followed the windmill block immediately. The tempered steel-alloy of the Falkniven entered Alain's neck above the Adam's apple. The weight of the knife propelled it through his mouth and into his brain at the cerebellum.

The traitor bent on matricide felt the initial shock of the knife, but felt nothing more as it penetrated his grey matter. His body went rigid. As Samara pulled, his body fell backward landing heavily on the tiled floor.

"Thank you, Elie," she said.

"You did good," Doc said, pulling herself to a seated position. "We need to get help for your mother. Any people here you can trust?"

"Plenty," she answered. "It's still home, in spite of Alain's stupidity."

Chapter 32

When the battlecruiser fired four keel-mounted laser cannon at surface defense locations, the ship's commander also fired the two cannon located on the ship's top deck at the Helacene patrol boats. Because the patrol boat captains did not trust the Kashōn, neither had lowered force fields. Their decision saved ships and crews, but the force of the laser burst, fired at such close range, pushed the smaller vessels several thousand miles into space. The impact rocked interiors, sending unsecured personnel and objects tumbling.

Engineers and pilots fought to bring the ships under control. Gunners fired laser cannons on the enemy cruiser. Like the patrol boats, the twin cannons affixed to the port and starboard hulls were smaller than their Kashōn opponent. However, the shorter cycle time required for the lighter-duty cannon to recharge and fire proved to be a benefit. The two Helacene ships rained lasers onto the battlecruiser. Two bursts impacted the outer hull as they trailed immediately behind strikes creating short-term gaps in the enemy's shields.

Captain Phistol, standing on the bridge, located on the cruiser's superstructure, was unimpressed by the ship's captain.

"You've taken damage," he said, watching the data fed to the command bridge. "A Shroud battlecruiser wounded by ships one-fifth its size. Do you plan on continuing to push them away, Captain?"

"I plan on destroying them," Captain Prauma replied. "Keep your comments to yourself, Captain Phistol. As a Shroud Fleet Captain I outrank you, and as a ground trooper, you have little to offer on the bridge."

Phistol's temper itched for release, but he maintained control. Prauma spoke the truth, except Phistol was Ashemacher and relative of the King. He would explain those things to the Captain later.

"Weapons, surface report," Prauma ordered.

"Four confirmed hits against surface emplacements designated as defensive cannon sites," the officer to his immediate left responded. "This side of the planet has two additional sites. The data provided by Commander Athodite indicates six more over the planet's horizons."

"Time for our cannons to complete recycle?"

"Four-minutes-seven-seconds," the reply. "The four sites targeted sustained considerable damage. I do not believe they can operate their cannons. Two appear to have power for shields. The other two show no signs of life. We estimate the two operational installations require another eight-minutes before they reach firing status. However, their shields are strengthening as the power converter increases output."

"The two patrol boats?"

"Since we are no longer stationary, the laser fire from the two Helacene vessels is less effective," the response from a female Kashōn seated at a console to Prauma's right. "Even without EM-drive, we are much faster. They maneuver more quickly, but they cannot harm us at distance."

"The wormhole?" the ship's commander asked.

"The battlecruiser Cinder exited the gate. They will be within range to engage the two patrol ships in three-hours," the answer from the same female officer. "There is a twelve-minute lag in visual and a four-hour lag in verbal."

"Weapons, train all six laser cannon on the two remaining surface installations. Three each. The added strength should handle the increased shield density. Target the two patrol boats with nuclear-tipped missiles. Six for each boat."

"It will leave us only eight missiles," the weapons officer responded.

"I know my armament count, Lieutenant," Prauma growled. "Once these two are destroyed, and Cinder wipes away the other two, the system will be all ours. Eight missiles will be sufficient. The bigger problem will be destroying the surface emplacements on the far side of the planet. Unless Commander Athodite becomes Suzerain before we need to concern ourselves." This final comment made while Prauma stared at Phistol.

"If he is, the cannon will be off line," Phistol answered the implied question. "If he is not, we will wait on Cinder. Between two Shroud Battleships I think you should be able to eliminate six land-based installations."

Prauma turned away. "Weapons, fire the missiles," he ordered. "As soon as cycle is complete, fire all cannons."

"Six missiles headed our way," Ensign Durad aboard the Helacene Patrol Ship Arvakr called. "Six more targeting Alsvior."

"Fire a spread of lasers," Captain Niamh ordered. She turned the ship to port to provide a better angle for her tactical officer.

"No hits," Durad reported. "The missiles use independent guidance systems. They avoided the lasers. Scans show nuclear signatures, Captain. If they hit, our shields will be disrupted by the EMP concussion."

Niamh pushed her ship down, a relative term in space, but if her head was up and her ass was down, then down it was.

"Missiles redirecting and following," Durad reported. "They have lock. I don't think we can outrun them."

"What is Alsvior doing?" Niamh asked, hoping for inspiration from the more experienced Captain in command of their sister boat.

"Erratic patterns. The missiles tracking Alsvior are changing speed. Two are maintaining and the other four are beginning to drop back."

"First two will disrupt the electro-magnetic force fields," Niamh said. "The force of the nuclear explosions will also damage internal systems and, most likely, shut down the engine. The missiles following will do the rest. What about our problem?"

"I'm continuing to fire lasers, but speeds are too great for accuracy," the ensign reported. "Missiles are closing, Captain. They are beginning to separate into two groups. The Kashōn battlecruiser has moved toward Hela."

"The commander considers us dead," the patrol captain said. "Maybe we are, but we can still take a bite out of their ass."

She pointed her ship at the battlecruiser and pushed her engine to maximum output. She hoped to increase shield density and reach her target before the missiles reached theirs.

"Captain?" the ensign asked.

"We don't have a chance against the missiles. I'm hoping if we impact the battlecruiser at the same time those nuclear tips explode, we produce the same effect on the Kashōn. If I can time it perfectly, we disrupt their shields and their own missiles will cause enough damage to prevent them from continuing the attack on Hela."

"Yes, ma'am," Durad replied weakly. Unable to consider her young life about to be over, she fell back on her training. "Alsvior has taken two hits," she reported. "All stop in space and shields down. Reports of casualties and damaged operating systems. Hull did not breach. Three-minutes-ten-seconds until the following missiles contact."

"We're fifteen-minutes from the cruiser," Niamh said aloud. "Let me know when the Alsvior is gone."

Three-minutes-thirty-seconds later, the Captain asked, "Durad. The Alsvior?"

"Still there, Captain," the awed ensign replied. "The four missiles exploded. They went off before reaching Alsvior. I have no idea what Captain Ossian did to stop them?"

Cassie did not bother materializing. There would be no point. As AI-Avatar she would take the Wraith into battle for the first time without a human or alien at the yoke. She operated once as a drone surveillance ship prior to being given to Daniel Cooper by Nathan Trent, but with strict operational orders to avoid contact.

She accessed Coop's battle histories and past strategic explanations in after-action reports.

The Wraith slipped through the atmosphere and turned toward the smaller Hela ship nearest the enemy battlecruiser. The first two missiles exploded, taking down the electro-magnetic shield protecting the ship. The nuclear detonation damaged several internal systems and knocked the engine off-line.

Cassie fired all four laser cannon hard-fixed beneath her wings. The four missiles following the two impacting the patrol boat disintegrated. The concussive waves shook the vessel. The ship lived. Without shields or power, it would not survive long if the Kashōn directed more weapons at the drifting ship.

"Captain of the patrol boat making the suicide run on the cruiser, I am United Earth Space Fleet ship Cassandra. I am a friend. You have exactly fifteen-seconds to do as I say before the Kashōn fire on Hela. Do not ram the cruiser. Angle beneath the ship's keel-line, cross and execute a ninety-degree elevated course change on my count, five . . . four . . ."

Niamh listened to the incoming message from the stranger, muttered, "Why the fuck not?" She angled the nose of her ship down.

". . . three . . . two . . . one . . . now."

Designed to be highly maneuverable, the potential results of a ninety-degree turn with a massive ship's keel within spitting distance never appeared on the operating specs for a Hela system patrol vessel.

Arvakr responded, straining to pull out of the dive and into the rise. The gravity-control systems could not compensate quickly enough. Anyone and anything aboard not strapped down tumbled.

The first two nuclear missiles detonated against the outer layer of the Kashōn ship's shield. As each following missiles impacted, the integrity decreased. The sixth and final self-propelled ship-killer reached the external hull, blasting away a section of the external airframe and rocking the big vessel.

The battlecruiser's six laser cannons fired automatically when they completed the power-recycle sequence. Four beams cut through space, missing the planet due to the change of station when the ship pitched violently. Two beams reached the surface. One impacted farm land. The other destroyed half a village near an ocean.

Cassie used the opening in the shields to launch twenty short-rod penetrators from her twin rail-guns. Without a forcefield to deflect the heavy alloy rods, they tore into the ship. Kinetic energy propelled the projectiles through the skin of the interior hull, then through decks, walls, bodies, machines, and anything else in their paths.

On the battleship's bridge, a shaken Captain Phistol yelled at the ship's commanding officer.

"Your own missiles! You stupid piece of shit! Get us away and find a place we can reevaluate before something worse happens."

"It is already happening," Prauma replied. Oddly, his voice indicated no strain. "The surface cannon are preparing to fire. I estimate five minutes."

"Can we outrun the lasers?" Phistol asked. "Will the shields hold?"

"Whatever hit us with those rods hurt us badly," Prauma answered. "I'm turning the ship to place our undamaged hull toward the planet. I am also redirecting eighty-percent of our energy to the shields. It will be our best chance. Unless you care to surrender?"

"Captain of the patrol boat, this is Cassandra. I suggest you assist your damaged friend. This part of space is going to become extremely hot."

"Niamh," the captain responded. "My name is Captain Niamh, Cassandra. Thank you."

"You're welcome, Captain Niamh, but it isn't over yet," Cassie answered.

"Captain, I think I have the Cassandra on our radiation wave scanners," Ens. Durad said. "They are the most sensitive scanners we have, and it is the only thing that makes sense. The ship's echo is incredibly minor."

"Where is she?" Niamh asked as she turned Arvakr toward Alsvior to provide aid and assistance.

"Between the Kashōn cruiser and Hela," Durad replied. "She's right in the middle of fire."

Cassie waited. The Wraith in place and everything ready. It would come down to timing.

Twin beams fired from the surface exploded in a laser light show against the battlecruiser's forcefield. The big vessel pushed back into the void as the beam contacting the shields created a colorful spiderweb effect. The continuous ray cut into the forcefield, placing greater strain on the EM generators, dynamos, and converters pumping all excess power to saving the ship. The beam dissipated before it could penetrate the final layer of shielding, but the attack exhausted the ship's energy reserves. For a brief time the forcefield winked out as systems rebooted.

Cassandra's tachyon cannon sat ready on its platform, lowered from the keel through bomb bay doors.

The neutral-particle-beam weapon ionized atoms by allowing them to capture an extra electron. The charged particles were then accelerated, and neutralized again by adding or removing electrons.

A cyclotron particle-accelerator escalated the speed of positively charged hydrogen ions until their velocity approached the speed of light. Individual ions contained a kinetic energy range of 100-MeV to 1000-MeV. The resulting high energy tachyon particles captured electrons from electron emitter electrodes. These electrons were then electrically neutralized. This created an electrically neutral beam of high energy hydrogen-based tachyons. The cannon fired these weaponized tachyon in a straight line at near the speed of light to smash into its target.

These particles travel with tremendous kinetic energy. The energy is imparted to matter in the target's surface on impact, inducing near-instantaneous and catastrophic superheating.

While the Kashōn systems rebooted, Cassie fired. The tachyon stream hit and infused the atomic structure of the unsecured hull. The now superheated structure disintegrated all organic life within the ship and melted everything else to slag. The cold air of space rushed to suck away the heat, cracking the ship like an egg.

On board the two patrol boats, and at several locations on the surface, including the communications and operations sub-center located in the basement of the Suzerain's manor, people vocalized many things, but all could be summed up by Samara's "Holy shit."

"Nice going, Cassie."

"Coop?" Cassie's scanners flared to maximum, sweeping space for the source of her captain's voice. "Where are you?"

"Assisting the last patrol boat near the wormhole," he replied. "I was too late to stop them from destroying one boat. I've damaged the Kashōn battlecruisers power plants and eliminated weapons-control systems. Not as spectacular as your show, but effective. They will drift until someone comes to collect them. The captain of the remaining patrol boat will keep watch until someone comes to collect them."

"How did you get here?"

"I'll be there is two hours. We can all meet and bring each other up to speed. I'll see you at the Suzerain's estate."

Chapter 33

The Wraith, looking more like a dangerous animal ready to pounce than ever, sat on the grassy area left of the landing port. Suzerain Palla Athodite, her daughter, Princess Samara, and Doc with a squad of trusted military Regulars (to replace the Royal Guard) waited at the rear entrance to the estate garden. Coop called before entering the atmosphere to inform them of his arrival.

"Thank you for putting on pants," Palla whispered to Samara. "That bodysuit is a bit revealing. I believe a blouse would also be advisable."

Smirking, enjoying her mother's chagrin, the princess replied, "It's quite comfortable. I think it looks cute with the cargo pants and trooper boots."

"The holster with laser pistol and the savage knife? Are they cute as well?"

"I hope so," the teen answered.

A ship emerged through the high clouds on the western horizon. The circular grey bottom tilted to reveal a cream-white upper section in the shape of a downside-up shallow saucer. Lights, or a luminescent energy source, flickered along a girth-line separating the top and bottom of the ship where grey turned to white.

As it neared, the size became apparent. Larger than Cassandra. Different configuration, but along the volume of Menace or one of the Helacene patrol ships. Too large for the shuttle landing-zone built to service the Suzerain's estate.

The vessel halted above and yards beyond the LZ. It lowered, stopping ten-feet above the ground. No wind moved. No engine sounds. An eerie sight considering the size and proximity of the flying saucer.

A doorway appeared above the line of lights facing the assembled group. A section of the hull slid inward and aside. A ramp extended from the hatch, reaching thirty-feet before tilting and lowering the leading edge to the surface. At the opening, Coop appeared and began the long walk. Dressed in his METS, without weapons. His short, shaggy hair needed a trim, and his stubbled chin darker, going another day unshaven.

"I see why looking cute is important," Palla said sotto voce to her daughter.

Doc met him at the end of the gangplank with a hug.

"It is good to see you. Is Key coming out?"

"Key isn't coming, Doc," he said. "I'm sorry."

Doc held herself straight, keeping her emotions under control. "Tell me what happened when you can," she said.

Samara, who did not hear Coop tell Doc about Key, pushed in to give him a hug.

"Is Trak with you?"

"He stayed on Enparatus," Coop answered as he extracted himself. "He was injured, but he's okay. He gave me the key to the saucer. But I'll explain it all later. I think I should meet your mother."

Taking him by the forearm, with Doc following, Samara led them to her waiting mother.

"Mother, this is Daniel Cooper from the planet Earth. He is captain of the Wraith ship, Cassandra, and my friend. He is also the one who rescued Alucha and Mandara. Coop, this is Palla Athodite, Suzerain of the Helacene Alliance."

"I'm not sure of the proper protocol," he began, cut off when the tall woman hugged him.

"It seems to be the new protocol," she said, stepping back from the embrace. "Especially for the one who saved my daughters."

"I had a lot of help," Coop replied. "Including Doc, Samara, and important people who died or were injured. I assume you know about your son, Alain."

"I killed him," Samara said, her left hand resting reflexively on the hilt of the knife sheathed on her waste.

"Before he killed me," the Suzerain added.

"We have another threat to discuss," Coop said. "Your fleet is sailing into a trap. You need to warn them."

"There isn't time," Palla said. "Samara told me everything already. Even our communication drones cannot get the message to them in time."

"I contacted Taah on Clyde after I departed Enparatus," Coop told them. "D'Sey and the others are on their way to Geras. They can't get a message to them any faster. He's hoping to get there in time to warn them before the Shroud attacks."

"If our fleet is destroyed, Phortis will not be concerned about taking Nessur," the Suzerain said. "He'll bring the Shroud here to finish what Alain began."

"I need to get equipment off Cassandra," Coop said. "Doc, get the pass-codes and frequencies used by the Alliance ships. Meet me back here in twenty. We'll take the Wraith and the saucer to Geras. With Menace, and the information D'Sey picked up on Chōntorham, we might make the difference."

"I'm going," Samara said. "I don't want to fight with you or Mother, but I've done enough to prove I can help."

"Having a Helacene princess on board would stop Admiral Epperan from firing on you," the Suzerain said, surprising her youngest daughter.

"Agreed, and she is good in a fight," Coop added, surprising her more. "Sam, whatever supplies you need, go get them. Be back in twenty or stay behind."

The young woman kissed her mother's cheek and raced toward the manor. Doc followed at a less hurried pace, smiling and shaking her head.

"No need to say it," Coop said to Palla. "I'll make sure she gets home, regardless of what else happens. I'm not losing another team member on this mission."

The woman nodded, accepting the word of a man she did not know from a world she never heard of before today.

Cassie, fully materialized and completely nude met him in the cockpit, had him undressed and on a bunk before he could say a word. Ten of twenty minutes used up with the furious coupling.

"I missed you, too," he said. "We have a lot to do, and we now have only a few minutes."

Back outside the garden's back entrance, Coop waited with his go-bag at his feet. Doc returned first, handing him a data-chip.

"All the communication codes, call signs, and anything else the military liaison could think of," she said. "I have a copy for Cassie. Do you want to send it to Taah, or have me do it?"

"I will. Clyde and the saucer are both Nakki. They communicate quickly."

"I wondered about the ship," she said. "Tell me the whole story when you tell me about Key. What's the plan, Captain?"

"You and Sam with Cassie," he said. "You saw what she did to that battlecruiser, so you know this little ship has a big bite. Cassie pilots. Sam can handle communications from the com-tact set-up in the galley. She will coordinate with the Alliance Fleet ships. You do the shooting."

"Seems like I should fly and Cassie should shoot," Doc argued. "I'm not the best shot, and she seems capable."

"Against one or two ships, maybe. Not in a dog-fight with multiple boogies. There is a minuscule but predictable lag time between target acquisition and pulling the trigger with AIs and avatars. Partly the thought process, but mainly due to codes added because artificial intelligence machines once killed a lot of humans. You go on instinct. See the target, kill the target."

"Why does it sound simpler than it probably is?" she asked.

"It is that simple, Doc," Coop said. "You save lives each time you take out a bad guy. You will have a day to get comfortable with the weapons' capabilities. Cassie will help. Here comes Sam."

Wavy hair pulled under control with a cap, curved bill, and a go-bag of her own, the princess dropped hers next to his.

"Nice knife," he said, nodding at her belt sheath.

"Cassie let me borrow it," Samara replied. "I'll put it back in the armory when I board."

"Don't," Coop answered, noting the catch in the girl's words as she promised to return the weapon. "Elie would want you to have it, and I can make her another."

The beaming smile answered in more ways than any words she could have used.

"Sam, I'm counting on you to watch Doc's back," he told her. "Doc will be shooter, and you need to handle coms and coordinations with the other alliance ships. If you see or hear anything you think she or Cassie needs to know, pass it on. Don't hesitate, and don't over think. In a battle you act, or you die. Worse, you get someone else killed."

Thinking about the short, deadly encounter with her brother, Samara grasped the concept and understood the importance of

Coop's words. With her hand firmly wrapped around the exposed hilt of Elie's, now her, knife, she answered, "Yes, sir."

Coop hugged Sam and then Doc. As they made for Cassandra he collected his bag and jogged up the gangway to the Nakki saucer.

Standing alone on the veranda, Suzerain Palla watched the two alien ships depart. The future of the Helacene Alliance in the hands of pirates, a stranger, and her teenage daughter. Instead of worry, she experienced a moment of tranquility.

Chapter 34

"Arrival in the Geras system will occur three-point-four-one-hours prior to the Wraith," a male voice informed him.

Coop sat in the pilot's seat. The only seat in the Nakki ship. Located center forward on the deck forming the highest level within the rounded ship. After starting the ship's engines, the seat molded to his body, creating a comfortable perch.

"From the information provided by CLIDD Alpha-Two, I calculate the arrival of Menace and Agent D'Sey at two-point-five-zero hours prior to our arrival."

The voice began talking shortly after Coop turned the obsidian key and pressed the button he translated roughly as labeled CY-CLE-UP. The voice spoke in a language his Fellen-designed translator could not decipher. He began to explain who he was, and continued into a synopsis of the past week. The voice interrupted in Earth english with a single instruction; "Patience."

Taking it as an order and not a philosophical imperative, he sat while lights flicked on and off. A low hum rose from the levels below. It lasted two minutes, diminished, and disappeared. The walls around him vanished. Trak, too injured to enter the ship with him, sat against a stone wall. The nomad made no sign he could see Coop. He assumed the disappearing walls constituted a one-way effect.

"I made contact with CLIDD Alpha-Two," the voice said when it returned. "It required six-minutes-three-seconds while I updated my files. It appears two-hundred-thousand-thirty-seven-hundred-years and sixteen-days passed since my last update. CLIDD Alpha-Two informed me the last thirteen months required my immediate attention."

The cavern ceiling overhead began to retract. Trak, stood to keep from being pelted by incoming sand and debris. He waved and disappeared behind the door they entered through earlier.

"You are Captain Daniel Marcel Cooper, formerly of the United Earth's Space Fleet. You are designated a Space Ranger. Enhanced human. Your species discovered a similar Nakki hangar and reverse engineered many of the devices found to speed advances in your own technological evolution. You also possess advanced brain function following the revivification of your left cortex. It will make this easier."

"Make what easier?" Coop asked.

The walls, floors, and consoles around him disappeared. He sat in the command chair surrounded by the limestone walls of the cavern. When he looked down, between his legs, he could see the ground beneath the ship. He levitated, passing over the rim at the top of the cavern. Beneath him, the ceiling began to close. The sky, world, and stars above blurred as the saucer headed for space.

Coop, too excited by the thrill of flying, never considered fear. The void of space morphed into a spray of blue ribbons.

"We are in space-fold," the voice said. "Based on your history, I thought you would enjoy virtual flight."

The interior of the saucer returned.

"Space-fold itself is rather boring," his travel guide explained. "It can be mentally taxing as well. Better you experience the remainder of the flight in reality."

"Who are you?"

"I am, obviously, the ship. I am a guide, companion, pilot, explorer, maintenance engineer, teacher, student, and advance scout ship for the Nakki civilization. My personality is based upon the Nakki philosopher Ninart. Ninart is a great hunter. He hunts for the truth, as well as for the enemy of the Nakki. As you are now the pilot, I am to assist you in your mission."

"The mission being?"

"To protect the Helacene Alliance from the Kashōn Empire. Amazing to realize after more than two-hundred-thousand-years, a confrontation in the future is an echo of the war between the Nakki and the Basfor Flynn. It is humbling to think I will play a role in the outcome."

"Do you have a name?"

"A designation. I am KSS-delta-one-nine-one-six."

"Not Ninart?"

"Certainly not," the voice sounded aggrieved. "There is a Ninart, and I am certainly not he."

"Your designation is too long. Unless you have an objection, I'll call you Arty. CLIDD Alpha-Two is Clyde. The Wraith ship is Cassandra, and I am Coop. Got all of that Arty?"

"I do."

"Great. Now how do I fly this ship? How do I tell you where I need you to go? Do you have weapons?"

Chapter 35

The First Battle of Geras

Admiral CerVia Epperan grew up on the planet Sto Parquatil Bon, the Happy Place. Her race, the Paquatil connected to the Parq nomads of Enparatus somewhere in the forgotten past. Genetic tests proved the two peoples shared ancestry beyond the shared genes from seeding.

While the Parq turned away from technology and returned to a minimalistic style of life, the Parquatil evolved into a highly sophisticated, technologically advanced society. What the separated tribes maintained in common was a deep respect for nature. The Parquatil never allowed advancement to occur at the expense of their environment. As a result it remained a happy place.

CerVia shared more traits with her Enparatus kinsmen. A nomad's heart and itchy feet. As a youngster she spent hours at the space port near her home, watching ships of the Helacene Alliance come and go. Coming from faraway places filled with adventure, and traveling to exotic worlds inhabited by aliens.

She enrolled in the confederated worlds' military academy as soon as she reached legal maturity. Accepted, she left Sto Parquatil Bon for a distant planet and the training academy of future service personnel. CerVia graduated, joined the Alliance fleet as a rookie pilot, and grew in experience and rank as the fleet grew around her.

No one expected anything less from Epperan than her rise to a commission as Fleet Admiral.

One year and one day after the ceremony, she commanded the largest gathering of warships and personnel from the twenty-six inhabited planets forming the confederation. On her shoulders rested the responsibility to protect the Helacene Alliance.

"Geras gate in fifteen-minutes, Admiral." The news given her by the Prudent's captain. Epperan sat in her Admiral's chair, dead center of the Command and Operations Bridge of the RS Prudent, the only Carrier-Cruiser in the fleet. The ship designed, constructed, and launched by the people of Sto Parquatil Bon.

"Too bad they haven't completed construction of the fighters," Captain Aether said. "It would have been nice to actually be a Carrier."

"They'll be waiting on us, Captain," Epperan said. "In the mean time you command the most advanced Cruiser in the fleet. Are we in contact with the other ships?"

"Most of them," he replied. "There are a few stragglers joining us from the outer systems. We do not have drone repeaters in every channel."

The proximity alarm sounded. It did not include a warning regarding any obstructions. The pilot activated the gate, and the RS Prudent re-entered normal space at the edge of the Geras system. The Geras star, a yellow giant, shone brightly in the distance. A massive planet crossed between them and the star. The juxtaposition made it appear like a black iris within a glowing eye ball.

"Nothing on any scans," reported the officer on station. "The planet is devoid of any life. Large deposits of minerals, but all base metals. Molten core, slow rotation. The density and composition makes it impossible to scan beyond the core. The other two planets are proximal the star. One on this side and one with three moons on the far side. Other than us, three dead planets, and three unlivable moons, the system is empty."

"Captain, take a position up one-million miles out, on a line between the gate and the planet. The distance will allow room for the following ships to gather without creating a jamb at the wormhole. The alignment will make it simpler to reverse course when we depart.

"Aye, Admiral. Pilot, you heard the order. Proceed. Do you want to dispatch a ship to scout the planet?"

"It would take a fast ship forty-hours to get there," the Admiral said. "I intend to be on our way to Nessur sooner."

Aether hesitated, but nodded. A stickler for rules, operational guidelines said survey nearby objects when scans could not do a complete job. The timeline did indicate a ship sent would be left behind before it could reach the planet and make a complete circuit.

"Expect to require ten hours for all fleet ships to arrive," Epperan said. "I'm going to attempt to sleep. I suggest you pass that order around to your crew and to the incoming commanders. There may not be a chance for a long respite after we depart for Nessur. Inform all ships' captains and first officers to prep for conference in twelve hours. The bridge is yours, Captain."

The bridge security officer called "Attention!" Everyone not standing, rose, stood tall, and placed an open palm on their upper chest, fingers pointed at their shoulder.

"Back to stations," Captain Aether said as the door sealed behind the Admiral's departure.

Epperan returned to the bridge ten hours later. The command bridge placed amidship by the designers, believing it wiser for the ship's operation center best located as far from enemy fire as possible. Most vessels still used the outdated, traditional design with command placed on or near the top deck. A useless tradition considering there never truly was a top or bottom when in space.

"Everyone here, Captain?" she asked, taking her seat after placing the crew at ease.

"One Corvette dropped out of wormhole for maintenance issues. Two gunboats and nine frigates still in transit. We have a total of ninety-six ships on site."

"Give me a quick breakdown. Class and numbers will suffice."

"Eighteen Battleships, thirty Corvettes, twelve Missile Boats, six Gunboats, twenty-nine Frigates, and one Carrier-Cruiser," the Captain responded. "The largest Alliance Armada in history," he added.

"Will all ships be able to conference?"

"Aye, ma'am. Communications already tested every connection. One-hour-forty-three minutes until mission conference begins."

"Captain, your attention please." The lieutenant overseeing electronic scans called for her commander.

Aether joined the officer. They engaged in a hushed, heated discussion as both studied the latest intel.

The ship's captain issued an order to his communications team. "Long-range optical scans on the planet, now. Put the video stream up."

The planet, eight-million-two-hundred-thousand-miles away came into view. Instead of waiting for a holographic or 3-D display, the tech running the incoming video sent it to the forward screen as a flat display. All eyes went to the picture.

Black dots moved away from the planet from every direction. They moved out, and more continued to come. In thirty-minutes the numbers of dots appearing on screen made the star behind the planet appear covered by netting.

"The Shroud," Aether said. "The Kashōn Shroud Fleet."

"How many ships?" Epperan requested.

"Six-hundred-sixteen," the lieutenant answered.

"They were waiting until our entire fleet gathered," Aether said. "We have thirty-six to forty-hours before they can arrive. They can launch long-range weapons from half the distance. It may give us time to reach the gate."

"We aren't retreating, Captain," Admiral Epperan said, bringing the bridge from excited murmurs to complete silence. "We knew we might face the Shroud when they attacked Nessur. This may be a different system, but it falls within Alliance space. In fact, because there is no life in Geras, this may be the best place possible for us to confront the Kashōn. Inform the battle group the mission conference will begin in fifteen-minutes. We will adjust. We will face them, and we will defeat them."

"Admiral, you need to make the conference a quick one," the lieutenant said. "The first line of Kashōn ships are advancing at three-times the speeds indicated as top velocity by our reports. They will be here in twelve hours. Within targeting distances in six-to-seven hours. If those reports are accurate."

Admiral Pitaritis ordered his five SuperCruisers forward. His own Juggernaut remained to the rear, for the safety of the King.

The EMDrives neared depletion. They would be unavailable following the charge from the planet to where the Alliance ships gathered.

The five attacked in the Kashōn wheel formation. One ship in the center. The other four flanking at the four points of the compass. As the formation punched into a fleet of enemy ships, the four outer vessels would break off destroying their enemy in a wide swath.

Epperan had no intention of presenting a pretty package of ships for them to plow through.

"Battle positions A-One," she ordered. "Tactical, report."

"Ships deploying," responded Tac-Officer. Tac-Off the position in charge of monitoring asset placement and maintaining numbers from ships, to crew members, to armaments available. "Scatter pattern with Prudent center point. Loose alignment into sub-battle groups. Fifteen Battleships forward with force fields at maximum and density reconfigured for greater depth facing incoming enemy ships. Each Battleship has two Corvettes protecting their stern."

"Are the smaller ships moving into place?"

"Aye, Admiral. Ten of the twelve Missile Boats and five Gunboats have attached to assigned Battleships. Fifteen Frigates are deployed, and fourteen remain in reserve. Four of those are re-supply ships and two are medical-hospital. We have eight Frigates rigged for combat."

Tac-Off's heads-up display would provide a visual of the battlefield with ships designated by code and number. A running total of losses and remaining armament would run continuously along the left outer edge.

On the Admiral's virtual holo-display ships would be represented in icon form with their names beneath each floating figure.

Prudent sat forward with two Battleships starboard, below, and back. Directly behind the Carrier-Cruiser ran two Frigates and a Missile Boat. Behind the Battleships two more battle-ready Frigates matched course.

Fifteen Battleship Sub-Battle Groups (BSSVG) spread out around the Flag Ship.

In reserve: One Battleships, one Missile Boats, one Gunboat, and the ten remaining Frigates, including those tasked to supply or medical."

"Do I have the spread?" Epperan asked.

"A-One is complete," Tac responded. "Enemy SuperCruisers are four-hours-eleven-minutes out. Maintaining the circle grouping. Scans detect enemy fire, Admiral. Lasers targeting our Battle-ships."

The Captain in command of the initial wave ordered his gun-ners, and those of the other four SuperCruisers, to fire laser can-non. Each SC-Class vessel could rotate nine-of-twelve cannon forward. Forty-five weapons assigned to sixteen targets.

"All ships are firing, Captain," his Operations officer reported. "Lasers have reached the enemy line. We have forty-percent im-pact, with no evident damage."

"Forty-percent!" the Shroud veteran howled. "Forty-five can-non and only eighteen made contact. I thought SuperCruisers were provided the best gunners."

"The enemy ships are widely separated," Ops answered. "From this distance they were able to adjust courses. They have plenty of space to maneuver. The telemetry data shows their shields are able to configure to provide additional density against incoming fire."

"They can do that?" the frustrated Captain asked. "Can we?"

"No, sir," the Bridge engineer answered. "Our power couplers distribute the force fields evenly. The electro-magnetic charges are bounced off the hull and the result is a unilateral distribution across the entire ship."

"No would have been enough," the Captain shouted at the en-gineer. "I don't need a fucking science lesson every time I ask a question. Did any of their ships return fire?"

"No, sir," responded Ops, and not a word more.

"Not a particularly impressive first strike by the SuperCruis-ers," Phortis said to his brother.

"Nothing more than a preliminary jab," Pitaritis replied. "When they get closer, their weapons will decimate the Alliance's big ships. Our Battlecruisers and Destroyers will follow, over-whelming the smaller ships. By the time the Penetrators and Swarm arrive, there will be nothing but lifeboats and stragglers for them to wipe away."

"I commend your confidence, Brother," the King said. "Was it wise to send only five ships in your initial wave. The Kashōn way has always been to crush the enemy under the shroud of hundreds of ships."

"In a time before SuperCruisers," the Admiral replied. "Those five ships contain as much firepower as one-hundred Destroyers. With their additional speed, they can engage an enemy before it is prepared. An advantage worth another one-hundred ships."

"The additional speed is about to be used up," Phortis countered. "If your calculations are correct, the number of Alliance ships will make the initial thrust practically a one-to-one match."

"I may lose a couple of ships," Pitaritis conceded. "My Battlecruisers will arrive five hours into the initial confrontation. The Destroyers follow ten hours later. Our fleet will roll over the enemy like storm waves battering the shore. With each wave of fresh assets, the Alliance will lose more of their vessels. Those remaining will become exhausted, and exhaustion will cause mistakes."

"Mistakes made in battle get you killed," Phortis repeated an ages-old tenet of Kashōn military lore.

"If you will excuse me, my King, I need to speak with my armory officers. They have been going over the data provided by your spy. By now I expect them to have discovered additional weaknesses we can exploit."

"By all means, Brother," Phortis replied. "We need every advantage we can find."

The Admiral departed, his departure ignored by the bridge staff as the ship was at battle alert.

"Captain Aritis," Phortis called to the ship's commanding officer.

The captain left the Ops console and walked at a deliberate, but unhurried, pace to his King.

At attention before the seated sire, he said, "Your Service, my King."

"Relax, Avae," Phortis said, his voice lowered to prevent his words reaching others on the bridge. "It must be difficult for you, cousin. Your ship, but operating with the Admiral and the Emperor aboard."

"It is an honor to have you aboard Jagannatha, King Phortis," the officer replied, not accepting the King's recognition of their relationship as an offer to relax. "It is my pleasure to serve as captain of the Admiral's flag ship."

"You, Avae, spread almost as much shit as your sister, Vistol," Phortis replied. "Without the crap, what is your professional judgement of our strategy to this point?"

"The Shroud Fleet has never faced opposition from an entire federation of planets," the captain answered. He kept his voice down to assure only Phortis heard. "Our victories always came from superior numbers attacking a single system. Even the most advanced civilizations we engaged sent fewer than twenty battle-worthy vessels to oppose us."

"And my brother's boast a new SuperCruisers is worth twenty-Destroyers?"

"Certainly five-times, and with the plasma cannon, perhaps ten," Captain de Aritis answered.

Phortis leaned forward and lowered his voice further. "Have we taken on too much, Avae?" the King asked.

"I don't believe so, my King. It may prove to be a more difficult battle than anticipated, but we are better equipped. The Alliance Fleet was unprepared for our ambush. We do outnumber them six-to-one."

"We have a long and storied past steeped in blood," Phortis said, feeling better about the current situation. "The Helacene Alliance has never been tested in battle. I agree, Avae. We will win."

Aboard the Prudent, the people on the bridge worked to display a calm no one felt. "The sub-battle groups have repositioned to scenario A-Two," Tactical reported. "Three sub-groups combined into each Triad. Five Triads to match the incoming enemy vessels. The enemy ships are separating to attack different sectors. Our ships created the bowl-effect you ordered, Admiral. The SuperCruisers will be attacking on a single-plane, while the Fleet ships respond from intersecting and parallel planes."

"Your plan gives us more angles and takes advantage of three-dimensional space," Aether said, "but it doesn't take away their weapons, Admiral."

"It gives us the opportunity to probe their defenses, Captain," the Admiral explained. "The multiple sub-battle groups will be able to fire on the Kashōn from different angles and with different weapons. Telemetry will follow every encounter, measure effects, and, hopefully, give us a strategy to attack more effectively."

"We're going to take casualties while we conduct these probes, Admiral."

"I'm not trying to sacrifice our people, Captain Aether," the Fleet Command Officer responded. "We aren't going to retreat, and we cannot win if we do not find holes in their defenses. Our ship commanders are top-flight. I expect them to avoid as much incoming fire as possible. Let's hope our forcefields stand up to the hits not avoided."

"SuperCruiser engaged by Triad Three," Tac called.

The SuperCruiser fired a spread of lasers as it neared a group of Helacene Alliance ships. The fifteen mixed Alliance ships fanned across the void in front of the massive cruiser. They remained in three loose sub-groups of five ships. While the lasers from the Kashōn SuperCruiser expanded to cover more area, the Alliance Battleships proved to be the primary targets.

"Super Cruisers have twelve laser cannon on surface-mounted platforms," Tac informed the Admiral as information arrived from the initial confrontation. "Three Battleships received hits, but shields held. Energy directed to protection reduced power to drive systems. Our smaller ships were missed."

The four additional Super Cruisers actively engaged Alliance ships minutes after the first ship fired.

"One of Triad One's Battleships has been targeted one-hundred-percent. The SuperCruiser ignored all other vessels."

"They appear to be doing their own probing," Aether commented. "Result, Tac?"

"The Battleship Catia's power generator is critical. The automatic diversion of power to shields attempted to keep pace with the extensive bombardment. Several sub-systems burned out. Catia has minimal maneuvering and shields are thin."

"Order the Captain to back off," Epperan said.

"The Kashōn must be getting the same information," Tac said. "The cruiser is ignoring incoming fire from the Triad and pursuing the Catia. Concentrated fire again. The Catia is breached, Admiral. Several sections open to space. Captain is ordering survivors to lifeboats."

"The other ships are firing on the Kashōn," Captain Aether interrupted the bad news. "Are we getting anything useful?"

"Our ships are firing lasers, thermal-nuclear and explosive missiles, and penetrator rods. The computers are receiving and analyzing all the results," Tac responded.

Epperan studied the five battlefields depicted by two-dimensional graphs on the forward display.

"We've lost two Corvettes and a Gunboat," she said. "Were they unable to avoid the lasers?"

"Missile kills," Tac reported. "The Kashōn launched self-guided missiles with mix-loads. The initial explosion is nuclear, disrupting the EM-generated shields. The first strike is followed by one, two, or three trailing missiles. An explosive missile penetrated one Corvette's hull. The explosive head detonated inside the ship. The other Corvette retained minimal shields, but three concurrent explosions created shockwaves strong enough to damage the ship's systems. The power generator was tied into one of those systems. After it shut down the shields failed. A SuperCruiser's centrifugal gun fired dozens of projectiles, shredding the ship. The Gunboat suffered erratic energy generation, most likely from proximity to the nuclear explosion crippling a Corvette. A laser burst shattered the keel."

"How the hell could they find weaknesses and exploit them so quickly?" Aether demanded from no one and everyone. "We have incredibly efficient computers and tactical software analyzing every shot fired, and we haven't found an answer to throw back at them. When did they become more sophisticated?"

On Jagannatha, Pitaritis, returned to the command bridge after updates from his armory experts, preened before his brother, the King.

"Our new Super Cruisers may win the war before the Battlecruisers arrive," Pitaritis said. An opportunity to shine in front of others, especially while his brother watched, never a moment to waste.

"I am pleased to see my decision to fund their construction was a wise one," Phortis countered. "I recall you were concerned about incorporating alien engineers and workers into the design and building of Shroud vessels."

"The additional security I authorized appears to have prevented any tampering," the Admiral replied. "As always, cooperation among the Ashemachers results in another achievement for the Kashōn Empire."

"The fleet is currently at eight kills, Pitaritis," the King said. "I believe that leaves eighty-eight enemy vessels. I would not count this as an achievement yet."

"The information the traitor, Alain Athodite, provided is proving reliable," Pitaritis responded, his demeanor less prideful and more commanding. "We know the enemy's weakest points. Our weapons appear capable of taking advantage of those weaknesses. My Battlecruisers are within firing range. In two more hours they will be on site. The combination of ships will slash through the Alliance fleet like a sharp sickle cutting shafts of grain."

"Giving the young Athodite a couple of planets is a cheap price for victory," Phortis said. "I was worried about your overconfidence, Pitaritis. I'm glad it was needless. The Shroud has evolved from victories achieved only through greater numbers to also winning with superior vessels. The combination of Super Cruisers and the largest fleet of warships in the galaxy will allow me to expand the Empire in every direction."

"Thank you for the vote of confidence," the younger brother said. "I believe we can begin moving Jagannatha closer to the action. You may enjoy seeing the Shroud sweep out the trash."

"And puts us nearer the wormhole gate," Phortis added. "When we finish here, we can move to take the Nessur system. The rest of the confederated worlds will fall into line quickly without a fleet to defend them. I will be returning to Chōntorham sooner than expected."

On the bridge of the HS Prudent, Admiral Epperan stood, unable to remain in her chair as ships died. Captain Aether joined her in front of the display.

"The Kashōn are breaking off contact," he told her. "Thirty Battlecruisers are inbound. I believe they are waiting to add their weapons for a final push."

"Losses?" she asked.

"We are now down a total of sixteen ships. Four Battleships, two Corvettes, two Missile Boats, four GunBoats and four Frigates," he answered. "It would have been a lot more if not for your strategy of dividing the fleet into sub-groups. Our commanders used space to our advantage. It confused the enemy ships, and they wasted a lot of munitions."

"It slowed them, but did not stop them," Epperan replied. "The wasted armaments will be nothing compared to what thirty additional ships will bring. Did we find any weaknesses?"

"They are not proficient at operating in multiple directions," he answered. "Our ships were successful at getting inside their defenses. We logged hundreds of hits against their shields."

"Their shields held," Epperan countered.

"Yes," Aether agreed. "We don't have a weapon with the strength to penetrate their force fields. We tried the nuclear-tipped missiles, followed by explosive missiles or penetrator rods. Their generators are too strong, or they use multiple power sources to allow maneuvering and shield generation to retain maximum capabilities. We timed the one-two punches as proximal as possible. The secondary weapons could not follow too closely or they would be caught in the initial explosion. By the time trailing missiles or rods arrived, the Kashōn's shields recovered."

"No soft spots in their forcefields?"

"Maybe," he answered. "The ships are simple designs. The SuperCruiser is a basic wedge, expanding in size as you move from nose to stern. Our techs believe the command bridge, operating systems, housing, and all non-technical, non-engineering activity is assigned the forward quarter of the ship. The remaining three-quarters hold engines, dynamos, munitions, and vital operational systems. Their forcefields are similar to our own, using electro-magnetic generated buffers. Theirs seem to increase or decrease in intensity depending on the surface area and thickness of the hull."

"The bridge and living areas are less protected than machinery," the Admiral surmised. "How much of a difference?"

"Not enough for our weapons to penetrate," he answered. "If the dynamos produced less power, the forward areas, especially the nose, would become vulnerable. We would need to damage the magno-electrical system to weaken their shield."

"Power systems located in areas protected by thicker hulls and denser shields," Epperan concluded. "The Kashōn are smarter than I ever realized."

"More likely, smart enough to use technology and brains from worlds they have conquered," Aether said.

"Same difference," the Admiral responded. "Order our ships to begin heading for the wormhole gate. The least protected first. Battleships and Corvettes will cover the retreat."

"Even if they can reach the gate and escape, those ships will not provide much protection for the Alliance," Aether said.

"No. But they will be alive," Epperan replied. "Move Prudent forward, Captain Aether. It's time to get bloody."

Aboard the lead SuperCruiser, the Captain received word of the Alliance ships in retreat. He did not hurry to the bridge. He felt no need to rush. They won the initial battle. The victory resulted in the Alliance retreat, a harbinger to the Empire winning the war.

"REPORT," he bellowed upon entering his command center.

"Eighty enemy vessels remain," Ops answered. "Smaller ships are breaking formation and making for the wormhole gates. The ships designated as Battleships and Corvettes remain. One additional ship is moving forward. Intel believes it to be the HS Prudent, based on specs for the Carrier-Cruiser Class among the Alliance fleet files King Phortis provided. Communication scans indicate significant chatter to and from this ship. Conclusion is it is the flag ship of their fleet commander."

"Force numbers?" he demanded, taking his seat. "And turn on the forward optics. I want to see the end of the Helacene bastards."

"Five Super Cruisers remain at one-hundred-percent operational status. Your display will provide details on the armaments available for each vessel. Thirty Battlecruisers will arrive on station in twenty-eight minutes. The BVG (Battlecruiser Battle Group) lead captain is available for you whenever you wish."

"Enemy formation?"

"We currently face the Carrier-Cruiser, three Battleships accompanying it, and the eleven Battleships surviving the first engagement. Twenty-eight Corvettes. A total of forty-three ships."

The interior nose of the SuperCarrier morphed from blank wall into a window. The window effect created by cameras and optic-software. The limited view allowed those on the command bridge to see ten of the forty-three ships, including the Prudent and three Battleships flanking her.

"Tell Captain Stongbä to move his ship to my port side," the Captain ordered. "Our two Super Cruisers will handle the Carrier-Cruiser and escorts. The other enemy ships will be divided between the other Super Cruisers and the Battlecruisers. Have our tactical computer assign primary targets. Their Battleships are our first concern. Corvettes secondary, and reassign ships as they become available."

Chapter 36

The Second Battle of Geras

"This is Admiral Epperan. I have ordered all communication channels open to allow every member of the fleet to hear. First, a moment of silence for those comrades lost today." All things stopped for ten-seconds aboard every ship present, including those coursing for the wormhole.

"Commendations to you all. Your service to the Helacene Alliance, and to the protection of the billions of people you represent will never be forgotten. To those who enter the wormhole, know you retreat to fight another time. You are not abandoning your fellow service people. I expect you to find safe haven, and from those ports continue the resistance to the Kashōn Empire's invasion of the confederation. Go with our blessings."

Epperan swiped her arm-pad control, removing the fleeing ships from her following announcements.

"Our mission now is to provide time for those ships in retreat to reach the wormhole and make their escape. Captains, remove power from laser canons. A laser is a powerful weapon, but not accurate. Reduce energy requirements to sustain life and gravity within your ships, and nothing more. The Kashōn are exploiting a weakness in our technology. By detonating their nuclear missiles against our shields, the resulting gamma radiation within the electro-magnetic pulse interrupts our electro-magnetic generated force fields. You will use missiles and solid penetrators to intercept incoming missiles before they can explode against your ship. I do not know if we have sufficient armament to match theirs. It will be nearly impossible to take out every nuclear missile before contact. Nor can we expect to eliminate those following. Do what you can with what you have."

The Admiral paused to allow her words to sink in to the thousands of ears listening.

"When you exhaust your supply, I expect you to disengage and seek safety. Whether you can hide in this solar system, or feel you need to run for the void of outer space, each Captain will decide. Your mission, at that point, is survival. When the Enemy ships depart Geras, return to the gate and join our sisters and brothers. Dying to shield the crews attempting to escape is an honorable death. Dying instead of fleeing when you can have no positive effect wastes valuable assets. Ships and, more importantly, people. You have your orders. You also have my respect. Fleet Admiral Epperan. Out."

She swiped her pad once more and tapped the icon for an armament update for the ships remaining. She ignored the individual stats and scrolled to totals available following the first battle.

Missiles with Superheated Plasma Generators: 30

Nuclear-Tip Missiles: 212

Explosive-Tip Missiles: 794

Projectiles (Long Rods): 13,972

Projectiles (Short Rods): 23,650

Nearly half of their armories used up during the initial confrontation.

Another icon provided an estimate on the number of missiles the Kashōn Shroud ships carried.

The tactical computer analysis, within a twelve-percent plus-or-minus for accuracy, indicated the five Super Cruisers carried a total of thirty-two missiles capable of delivering a nuclear payload. The Battlecruisers joining them would bring three-thousand missiles, one-third to one-half nuclear. One-thousand to fifteen-hundred.

The optimist in her said they stood a chance. The pessimist said they only stood a chance.

Three-Hours-Nine-Minutes into the second battle of Geras.

Prudent vibrated from the shock wave. Officers and enlisted on the bridge held onto anything solid. With reductions to the gravity stabilizers within the ship, falling could find you landing hard in a number of directions.

"The nuclear missile got through," Aether said. No one commented on the obvious nature of his statement. "Projectiles fired."

The Prudent exhausted its supply of explosive missiles intercepting barrage after barrage of incoming nuclear and trailing missiles. Based on the number of enemy ships targeting the Prudent, the Kashōn fleet commander deduced the Alliance Fleet Admiral was aboard the Carrier-Cruiser. Prudent, limited to long and short rod projectiles for defense, could not prevent all incoming nuclear-tipped missiles from making impact. The big ship received four nuclear blasts against her shields. Weapons systems were able to counter trailing missiles before a devastating hit could be made against the depleted shields.

Two hours earlier, one hour into the second battle of Geras, Epperan ordered her ships to go on offense. Using the same technique used against them, she launched nuclear missiles against Shroud space craft. Many had no effect, but a few did. The older Battlecruisers did not have the stronger defensive systems as the later models.

"Tac?" she asked.

The Tactical Officer, his head bandaged, refreshed his data. The first nuclear missile to impact the ship rocked her hard. With gravity lessened, he was tossed into the starboard bulkhead. Medics stopped the bleeding, placed an old-fashion wrap over a bandage, and, by his demand, placed him back at his console. His battle harness now secured to prevent any future unexpected travels.

"Seven Battleships destroyed. Four depleted and breaking for space. Twelve Corvettes down. Prudent, three battleships, and sixteen Corvettes remain engaged. The first wave of our retreating ships will be at the gate in one-hour-fifty-one minutes. The Kashōn will not be able to stop them from exiting," he added.

"Anything more from the ship which entered the system?" Epperan asked.

"No, ma'am. Sure it is a Kashōn design, but not a battle ship. More like a private craft, or possibly a light commercial ship. It moved away from the gate, but has not moved closer. It appears to be monitoring the action. No hails returned, and nothing hostile toward the retreating ships."

"Enemy numbers?"

"Our ships destroyed twelve of the enemy Battle Cruisers. Seven more damaged, but continuing to launch missiles. One of the Super Cruisers took damage to its stern keel section. A nuclear missile and plasma missile combo landed during a system failure, or perhaps while a dynamo recycled. The ship does not appear to have steering. It continues to fire on Alliance ships. Eleven fully operational Battlecruisers and four fully operational SuperCruisers."

The Admiral checked the running total of available armaments. The Prudent's two plasma missiles, two nuclear missiles, four explosive missiles, and 800-rounds of long rods available. The three Battleships combined for a total of four plasma missiles, twenty-two nuclear missiles, and thirty-six explosive missiles. Nine-hundred long rods left between them. The Corvettes had sixty-four missiles, and eight-thousand metal balls for their rail-guns.

Epperan's final ploy involved all ships firing on the four SuperCruiser with their remaining nuclear missiles. The nukes trailed by plasma missiles. The combined effect might take out the ships, but, equally important, the EMP from the nuclear detonations followed immediately by a superheated plasma explosion would create a screen. A concussive wave disruptive enough to allow the Alliance vessels a head start as they made to escape the Shroud fleet. The ships ordered to retreat earlier would be safe at the wormhole. She could think of nothing more they could accomplish before the eighty incoming Kashōn Destroyers arrived.

On the verge of sending out the order, the Prudent rocked violently.

"Four nuclear explosions on our bow," Captain Aether called. "Several missiles incoming from multiple angles. Where are my gunners?"

"Rail-gun port-side off-line," Tac answered. "Rail-gun starboard does not have an angle. Shield integrity at less than ten-percent. Multiple hull impacts in twenty-seconds."

Aether turned to look at Epperan, the unspoken truth passed between the two career officers. The Carrier-Cruiser would not survive.

Braced, Epperan gave a silent prayer for the future of the Alliance. As the twenty-seconds came and went, with no apocalyptic explosions, she turned a furrowed brow to her Captain and Tactical Officer.

"An unknown ship intercepted the incoming missiles," Aether said, looking over his Tac's shoulder. The ship paced the missiles and eliminated all eleven with multiple laser bursts."

"To the Helacene Alliance ships engaged with the Kashōn, I am an ally sent by Suzerain Palla." The voice crossed all channels, emitted through speakers, and heard by anyone with earphones or implants. "I do not have time for a conversation, Admiral Epperan. In thirty-seconds the five SuperCruisers will experience acute systems failures. Several, but not all of the Battlecruisers will suffer the same failures. Prepare your remaining missiles."

Aether regarded his commander. Epperan shrugged and passed the order to all ships, "Prepare missiles. Target all Super-Cruisers. Be prepared to fire on any Battlecruiser without shields."

Aboard Menace D'Sey piloted the ship into the midst of the Kashōn. Duly sat at the weapons console. Rox initiated a signal using the secret communications band provided by Dr. Scandeki Pau. The message contained a code designed to invade the operating systems on Shroud ships built over the past decade. The short embedded code the key given to them by the Ve, Docha. An off switch.

"Did it work?" Duly asked.

The SuperCruiser's bridge remained eerily silent. Expectation of cheers on the destruction of the Helacene Alliance's flag ship, dissolved to an uneasy hush.

"Where did that ship come from?" the Kashōn captain demanded.

His operations officer held a hand to request a moment while he scanned every data point of electronic surveillance the big ship possessed.

"I do not know," he finally answered. "The wormhole did not open. My only guess is they were here, hiding, since before we arrived. Even now our scans are having a difficult time tracking it."

The sudden jolt pushed the Captain from his seat. The large ram landed on his knees. Bridge lights dimmed, then returned. Soft whirls and whistling noises followed. Indicators of consoles and other electronics rebooting following an ugly shutdown.

"Now what?" the Captain asked, rising from the floor.

Ops needed a second for his display to recover. When it did, he wished it had not.

"The conduits from the magno-generators are closed. Power is no longer shunted to the converters for redistribution to systems. There is no electricity, and no electro-magnetic power to maintain shields. Bridge and essential systems currently using back-up batteries. Force field is down fifty-percent and dropping quickly."

"Coms, tell the other ships we need protection. Have them reposition to stand between us and the Alliance while we make repairs," the Captain ordered.

"The other Super Cruisers are experiencing the same cataclysmic failures," Coms reported. "Some of the Battlecruisers are, and others are not."

"Ops. Can you find the problem?"

"Yes," came the immediate reply. "A valve closed in the main conduit from each of the generators. Maintenance codes have been corrupted. The valve will not respond to commands to open."

"Then have someone open it by hand!" the Captain screamed.

"It's too late," Ops said, falling back into his chair. "Missiles incoming."

The Helacene Alliance ships coordinated firing solutions in seconds. Three nuclear missiles per SuperCruiser impacted, fired from Prudent, and the Battleships. The Corvettes reacted to the Shroud Battlecruisers. Of the eighteen Imperial vessels operational following the first battle, eight experienced electro-magnetic system failures. The eight Corvettes nearest the stricken enemy ships fired two nuclear missiles per target.

On the heels of the first swarm of missiles, five plasma missiles plowed into the five SuperCruisers. Conventional missiles with high-explosive tips crossed through the vacuum of space to slam into eight Battlecruisers crippled by the computer worm and immobilized by nuclear detonations.

Cheers erupted throughout the Alliance ships as thirteen of the Shroud Fleet's greatest ships cracked. The metal skins and frameworks superheated and expanded. As a result, they developed devastating fractures as the cold air of space rushed to quench the heat. Like an egg hit by a hammer, the vessels imploded first, and then exploded, spewing inorganic and organic material outward.

The remaining Battleships, every captain stunned by the sudden, catastrophic loss of their fellow fleet-members, backed away from the carnage. There would be no survivors to pick up. There was the distinct possibility they might be next.

Captain Aether needed to yell twice for the bridge crew to quiet.

"There are still enemy ships out there," he yowled. "Get to stations and tell me what they are doing. And where is that strange ship?"

"Six Battlecruisers are gathering 230,000 miles linear to star," Tac called. "Four of the seven damaged Battlecruisers remain in the battlefield. The other three were destroyed. The Shroud designated Destroyers are five hours from contact. Eighty of them, Captain. Another five-hundred smaller ships follow at sixteen to eighteen-hours. A single SuperCruiser has left the planet and is also headed this direction."

"The ship sent by the Suzerain? Do you have anything?"

"Must be a mistake," Tac answered. "I meshed the scans from the other ships with ours, and . . ."

"Go ahead, Tac," Epperan said from her chair. "Tell us all."

"The design matches only one in our records," Tac said. "The pirate ship Virago."

"The pirate Slate? You have got to be mistaken," Aether said.

"He's not mistaken, Captain Aether," the voice from earlier said over the bridge speakers. "He is misinformed. My ship is called Menace and my name is Veresk D'Sey, not Slate. Virago and Slate were names your people made up."

"Captain D'Sey, this is Admiral Epperan. How did you get access to our secure communications? And how did you get to the Geras system?"

"As I said, Admiral, Suzerain Palla asked for my help. She provided your secure channels, and everything else I needed. I'm here to help, but my ship, special as she is, cannot take on the remaining Shroud fleet. Considering your depleted stores, and your crews nearing exhaustion, you cannot either."

"Suggestions, Captain?"

"Retreat, Admiral. I will cover your back. Recall those ships in hiding and if they can reach the wormhole gate before the Destroyers, have them join you. You've done all you can. Considering you sailed into an ambush by a well-informed enemy with a hell of a lot more firepower, I would say you did the impossible. You survived."

"Is your ship special enough to hold off ten Battlecruisers, a SuperCruiser, and nearly six-hundred more warcraft?" she asked.

"I don't need to hold them off as much as delay them."

"Long enough for my ships to gate out of the system?"

"We can only hope, Admiral."

On the Jagannatha, Phortis demanded, "What just happened, Pitaritis?"

"What just happened? The Alliance ships destroyed five SuperCruisers and eight Battlecruisers," Pitaritis hissed. Our remaining Battlecruisers retreated. The Alliance ships are moving away, back toward the wormhole gate."

"And before?" the King demanded.

"The ship my analysts swear is the same pirate ship harassing us for decades broadcasted a signal to our ships. It contained a message using our secret codes. The message contained an order directed at the chip controlling the emergency shut-off valves on the energy conduits attached to the generators. After closing the valves, the code embedded a virus to prevent the valves being reopened."

Pitaritis completed the explanation, then spoke with his security chief. The chief left immediately after the Admiral stopped talking.

"How did the pirate get our codes?" the King asked.

"Probably from the same people who gave him the means of closing the valve. The same ones who installed a back-door switch able to close the valve. Most likely done when the valve was installed in the ship. Someone with access to our newest, most technologically advanced ships."

"Sentütol's alien tech and science program," Phortis spat. "Those fucking aliens sabotaged my fleet. Wait. This ship, Jagannatha is the latest one launched."

"I ordered my security people to kill every alien on board," Pitaritis answered. "Security will then supervise Kashōn engineers as they either replace the valves or build by-pass conduits. The same orders have been issued to all Shroud ships, old and new."

Chapter 37

Before The Third Battle of Geras

The Kashōn Shroud Destroyer represented the might of the Empire for centuries prior to the arrival of Battlecruisers. The ships constructed on simple designs. A V-Shape bow swept out as it rose on both sides. The exterior hulls extended one-thousand-feet back to a U-shaped stern with a flattened rear. The keel curved inward. Exhaust ports, one-hundred-foot cylinders, twenty-feet in diameter sat along the line where the ship's sides began to curve, extending twenty feet beyond the flat rear. The venting expelled heat and gas created by the four large ion-conversion generators powering the ship's systems, shields, and weapons. The contrails created when hydrogen particles and heat mixed added to the Shroud lore, as the deep mist made the killing machine appear to emerge from a grey hole in space.

Twin missile tubes at the bow, below the top-deck resembled flat-black irises. A massive centrifugal gun emplacement dominated the forward uppermost deck. The large pie-shaped base split, with automatic belt feed for three different types of penetrating rods. Five-hundred short-rod penetrators (SRPs), five-hundred long-rod penetrators (LRPs) and unique booster-assisted long rods (BLRPs) the size of tree trunks were fed from the ship's armory into the lower section of the gun mount. The upper section could rotate three-hundred-sixty degrees, and the barrel of the gun could elevate from zero-degrees to seventy-five degrees.

The upper section spun at an extremely high revolution and a rod fed into the breach would be ejected by centrifugal force. The kinetic energy created equalled a modern rail-gun but required one-fifth the power. The design allowed for rods of extreme size to be fired. Fired from space, these rods could destroy an entire metroplex on the surface of a planet.

The Command super structure sat behind the centrifugal gun. The vessel's most unique weapon located next in line. A laser cannon on rails which circled the ship. The wide-beam cannon could be placed anywhere on those rails, offering an unlimited field of fire.

"Duly, ordinance and specs for the Destroyers?" D'Sey asked. He knew the answer, and the Howler knew he knew. This was their way of remaining calm before a fight.

"Sixteen missiles," Duly began. "The mix can be nuclear, tactical nuclear, explosive, concussive, or flammable. No way to know the ratio. Each Captain arms for their personal preference."

"Estimated payload size?"

"Big. Average equivalent of twenty-thousand-tons of normal munitions. The Empire believes in overkill. The newer missiles come with guidance systems and thrusters. The initial firing provides most of the energy to cover the distance to the target. The thrusters allow the missiles to make minor adjustments in flight. A crucial advantage for long-range target acquisition. They operate autonomically after launch. Once they leave the tubes, the gunners forget them."

"Why don't they use remote guidance?" Rox asked. "Seems like it would be more accurate."

"Probably, but you need personnel to do the work," Duly answered. "Destroyers work with minimal crews. They need space for power and weapons."

"Go on," D'Sey said. He allowed Menace to drift. The ship monitored the remaining Shroud Battlecruisers in case a commander decided to launch something in their direction. Nothing offensive came from any of them since the end of the second Battle of Geras. Might be an indication of depleted armaments, or they could be waiting for reinforcements before throwing leftovers at them.

"The centrifugal gun has been around for centuries. Great design, allowing a ship to fire large rods with minimal energy required. Because the centrifuge spins at a high rate, it can fire dozens of small rounds per minute. Because they use centrifugal force, there is no recoil. The gun barrels can be adapted to two widths. One for normal rods and one wider for the over-sized penetrators. The information we stole from the outpost we raided a few months ago hinted the Kashōn added booster rockets to the super-long rods. Seems like a waste of energy for a kinetic weapon."

"Flight adjustments?" Rox suggested. "Like the missile boosters."

Duly only shrugged. The stolen data did not include the theory or practical application expected from the boosters.

"The final weapon, the laser cannon can circle the entire ship. It is a slotted muzzle design and emits a wide beam. The Destroyers use four magneto-electric generators. One is dedicated to the laser cannon. One is dedicated to maintaining the ship's forcefield."

"Weaknesses?" D'Sey asked.

"Relatively slow in comparison to more modern ships," the Xentarene replied. "They are built to plow, not to race. Eighty of them at once means one damn-big field they can cover. No records of Destroyers being defeated in battle. I'm not sure if we can distract them."

"I might be able to help out."

The voice interrupting came through the pirates' trans-com implants, and it was easily recognized.

"Cooper," Duly replied. "Where the fuck are you?"

"If you had windows, I'd be the guy sitting next to you," he answered.

"Display exterior," D'Sey ordered. The interior walls of the bridge shimmered and turned into windows. Actually three-dimensional high definition video reproduction of space as fed to the simulator from external cameras. A white and grey disc hovered fewer than one-hundred yards off Menace's starboard.

"A Nakki scout ship," D'Sey said aloud. "How did you get your hands on a Nakki ship? And how did you get close without my ship setting off alarms?"

"Arty informed Menace who we were and requested she not warn you. You remember telling me about abandoned Nakki outposts scattered around the Milky Way. Ones similar to the Martian hangar?" Coop's tone indicated he thoroughly enjoyed surprising the pirates. Perhaps payback for ripping Cassandra from space-fold without a warning.

"Yes, and who the fuck is Arty?" D'Sey was not amused by the situation. He was also not used to being the one surprised. Duly and Rox thoroughly enjoyed it, holding back amused noises, but not wide smiles at D'Sey's discomfort.

"Arty is the ship's guide," Coop answered without extrapolating. "The ship was left in a hidden hangar similar to the one found on Mars. It was on Enparatus, and, according to Arty, left behind over two-hundred-thousand-years ago. Unlike the saucer on Mars, this one came with a key. I'll explain more and potential tactics we can use against the Kashōn, but there is something more important I need to tell you. Key died on Enparatus."

D'Sey gave no outward emotional sign. Anger or sadness. Rox and Duly lost their smiles, dropped their heads as one. Everyone on Menace's crew knew loss, but it never made the death of a friend easier.

"Doc, Taah, and Teak know," Coop added. "He died protecting my back."

"We knew the princesses were safe, and Doc told us about Alain Athodite's treason," D'Sey said. "Key was a good being. He was a better friend."

"The Destroyers are less than three-hours out," Duly said, distancing himself from the loss of Key with a more immediate problem. "You said you have a plan."

Chapter 38

The Third Battle Of Geras

"The first wave of Alliance ships is beginning to enter the wormhole," Rox reported. "The Admiral's Cruiser and the remaining Battleships are further away than hoped. Those ships are pretty beat up. The one's with full power continue to escort those with damaged flight systems. The four ships able to escape into the system during the battle are now incoming. Dee, if the Shroud Destroyers get through us, they could catch the Alliance ships before they can exit."

"Let's hope Coop's plan works," the pirate captain and Nakki agent replied. "Never heard of anything like it before, but I am only a few thousand years old. Duly, do you have the weapons set?"

"Pulse cannon and rail-gun ready to integrate with Coop," the large armament expert answered. "I finished uploading the improvements from the scout ship. I don't understand how an ancient Nakki ship has better targeting capabilities than Menace. She is a Nakki ship, too, and much newer than the saucer."

"Nakki are too smart for us," Rox responded. "Always they are so superior. They did not think anyone but a Nakki could handle their more advanced weapons. Shanks."

"What can we expect from the upgrades?" D'Sey asked.

"Laser accuracy and improved range limitation. The added inline coherent targeting system adjusts with each shot. By determining a proper range, the beams don't simply keep going if they miss. More punch and more precise. Menace also now has linear quadratic estimation neuromorphic chips."

"Say that again," Rox bantered. "I'll bet anything you can't get it all out the same way twice."

Duly grinned and agreed, "Probably not. But it is cool what it does. The chips improve the operating computer's cognitive adaptation relative to adjustments made on any of our firing platforms to make firing patterns more exact. We are now quicker on the draw, and can adjust aim between shots, regardless of the weapon or the speed of fire."

"There is a lot of physics, and science, and words I don't get," Rox admitted. "Guess what matters is will it all work?"

"About to find out," D'Sey said. "Shroud Destroyers have broken into two major groups of forty ships. The first forty are within range and firing missiles. Duly, try out your improved laser cannon. I count twelve incoming missiles from six Destroyers."

"Done," Duly replied, pressing one icon and two keys. "Lasers fired, and, wait for it, twelve-of-twelve hits. We can hit tin cans in space, Dee."

"Nice shooting," Coop said. "The Destroyers are spread, but arranged in pods of four. Heading for sixty-five-by-one-by-eight (the three points representing a position is space relative to the two Nakki ships at zero). D'Sey take them from port to starboard."

D'Sey did not answer, but pushed his sleek craft forward, leading the flying disc to the designated battle group pod .

"Start sequence now," he ordered.

Duly fired their pulse cannon. The electromagnetic pulse, a non-nuclear level wave, contacted the Destroyer's EM-generated forcefield. The contact created a burst of electrical energy which, in turn, charged electrons and ion particles in contact with the shield.

Coop swooped around and in front of Menace, firing the scout ship's laser ray gun. Unlike laser weapons he was accustomed to handling, the gun aboard the Nakki ship included a variant range from a low end, where the laser beam did little more than act as a pointer, to a high end emitting a ray in excess of one-hundred-fifty-million degrees Celsius. When the super-heated laser hit the EM-excited ions they turned to gas and continued to morph into dense plasma radiation. The effect bathed the Destroyer in an aurorae of green, blue, red, and purple.

As the saucer cleared, Duly fired a dozen Long-Range Penetration (LRP) rods into the colorful display. The plasma cloud diffused the dense metal rods, turning them into grey dust. The dust particles attached themselves to the ship's forcefield, magnetized to the EM-electrically charged electrons within the shield.

"They're blind," Coop announced. "Total particle adherence. None of their scanners, optics, coms, nothing electronic can enter or exit through the coating."

"They can still fire weapons," Duly said.

"Yep. But missiles will get their own coat as they pass through making guidance systems inactive. Rods and lasers will be fired blindly. They might hit their own ships. But every time they do fire, a hole will be carved into the forcefield. It will only take a few seconds for the generators to fill it in, but it creates an opening where they are vulnerable to incoming fire."

"You sure they can't shake the dust off?" Rox asked.

"I'm going on information Arty provided about how the Nakki fought the Basfor Flyn, and I'm adapting with the weapons we have available. The science is good, but I can't promise anything. The only way I can see for them to get out from the particle sheet is to drop their forcefield and cruise far enough away the dust is no longer attracted to the shield."

"Leaving them with no protection," Duly added. "Now what?"

"The other Destroyers have no idea what happened, and this guy can't tell them," Coop replied. "But they know it isn't good for them. I read dozens of incoming missiles, as well as laser fire attempting to bracket us. We're both fast and small. We take advantage of those qualities. Let's hit these other three Destroyers. Keep your scans tuned for any weapons fired from a coated ship. You'll have three, maybe four-seconds to fire your lasers into the hole left by the wake."

D'Sey began the ballet. He repositioned Menace for the jab, an EM blast from the pulse cannon. Coop swung through and superheated the EM with the saucer's laser, and Duly landed the next punch with the LRPs.

The Destroyers attacked by the two small ships could not adjust and fire at the ships quickly enough. The enemy fighters flew within yards of the much larger Destroyers. The code-writers for the targeting systems never considered aiming at anything within five-hundred-yards of a ship.

Other ships disengaged from their four-vessel pods to fire from distance. Being careful not to fire into their own ships, they launched dozens of guidance-aided missiles at the two enemy spacecraft. Laser beams flashed through the void of space, and while none made contact, the concussive waves created by the sheer number of beams made for a shaky ride.

"Coated ship firing missiles," Coop called. "Targeting the funnel with laser fire."

"Rox, results?" D'Sey called to Silvanaē.

"Oh. My. Word. To. Thau." she said each word staccato in her awe. "The laser was still set at the maximum heat level. The Destroyer is boiling inside the coated forcefield. I have no other way to describe it. The shields, with the magnetized dust sheet are acting like a microwave container. Dee, you ever put something in a microwave prep station and set the timer for too long?"

"It explodes," he answered.

"Messes up the whole inside of the station," Duly added.

"The inside of the Destroyer looks like the inside of a microwave prep station after something big and juicy went boom," Rox said.

"So it works," Duly said, and added a toothy grin. "Another ship fired its laser. Got a pretty slotted hole in the shield. Wonder what a laser without the super-heat knob on it can do. Firing."

The advanced targeting capabilities placed three laser bursts through the slot before the dedicated generator could close the hole.

"Got a reading before the metal particles closed over the new shielded area," Rox said. "I can't promise, but I think you took out their laser cannon. Maybe a section of the port hull, but I don't see any sign of implosions."

Menace and the scout ship continued to dance around the Shroud fleet. The three step waltz consisted of coating a forcefield, avoiding incoming enemy fire, and shooting at any opportunity to take advantage of a rift in a shield. Two hours into the third battle of the Geras system, Menace got rocked.

An explosive tipped missile detonated on the pirate ship's lower starboard side. The concussion pushed the ship into a spiral until D'Sey could right them. He dropped the ship in an elevator to avoid a second explosion.

"They set the missiles for proximity detonation," he said. "They don't care if they hit us, or if the missiles go off near one of their own. Rox, do you have an update?"

"We've coated twenty-eight Destroyers," she answered. "Between Coop and us, eight have been destroyed, and eight damaged. The second wave of Destroyers continue to make for the wormhole and the Alliance ships. At this rate they may get enough ships through to cause serious harm to the Helacene ships waiting to gate out."

"We have another problem," Coop said trans-ship. "The SuperCruiser that did not join the first battle is moving this way, and coming fast. EMDrive. I ran the numbers, and she's too big for the metal dust coat to work. Too much surface area. If we are forced to face it, the remaining Destroyers will tear the last of the Alliance ships to pieces."

"The Shroud Destroyers are repositioning," Rox called. "The twelve ships from the first wave are converging. Aligning to create three intersecting diamonds. Twenty ships dropped from the second wave. Pairing up and setting up roughly between our two ships and the wormhole. The paired Destroyers are taking positions over a wide expanse. The region is too large to box us in, but the ten pairs and the triple-diamond group will place us in the middle of their sights."

"The SuperCruiser will be here within two hours. They are within target acquisition range for most of the weapons I've seen used," Coop interjected from the saucer. "I don't know if they are able to fire while using the EMDrive."

"Twenty Destroyers continue to head for the wormhole," Rox added to the running account of current battlefield conditions. "I detect missile signatures."

"Confirmed," Coop replied. "They fired on the retreating ships. Two per ship. They are firing a second salvo."

Duly and D'Sey held back any comments or questions as they watched Rox watch her heads-up display. Coop would be doing something similar on the Nakki scout ship. Three-minutes ticked away. Rox waited another full minute before saying, "Four missiles per ship. Eighty total. Radiation levels indicate the initial payloads are nuclear. The trailing forty are non-nuclear. Can't tell what they are packed with."

"They targeted Alliance survivors queued at the gate," Coop said. "With the distance and time, can the remaining ships defend themselves?"

"Tactical analysis estimates the Battleships and Corvettes combined carry fewer than two-dozen missiles," Rox informed both ships. "The Battleships have laser cannon, but nothing super accurate. The Corvettes still have thousands of LRP projectiles."

"The Kashōn missiles have booster rockets and on-board guidance," D'Sey interjected. "Guidance means avoidance. If the Admiral orders missiles and long range penetrators fired for intercept too soon, the majority of the incoming missiles will evade and proceed. If she waits too long, they may not be able to intercept enough for it to matter."

"At best they might take out half," Duly said. "I'm talking about half of the ones in flight. Those twenty ships alone carry another two-hundred-forty. If we leave to help, the thirty-two surrounding us will fill the void with everything they have. It's what I would do. I'd set every tip with a proximity switch."

"They would be wiping out the coated Destroyers if they do," Rox countered. "Those proximity sensors can't distinguish us from them."

"The SuperCruiser has Phortis aboard," D'Sey reminded them. "He'll destroy half his fleet if it kills us at the same time. Cooper, we've spent the last hundred years operating as marauders. You're the military expert. You decide. We'll follow."

"Arty will contact Admiral Epperan. The Alliance ships will need to take out as many nuclear-tipped missiles as they can. If they can't distinguish, he'll provide the telemetry for their gunners. If they can preserve shield integrity, they might be able to ride-out the hammering the next wave of missiles deliver. It may provide a little time before the Destroyers repeat the attack."

"They won't have anything to defend against a second barrage," Rox said. "And the Kashōn Destroyers will be much closer."

"One battle at a time, Rox," Coop answered. "I don't know how good your ship is, D'Sey, but if she's half as quick as this scout ship, we go old school. We attack the Destroyers attempting to box us. We go at fastest possible velocity short of space-fold. We do not slow down. We get in close and we hit exactly what we aim for. Then move on to the next boogie, regardless of the results."

"Menace is more than capable of keeping up," D'Sey assured his counterpart.

"You take the twelve in the tri-diamond pattern," Coop replied. "Watch for the SuperCruiser. It will arrive from the same direction. Sync your pulse cannon with your rod guns. If you get tight enough, you will be able to dent their shields enough for a rod or rods to reach the hulls. If they do, physics will take over."

Rox lifted a thumb, and Duly followed two-seconds later.

"Say when," D'Sey said, taking the ship's piloting controls away from any system interference or lag by placing the articulating flight controller in his hand.

"The Admiral has acknowledged Arty's instructions," Coop said. "Mission green in five - four - three - two

Chapter 39

The Fourth Battle of Geras

Daniel Cooper flew all sorts of ships, from in-atmosphere jets to space fighters, like Cassandra and Angel 7, to battle-worthy craft like PT-109, the John F. Kennedy. He flew at space-normal speeds as high as 300,000mph. The saucer traveled nearly twice as fast, placing him half-way to the scattered pair-groupings of Shroud ships before startled sailors realized the importance in the rapidly changing read-outs on their monitors.

By the time a warning relayed from tactical to command, the flying disc could be seen as a streaking blur on optics. By the time the first pair of captains ordered weapons to fire on the impossibly fast target, Coop had flown his borrowed ship beneath the keel of the nearest Destroyer. He fired a narrow-beam of charged electrons from a microwave emitter into the enemy's underbelly. The ship moved too fast for him, regardless of enhanced reflexes, to fire a second weapon. Arty, however, did not possess reflexes. The non-corporal guide, instructor, and team member was an integrated component of the Nakki craft. He was not an artificial intelligence with a lapse coded into his programming to delay killing others. There existed no lag between need to act and action.

Coop flew and triggered the microwave emitter. Arty released a weapon unique to anything in the experience of Daniel Cooper. The saucer, acting on the subtle variation in brain wave patterns as Coop called on the microwave emitter, fired a laser ray gun. The timing allowed the microwaves, which were faster, to pass the laser beam and impact the target nano-seconds before the beam arrived.

When the super-heated laser reacted with the electromagnetic pulse earlier, it resulted in a plasma aurorae. This time when the laser reached the shield, dented by the microwave, it created a different reaction. Instead of the intense heat creating a gas, it created a solid. Super-heated plasma-based liquid metal which rapidly solidified in the frozen vacuum of space.

The speed of the delivery turned the once liquid plasma into a spear. It pierced the depleted forcefield as an arrow would an apple. Physics took over.

The impact of the spear at extreme velocity resulted in several types of energy distributed throughout the Destroyer. Kinetic movement meant the solid plasma did not stop at penetration. It continued piercing the ship. Thick metal walls or organic matter split like butter.

The thermodynamic energy (heat) burned everything in its path for several yards. The intense heat continued to expand, broiling, boiling, and roasting the ship's interior, systems, and crew.

Acoustic energy created concussive waves capable of crumpling the densest frames and buckling hulls built to withstand the rigors of space.

All of these physics came into play within the milliseconds needed for the spear to pass through the ship, leaving a lifeless husk behind. The Destroyer lay dead in space, no oxygen left to create implosions. The once fearsome warcraft forge-welded into a single, massive billet.

The human pilot and audio-entity repeated the unique assault against the ship flanking the first. The blitz resulted in a similar heap of slag floating in space.

"That worked almost too well," Coop said.

"Similar to a tactic used by the Nakki against Basfor Flyn ships after they invaded the greater Milky Way," Arty said. "This ship never engaged in such an action, but we do possess everything necessary. Obviously."

Menace did not have the speed of the scout ship, but not far off. The sleek corsair streaked for the center of the three diamonds. The ships within the sub-battle group had more time to recognize the attack than those facing the flying saucer.

Lasers and missiles belched into the path of the pirate ship from all twelve ships as they tried to prevent the privateer from getting near.

D'Sey dodged the lasers and ignored the missiles, flashing past the over-sized darts and gone before the proximity switches detonated the warheads. Plumes of silent explosions peppered the dark skies behind the cream-colored spaceship.

The diamond pattern, meant to hold the enemy at bay, worked against the Kashōn. D'Sey understood the vagaries of outer space better than most, having lived among the stars longer than certain civilizations existed. He sent Menace into a pirouette. Prepared, Duly fired LRP rounds and EM pulse blasts as Rox fed the distance-to-targets to his console. Of the three, the Dualönges faced the most difficult task. She had to anticipate D'Sey's move. Next, she needed to set scans for the enemy Destroyer most likely to come up as the initial target. Quickly routing the distance to Duly, and as quickly determine the next quarry.

Menace spiraled. Rods released, pulse wave catching and passing the dense metal projectiles to impact the hunter-turned-prey's shields. Rods penetrated the outer hulls, blowing through inner liners, and continued through everything they encountered. Rods spent their momentum within the ships. The damage ranged from unusable sections closed off to prevent loss of atmosphere, to vital systems damaged to a degree the result would be terminal.

Others blasted through the opposite hull, leaving a gaping wound too large for emergency measures to shutter affected sections. These ships imploded. In all, the first group lost two Destroyers to catastrophic violent inward collapses. Another died slowly as system after system degraded and quit. Lights and lives snuffed out. The last one limped away, but with forcefield renewed. Engineers could save it.

"Bammies," Duly said.

"Whoop. Whoop," Rox added.

The Jagannatha's Tac officer said, "The jaghtschip [fast pirate ship] is too maneuverable for the Destroyers." He spoke aloud for either the Captain, the Admiral, or the King to hear the report. "It has a forcefield which appears to be reinforced. There is a magno-electric quality to the outer portion, but a different construct in the layers beneath. The proximal nuclear explosions weaken it.

However, laser or explosive charges at or near the enervated portions do not penetrate. The second layer appears to have an acoustic quality."

"A forcefield made of sound?" Phortis asked the question, but it came forth as questioning the Tac officer's information.

"Yes, your Highness," the ram replied. "It vibrates and scanners detect harmonic waves. It is not anything I have seen, or heard, before."

"Tell me about the disc-shaped ship?" Pitaritis demanded.

"Incredible speed, similar forcefield," the officer reported. "Unknown construction. Nothing with this exact design in our files. No known origin. Extremely difficult to scan. Unique weapons."

"You have told me nothing, Lieutenant," the Admiral replied, venom in the response. "Does your tactical analysis include any suggestions on fighting it?"

"Both ships, the saucer-shaped one and the one we believe to be the pirate vessel Virago, are B-Class sized. Similar in size to the larger yachts or smaller transport freighters. Their size is more of an advantage with their superior speed. They can fire accurately during acceleration and high-speed maneuvering."

"You continue to tell me what they can do," the Admiral nearly howled across the bridge. "What can WE do?"

"Overwhelm them, sir," the tactical officer answered. "A depleted Shroud Fleet maintains an enormous advantage in numbers and weapons."

Pitaritis activated his personal command channel and ordered two of the Destroyers in the dissected diamond pattern facing off against the pirates to move forward at best speed and engage the enemy.

He issued the same order to two Destroyers among the eighteen left fighting the saucer.

Pitaritis ended all communications with the four ships sent to draw the attention of the smaller enemy spacecraft.

"Captains," he said to the forty-two remaining Destroyers, the enemy ships are difficult to target, and difficult to hit. When scans indicate the four ships deployed to face them come under attack, flood the area with every weapon you have available. Use our Destroyers as the center point for your range of fire. The Jagannatha will add our compliment of weapons to yours. To the ships in pursuit of the Alliance ships trying to escape through the wormhole. On my order, fire half of your ordinance at those ships. The remaining armaments will be used against the two enemy fighters."

"Bait," Phortis said. "You are sacrificing four of your Destroyers to pull the bastards into a space small enough for the rest of the Fleet to permeate with firepower. I like it, Brother."

"Eradicating the fucking Helacene Alliance at the same time," Pitaritis replied. "The Shroud will add to our history today."

Menace completed her pirouette. D'Sey pulled his ship away from a second confrontation as the forward twenty Destroyers released a wave of missiles toward the wormhole gate.

"Cooper, the remaining fleet ships don't have enough firepower to stop those missiles," D'Sey called. "We need to finish here and use space-fold to get ahead of the attack. With the improved targeting acquisition, we might be able to prevent most of the missiles from reaching Helacene ships."

"Agreed," Coop answered. "Lining the two aspect-high incoming Destroyers up for the kill now. A soon as I'm done, I'll fold for the wormhole."

The micro-wave emitter activated, and Arty triggered a super-heated laser beam.

Aboard Mcnace, Duly and Rox repeated their earlier duet. They targeted the Destroyer port-side, low, and charging. Before the rounds could make contact, she began adjusting to direct weapons toward the starboard enemy ship. Then the Geras system erupted.

Captain Aether dropped into his command chair. "It's over, Admiral," he said. He sat unmoving in his chair, defeated. Exhausted from days with little rest and never-ending tension. "Two-hundred-forty missiles incoming with mixed warheads. More than enough radiation signatures to eliminate all of our shields. The region where the pirate D'Sey and the unknown saucer confronted the Kashōn reads hotter than the star. The Shroud Destroyers, all of them, fired everything into an area tighter than a small moon. The last SuperCruiser added lasers, missiles, and centrifugal-fired LRPs."

"The SuperCruiser fired its Ion-Plasma cannon into the region," Ops reported. "The recoil visibly rocked the ship."

"The Ion-Plasma weapon is designed for space-to-surface attacks," Aether said. "Anything inside the killing zone will be vaporized. At least they tried to gain us extra time to escape."

"Captain. Admiral. One-hundred-six incoming missiles have exploded." The bridge officer in charge of telemetry spoke as she rose from her seat. The holo-display hovering above her console sped blue-highlighted numbers across the air. Red bursts, and multiple color digital reports ran along one side.

"How many ships lost?" Aether asked.

"No, Sir, you misunderstood. Or I said it wrong. Or . . . I don't know, Sir, but the missiles exploded before reaching any of our ships," the excited younger officer explained.

"Visual," Epperan ordered. The SHD screen appeared. The tech in charge spun his track-ball until silent plumes lit distant space. Zoom, and the plumes grew, changing into colors indicative of the type of payload exploding.

"Is that a ship?" the Admiral asked. The object in question danced between the cameras and the explosions, backlit for a few moments as it moved from port to starboard and gained altitude, relative to their position.

"Low-profile fighter," Telemetry answered. "Unknown origin. I know its vicinity where it is, but scans barely see it. Surface is reflective and absorbent. If it wasn't for the heat variance between it, space, and the explosions, I don't think I could find it at all. It's firing a combination of lasers and kinetic rods. Extreme accuracy with both. Estimated velocity of the craft is two-eighty-six-thousand-mph."

"You're being hailed, Admiral. It's on the Suzerain's private channel," the Coms officer informed her superior.

"This is Admiral Epperan."

"Hi, Admiral, this is Princess Samara. I'm on the ship Cassandra. We're trying to shoot down as many of the nuclear-tipped missiles as we can. We're having to take out others 'cause they keep getting in the way."

In the background, the crew on the bridge of Prudent heard someone say, emphatically, "SAM!"

"Oh, sorry, Doc. Guess I'm excited. Sorry, Admiral. Anyway, Cassie says you need to tell your ships to fire lasers at the torpe-does . . . what, oh, does it matter? . . . the missiles."

"Princess Samara, we cannot hold our scans on your ship. If we fire lasers into the swarm of missiles, we might hit you accidentally," Captain Aether interrupted.

"Cassie says no worries. Gotta go."

"Cassie? Doc?" Aether asked.

"No worries?" Coms asked.

"Ops. Order all ships to fire laser at the incoming missiles," Epperan called. The bridge came to a halt as all eyes watched the display.

Hundreds of plumes erupted across the void as the small fighter targeted and destroyed nuclear warheads, and any missile getting in the way. Laser fire from the remaining Fleet Battleships sliced into the pack of missiles. The Missile Boats, Gunboats, and Frigates waiting for the gate also added their lasers.

The guidance and avoidance systems on board the Kashōn missiles became erratic to the point of uselessness. When the nuclear-armed weapons ignited, they released EM concussive waves into the space occupied by the crowd of missiles. The EM pulses disrupted electric and magnetic fields, including the power and operating chips for navigation.

Of the two-hundred-forty missiles launched to eradicate the last remaining Helacene Alliance ships, twelve made contact. These exploded on shield impact. With the force fields intact, damage proved minimal.

"Princess Samara," Epperan called across the Royal Command channel. "Are you there?"

"We're here, Admiral," replied the young voice. A group sigh of relief coursed through the bridge. "We're going to join D'Sey and Coop."

"I know who D'Sey is, and assume Coop means the disc-shaped craft, but they are gone, Princess. The Shroud decimated everything in the region they were last seen. The SuperCruiser also fired its ion-plasma cannon into the sector. No one could have survived."

"They jumped half-way to the star," Samara responded. "They weren't in the area when the Kashōn blew it up. We're going to meet them in a few seconds and take care of the rest of the Shroud ships, Admiral. Samara, out."

"Jumped half-way to the star?" Aether and the telemetry officer asked in unison.

Epperan shrugged her shoulders.

Coop said, "The good news is the Kashōn fired everything they have."

"I think the good news is we are still alive," Rox countered. "Without space-fold, we'd be slag."

"Now what?" Doc asked. "We still have Kashōn Destroyers, a SuperCruiser, and five-hundred smaller ships inbound. Cassandra is low on SRPs."

"We do what we planned on doing from the beginning," D'Sey interjected. "We brought Coop and Cassie here to rescue the Helacene princesses. Mission accomplished. The second part of the job was to eliminate Phortis and as many Ashemachers as we could to slow down the Kashōn Empire's push to conquer more systems. Our intel says King Phortis C and his brother, Admiral Pitaritis are aboard that SuperCruiser. They are the target. Once we eliminate them, the Shroud will fall back."

"The valve control backdoor no longer works," Rox reminded them.

"The SuperCruiser has joined the remaining Destroyers. The ships are deployed to provide maximum cover for the King," Cassie informed them.

"Captain Cooper," D'Sey spoke for all to hear. "You are still the military strategist with the experience. What do you say?"

"Arty has a high-probability the command bridge for the SuperCruiser is one-quarter to one-third the distance behind of the ship's point forward, and three-to-five decks below top deck. Anyone else?" Coop asked.

"Agreed," Rox answered. "The communications and activity scans indicate the greatest amount of chatter comes from that section of the ship."

"We just arrived," Doc said. "We go with Arty. By the way, who is Arty?"

"I'll introduce you later," Coop promised. "We're currently six-million-miles away." The three ships rendezvoused at this point after Cassie made contact with the saucer and Menace following their emergency jumps to the far side of the dead planet. "Using space-fold, we can be on them in four-minutes-thirty-seconds. I'm getting tired, people. I say we do this fast, dirty, and done."

Agreement returned from beings representing five species, a hologram, and the audio-representation of a Nakki philosopher.

"Teak and I also agree," Taah added from her oversight position on Clyde. "We're getting tired of being stuck out here alone. Kill the bastards and come home."

Chapter 40

The Fifth And Final Battle Of Geras

Cassandra reentered natural space first.

The Wraith appeared fewer than fifty-thousand-miles from the SuperCruiser battle group. She drove toward the forward section, the nose, of the giant ship. To reach her objective she needed to plow through dozens of Destroyers. Before scans warned the ships' commanders a vessel smaller than storage compartments within their warcraft initiated an attack, the tachyon cannon deployed beneath her keel opened fired. With a velocity near speed of light, the pulse slammed ships aside. Force fields unable to deflect the weapon simply rebounded away. With a clear path, the double-barrel rail-guns fired non-stop EM bursts at the juggernaut.

Menace followed two-miles behind the Wraith. D'Sey avoided any ships or debris while Duly aimed their pulse cannon at the lower half of the SuperCruiser's nose section. The EM pulse wave constricted to travel below Cassandra.

The Nakki saucer rode the pirate ship's tail.

Cassandra banked port with an azimuth bearing of ninety-degrees. Menace banked starboard at one-eighty.

Coop triggered the laser gun. The one-hundred-fifty-million-degree (C°) beam connected with the depleted forcefield protecting the Fleet Command Ship, it turned from ionized-light, into a gas for a brief moment, and then into a super-heated liquid. As the liquid made for the nose of the ship, frigid space rapidly cooled the liquid.

The speed of the attack allowed only the external liquid layer to solidify. The high-velocity spear pierced the hull with ease. The morphed light entered the ship and continued forward. The hardened point cut through everything in its path on the way to an explosive exit through the rear engine bays.

The concussive force wave generated by the spear, along with the acoustic waves created by sympathetic response, blew hulls apart, collapsed decks, and compressed organic material to soup. Liquid metal not solidified by contact with outer space did not splash. It acted as drops of acid flying through the air at Mach 12+ velocity. The liquid pitted walls, ceiling, and decks. It destroyed systems. It killed Kashōn on contact, including everyone on the interior command bridge.

As Admiral Pitaritis turned to tell his brother, King Phortis C of the Kashōn Empire not to worry about the tiny ship attacking them . . . in that short amount of time, the Empire came to a stop. Fast. Dirty. Done.

Chapter 41

Aboard Prudent

The Carrier-Cruiser Prudent sailed into battle without the wing of fighters the ship was designed to carry. The landing deck and open bays provided sufficient space for Cassandra, Menace, and the Nakki ship to land and dock within the atmospherically controlled hangar.

Coop, D'Sey, Duly, Rox, Krest, Doc, and Samara met on the deck in front of the flying saucer. Cassie could not materialize outside of the Wraith, and Arty manifested no corporal self. Both artificial intelligences could communicate. While the humanoids reunited and Princess Samara Athodite introduced to the crew of Menace, the avatar and the voice got to know one another.

"Menace took a beating," Doc said. The craft hovered two feet above the deck, its cream-colored surface scarred with long scorch marks. The shields prevented catastrophic failure from the multitude of hits by a variety of weapons. Burned and pitted alloy proved many of those strikes, though weakened, landed.

"She was too pretty," Duly said. "I prefer the new mean-girl look."

A squad of Fleet Marines escorted the crews to the ship's conference center. The group quieter than normal as the shadow of Key Largo's loss settled over them.

The meeting with the Helacene Alliance Fleet Admiral began amusingly.

Captain Aether attended, and neither he nor the Admiral knew precisely, from a protocol point of view, how to deal with the presence of Princess Samara. She was royal, but not the heir nor the spare. Samara's existence more often forgotten than remarked upon by military personnel. Her arrival as the Suzerain's representative, a royal princess, and a savior left the two officers shuffling between bows, kneeling, salutes, and standing at attention.

Her appearance in the snug skin-suit top, tactical pants, combat boots, and carrying a sidearm and business-like knife added to their discomfort.

Rox Silvanaē shook her head and snuffled at the sight. Duly could not contain his laughter, while the others tried to hide grins. Samara took control of the situation. She hugged Aether, then hugged Epperan.

"I am happy you are alive," she said. "Mother will be, too. The Fleet did incredibly well against so many ships. Falling into Alain's trap. Ambushed. Outnumbered. Every member of the Fleet should be proud today."

"Alain's trap?" Epperan queried, brow furrowed.

"My brother was a traitor and a Kashōn spy," she said. "I'll tell you all about it later," she promised.

"The remaining Kashōn ships?" Coop asked.

"The Destroyers are moving to meet up with the smaller ships. They broadcast a message promising to remain in the system until all Alliance ships exit. They also promised to return to Chōntorham," Aether answered. "You are?"

"Daniel Cooper," he replied, stepping forward to shake hands with Aether, and then Admiral Epperan. Both returned the handshake, though unsure of the custom.

Duly, Doc, and Rox introduced themselves by first name and from across the small room.

D'Sey saluted. "Captain Veresk D'Sey."

"The pirate Slate, I presume," Epperan said in reply.

"Privateer and agent of the Helacene Alliance," he responded. "I work for the Suzerain as a private contractor."

"You do?" Epperan said, questioningly.

"You do?" Samara said amazed.

"You do?" Duly, Doc, and Rox chimed in, surprised.

"I do," he answered all. "Among other things."

"There was another Kashōn ship in the system" Coop said.

"Red space yacht," Aether answered. "Never made contact. When the King's SuperCruiser was destroyed, it sailed to the gate and exited. We warned it off, but it sailed through our ships and made no act of aggression. Acted as if it did not care what we did or did not do."

"A dispatch has been sent to Hela," Epperan informed the gathered. "It contains the details of the confrontation. It includes my recommendation all of you receive the Alliance Star for saving the lives of thousands of Fleet personnel."

"The Star is so cool," Samara gushed. "It's a star-burst medal made from a super-rare mineral. It contains nineteen Tistian diamonds. The tiniest cut diamonds in the galaxy. It's presented for heroic action while protecting the Helacene Alliance. You know the best thing about it?"

"What?" Duly asked. The oversized grey alien bent low and caught up in the princess' excitement.

"If you are wearing the Star, you never pay for anything on any confederated planet ever," she answered.

"No!" Duly responded. "Ever? I'd make one and wear it. If I wasn't going to get my own," he added.

"Anyone wearing an unearned Star is subject to life in prison," Epperan said. "And you don't have one, yet. All I can do is make the recommendation. The Suzerain makes the final decision."

"We appreciate the honor, Admiral, regardless of the result," D'Sey said. "We have to leave. Suzerain Palla will be wanting her daughters, all of them, back home. After we collect Princesses Alucha and Mandara and return them to Hela, we have another job to do on Chōntorham."

"What could possibly make you go to the Kashōn home world?" Captain Aether asked. "When word of Geras and the death of Phortis reaches the Empire, you and your crew will be the most wanted ship on this side of the black hole."

"I think I know who was on that red space yacht," D'Sey answered. "We received valuable help from people held prisoner by the Kashōn. Help that made the difference here, and probably saved the Helacene Alliance. We need to get those people off Chōntorham before word of Phortis' death arrives."

"The yacht is already in the wormhole channel," Epperan reminded the pirate. "You said you need to take the princesses home first. You believe you can reach the prisoners first?"

"We work best under pressure," Rox answered for D'Sey.

"I must return the saucer," Coop interjected. "It's borrowed and I promised to bring it back." He avoided mentioning Enparatus. D'Sey's group knew the saucer's history, but the Alliance did not. It would be left to Trak and the Parq to decide if the secret would be shared.

"Then back to Earth?" Doc asked.

Coop nodded.

"You all have things to accomplish," Epperan said. She walked to each of the special operators, placing an open hand over her chest with small bow of respect to each, including Princess Samara.

In the hallway they were awed by the sight of uniformed Alliance military and civilian contractors lining both sides of the corridor. As Captain Aether led them to the lift and the ride to the hangar, applause began like the first drops of a summer rain. It rose into a deluge of hand claps, shouts of thanks and cries of victory as they neared the elevator doors. The chorus continued as the door closed and they lowered.

Samara fought tears and found Doc's hand holding hers. Duly and Rox preened. Living as pirates meant never receiving recognition for their real work. Coop and D'Sey appeared thoughtful. Krest remained contained; trying, and failing, to go unnoticed.

The lift opened and a gathering of personnel greeted them with more applause. They accepted thanks and back-slaps as they walked through the throng. The first person to slap Samara on her upper back, a young engineer, froze as he realized he struck a royal princess. A hush cascaded through the congregation.

Samara turned on the pale man, smiled, slapped him on the shoulder, and rewarded him with a hug. As she stepped away from the stunned serviceperson, the cacophony of claps and shouts returned, louder than before.

D'Sey and Coop ducked behind Cassandra's starboard strut to escape the noise.

"Doc will come with you," D'Sey said. "She can ride with Cassie to Enparatus. I want her to bring Key back for a proper funeral. If you don't object."

"My honor," Coop replied. "As soon as I put the saucer back in the hangar and check on Trak and the academy staff, I'll collect Key. I'll show Doc where the Ve engineers are buried. If their families can be located, they will want them brought home as well."

"I know where one relative is already," D'Sey responded. "Ve is under control of the Empire, but we'll get them home as soon as possible," he promised. "By the time you reach Clyde, we'll be gone. Taah and Teak will wait for Doc and Key. They will use a light-ship and join us on Hela. Clyde will take you home. You're going to miss out on your medal, Captain Cooper."

D'Sey extended his hand an said, "Thank you, Coop. It may have been a rocky first meeting, but I could not have asked for a better person to watch my back."

Coop accepted the grip.

"Hell of an adventure," he replied. "Maybe exactly what I needed."

"Any thought about becoming a Nakki agent?" D'Sey asked.

"Might actually be fun, one day," the Earther answered, releasing the handshake. "Currently I have enough problems waiting. Can I expect you to stay in touch?"

"I may have shanghaied you, but you are officially a pirate now, Daniel Marcel Cooper," D'Sey spoke, adding a wry smile to the glint in his eyes. "Besides, I believe that once Princess Samara comes of age, she might come looking for you herself."

"Take care of them," Coop said. "You have good people, Captain. They have a good leader. Next time you need help, ask. I never want to get yanked out of space-fold again. It hurts."

D'Sey spoke with Doc as Coop called down the access ladder. He turned into a full-body embrace and a soul-filled kiss by a teenage girl.

"Don't say anything," she said. "I'll break into tears and embarrass both of us if you talk."

Coop nodded. He watched her climb the ladder. She had to return the METS, the laser pistol, and collect her leathers.

"What are you thinking?" Doc asked.

"Her ass does look good," he said. He received a sharp blow to his triceps.

"Until she's old enough, you keep those thoughts to yourself," the teal woman said, smiling the entire time.

"What thoughts?" Duly asked, joining them beneath the Wraith with Rox a step behind.

Coop performed a quickdraw. The laser pistol cleared the holster, the hinged power box dropped into place, and the muzzle rested against the giant's torso before anyone present realized what happened.

Duly's wide eyes lowered to stare at the pistol. Coop spun the gun, then twisted to hold it by the barrel, handle toward the Xentarene.

"The power source is a black crystal placed in the converter in front of the trigger guard," he said. "Don't know if you have anything like it on this side of the galaxy, but if you can find them, you can upgrade all of your weapons."

The grey shaggy hair shook, and the troll-like face beamed. A large hand took the gift, holding it like a precious child. Unable to talk, Duly took Coop into a bear-hug (Howler-hug?) and lifted him from the deck.

Krest caught Coop's eye. Standing in the shadow of Cassandra's wing, the alien gave a nod. The gesture returned in kind.

On the ground, before catching his breath, Rox swept in with her own hug. She added a kiss and pressed her chest against his.

"If you can't find anyone like me on your side of the galaxy, come back," she said, letting him free and stepping away. "I'll upgrade your sex-life."

Doc sneezed, Duly laughed, and Rox licked her lips.

Samara's return saved Coop from making a response.

At the bottom of the ladder, she turned, wondered what the amusement had been about, but shrugged it off. She held the Falkniven.

"I know you said I could have it, but . . .," she said, holding the blade out.

Coop took the knife. He reached out and took Sam's arm, lifting it up and forcing her fingers open, palm turned up.

"This knife was made for a warrior," he told her. "When it was forged and shaped, I had one person in mind. The handle was hand-sanded and wrapped to fit her grip. The final test to see if the knife and the woman were matched was to test the balance."

He placed the tip of the blade against her palm.

"If the knife remained upright, it was in tune with the person. If the two did not belong together, the tip would break the skin and the blade would fall over."

He let go. Sam froze. Time froze. The knife did not move.

Coop took the handle and flipped it around to present the leather grip to Samara.

"It appears it was made for two warriors," he said.

Chapter 42

Cassandra settled on her tripods inside Clyde's hangar. Taah and Teak awaited on deck.

The saucer once more rested in the hidden cavern on Enparatus.

Arty provided a detailed diagram for a Nakki scout ship key, including the components necessary to make one. If Coop wished to start the saucer on Mars, he had the means.

The guide assured him returning to stasis was fine, and that Cassandra's storage files contained a few secrets humans had not reverse-engineered to date.

Trak, appearing healed from his injury, greeted him after he exited the ship. Together they returned to the oasis and awaited the arrival of Cassandra. Coop caught the nomad tribal leader up on events following the saucer's departure to Hela.

Coop joined Doc on board the Wraith, after the ship's arrival and the Kanistari saying her good-bye to the Parz nomad.

A short trip to collect Key's body, followed by a somber trip across space-fold to rendezvous with Clyde.

Taah accepted the grav-sled with Key Largo's covered remains, pushed from the rear storage and down the loading ramp by Doc. Without comment, she guided the sled toward a small ship nestled in the shadows of the hangar. Another shadow accompanied her.

"You sure about leaving him in the METS?" she asked.

"I want him to be in something from Earth," Coop answered. "I removed the SIM-cards, and operating chips. It's only a body-suit now."

"He would have appreciated it," Doc replied.

"There's more to D'Sey's defending the Helacene Alliance than Nakki concerns," Coop said, turning to face the woman. "You told me once D'Sey loved the Suzerain. Care to expand?"

"You never met the youngest son, Mandrake," Doc said. "He looks so much like Dee I'm surprised Samara didn't say something when she first saw Veresk D'Sey."

"D'Sey is Mandrake's father."

"Pella Athodite's children each come from a different sire," Doc explained. "It's part of the royal tradition of the Suzerain. I believe there is more between Dee and Pella than tradition."

"Sounds like Menace will be remaining in this region of the Milky Way for a while longer."

"It's not a bad place to be," Doc replied. "With Phortis and his brother, Pitaritis both dead, it will be interesting to see how the Ashemacher react. Whatever comes next, it will take time for the Empire to recover from the loss in Geras."

"Time to improve the Helacene Alliance's ability to stand against the renewed Kashōn Empire?"

Doc smiled and nodded.

"The Gavari Federation is between the Helacene Alliance and the Trade Worlds. Sounds like they may be on the agenda soon," Coop said.

"Maybe," Doc replied without committing to any desire to face the aliens who enslaved her home.

"D'Sey kept referring to the Devee as a potential threat to Earth."

"He ordered Clyde to provide information on Devistar and the Devee to Cassie," the Kanistari told him. "Part of your payment for services."

Cassie joined them as Taah and Teak returned from the shadows with Cassandra's grav-sled. Key's body replaced with an assortment of objects.

"Tech odds and ends we've pirated over the years," the short green alien said, sliding the sled toward him. "A couple of interesting weapons Duly added."

"What now?" Coop asked.

"We'll meet up with Menace," Doc answered. "D'Sey had some scheme to get as many of the alien workforce off Chōntorham as possible before word of the Shroud Fleet's defeat reached the planet. Not sure what he had in mind, but Duly seemed unhappy about reprising his role as a Kashōn ram. Clyde will return you to about the same spot he yanked you out of space-fold."

Taah hugged Coop and then Cassie. She did not say anything, rushing away. Teak hovered nearby. The Andromedan wavered, a lighter dark outlined by the deeper shadows of the hangar behind him. There was no overt communications, but Coop knew he said thank you and good-bye.

"Good-bye, Teak," he said. "I hope you find a way home."

Doc embraced the holo-avatar, whispered to her, and kissed her on the cheek. She gave Coop a hug, a kiss on the cheek, and said, "The Milky Way is getting smaller, even as it continues to expand. We'll see each other again, Coop. I'm sure of it."

Without waiting on a reply, she pivoted and walked toward the light ship that would take them to the rendezvous with the pirate ship. Teak ghosted in her wake.

"We need to leave the hangar," Cassie said, leading the way to the doorway connecting to the lounge.

Coop closed the door, went behind the bar and liberated a bottle of soda.

"If we have to travel from one side of the galaxy to the other, not a bad method," he said.

Cassie pulled her top over her head. "I need a shower," she said, and headed for the other door. Coop on her heels.

Chapter 43

The Kashōn supply vessel made for the wormhole gate as fast as Krest could force the utilitarian engines to fly.

Duly, head of a Xentarene and body covered in the armor and trousers of an Imperial trooper, stood beside the control board for the ship's single laser cannon. Grumbling over the fact they had only one laser.

Rox sat at the ship's systems station. She waited to see if any vessels from the surface or those already in space suddenly made for their location. The Dualönges also listened for emergency hails, or calls for action against the supply ship.

Aboard Menace, D'Sey mirrored Rox, watching and listening for signs of pursuit while he kept pace with the military resupply and refit vessel with his crew in charge and its storage bays filled with a variety of aliens.

Menace currently appeared to be a Kashōn system patrol boat on visual scans. She pinged as the Patrol and Protection Vessel, Pantortis.

"I can't believe we're here," Docha said. The short Ve engineer stood at the rear of the small command bridge aboard the hijacked supply ship.

"I thought we were dead," Dr. Pau said, standing next to her colleague. "When the security guards came for us, I feared Phortis discovered the worm we designed to sabotage fleet ships."

Docha gazed up at the taller Aekran and added, "I thought we were done, too. I didn't know what to think when we were joined in the lobby by every alien kept in the ARC."

"I was pretty convincing," Duly said, listening in on the conversation. "Marched into that building and ordered the guards to collect every fucking alien in the building by command of King Phortis C. 'Don't let the bastards touch anything,' I yelled. 'The King wants them moved immediately.' I don't know if how scared those Kashōn security agents acted or seeing Rox in an Imperial uniform was funnier."

"Damn thing still itches," she said, never turning away from the monitors. The helmet, armored tunic, forearm greaves, and one of Duly's overly large multi-barrel laser rifles lay on the deck behind her. She wore a tight-fitted top, Imperial Trooper trousers and boots. White cotton balls remained glued to her forehead and chin.

"While we snookered the guards into bringing everybody to us, Dee and Krest stole a supply ship. That's the story I want to hear when we're out of this system."

If Krest listened, he did not take the bait to join the discussion.

"Actually, I think the march across the space port was funnier," Rox said. "You in front with that cannon, the aliens bunched together like pysiga going to slaughter, the dumb-ass Kashōn guards on either side, and me bringing up the rear. People scattered like insects to get out of the way."

"Thank Thau no one tried to escape," Dr. Pau said.

"Didn't know where I was leading everybody until Dee called with the location," Duly snickered. "Otherwise we might be back there still marching."

"I cannot tell you how relieved I was when Captain D'Sey pulled me aside after we entered the supply ship," Docha said.

"Piece of cake after getting everyone on board," Duly said.

"Except Dee had to get back to Menace, and Krest had to bluff his way off the planet," Rox said. "Menace showing up, looking like a Patrol Vessel sent to escort the prisoners, was a great touch."

"Now what?" Docha asked.

"We attempt to gate out without being fired upon," Krest answered. "I suggest that Docha and Dr. Pau return to the storage area. They should reassure the other aliens."

Rox tossed a communication chip to Duly, who delivered it to Scandeki Pau.

"If you need us, call," he said.

Several hours later the two ships exited the system. The military supply ship via the wormhole gate. Menace entered space-fold at the same time, expecting planet monitoring stations to assume the Patrol vessel entered the wormhole.

The portal closed, and before the gamma radiation shunted from the immediate vicinity of the gate, it reopened.

A blood red ship emerged.

Home

Coop sat in the pilot's seat. The Wraith positioned to exit the Nakki transport ship when the hangar doors parted. Cassie sat to his right, eyes closed. I Can See Clearly Now by Johnny Nash played over the ship's speakers. The song pulled from Key's reggae collection.

"Almost home," Coop said.

"There will be things I miss when we return," Cassie said.

"I'm pretty sure I can talk Manny Hernandez into installing a shower that uses real water," Coop replied.

The avatar smiled and opened her eyes. "Hangar doors opening," she said. "Clyde says we're in the void between the Aster Farum and Fell systems. He also says 'Good luck.'"

"Not good-bye," Coop murmured as he pushed the fighter across the deck and into space.

Cassandra sped into the starry expanse. Clyde disappeared.

"What?" Coop asked, noticing Cassie's pinched expression while she stared into space.

"We're in the right place," she said, "but my chronometer is rebooting."

"So?"

"The alignment of stars is making my operating systems recalculate and reset time functions."

"And?"

"The ten days we were gone just became eight-months-thirteen-days and six-hours."

Jimmy Cliff replaced Johnny Nash, singing Many Rivers To Cross.

The End

Feb. 14, 2018

I hope you enjoyed the story. I'd like to thank you for taking the time to read a Space Fleet Saga adventure. As a writer trying to build a reputation, nothing works as well as reviews to entice other readers to try a new book. If you would take a moment to leave a review at Amazon, Barnes & Noble, or Goodreads it will go a long way in keeping the series alive.

To stay in touch with the Space Fleet Saga universe, and for a chance to win free books, go to donfoxe.com, and leave your email to join the newsletter group -- form is on the CONTACT page.

Sincerely,

Don